THE MISADVENTURES OF SULLIVER PONG

A NOVEL

LELAND CHEUK

CHICAGO CENTER FOR LITERATURE AND PHOTOGRAPHY
2015

Printed and distributed by the Chicago Center for
Literature and Photography. *First paperback edition, first
printing: November 2015.*

Cover design: Coon Lam

ISBN: 978-1-939987-37-2

This collection is also available in a variety of electronic
formats, including EPUB for mobile devices, MOBI
for Kindles, and PDFs for both American and
European laserprinters. Find them all, plus a plethora of
supplemental information such as interviews, videos and
reviews, at:

cclapcenter.com/pong

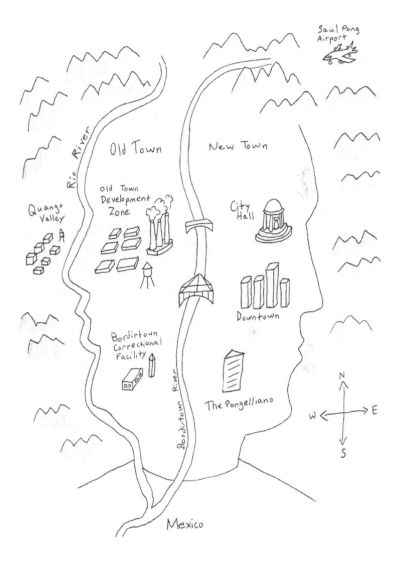

Map of Bordirtoun

0.

BORDIRTOUN. POPULATION 157,000. My birthplace, the safest rest stop for the dubious intentions and the miserable legacy of the Pong family. My great-great-granduncle Millmore was the first American Pong. He arrived in 1861 from Guangzhou, China and worked a little-known railroad that ran from the New Mexico territories to Los Angeles, sticking dynamite in the most stubborn mountain faces of the southwest. A quiet man who rarely complained, Millmore chose not to join an unsuccessful worker strike because his pregnant wife was due, and the railroad company rewarded his loyalty with a transfer to the safer occupation of bridge construction. The following week, just two days after his son was born, at his new job, Millmore's safety harness was chafing his crotch, and while adjusting it, he inadvertently undid the belt and plummeted to his death, off the railroad bridge that traverses what is now Bordirtoun River.

Millmore's son Parris grew up to run one of the many brothels for which Bordirtoun became renowned. He was the head of the local Chinese business association and a notoriously poor speller.

When the town was just a single dirt road, Parris Pong painted a large sign on the wall of one of the saloons that read: "Sects wif Beast Layddys af Parris's Bordirtoun Brofful." Parris's misspelling of border town stuck, and the Chinese business association officially named the village Bordirtoun in 1895. Today, the faded sign hangs in the Museum of Bordirtoun History, which is not much larger than the principal's office at my old middle school.

The railroads brought caboose-fulls of whites, Native Americans, and Mexicans, and over time these people formed a full-fledged city government. Parris's son Francisco became Bordirtoun's most popular evangelical pastor, and he dreamed of bringing the extended Pong clan to America. During a time when Chinese immigrants were less welcome in the country than even the despised Mexicans, Francisco successfully sponsored the immigration of numerous Pongs. Today, many of them are scattered across the West Coast, no doubt lowering the average IQ of Chinese-Americans in Seattle, Portland, San Francisco, Los Angeles, and San Diego.

Francisco was the first Pong to speak fluent English. After the Japanese attacked Pearl Harbor, Francisco's fluency was tested by officials convinced that his thick, sloped brows and high, round cheekbones indicated he was a member of the enemy. Under a blazing white sky without clouds, Francisco shuffled down the cobblestone road near his church, likely confident that God would resolve his case of mistaken identity, if not that day, then some day soon. The day was February 20, 1942, the morning after President Roosevelt issued Executive Order 9066, the order to intern Japanese-Americans. Francisco was arrested and shipped to the Rio River internment camps, where he contracted pneumonia and died soon after, leaving no one to deal with the impending arrival of his cousin (my grandfather Robinson) and his cousin's son (my father, Saul).

There's a dearth of archived information regarding Robinson

Pong. My father has generally avoided all mention of my grandfather over the years, and all that's known of him is that he owned a general store for over a decade before going to work one day and never coming home. A missing persons report was filed. A few days later, a local waitress also disappeared without notice, without a trace, leaving a son and a husband, and for several weeks, police worried that there might be a serial killer or kidnapper loose in Bordirtoun. No sign of either Robinson or the woman was ever found, nor was there any evidence of a bone collector, a night stalker, or any such criminal.

Saul was the lucky Pong. History holds that engineer and entrepreneur Nolan Bushnell conceived one of the first video games, PONG, for his company Atari in 1972. What history fails to note is that my father and Bushnell were inseparable as electrical engineering students at the University of Utah and that he hired Saul (the Utes' ping-pong champion 1966) as a table-tennis verisimilitude consultant in 1970. When the time arrived to name the landmark game, my father suggested his now-famous surname. Just before the patent for PONG was filed in 1973, Bushnell and Saul had a mysterious falling out, and the executives at Atari felt enough antipathy toward my father to pay him royally to leave the company and expunge his employee records. My father has never told me what happened between him and Bushnell, but for many years, in his home office, Saul kept a framed candid of himself and Bushnell's first wife, Paula, looking into each other's eyes and smiling in front of an Atari office building.

My father landed as he always landed: on his feet and ready to run. He invested the payoff into real estate and went into politics. By the turn of the century, my father had become the mayor of Bordirtoun. I found out via e-mail, sent from Saul with the subject line, "I DUN IT! I WON MAJUR," followed by a link to the *Bordirtoun Daily* article with a photo of my father beaming and holding up my frowning mother's hand.

Why would Saul want to preside over a place with such a peculiar brand of mediocrity? I never felt safe within Bordirtoun's confines, with its chemical plant stacks ever-spewing, its serpentine and never-ending outbound highways, the leering black mountains, and the acerbic atmosphere of cow patty and metal. Most of Bordirtoun's cultural events included the following as narrative fulcra: a cowboy, a sinister Mariachi, or nude painted dancers as performance artists. In my early teens, I loitered after school in front of City Hall, tossing eggs at the statue of Leland Stanford, the man who had brought the railroads through Bordirtoun. When I was done, I sat at the base of the statue, hugging my belly, brutally constipated (as I often was due to the low quality butcheries and brittle produce endemic to the region), and I stared out at the turdy brown of the river separating the city's eastern middle-class neighborhoods and its poorer western districts. I recall digging my heels into the pedestal and thinking: when I grow up, I will not be here.

Why would Bordirtoun want to be presided over by my father and his peculiar brand of mediocrity? Prior to my adolescent battles with orthodontic gingivitis, halitosis, and acne vulgaris, Saul took me on dates with his mistresses (many of them notably unattractive) and made me wait in unfamiliar backyards while he hoed sundry longhaired and breasted gardens. Naturally my mother protested, and many of my childhood nights were spent covering my ears with limp pillows. The way Saul treated my mother was the main reason I fled Bordirtoun. I aspired to be a better man, and for a long time, I was more or less successful.

What has become of me, you ask? Where do I, Sulliver Pong, fall in the spectrum of Bordirtoun Pong legacies? Allow me to provide an answer, however incomplete.

Twenty years, two business schools, a myriad of big city consultancies, and thousands of airport sandwiches later, I discovered myself in Copenhagen, of all places, with my wife, my Danish language instructor, Lene. I had always preferred tall women with Anglo-Saxon features, and since I was bald, short, Asian, and, at the time, obese, I often faced difficult odds. But Lene was my lucky play. I adored her allergy to confusion. Early in our courtship, while I hemmed and hawed over our evident differences, Lene revealed she had long since chosen me.

"When I was young, I had a teacher who had dark hair and bad teeth like you," she said. "All my friends said he was very ugly. To me, he looked mysterious. I knew the man I married would have mystery. Tell me, will you stay or shall I look for another?"

Together for eleven years, married for eight, in that time, I rarely regretted Lene's choice. Whenever we stood on our balcony, our bent elbows linked, my head resting on her shoulder as we stared out at the milky horizon toward just-invisible Sweden, smoking Prince cigarettes after a daylight-drenched summer dinner, I was reminded to appreciate how far I'd come: a Bordirtoun hick done good.

Before I go further and mislead you into thinking that all's well that ends well, I feel it's fair to note that I am, at this moment, writing belly-down on the top bunk of a jail cell, ignoring the stuttering breathing of my cellmate, Manny, who is masturbating. The prison is minimum security, but I've long since learned that it is so to my detriment. I can still stare out at the horizon here, through a human-proof window. If I somehow managed to pry open this glass and run, I'd be gunned down at a hundred yards, or, with my luck, eighty. Lene is long gone. I am no longer in Denmark. I am where I was born. In America. In Bordirtoun.

I am an innocent man with no prior criminal history. I have eighteen months remaining in my four-year sentence. Every six months I apply for parole, like a regularly scheduled dental cleaning, and each time, I've been assigned a less competent attorney, and laughed out of the parole hearing. My most recent legal representative was in the midst of a career change; he was a defrocked priest. Another attorney was so severely dyslexic that he couldn't read his own notes. My latest lawyer is named Janning Jaynuss (pronounced Yawning Yay-ness) and he seems to believe that the reason I haven't been paroled is that the board doesn't *know me* well enough.

"I see the parole board more than I see my parents," I said over the phone earlier today.

"Who were you before you came to prison?" he replied. Music (meringue or salsa?) was audible in the background. "How did you end up inside? How have you changed? How has prison reformed and rehabilitated your character?"

"I'm innocent of the crime for which I was convicted."

I heard chips crunching over the line.

"Hello?" I said.

"That's great. Just great."

"What's great?"

"That you're innocent."

"I pled innocent."

"You did?"

"Haven't you read my file?"

"Well, Mr. Pong, set the record straight," he said. "Write it down. Tell your story. Leave no story stone unturned."

I questioned whether storytelling was a good use of my time.

The music stopped. "Look, Pong, you got better things to do?" Jaynuss said. "You haven't given me much to work with here. The parole board doesn't care whether you're innocent or not. You've been convicted, and the board assumes that the process has been fair to you, even if it hasn't. You've shown no remorse for anything that happened. You've shown no signs of even reflecting on how you got in the mess you're in. All these hearings and not once has one of your

family members sent a letter to the board asking for leniency. In fact, no one has shown up on your behalf. Not your ex-wife, not your father, not your mother."

To that, I had no rebuttal.

"Leave no story stone unturned, Pong," Jaynuss repeated before hanging up.

Fine. I will turn over all story stones, perhaps even a few other stones. Just for you, Jaynuss (pronounced Yoost for you, Yay-ness). Yoost for you too, reader. Once and for all.

I.

REWIND: TWO YEARS AGO. A morning of first-in-awhiles. For the first time in at least a year, I was biking around the lake near downtown Copenhagen, with vague hopes of trimming my winter-grown paunch, so unbecoming on an already truncated customer like myself. My groin was a bit tight from another first-in-awhile: sex with Lene. I inhaled deeply the crisp morning air, made strangely sweet by the faint traces of diesel from the traffic, and I took in the bebopping urban trees and the verdant surface of the lake. Riding felt safe here; the bike lanes were roughly twice the width of an average American sidewalk. I passed Lene's favorite housewares shop with its large spoons hanging in the window—some wooden, some plastic and colorful in that Scandinavian way: bright yellows and blues, a lovely contrast to the long white winters. I decided, when the stoplight turned green, that the next time I passed the store, I would buy her the entire display.

I turned right at the next corner, ringing my bell, passing a

middle-aged woman with sizable calves. As I moved ahead, the knot in my groin clenched. I slowed and was promptly slammed from behind. Down I went, in a metallic and fleshy tangle. The woman and I ended up on the curb. She bounced up, dusted herself off, and cursed me in Danish. I couldn't follow all the expletives. She spoke some rural dialect, and from what I could understand, she was either cursing my ancestors or my ancestry, possibly both. Tightening the salt-and-pepper bun on the back of her head, she bent over, mounted her bicycle, and rode off.

I got up slowly, stiffer than before. I was skinned at my few angles. My hips and knees were bleeding. The damage could have been much worse. I picked up my bike and noticed that the front wheel spokes were slightly crooked, handlebars bent. A wicker basket was attached to the back. The bike wasn't mine. The frame was painted pink with multicolored flowers. "Fuck," I said, looking down the road. The woman had already disappeared.

Lene might be bothered by this, I thought. She had given me the bike for one of our anniversaries (or was it one of my birthdays?). Don't you care about my gift, she might ask? Well, of course I care, honey, I'd reply. You don't even remember the occasion for which I purchased the gift, she'd say. Of course I do, dear. What was it, she'd ask? I would then, in all probability, incorrectly guess that she had purchased the bike for our fifth anniversary, and argue that I was correct until Lene backed down.

I lifted my leg slowly over the bike seat and tried to pedal, but my groin grabbed. I limped the vehicle over to a nearby bench and sat. My cell phone vibrated in my pocket—Lene calling. I considered letting it go to voicemail but a well-endowed runner bounded and jiggled past, and I recalled Lene on top of me, just hours before, spreading my legs again into her favorite lotus position, which, despite its unnecessarily gymnastic and painful nature, still made for

a successful sexual encounter. I decided to answer.

"*Skat*," I said.

"Are you okay?"

"My groin."

"Do you want me to come get you?"

"No, no," I said. I added with a purr, "I guess I couldn't handle your love this morning."

Lene didn't reply. I considered what to tell her about the bike. Better to say nothing, I decided.

"Someone called for you," she said. "She claimed to be your father's assistant."

"My father's assistant?" While I'd received the occasional email from him, I hadn't spoken to Saul in at least five years. My parents had not been invited to our wedding.

"Said it was urgent."

I felt queasy. Urgent meant he wanted something from me.

"Do you plan to call him?" Lene asked.

"You think I should?"

"Sully, remember the last time you returned his call?"

He had asked me whether I would consider investing in land of an undisclosed size for an undisclosed purpose for an undisclosed sum. I asked him to send me more information just to get him off the phone. He proceeded to fax me a letter of intent to invest in a 100,000 square foot piece of distressed real estate that appeared to be owned by an ethnic group (Native American tribe?) I'd never heard of. At the bottom of the letter was my signature, already forged by my father (as he often did during my college years—moving money in and out of our various joint accounts to pay the tuition). I called and informed him I had not agreed to anything and that I wanted the letter shredded. To which Saul responded, "I need your bank routing numbers so I can wire the money." I had to have my lawyer

threaten to sue before Saul finally gave up.

"Yes, you're right," I said to Lene. I declared that I would not call him back.

"Good!" Lene said. "Oh wait! The woman said your father wanted to talk to you about your mother."

"Momma?" I sat forward and knocked over the bike with a clang. I waited for the noise to pass.

"What was that?" she said.

"Construction," I said. "Call me later?"

"Uh-huh."

I heard Lene turn on the television, and I bade her farewell.

I left the woman's bike. At the underground, I calculated that if I let the next two trains pass, Lene would have departed for the university by the time I got home.

As planned, when I arrived at the flat, my wife was gone. In my home office, I tried not to think about my father's assistant's call about Momma. I still talked with my mother over the phone every few weeks. Though I dreaded returning her calls and hearing her loving reminders of filial bonds (like "Why haven't you called me in so long, Sully? Have you forgotten your family?" or "Call me back, you useless son! Why are you so useless? I told you to work for your father so you wouldn't be so useless," or Lene's personal favorite, "That woman's telling you not to call me back, isn't she?"), I saw it as my duty to keep the communication lines open with her, just long enough to make sure she was still alive. I feel it's fair to note that I had not performed that particular duty quite as regularly in the weeks prior to my father's outreach. I hadn't returned Momma's calls in at least two months. She was getting older, closing in on seventy, and though she had a history of good health, she wouldn't be alive forever. I wondered if her displeasure with me had been escalated to my father, and Saul had had his assistant call on Momma's behalf.

After cleansing my wounds with antiseptic (cussing loudly in English and Danish) and bandaging my knees and elbows, I bulletpointed vague marketing plans for my foundering public relations consultancy, which specialized in translating Danish PR strategy for American audiences (i.e. dumbing it down and/or making the language as vague and circuitous as possible). I hadn't had a client in six months and had recently stopped prospecting without Lene's knowledge after qualifying for Denmark's sweet, sweet dole. I surfed the Internet and gave a three-star rating to *Ekstra Bladet*'s Page Nine girl (half-star deductions for underwhelming overall height and overwhelming height of hair). I called my connection at the tabloid (the attractive, way-too-young, not-that-I'd-ever-try intern who worked the personals) and posted a brief ad regarding the stolen bike. I contemplated having a go at myself to some streaming free PornTube vids but my groin began to feel hard and swollen, and I was still fuck-sore from the morning with Lene. I hobbled a small circle around my office, an icepack taped to my crotch.

My fellow inmates would likely be surprised to hear that I used to consider myself an exceedingly optimistic person. After I was jailed, I went through a bit of an apocalyptic phase; for the first three months, I grew a full beard and gave sermons after lights out about seven-headed beasts soon to rise from Bordirtoun River and the accompanying natural disasters about to lay waste to all who supported us Pongs. Anyway—back to my original point—I once identified myself as an optimist. I gave several consecutive American presidents the benefit of the doubt. I was habitually tardy because I always thought I had more time than I did. Though Lene and I didn't make love for months on end, all it took was one lustful morning, and I would expect her libido to return.

So during this idle, sexually sated day, feeling optimistic, I gave my father the benefit of the doubt. I called his assistant back.

"What is your name?" she asked.

My name caught in my throat. Had I really given *my father* the benefit of the doubt?

The assistant made a bone-sucking noise. "Your name, please?"

"I'm his son."

"This—is—the—last—time—I'm—asking."

"I'm sure my father wouldn't approve of your disposition."

"Have a nice day."

"My name is Sully!"

I heard rustling papers, shuffling feet, and whispering. "What's your mother's maiden name?"

"Chong," I added.

"Please hold." A tune played over the receiver. *Boxcars of 'em rolling through / tracks built for me and you / by the ChinaMAN, MexiCAN, AfriCAN coming round / to our blue, blue rivers of Bordirtoun.* The song was entitled, "The Death of Bordirtoun." We had to memorize it in grade school. Not until my senior year did my Mexican-American civics teacher inform me that the "me and you" meant "white people."

I was about to hang up, when my call waiting sounded. Lene had advised against this. Again, the beep. I tried to remember the last time I regretted taking her advice. I could not. For some reason, I recalled an incident shortly before our wedding, when Lene simply stared at me with an arched brow when I asked her whether I should consider Saul's offer to go halfsies on an organ donation center in Secaucus. A third beep. I clicked the hook.

"Sully!" my father bellowed. "You haven't had children without telling me, have you?" He giggled to himself.

"No," I said flatly.

"I'm in Amsterdam."

I imagined him calling from the edge of a whore's bed.

"I thought I'd drop by and visit you and Elena," he said.

"*Lene*," I corrected. "You can't just show up anytime you want. We have lives, you know. Busy lives, with schedules and such."

"Then when will you be available?"

"Depends."

"I'd appreciate it if you can fit me into your schedule next week," he said, talking nice and slow. "I have something urgent to *consult* with you about."

I pinched my gullet. "Your assistant said you called about Momma. But if it's business, I should be upfront and inform you that *my* business is going very, very well, and I am quite busy with my many clients, and I don't have time for your propositions."

"It's about Momma."

"Is it serious?"

"No, nothing serious, of course, just the type of thing she'd overreact to," my father said, chuckling.

"Then why did you call me?"

The sounds of a horn, traffic, and muffled Dutch. "Can't talk now, Sully!" he shouted. "How about Tuesday? I'll call you."

I stared at my blank wall calendar. "I'm quite busy."

"Connection's breaking up," he said clearly. "Call you and Elena on Tuesday!"

"It's *Lene*!" I shouted. "What's wrong with—"

"Looking forward!" My father hung up.

I ripped off my headset. The phone, still attached, skated off my desk, and cracked against the hardwood.

The front door unlocked with a clack. Lene's boot heels spanked perfect quarter beats in the hall. She appeared in the doorway, fastening an earring. Her hair was short back then, just beyond ear length, golden bangs, recently shorn. Her stylist had suggested the cut. I thought it made her look older (and she was already 45).

Naturally, I'd said she looked great.

"Have you seen my dossier—" Lene stopped and surveyed the state of things: the phone on the floor, me in my boxers, the icepack. "What happened?"

"My father is in Amsterdam. He's visiting Tuesday."

"Tuesday?" Lene's neck seemed to lengthen. "Did you call him?"

"No," I said. "He called me." Not entirely true. I cleared my throat. "I shouldn't have picked up the phone."

Worry lines stacked themselves on her forehead. "Where's your bike?"

"We're just having lunch, though."

"Your father took the bike?"

"Who cares about the goddamn bike? It was stolen, okay? Some old lady stole the bike. I got in an accident? You see my knee? You see this icepack? The old lady hit me with her bike. Then she got on my bike and rode off."

My voice was bouncing off the walls; my hands chopped left and right. I was bracing for a fight. But to my surprise, Lene walked to where I sat and placed her large, icy, dry palm on my scalp. Her figure cast a shadow over me. The lines beneath her eyes were faint but precise, like etchings on an eminently reliable instrument. She stared into my eyes until I looked away.

"How was I supposed to know if you didn't say anything?" she said.

I sighed loudly. "Do I have to say everything?"

"But you never say anything."

I pondered that statement. Did I really hide that much from Lene? Perhaps I did. Perhaps I would. I held her hand and apologized.

She inspected my face. "He's not staying, is he?"

I kissed her knuckles. "Of course not."

"Good." She mussed what was left of my hair. "Your parents

have caused so many problems for you."

Later, while I rested in my recliner, Lene and I watched an American family sitcom dubbed into Danish. We held hands over the arms of our separate chairs. My redwoodesque Lene threaded her fingers through her short hair with a seemingly contented smile.

"What do you think your father really wants?"

"Who knows?"

"Maybe he would like to build you a house so you can move back," Lene said. "But do graft on the development."

"Maybe a Ponzi scheme to sell the sequel to PONG?"

Lene laughed. She got up and perched on the arm of my chair. She leaned down and pulled on my ear lightly. I half-stood to kiss her neck, and she reached to touch my thigh.

"He said he had something to tell me about Momma."

Lene backed away. "He hasn't told you anything yet?"

"Nothing."

"Do you think there's really something wrong?"

"Probably not."

"She left a message a few weeks ago," she said. "Did you call her back?"

I sat. "No."

"Why don't you?" Lene asked.

I didn't have an answer, other than my cowardice and laziness. "I should," I said, my voice pitching high. A signal that I didn't want to be questioned further on the topic.

Lene sandwiched my cheeks in her palms. "Remember what you said when my father died?"

After her father passed away, only a year after her mother's death, Lene sat in my very seat for hours on end, staring silently at the television. Her parents had been good people. Maddening to each other, stubborn, but dutiful in life and love. Nothing like Saul and

Momma. Trying to make her feel better, I had said, "I'll be your family. You are mine.'"

Now, with my face in her hands, Lene repeated my words, mocking my nasal American accent. "I'll be your family. You are mine."

She laughed and kissed me, our teeth clicking. Later, we would make love, and as she thrust her pelvis against mine, her legs splayed over my outspread legs, my groin seared, but we did not rush.

My Lene. Her wrath, never quite as wrathful as I tended to anticipate. What did my overreactions say about me, about our marriage? When Lene said my parents had caused so many problems for me, she really meant they had caused so many problems for *us*. When Momma heard that I had married without her knowledge, she immediately blamed Lene.

"She didn't want us to come, did she?" Momma said. "She doesn't like Chinese people. She's in control of you."

Of course, I denied all of the above. And even if I neglected to deny all of the above some of the time, it made no difference. Denial was pointless with Momma. She never listens to me. Even now, when she visits me in prison, toting a glass jar of soup, and hemorrhoid cream, Momma never brings me what I always request: reams of thirty-two pound writing paper (the prison stationery is practically one-ply).

When Lene and I returned from our Italian honeymoon to find a small package from Momma, I had a strong sense that the contents were unlikely to be congratulatory.

"How nice of your parents," Lene said, smiling as she split the packing tape with scissors. When her face paled, I silently took from her the sharp instrument. Momma had airmailed my old senior prom photos. I had gone with a Chinese girl from the math club who didn't speak much English (she had asked me before I got around to asking the accessible overweight blond who lived down the street). Momma thought the Chinese girl was very good-looking and to this day, two decades later, she still occasionally asks what happened to her. The girl had a drinking problem and the dirtiest Cantonese mouth I'd ever heard. Even my father didn't swear in Cantonese as much as she did after a few drinks. On prom night, she vomited eight times, and I carried her to her parents' doorstep, laid her down, rang the doorbell, ran to my car, and drove away.

"Why don't you just tell her that you love me, and this behavior is unacceptable?" Lene said. "If you are in public relations, you are the worst public relations person ever!" I slept in the guest room for a week. To this day, Lene still refers to the Chinese girl as my ex-girlfriend (only partially in jest).

For the first several years of my marriage, every time Momma and Saul met someone who had a Chinese daughter roughly my age, they snapped a picture and sent it to me. When Saul discovered that I'd married, he found a way to pull Lene's financial records and discovered that she was "only" a teacher. He made it clear via email that he would not leave a dime of his estate to someone with such low earning potential. Saul offered to introduce me to the many beautiful young dentists and paralegals he knew in China and Taiwan. Numerous photos were attached to his email, and Saul was in all of them, hugging and saying cheese with a variety of long, sable-haired, porcelain-complected Asian women half his age.

I agreed to a half-hour late morning visit with Saul after he checked into his hotel (I pretended to have a previously scheduled lunch meeting). The doorbell rang at 11 a.m. sharp. My father stood

beyond the threshold, beaming with unnaturally white teeth; his silver hair appeared to be the product of a perm, shoulder-length and wavy, as though he were an aging actor playing a knight. His slouch was more pronounced and made him shorter than I remembered. His cheeks shone (injections?) and his dark, reptilian eyes bulged, lucid and darting as always. He wore a jacket with its brand name on the breast (Bolo Ralph Loren) and held a sizable rolling suitcase at his side.

I held the door open but didn't let him in. "Did you just come from the airport?"

My father blinked. I repeated my question and added, "You can't stay, you know."

"Let me sit and explain," Saul said.

"You didn't say you were staying."

My father rubbed his lower back. "Just let me sit, Sully. Are we going to stand here all day?"

I sighed and let him in. I rolled my father's suitcase down the hall. The case was so heavy that I had to stop outside the kitchen to rest.

"What's in here?" I asked.

My father placed an arm around my shoulder; his warmth made me shudder. "Are you okay?" he asked.

"I hurt myself biking."

My father looked me up and down. "Really?"

"Yes, I have been known to bike."

He patted me on the belly. "It would be good for you." He stepped into the kitchen and looked around. "Where's Elena?"

I eased myself down at the dining table. "At work."

"Oh, good, she works!" he exclaimed, nodding vigorously. "A real job?"

"She has a real job."

"I see," Saul said. He cupped one of the hanging blue ladles without removing it from its hook. Then he let it go like he didn't like what he saw. "Do you have a guest room?"

"We do."

"Plan on converting it?"

"To what?"

"A baby's room."

"I have no plans to have children." My voice started to spike. "God forbid I'm half as terrible at parenting as you were."

"Elena agrees?" Saul said, seeming not to hear my insult.

"For now, yes." Not sure why I said that. That time had passed for us. I never wanted children, never wanted to disappoint a child as much as my father had disappointed me. Lene had never felt strongly about kids and often joked that I was one child too many for her.

My father ran an index finger over the rounded counter's edge. My fastidious Lene had rendered the kitchen spotless, every dish put away. Still, my father wiped his finger on a towel before sitting across from me. I turned my chair away from the table and stretched my legs before noting that my father was also sitting the same way. I straightened. "About Momma—"

"Momma, yes, absolutely." My father nodded. "As I mentioned before, it's nothing serious. I'm glad you finally got married, Sully. She's not Chinese, but you did okay. She sounded pretty on the phone." He leaned his head closer. "How old are you now? Thirty-two?"

"Thirty-eight."

"Jesus!" my father said. "That means I'm—"

"A senior citizen."

My father clucked at the years gone by. "I feel early fifties." He folded his hands on the table. "My approval ratings are higher than ever. People like me because they think, 'Wow, a man who has accomplished so much and is a man of ideas and yet, he's still so

young.' Things are not perfect, of course. But a lot of good jobs have come into town during my administration. Now I'm thinking about my third term. I'm very capable of accomplishing whatever I set my mind to."

"Good for you."

"It's you that I'm worried about."

"*Me?*" I added a guffaw for good measure. "I'm quite happy."

"It's been my greatest fear that you'd use some of the questionable actions of our family's past as an excuse to spoil your future. I've always told you: learn only my good things, not the bad."

"What good things?"

My father glared at me for a moment before catching himself. My chest puffed a bit, proud that my verbal stab had struck bone. I informed him our allotted window would soon expire and that it was time to discuss Momma.

"My assistant botched my reservation," he said. "The hotel had me down for next week, and by then, I'll be gone."

My jaw clenched. "So you need a place to stay."

The edges of my father's lips curled upward. "Unfortunately, Sully, I must impose."

"I'm very busy this week. This month in fact."

My father's smirk mutated into a frown. "Well, Sully, I'm sorry to inconvenience you," he said. "You are my only son. And we need to talk about Momma."

My eyes bulged. "*Now* you want to talk about Momma?"

"You're just like your mother, always parsing my words." My father looked at his watch. "You should leave soon if you want to get to your meeting on time. You have a busy schedule. I'll just wait here."

I felt the color draining from my face. Now I had no choice but to leave Saul in my flat.

"Sully, can I trouble you for some juice before you go?"

I poured my father a glass of orange juice and left the apartment, cussing my ancestors and my ancestry. I would not have been the least bit surprised to learn that my father never bothered to make a reservation. Any other town, my father would have booked reservations weeks ahead. Not Copenhagen! His spineless slothful Sully lived in Copenhagen! I'm guessing he was supremely confident that he could manipulate me into letting him stay, just as he had worked me over like a speed bag from that phone booth in Amsterdam. In my weaker moments, walking the concrete halls of this prison, surrounded by evil men and those who have broken laws, lost their way, and failed to get what they want, I envy the confidence with which my father carried himself, unafraid to strut into a strange country without an itinerary, without any knowledge of the language, certain that he would find a way to get exactly what he wanted.

I cabbed to eight hotels in Østerbro, Nørrebro, Vesterbro and på Strøget without finding a single vacant room. A Swedish metal festival (the Midnight Sun of SatanFest) was in town. I came home to find my father in my office, at my desk, talking on my headset, no doubt long distance to America, his cell phone clipped to his belt. Nauseated by what my evening was about to become, I dragged his suitcase (still sitting in the kitchen where I'd left it) to the guest room.

As I was walking back to the office, keys jingled in the door.

The moment Lene saw the look on my face, her shoulders sagged. I tried to smile my way onto her good side, but she wouldn't look at me. After smoothing her skirt and taking a deep breath, she entered the office and introduced herself to Saul with a firm handshake and a smile as if he were a business associate instead of the father-in-law she'd never met. Then she stormed past me into our bedroom and shut the door. Later, when my father was in the bathroom, humming some Chinese tune I recognized from my childhood and emitting

occasional flatulence, Lene and I had the inevitable low-volume fight.

"Why do you do exactly opposite of what I tell you?" Lene whispered.

"What was I supposed to do?"

"I've been very quiet over the years about the way they've disrespected me and our marriage," she said. "But don't you, for one second, think I've forgotten. Now you invite him into our house?"

"Well, I wasn't handed a manual on how to treat situations like this," I said. "I didn't grow up with Mr. and Mrs. Perfekt Svanemüllerströp."

She jabbed a finger at me. "Don't talk about my parents like that. You know nothing about them." She turned her back. I attempted to soothe with gentle strokes of my palm against her broad shoulder blades. Beyond the wall, my father cleared his throat and flushed the toilet.

"I'll find out what he wants, find out about my mother, he'll go home, and that'll be all."

She stared at me, her lips pursed, eyes wide. "Why don't you just call her?" she asked again, this time slowly, each word distinct.

As I stared at her blankly, I assumed she wished she wasn't thinking what she thought of me. She sat on the bed, pulled back the sheets, and said disgustedly, "Good night."

The alarm clock read half past four.

Lene slid beneath the duvet and closed her eyes. Her hands were folded beneath the dunes of her breasts. She appeared ready for burial. I wanted to tell her many things as I watched her, my hands in my pockets, then out of pockets. I wanted to say, "Don't make this situation harder on me; you're supposed to be my family."

I heard a knock on the door. I turned out the light and walked into the hall.

"She's sleeping already?" my father said.

I told him Lene had been feeling ill.

"She's very tall," Saul said. "You look like her child."

I glared at him.

Into my ear, he added with a whisper, "Isn't she too old to have children? Is that why you don't want children?"

I shooed him down the hall. "I don't want children because I don't want children."

Saul rolled his eyes. "Wake her up and let's go eat," he said. "I'm starving."

"I'm not hungry," I said. "If you want to eat, you can go out to eat yourself."

My father followed me. "Well, I don't speak the language—"

"Everyone speaks English!" I barked before I could stop myself.

My father placed an index finger to his closed lips. "You'll wake Elena," he whispered.

I dropped myself into one of my two leather office chairs, which bookended a small table with a conference phone. Saul sat across from me. This was where I held meetings back when I had clients. I tried to convince myself that Saul was no worse than a bitchy, liver-spotted, paper-skinned client with warts on his knuckles. I looked out the window at the low roof across the street. Twilight already. I turned to my father, who draped his arms over the back of the chair like it was a throne of which he'd grown bored.

"Tell me about Momma," I said. "Just say it." I liked how assertive I sounded, so I repeated it louder. The next thing I knew, my face was quaking, and I was shouting, "Just fucking say it!"

My father's eyes narrowed, and I could tell he was mentally frisking me, probing my outburst, trying to decide whether to finally play his downturned card.

"Your mother was diagnosed with clinical depression," he said flatly.

"And that's not serious?!"

"I didn't want to worry you."

"Isn't that why you're here?" I said. "Because you're worried?"

"I had business in Europe as well."

"What do you mean by clinical depression?" I said. "Did something happen, and you called a doctor?"

"Yes," my father said, elongating the word as if unsure.

"So what happened?"

"Momma has been having a difficult time lately. I've been very busy, and she's been more alone than usual. I think she needs family to be with her now."

"Family meaning me."

"No, a foster family," my father said. "Of course, family meaning you!"

I pinched my sinuses and sighed. "What did the doctor recommend?"

"Therapy and pills."

I snickered. "Brilliant. Try not to be too specific."

Saul thrust himself forward to the edge of the seat, startling me. "I don't appreciate this constant stream of questioning and distrust," he said. "You're not the only one who cares about Momma, okay? She has been my wife of forty years. If you care so damn much, why haven't you come home? One phone call a year. That's all we get from our only son."

"Okay, enough—"

"No, not enough," my father said, wagging a long pinky nail at me. "Not enough. The point is not the preliminary diagnosis, because that has yet to be finalized. But I think we know at this juncture that the final diagnosis is just a formality in nature. The point is that it is now time for you to come home. At least for a visit. Before I left, she begged me, on her knees, begged me to bring you

back to Bordirtoun."

My cheek began to pulsate involuntarily. I imagined Momma, weeping on her knees, clinging to my father's sleeve as he left the house. I had witnessed such a scene when I was ten, when my father threatened to leave us for one of his gaggle of mistresses. He pushed Momma to the ground and left as I looked on, crying. He should have left us, but he never did. Truth was, I'd often suspected my mother was depressed. She was, at the very least, a deeply unhappy and unloved woman, thanks to Saul. I just never had the courage or the diligence to do anything about it (or, frankly, even bring it up). Instead I fled, lived my own life as selfishly as possible, and left her repeated calls unreturned. As I sat across from my father, I avoided looking at him.

"This is not about whatever gripe you have against me." Saul got up, shoved his hands into his pockets, and paced the room with his trademark slouch. I imagined this was the way he paced his office at Bordirtoun City Hall. "I'm sure you feel guilty like I do. You may not believe me but I wish I could make your mother happy too. This is about taking care of Momma and making her better."

"I just don't trust you."

My father raised his hands, palms facing me as if he was a criminal, and I was an approaching police officer. "There's no reasoning with you." He backpedaled toward the door. "I'll tell Momma it's my fault like everything else in everyone else's lives. I run a major metropolitan city but I can't get my own son, my only son, to come home, even to his sick mother." He shook his head at the ceiling. "Is it so wrong for us to want you near as we grow older? I know I haven't been an ideal father but when will my penance end?"

I stared at our elegant ceiling moldings, ornamented with three-dimensional serpentine gold braids, one of the reasons Lene and I chose this place. When I had nothing to say, no plan to move

forward, and no answers to any of Life's larger questions, I often reclined in my chair and sought answers in those ringlets. I knew Lene would not be happy if I agreed to go back to Bordirtoun, but were she in my position, would she turn away her own parents?

"I'll leave tomorrow morning," Saul said. "I can see I'm not welcome."

And yet, he didn't step through that doorway or go to dinner or bed; my father waited, hands in the air. I was fairly certain he would stand there for the rest of the night until I said something.

I took a deep, unsatisfying breath. "I'll ask Lene."

"She won't say yes," my father said. "She doesn't know us."

She knows you well enough, I thought.

"If she says no, you'll still come?"

I squirmed in my seat and didn't reply.

"I'm telling Momma you'll still come."

I sighed, and my chin tipped down in a manner that resembled a nod. My father's face froze. I can only presume he was as surprised as I was. "That's a yes," he said.

"No."

He pulled out his cell phone and began punching numbers. "Then I'll tell her you don't want to see her."

"Wait—"

"Perfect, then I'll make your flight arrangements," he said. "Momma will go crazy with excitement." He laughed at his own joke as I scowled at him silently.

"I have classes," Lene whispered in Danish through clenched teeth when I asked her if she would come with me. For one week, I'd said. We lay in the dark of our bedroom, our stomachs growling.

"You can find a substitute."

"No."

"Why not?"

"Because you didn't listen to me," she said. "You never listen to me."

I leaned over and touched her soft flank. "*Skat.*"

Lene brushed my hand away.

"It's only one week," I said. "They're getting older, and I don't want to be completely unavailable forever. I don't think it's too much to ask."

"One week in five years is 'available'?" Lene said. "You could just call your mother and ask how she's doing. Instead, you fly halfway around the world just because your dad tells you. It's half-hearted and over-the-top at the same time. Like everything you do."

I peeled aside the comforter and got out of bed. "I'm just trying to do the right thing."

My father snored in the next room. I shut my eyes, hoping I was in a bad dream. The floorboards creaked beneath our marital bed. I hoped for a response, any response, to affirm that Lene might actually understand me, even if I didn't fully understand myself. She stirred, swallowed audibly. Then her words resounded, sharp and forceful.

"He's playing with you, Sully."

This had been exactly what I wanted to avoid by moving to Europe. A life of poisonous Pongs. To this day, when it rains and we're not allowed outside to play wiffleball in the prison yard, the guards roll steel tables into the cafeteria with PONG consoles bolted to the tops. When I see that stupid game, that ridiculous white square slugging across that white line only to come back again, I feel like vomiting.

I feel like changing my last name.

2.

I CAN'T SLEEP.

Jaynuss called me today and told me that my first chapter was on track, that the parole board would empathize with my struggle to remain a good man despite my villainous father's influence. "Make sure he's the bad guy and you're the victim," he advised. He was breathing hard and grunting between words. Sounded like he was working out. "Make yourself seem like the unluckiest motherfucker on the planet. Make 'em think the stars of the Zodiac will never, ever, never align for Sulliver Pong."

"Are you at the gym?" I asked.

"Fuck," Jaynuss said. "Yeah. Gotta." He grunted again. "Go." Then he hung up.

I lean over my upper bunk and watch the curled, hulking mass of Manny. He is shivering and his blanket lays crumpled on the ground. Someone releases a guttural wail from a distant cell. It's hard to decipher whether the wail is from physical pain, ecstasy, or despair. A rat with gold fur skitters across the cement and vanishes into the wall. In the Chinese Zodiac, the Rat is a leader, a pioneer, even a conqueror.

Should you ever desire to disprove the validity of Chinese astrology, you can begin with the Pongs.

My great-great-granduncle Millmore was born in the Year of the Dragon. The Dragon is supposed to be stately, fiery, passionate, lucky and even intellectual. Unfortunately, according to the historical records of the Pong Library (which I requested from the Pong Foundation's "Prisoners Peroose Too" book lending program), Millmore was nothing like a Dragon; he was quiet to the point of muteness and suspected to be mildly retarded.

Parris Pong, the brothel owner, was born the Year of the Pig, the simple, honest, and loyal zodiac animal probably best assigned to Millmore. Parris, however, was probably most like a Dragon's dark side: ambitious, power-hungry, and egotistical—an all-around sore loser. There are numerous reports of Parris treating his ladies roughly when they decided to leave his brothel. In fact, Sunblaze Wilde, one of his former prostitutes, disappeared the day after she quit, and Parris was the last person to see her. While Parris was never charged with a crime, Wilde's case is still an unsolved mystery.

Francisco, the evangelical pastor, was born on a Monkey year. The Monkey is self-indulgent and tends to lack high morals—the polar opposite of Francisco's personality. From everything I've read, Francisco was always positive, ascetic, and devoted to God.

I was born in the Year of the Rat. The Rat can be highly ambitious, unapologetic about promoting his own agendas. Rats have total control over their emotions and may use them to exploit and manipulate their friends and foes. If anything, my father had the attributes of a Rat. He, however, happened to be a Sheep. The Sheep is supposed to be passive, indecisive, and over-sensitive—the wuss of the Zodiac. Saul and I must have accidentally swapped signs.

Lene was, again, right about my passive ways. Couldn't I have said, "No, father, no, I know you have some hidden agenda, and I'm not coming home?" Couldn't I have just called my mother to make my own judgment about her mental health? Well, of course I could have, but I didn't. It was too much trouble! If I were completely honest, I'd have admitted that I actually felt somewhat relieved to be leaving Denmark for a few days. No need to pretend to find a job. No need to fill my aimless hours bulletpointing goals I'd never achieve. No need to feign my equality in Denmark's allegedly egalitarian culture. Something to do!

But what? What was I planning to do? It pains me to admit that, to this day, I have no idea. Perhaps I naively hoped that my mere presence after two decades would make Momma feel better. More likely, I was just going home to assuage my guilt. Give Momma and Saul one week, and then I'd have bought myself another twenty years sans Pong, and I'd come home to Lene, and we'd live out the rest of our days in Denmark in peace. Alas, my father, like the Rat he should have been, had his own plans.

Manny cries out in his sleep, startling me. He is tossing, turning, torquing, and whimpering. He is having a nightmare—that much is obvious. Several rats emerge from the wall as if Manny is their master. They skitter across the floor and bound into his bed. He half-wakes, reaches and grabs his blanket off the cement ground, and balls it beneath his chin, like a child. Though the rats are running around to and fro in his bed, Manny goes still and begins to snore, finally at peace with his family of vermin.

A solitary descent into Bordirtoun. Just a hop (Zurich), skip (Dallas Fort-Worth) and a jump (commuter plane from El Paso) from

Copenhagen. I looked out the plane's window at the river in which my great-great-granduncle Millmore died. The color of it was a dark brown, even more like soiled toilet water than I remembered. The river split Bordirtoun into two halves. To the west, there was Old Town, the poorer side of the city, a sprawling and bleak flatness, a brown frontier quilt, punctuated by tubes of dark smoke rising. As a high schooler, when I felt adventurous, I took the bus over the river and walked alone through the nearly abandoned neighborhoods of Old Town. The air smelled of sulfur, lead and sunburnt rubber from the shallow piles of tires lying in the gutters and the nearby chemical plant. Stray dogs trotted down the middle of streets; even they kept to themselves in Old Town. The most memorable sounds of my early teen years were the whir of electric fans and the braying of a televangelist ("ya see the Gospel-says…") through the gaping windows of the shacks I walked past. Once, I peeped a man inside his living room wearing a cowboy hat, riding one of those coin-operating aluminum horses you find outside old supermarkets, belting out hymns. Yes, Old Town was once a strange little wasteland safari. From above, it didn't seem like much had changed, or that much would ever change. Of course, I would discover that that was far from the case.

On the other side of the river, in New Town, where I was born, the skyline was much more developed than before: four new mini-skyscrapers near downtown. On first glance, one might almost mistake this new Bordirtoun for a legitimate, eighth-tier American city like Santa Fe or Scottsdale. There were low black mountains to the town's northeast edge, the place where Momma used to take me hiking as a child. During one of our hikes, I walked ahead of her a few steps on the trail and when I turned around, she was gone. Where did she go? I waited for her for what seemed like an eternity. After a few minutes, I went back and forth on the trail, crying, in a full and frothy panic. Finally, she emerged from the bushes, tying the sash of her dress. She said she had gone to take a dump. As I eyed those hills from the airplane, I still felt a nip of the fear of getting lost. I looked at the empty seat next to me, the half-vacant cabin, and I took a deep breath and reminded myself it would only be a week before I was reunited with Lene, cooing my way back into her favor.

After nearly thirty-three hours of travel, my groin was killing me, and once we landed, I struggled to get off the plane. My clothes were damp with sweat, and at the newsstand, I bought some gum and an umbrella. I chewed three pieces of spearmint to steel myself against the agony. The umbrella served as a makeshift walking stick.

I stopped at a sign that read, "Welcome to Saul Pong Airport— Enjoy your stay in the PONG Capital of the World."

The last time I had been here, the airport was named after Davy Crockett!

The airport name wasn't the only place where I'd see my father's presence. In a mural, he stood tall above a throng of toddlers grasping at his legs. On a large well-lit advertisement, my father's beaming face endorsed Bordirtoun Bank and Trust. Another ad showed my father wearing a plaid shirt and jeans, a shovel in one hand and a shotgun slung over his shoulder (Bordirtoun Construction and Rifle Company). There was a blown-up black-and-white photo of Saul wearing bell bottoms, a denim shirt with enormous lapels, and giant sunglasses indoors, playing PONG. I recognized the photo from my childhood. On my way to the baggage claim, I nearly bumped into a glass box. Inside? According to the plaque, one of the first PONG consoles ever manufactured! I stopped to take several deep breaths; I felt like I was hyperventilating. My father's face was everywhere.

Outside the baggage claim, a thin man with a silver slug-shaped mustache waited for me behind a yellow divider. He was wearing a cowboy hat, a dark suit, sunglasses, and an earpiece, and he held a glossy white board bearing my name spelled with three Ls.

"Mr. Pong, your father sent me," he said. When I handed him my bag, he inspected me like I was modeling his Ross Dress for Less suit. "Do you need additional help?"

"What do you mean?"

"A wheelchair, perhaps?"

"Do I look like I need a wheelchair?" I followed the man toward the exit, hobbling so slowly that he had to pause several times to wait for me to catch up. A limo waited outside, and I exhaled, still trying to shake the sundry images of my father smiling. While the driver put my luggage in the trunk, I slid across the leather seat and dialed my father. "Sully?" he answered with a low tone.

"Nice airport," I said flatly.

"Thanks, son!" he exclaimed. Then, softly, he added, "I'm in a meeting. Come to the hotel." He hung up before I could ask which one. I dialed him again. Straight to voicemail.

The driver started the car. I asked him if he knew where "The Hotel" was. He didn't reply, but the limo moved forward and made occasional turns, so I assumed the driver did know. As we entered Bordirtoun's city limits, new tract homes the color of blanched flesh appeared, followed by an office park with giant obsidian windows. There was a Chinese supermarket named D. Duck 88 where the Cattleman's Diner used to be. The parking lot was full and multichromatic with cars, and there was a larger-than-life upside-down cartoon roast duck statue at its entrance. The duck was hanging by its bound feet from a giant rod. D. Duck had an "88" (eight was a lucky number because it rhymed with the word "rich" when spoken in Chinese) branded on its breast, and its head was upturned and smiling, winking at the public, evidently happy to be strung up like an ousted dictator.

The limo signaled at the downtown exit. Against the backdrop of a shadowy mountain peak, the bronze dome of City Hall stood tallest among the crowns of the office buildings. We stalled behind a line of brake lights at the off-ramp, waiting to merge. On the overpass, cars and trucks were bumper-to-bumper, the exhaust rising and crinkling in the heat. The passengers had just crossed the Mexican border into America.

We circled the downtown roundabout in the center of which stood the statue I recalled from my childhood. A bearded Leland Stanford, the man who brought the railroad to Bordirtoun. But upon closer inspection, Stanford no longer had a beard. The long hair, the slight slouch, the left leg turned outward to show off the ample cod piece (a la the Jefferson Memorial), the bulbous eyes, the wide grin. I lowered the window and stuck my head out of the car to get a closer look. The statue was of my father! Bronze Saul Pong was rotating, its right arm raising and lowering a thumbs up, the rusty joints squealing loud and long like an elephant's fart.

Saul, Saul, and more Saul! He was the subject of a Mao-sized illustrated portrait hanging from the front of City Hall. Painted likenesses of Saul, Millmore in a rice hat, Parris, and a collar-wearing Francisco Pong hung side-by-side beneath a sign on the marquee of the Museum of PONG. The exhibit was entitled, "A History of the Pongs—Bordirtoun's First Family." Waiting at a stoplight, an obese curly-haired couple wore matching sweat-mooned cotton tees that read "The Birthplace of PONG," beneath my father's silkscreened, smiling face.

I rapped on the glass between the driver and me. "Where are we going?"

He didn't turn around, but he did bellow out of the side of his mouth: "The *Pong*elliano."

A track of sweat ran down the back of my neck. It finally occurred to me then that Saul's hidden agenda might reveal itself at any moment, and I was, for some mysterious reason, ill-prepared.

I don't recall what I was expecting upon my Bordirtoun arrival. Perhaps I expected to be driven to my mother's house, where she'd feed me grapes, and I could sleep off the long trip, and perhaps rub one out into a tube sock on my creaky old twin bed from high school. Regardless of what my past-self expected, I certainly did not expect what actually happened that day.

With each passing stoplight, the dark hills grew closer and larger. The limo turned left and followed a sinuous path down past a giant turf golf course. At the end of the road, a red clubhouse and several high-rise buildings overlooked the river and the adjacent northbound highways. In thick gilded cursive, the sign read "The Pongelliano." A bronze face of my father smiled out from the frieze.

The driver stopped in front of the hotel entrance, got out, walked around the rear of the limo, and opened my door. I stepped out and followed him. Glacial air-conditioning made bumps rise on my arms as I limped my way through the lobby. Immediately, I noticed the lights from the slot machines, the green table felt, the black jackets of the croupiers, the faint traces of cigarette smoke and the buffet carvery. A casino?

As I passed an inexplicable ice sculpture of my tie-wearing father (rolled-up shirt sleeves) standing with a pick-axe resting on his shoulder, his voice startled me, and it took me a moment to realize it was coming not from the ice sculpture but from over the intercom. "Hi, I'm Saul Pong, the true inventor of the game PONG. Welcome to The Pongelliano, the Pong family's hotel. I hope you enjoy your stay. In fact, I feel personally responsible for your enjoyment. If there's anything I can do to make your stay more enjoyable, please do not hesitate to visit me at my personal suite on the eighth floor—"

The smell of talcum powder and too much perfume turned my head, and I was nearly trampled by a jangling headdress and the showgirl attached. The purple-lensed woman gave her sequined bra straps a quick upward tug, and my eyes drifted down to her fleshy belly and the glittery bikini bottom, tight enough to create an indentation at the hips.

"Careful, Mr. Pong," the driver said, motioning me toward a descending staircase.

A paunchy man in a spa robe wrapped an arm around the showgirl's shoulders and led her away, grinning and chewing with his mouth open. The driver led me down a series of hallways. The din of the casino faded.

"I'll pay you to tell me where we're going," I said.

He said nothing.

"How much do you want?" I asked.

"Sorry, Mr. Pong."

We went through a door, and I found myself in a room the size of a carnival booth, facing a heavy drape. My father was talking to someone, but I couldn't clearly hear what he was saying.

"I demand to know what is happening," I whispered to the driver.

He moistened his mustache with his lower lip. Then he grabbed my elbow and pulled me close. I tried to shake free but he held tight. He smelled oddly industrial, like leaking natural gas.

His jacket vibrated: his mobile. He whipped aside the drape and shoved me into the light. I halted my stumble with the umbrella and looked around.

I was on a stage. There was an audience before me, a diffuse gathering of note-scribbling reporters and television cameras. The room smelled of tortillas and pork. All the reporters facing me were white men wearing cowboy hats. They were uniformly old and wizened as if they had all graduated from the same pre-World War II journalism school and were attending an alumni reunion, and their faces were marked by embedded scowls and unkempt eyebrows. The others had their hunched backs turned to me. They were lined up to attack the spit-roasted pig. My father was standing behind a podium a few feet to my left. Off the side of the dais, Saul's besuited, dark-haired handlers were shoulder to shoulder, hands behind their backs and slouching, the same way my father stood. I was standing next to a photo on an easel. It was me, half-smiling, thirty pounds lighter, from my graduate school commencement. I'd had hair back then. Music played—the type one hears in movie trailers, heavy on the bass drums and cellos. I swallowed. My ears popped.

"There he is," Saul said, beaming without looking at me. "The man of the hour. Just off the plane from Europe. My only son, Sulliver Pong, and the new president of the Pong Foundation. The leader of the Old Town redevelopment project."

My father's handlers applauded. Flashbulbs went off. I shielded my eyes. One of the thinner reporters raised his hand and began jumping up and down. My father called on him.

"Why now Sulliver what made you say 'enough is enough I'm coming home I can't allow Old Town to be the ghetto of Bordirtoun anymore?'" The reporter blurted his words in a stream without pause. I didn't understand the question. I glimpsed one of the other reporters chomping down on a taco and splattering beans and salsa on his notebook.

One of my father's people pushed a microphone stand in front of me.

"Um…" I began. The speakers screeched with feedback.

"Mayor Pong has said that the new Old Town will be primarily a commercial zone," another reporter said. "What is your plan for affordable housing for the current Old Town residents?"

My father walked to my side and put his arm around me. More flashbulbs popped. "We apologize for the abbreviated press conference but my son is very tired from the very long flight from the Old World," he said with a chuckle. "Sulliver will be releasing a more detailed statement shortly."

As he guided me off-stage, I saw the large banner that read, "The Pong Fundation: Hope and Prospurrety Generation to Every Generation of Bordirtoun—the Pong Family Tradishion Across Generation."

In my father's dressing room, my groin hurt more with every limp, and I was suddenly desperate to urinate.

"A press conference?! A press conference?!" I shouted, my voice sharp and shrill, not unlike my father's when angered.

Saul pulled open the door and looked left and right. Then he locked it and flipped on the stereo. Chinese music blared as he reclined on the couch, arms wide. He crossed his legs and took a deep satisfied breath. "This will be good for the people," he began. "You haven't seen how poor Old Town has become. They are second-class citizens for all intense and purpose—"

"Intents!" I corrected. "I have a home. I have a family."

Saul leaned forward and squinted. "This is your home. Your family is here."

"My wife is my family."

My father laughed. "That *white* woman? She can't even have children."

I smashed the tip of my umbrella on the ground. Saul stopped smiling.

My father's eyes dropped, and he gripped and rubbed the back of his neck hard, like he was trying to open a jar of elusive asshole antidote. "I simply figured that while you were home, you could help me."

I buckled into the nearest chair, my shirt stuck to my sweaty back. I squeezed my aching thighs together. "I said one week."

"Remember how Old Town used to be?" he said. "Remember when we went to the black district and saw that…what was it? A jazz club?"

I had no recollection of ever going to Old Town with my father, and I told him so.

"You were there!"

"No, not so."

"Well, maybe it was someone else."

"One of your other sons?"

"Don't be ridiculous," Saul said. "This is my New Deal, my legacy, but forget about that, that's me. Elena will understand. You can help break ground on the revitality creation of the blacks and Mexicans, and I'll be re-elected, and you can go home. I promise."

"No!" I said. "No. No and no."

"I have some business meetings in Tokyo next month," he went on as if I had said nothing. "The groundbreaking must happen on schedule or the development won't be finished by election season. I need you to manage this project."

"Why me?"

"I didn't send you to the best schools, two of them, so you could live halfway around the world while I hire someone else to tend to our family's affairs," my father said. "Your education cost me over $200,000, not including interest. I can't believe I've put up with it as long as I have."

"I'm truly sorry for you having to put up with my education."

"At what cost, Sully?"

He almost sang that last sentence. I might have responded with a "Fuck you!" or "I'm leaving," but just as likely, I suppose, I might have said nothing. What I actually said seems insignificant now. Because once I sprung from that chair, the course of my life would change forever. In one week, I would no longer be cooing my way back into Lene's good graces. I would still be in Bordirtoun, and during that time, old regrets, old fires, old habits and the old rages I thought I had fled would return to have one more go at me.

I felt a pop in my pelvis and collapsed, crying out. My pants grew hot and wet, and I felt a deep nether release in the midst of the pain. Saul dropped to my side, exclaiming "no, no, no," and while I tried to remain motionless, he rolled me back and forth on the carpet as if I were on fire.

At the hospital, the doctor informed me that I had suffered a grade-three groin strain. One of my adductor muscles had ruptured, tearing away from the pelvic bone. Emergency surgery was necessary. She asked me if I played a lot of recreational football or soccer, and her eyes nearly popped out of her head when I told her I rarely exercised outside of the occasional short bike ride. She recommended against travel and said that rehabilitation could take up to three months.

Laid out on a gurney in the hospital hallway while I waited for surgery, I called Lene and delivered the bad news.

"I'll have to stay longer," I said through clenched breaths. My damaged muscle felt like it was dangling from my thigh. My piss-wet pant legs had been rent with scissors.

"I knew something like this would happen." Her voice was rising, tears en route.

I tried to pull off my own boxers but the nurse instructed me not to move. He unsheathed me, exposing my wet, shrinking penis.

"Don't cry," I said softly. "I wish you were here, and I could hold you."

The nurse frowned, blinking hard.

"I'm talking to my wife!" I exclaimed. A beep. The call dropped. "Prick."

"Jus' makin' sure I didn't forget nothin', sir," the nurse said as he dragged my gurney down the hall.

I tried to dial again but my phone read "No Service." The banks of halogen lights flickered, then died altogether. The nurse informed me in the dark that this was normal; the hospital was just conserving power for the critical ER quadrants and the ICU.

THE MISADVENTURES
OF MILLMORE PONG

THE YEAR WAS 1852, the Year of the Rat. As a Dragon, the Year of the Rat was supposed to be a fortuitous one for Millmore Pong in all areas of life. At twenty, he was the eldest son of the first wife of a port official in Guangzhou, one of the most important seaside cities in the world in the nineteenth century. A typical young man of Millmore's background would be working toward the district imperial examination, and if he was fortunate enough to be one of the passing five percent, Millmore would enter the gentry and soon enjoy some of the perks his father Pong Feng enjoyed: exemptions from criminal punishment, eligibility for state stipends, and very fashionable robes made of embroidered silk.

But Pong Jong Dong (Millmore's Chinese name loosely translated to the unusually blunt descriptor of "Eastern Male") was destined for a different path. He'd never been good in school, had trouble learning to read and write, and had, over time, become a retiring fellow, whose favorite activity was to do cartwheels and backflips alone in the courtyard of his family home. He had few, if any, friends, and even the servants feared that the people with whom Millmore seemed to quietly converse and playfight were imaginary.

One day, Millmore accompanied his father and his half-brother Yixin (Sulliver Pong's great-great-great-grandfather) to visit someone Pong Feng claimed was "very, very important to the family's future." Because he was bringing his two sons and the Pongs lived but a kilometer from the imperial office, Pong Feng decided to eschew the servant-shouldered palanquin and walk through the streets of downtown Guangzhou. Millmore's father thought that communing with the non-gentry (the poor and uneducated) was an uncomfortable but necessary exercise to demonstrate to his boys what a life outside the civil service would be like so they would study harder and with greater urgency. Still, the minute Pong Feng began walking through the throngs of meek street merchants, opium addicts, and perhaps worst of all, the growing number of long-haired Christians (both foreign and Chinese), he began to feel disgusted and a smidgeon fearful. Pong Feng ordered his sons to hold hands so as to avoid losing each other. Though Millmore was standing closest to him, Pong Feng clasped the hand of the taller, stockier Yixin, who was born several weeks after Millmore to Pong Feng's bovine fourth wife, and the interlinked trio weaved through the crowd. Millmore, who was at least a head shorter than both his half-brother and father, struggled to read the signs on the stores. Ginger Shop. Hat Store. Milk-Tea. Yixin jerked his arm hard enough to cause an audible pop from Millmore's elbow.

"Walk faster," Yixin said.

"Listen to your brother," Pong Feng said. "There's nothing to see here. Pay attention to the people, though. Remember, you do not want to become them."

Millmore held to his half-brother as best he could and trailed the focused, straight path of the other Pong men. He sidestepped a merchant shouldering a bamboo pole curved with the weight of basins. He nearly tripped over a longhaired man lying on the side of the road making sweet smoke from a pipe. They turned a corner and came upon a clearing, surrounded by tall buildings and banyan trees swaying in the wind at the Pearl River's edge. The waterfront was cluttered with large sailboats and smaller junks. Workers unloaded crates at the pier. Hundreds shuffled quickly from the river to the streets of Guangzhou, kicking up swirls of dirt into Millmore's eyes. The air smelled of fish pungency. Millmore inhaled deeply from the grit. To him, the air was sweet. Millmore failed to hear his father calling his name repeatedly.

"Jong Dong!" his father said. "This way!"

Millmore had absent-mindedly wandered from his half-brother. His father gripped him by the arm and pulled him away from the river. With Millmore in one hand and Yixin in the other, Pong Feng led his sons into the shaded entrance of the imperial office. He removed his flat-bottomed, bowl-shaped hat, straightened his queue, and mopped his large forehead with the horsehoof cuff of his robe. He licked his fingers and moistened his long whiskers. Then he fitted his hat, closed his eyes, and performed several tai chi movements, making loud breathing and hawking noises while his boys waited.

"Very important person," Millmore's father repeated when he was finished with his tai chi. Then he added, "Don't shame me."

Yixin nodded vigorously. "I won't shame you."

Pong Feng smiled and patted Yixin on the head. "I know you won't."

Millmore's attention had drifted again to the river.

"Jong Dong!"

Pong Feng fanned a finger and gave Millmore another warning look.

They walked up the stairs and into the chamber of the imperial commissioner. The newly appointed leader was Ye Mingchen, who had been tasked with taking a harder line on trade with the West after China's embarrassing defeat to the British in the First Opium War. China's loss had, however, been the Pong family's gain, as Pong Feng had amassed a small fortune over the past two decades from accepting silver from the British, French and Americans in exchange for port access for the purposes of illegal opium smuggling.

Wearing a much wider hat than Pong Feng and a dark and heavily embroidered imperial robe, the commissioner was a squat, round middle-aged man (roughly Millmore's height), who habitually cupped a short beard that made the rest of his face, thanks to his bulbous forehead, appear cartoonishly large. He also had a poorly aimed gaze that gave Millmore the impression that his nose was being stared at.

"Honorable Commissioner." Pong Feng kowtowed. "It is a great privilege. I have heard many good things."

The commissioner looked up at the taller Pong Feng. "I've heard much about you too."

"Good things."

"Is that a question?"

Pong Feng pinched the erect collar on his robe. "I suppose."

"I've heard enough to doubt your obedience regarding Our High and Mighty Emperor's edict to resist the barbarians," the commissioner said.

"I can only say that my family and I are very committed—"

"I've heard many tales of your gift for manipulation," the commissioner said. "It is evident that you have brought your sons here to gain undue influence."

Millmore noticed a centipede of sweat crawl down his father's jaw. "With respect, Commissioner, I've brought my eldest son,

Yixin, here today to meet you as a hero of Our Celestial Empire. I've informed him how much I admire your achievements, and I believe he will be very well-qualified to work with us one day should he pass the district imperial examination," Pong Feng said.

Something about what his father said didn't sound right to Millmore. Before Millmore could articulate his intuition and assert that he, and not his half-brother, was the eldest son, Yixin kowtowed to the commissioner and recited a line from the emperor's recently publicized statements about the wickedness of Britain's opium trade.

"Very good, young one," the commissioner said with a smile. "Why is your other son here?"

Pong Feng stared blankly at the commissioner for a moment, before turning to Millmore. "His mother, my main wife, asked me to bring him today. She says it's good for him to meet important people. He's a good boy. Just slow."

Millmore's face turned a deep shade of crimson. He realized that his father had chosen Yixin to be his top heir. Millmore did not hate his father, but from this moment forward, he could not love him either. Millmore began softly humming an unknown song to the rhythm of the merchants' cawing outside, audible through an open window on this very warm and humid day.

"He's very close to his mother," Pong Feng went on. "Rarely leaves her side. Likes to dance. Likes to bathe several times a day in perfumed water. I don't think he'll pass the examination."

"Perhaps one day," the commissioner said.

Pong Feng glanced askance at his true eldest son. "No, I don't think so."

Though Millmore's father had taken all manner of gifts from all manner of foreigners during his career, Pong Feng was not about to sacrifice his livelihood for a few extra taels of silver with the virtuous new commissioner in office. For the next four years, he ingratiated himself to Commissioner Ye, and his work paid off as Yixin passed the imperial exam and gained a tariff-collecting post at the port. Millmore meanwhile continued to languish at home, lacking the book-smarts for the civil service elite. Yes, he may have been well-suited for the physical labor of the non-gentry classes, but his father opined that such work was beneath a member of the Pong family. After all, having a son do physical labor was not why Pong Feng had studied so hard to rank first class in his examinations and certainly not why he had worked so hard at being a corrupt official over the years.

Soon, however, Pong Feng would have far less time to dictate Millmore's path in life. His devotion to the bureaucracy would place the Pongs where they would become accustomed over the next several generations: on the wrong end of history's truncheon in China. The British didn't make nearly the effort that Pong Feng did to ingratiate themselves to the new commissioner, and in 1856, they opened naval hostilities again with China, and the Queen's Navy proceeded to bludgeon the country in the Second Opium War. Commissioner Ye was captured as a prisoner of war, and Pong Feng and Yixin were reassigned to rural villages in the Guangxi Province in Southwest China. They were forced to spend much of the year away from Guangzhou and Pong Feng's five wives, eleven children (nine of them girls) and the family's many servants.

Banished to the hinterlands, Pong Feng backslid into turpitude and addiction. He soon cultivated an emperor-sized opium habit that led to the sale and seizure of many of the family's possessions, including, eventually, Millmore's favorite porcelain bathtub. At his new rural post, Pong Feng kept a second family that consisted of three more wives and to his continued consternation, two additional daughters. Millmore's mother tried to get Pong Feng to stop smoking opium, which only stoked the fires of his rage toward his first son.

"You spoiled that boy," Pong Feng snarled at Millmore's mother. "Look at him. Lounging about like a dumb monkey. It's not possible that he's truly my son. How can my son be so slow? You must have defective people in your family."

Millmore observed his parents fight behind a gridded screen that separated his mother's bedroom and bathing quarters, where he was sitting in a barrel full of perfumed water.

"Why do you hate him so much?" Millmore's mother cried. "He's your oldest son!"

"My oldest son can't be dumb and mute!" Pong Feng shouted. "I am a Pong! I am a presented scholar!"

"A scholar of thievery and poison!"

Pong Feng threatened to slap his wife. Then he repeated his threat and added that if she didn't walk before him, with her bound feet in lotus shoes, slowly and swaying in an arousing manner, he'd beat Millmore as well. Out in the country, the women didn't bind their feet because they had to work in the fields. As his wife teetered back and forth in front of him, Pong Feng was glad to be back in urban civilization with his original local family. Millmore became nauseous at the sight of his seated father, whose hand was moving beneath his robe like a lost mole.

When he was finished, Pong Feng asked Millmore and his mother to leave the room and summon the second wife.

The year was 1861, the Year of the Monkey, which, according to the Chinese horoscope, forecasted to be a very unfortunate year for Dragons. Instead, it was the year that changed Millmore's life forever, the year he finally became more than Pong Feng's slow son. Millmore and his mother took the sedan chair to nearby Dongshan Lake. The two left their servants and walked slowly around the water's edge, occasionally stopping to observe their surroundings. His mother pointed out that the shape of junks in the lake looked like the cockroaches in their kitchen.

As Millmore tried to skip a pebble across the surface of the water, his mother added, "I love you, Jong Dong."

"I love you too," Millmore said. When he turned to his mother, he saw that her cheeks were the color of guava rind and her eyes moist. She wrapped her twig-like arms around him, stroking and petting his head. She rarely displayed that level of affection. Millmore knew something was wrong.

"Do you like the lake, son?"

"I like the earth," he said. "I like the water. I like that it's always moving. I like always moving."

His mother began to weep. Millmore didn't know how to respond. He waited for her to regain composure.

"Your uncle runs a business," she said. "He puts people on boats to America to work there. He thinks that you should go to Gold Mountain."

Millmore was silent. Though he could not call home a particularly happy place, and he knew he could be nothing more than a disappointment to his father, the notion of leaving filled him with fear.

"Are you coming with me?"

"No, Jong Dong," she said. "I must stay with the family."

Millmore began to realize what his mother was asking him to do. "Then I don't want to go."

"You must," she said. "Your father is not good to you. I can't watch it anymore."

"He's not good to you either."

Millmore's mother gripped his shoulders, pushed him to arm's length, and looked into his eyes. "But I am only a woman."

A month later, with his mother looking on from Guangzhou Harbor, Millmore boarded the boat to America with nothing but his credit-ticket, a change of clothes, a bag of food consisting of cured seafood and dried fruit, and an English-language book about the American government that his mother had given him ("Perhaps you can learn to read English instead," she'd suggested optimistically). A hundred days later, Millmore arrived in San Francisco. Behind a desk at the immigration station, a tall, thin white man with a thick mustache and a monocle requested Millmore's name.

He didn't know what the man was asking. He began emptying his bag, thinking that perhaps something inside would answer the question. The book about American government fell out and landed open on a page with a picture of a doughy-cheeked older gentleman with pouchy eyes and a haircut that fluted outward at the ears like the rim of a bell.

The man looked at the book. Millmore took his attention as a positive sign that something in the pages answered the question. He pointed to the words under the picture.

"Your name is Millard Fillmore?" the man said dubiously.

Millmore nodded and said, "Pong Jong Dong."

"Last name: Pong, okay," the man said. "First name?"

Millmore pointed again at the name, first to the "Mill," then to the "more."

"Millmore?" the man said, writing it down. He adjusted his monocle and slitted his eyes. Millmore nodded an unknowing approval. The man shrugged and chuckled. "I wish you luck, Millmore."

In 1865, two years after the Central Pacific Railroad laid its first rails trying to connect San Francisco and Promontory, Utah, Leland Stanford and his company began hiring Chinese workers. Millmore had made a name for himself as one of the most reliable and athletic Chinese construction workers in San Francisco. So when word struck that Central Pacific was hiring, Millmore and the company for which he'd worked came highly recommended.

In the Sierra Nevadas, the job was dangerous. Carrying sticks of dynamite and a pick, Chinamen were lowered down the side of a mountain in reed baskets. Dangling, the worker would chip at the face of the mountain, place the dynamite in the fresh crevice, light the fuse and signal for the team at the crest to hoist him up. If the team didn't pull fast enough, the Chinaman died in the blast.

Of his cohort, Millmore was the only worker never to suffer so much as a scratch. He relished the job as if he was born to do it. He loved the smell of dirt and gunpowder on his hands, the feeling of thin air in his lungs. He even wove his own reed basket.

In addition to being one of the best workers, Millmore also smelled the best. He bathed twice daily in tea leaves that his mother would send from China. Millmore was hygienically meticulous; he wore cotton pants that he hand-laundered every other day so that the fabric, once imbued with sweat, wouldn't chafe his skin. Even his fellow Chinese workers ridiculed his feminine standard of cleanliness.

The other Chinamen also ridiculed Millmore's asceticism. Having seen the havoc that opium had wrecked on the Pong family in China, Millmore never touched the drug. He neither drank nor gambled. He even taught and extolled the virtues of tai chi to the Irishmen. He was a man who kept to his good-smelling, hard-working self while the other workers blew their meager earnings on gambling, opium, and prostitutes. Millmore was quietly convinced that his asceticism kept him alive longer than the many workers who perished either from the accidents with explosives or from illnesses during the harsh Sierra winters. In 1869, when Leland Stanford drove the final Golden Stake into the ground at Promontory, Millmore was already on his way to his next job in Los Angeles.

On the southbound train from Reno to L.A., Millmore noticed a woman. She was dressed like a westerner in a full, bustled skirt. She wore her hair up braided into a crown. Her skin was pale and reddish like that of a white woman. Upon closer examination, however, Millmore saw that she was Chinese, and something about her calm expression reminded him of his mother. He took off his rice hat and placed it in the rack above his seat. He considered initiating conversation, but decided not to. He was thirty-eight and had never been with a woman.

"You smell nice," the woman said in Cantonese. "Like a woman."

Millmore flushed. "I enjoy a nice bath. I work the railroads, and that's hard work. You smell like my mother."

She giggled, covering her mouth with four fingers. "And how does she smell?"

"Like tea. Like home." Millmore found himself struggling not to cry in front of this attractive woman. He looked out the window to hide his whimpers. Flatness and dirt unfurled before him. Then the mountains, they rose. A great wall.

Millmore wiped his tears with oversized cuffs. That was when he noticed the woman had seated herself next to him. She rested her head on Millmore's shoulder. He was surprised by her forward nature. Her head was light. If he moved, he felt her head would fall away. She offered a white-gloved hand.

"My name is Martha."

Millmore and Martha got married, and over the next several years, they followed the railroad from Los Angeles, to Tuscon, and finally, to an area near the Mexican border where Central Pacific planned to build a tunnel for its track from Los Angeles to the New

Mexico territories. Once the company set up camp at the work site, Martha quickly got pregnant, even though Millmore was often so bone-tired from work that he would have liked nothing more than to fall asleep without dinner. Martha's sexual appetite surprised Millmore. He'd gone from having no sex ever to having sex before breakfast, dinner and perhaps several times during the night. He was surprised they hadn't had several children already given how much sex they'd had.

One afternoon, Millmore returned to his tent and immediately began stripping his sweat-drenched work clothes. An itch had been bothering him for several weeks. Much of his groin had become red with a rash. "My clothes must not be clean," he said to his wife, who was sitting in a rocking chair, seven months pregnant. "I'll have to clean them tonight." He filled a whiskey barrel with water, hoping to take a bath before Martha came after him for sex. Outside, workers complained loudly about wages and the laziness of the Irishmen.

"You're so quiet and agreeable, and the only way I can tell you're happy is when you let me see that one tiny half-smile at the end of the night before we blow out the lamp," Martha said, palming her navel. "Sometimes I wish you'd say more."

Millmore heard none of what Martha was saying because his ears were still ringing from the day's dynamite blasts. "I love you, wife," he said, idly scratching his inner thigh.

"I know you'll be a quiet and strong father for our baby, husband," Martha said.

There was the din of laughter from the camp. The men were joking about how much they enjoyed having a few women around, how much they enjoyed seducing each other's wives.

Millmore got into his bath, shut his eyes and groaned. He heard nothing when Martha said that she had something to confess.

3.

THE BORDIRTOUN PONGS have long been known for being artists of denial. To be such an artist, one must be nearly developmentally disabled at heeding the advice and/or warnings of others. When Millmore's co-workers repeatedly told him that bridge construction was in no way safer than building railroad tunnels, my great-great-granduncle simply nodded and went on his merry way. Probably because, by most accounts, he didn't understand much English and was partially deaf thanks to his repeated exposure to dynamite blasts. When Parris Pong was told by his most loyal customers that he needed to stop bruising his prized prostitutes, he agreed and slapped them face-side instead. Before Francisco Pong was interned, members of his congregation had warned him that his own congregants were questioning his ethnicity. But he persisted, insisting that God saw no color, and all His children would be able to distinguish between Japanese-Americans and Chinese-Americans. Of course, Saul was warned numerous times by Nolan Bushnell himself to stay away from his wife, a warning left unheeded.

Since I've started writing these pages, I have found myself becoming attuned to the patterns of denial in my fellow inmates. There's a wing of sex offenders at Bordirtoun Correctional who have pled not guilty, who spend group therapy sessions maintaining that they did not go over to that teen's house with sexual intentions, never mind that they had condoms in their pockets.

What about my patterns of denial, you ask? Well, you will soon read that once I found myself in repose, in Bordirtoun, for an extended period, certain truths about my character began to assert themselves. Truths I had long ignored, and soon, I would find myself deeper, embedded. You will find that I am similarly skilled at this Pong-ian art of denial. After all, I was the one who came halfway around the world, assuming that my father was telling the truth, knowing full well that he was a world-class liar and cheat.

When I came to, my father was hovering over my bed, his eyes small with examination. He was staring at my right arm and tried to stick a pen in my hand. "The doctor says you are going to stay awhile."

"No," I mumbled. I closed my eyes and tried to sleep.

I felt my father closing my fingers over his pen.

"I said no!" I sat up, wincing, feeling the stitches below.

My father pulled out my meal tray and laid down a clipboarded stack of papers. "Initial on the 'X.'"

"What is this?"

"Building permits."

"No."

"Work can start while you're recovering."

"I'm not signing anything. You're trying to trap me."

"Trap you? Is that what you call our family love?" He clicked the pen. "Sign."

"No."

"What if I paid you?"

"No!"

My father sighed loudly; his mint-masked old man's breath made me turn away. "Fine." He snatched the pen. "Maybe you should tell Momma you don't want to stay."

Saul took the clipboard and stormed out of the room. I expected Momma to come in after him, waiting outside as his plan B. But she didn't show, so I fell back asleep. When I woke, Momma was teetering at my bedside. She was much older, thinner, and shorter than I remembered, her hair a crew-cut white. Her deeply set eyes and bulbous nose were like my own, as were the prominent cheekbones (at least like the ones I'd had before I ballooned). She reached for me, and in my haze, I reached weakly for her. We had both seen better days. Then her fingers curled, and her talons sunk into my arm.

"Momma." I winced.

"Why don't you exercise?" she yelled in Cantonese. "I've always told you to exercise but you don't listen, and now you're so fat, you don't listen, just like your father—"

"I exercise—"

"I don't understand what you're saying," Momma said. "Speak Chinese."

"Dad tells me you're not well," I went on in English.

"I'm not well?" she said, pointing at her throat. "*I'm* not well?"

"Dad told me—"

She gripped my arm again; this time she pulled. "Let's go. I'll show you who's not well."

"I just got out of surgery!"

She sat in the chair by my nightstand. Her face pinkened, and she began to cry.

"I hate you for being away so long," Momma said. "You are a terrible son."

"Momma—"

"How many years have you been married?" she said. "Ten? Fifteen? Where are my grandchildren? When will I get to take care of my grandsons? Why won't you let me see them? What's the point of getting married if you haven't had children? You haven't had them yet, have you?"

"No, Momma, I don't want to be a father," I said.

"She can't have them, can she?" she said. "She's not even a real woman. She's dry and barren, barren and dry."

"Stop, just stop!" I said. "This is why I don't come back."

"And you don't call. If I died, you wouldn't even know."

She kicked the bed with surprising force. My stitches throbbed.

"I'm sorry, Momma, okay? Is that what you want to hear? I'm sorry."

"You should be."

I sighed loudly. "Can't you just say 'It's okay?'"

"It's not okay."

"Dad said you went to the doctor, and he said you were having problems," I said. "What exactly did the doctor say?"

"I didn't go to any doctor."

"Excuse me?"

Momma shook her head. "I went to the dentist last month."

"Don't lie to me," I said. "When Dad came to Europe, he told me you were sick. He told me you were depressed."

"Depressed?"

"Yes, depressed. It's the only reason I came back."

"I have to be depressed for you to visit?" She slapped me on my leg, and I cried out.

"Look, Lene is upset at me for leaving her."

"Who's Lay-na?"

"My wife."

"What kind of name is that?"

"Danish."

"Where's that?"

"Denmark. Where I live."

"Why is she upset that you visit your mother?" she said. "Why is she so important that you have to live so far away that I never see you?"

"She's my wife," I repeated.

"Your wife I've never even met!" Momma shouted. "All my life I waited for you to get married. I dreamed that you'd get married in a church or on a cruise ship. I waited and dreamed, and you got married and didn't even invite us. I know it was her fault. I know it would never have been your idea. I will never see my only son get married again."

The familylessness of my wedding had been very much at my insistence. Momma had been against my decision to stay in Europe, and she had called every few days to leave messages about the three or four documented cases of Nazi persecution of the European Chinese Jews during World War II. She begged me not to become a citizen of what she called "the white continent."

"Are you sure you don't want to invite your parents?" Lene had asked while we addressed the invitations.

"Yes, I'm sure," I said.

"They're going to blame me, you know that, right?" Lene said. "Don't you think you're being too cold?"

Too cold? Was there such a thing? I paused and replayed Momma's messages in my head. I imagined a wedding day of Momma blabbering that Lene was too tall and old for me, and Saul groping the bridesmaids. I did not believe in their capacity to support and respect my life decisions. They have, even to this day, shown no such ability. At the time, I didn't even pause to consider how they might blame

Lene. After all, why would I? I had planned to keep them at arm's length for the rest of our lives. At least, until their health began to fail, and by then, they'd need me, and I'd shut them up once and for all by dangling the blade of the nursing home guillotine over them.

I know this does not make me an ideal son or husband. In any case, I told Lene that I felt quite appropriately cold.

Lene shook her head and shrugged. "Sully."

"No, thank you," I replied as if Lene had been asking me whether I wanted a glass of milk.

"That woman has broken up our family," Momma said, interrupting my recollections.

"She has done nothing of the sort."

"You're just protecting her."

"She doesn't need my protection."

"Then come home!" she said. "Every day your father says he doesn't have enough help. 'If only Sully wasn't in Europe.' 'If only Sully came home.' And you know who he blames? Me! 'You drove him away, you cunt!' 'He doesn't want to come home because you nag him!' That's simply not true. Not true, is it, Sully?"

"I just came home to make sure you're healthy," I said. "And you're fine, right?"

"Don't I look fine?"

I didn't answer.

"Well, I am fine, Sully," she said. "I'm very fine."

"Fine, Momma," I said. "I'm glad. Despite our differences, I still wish you good health and a long life. I really do."

"But you won't come home," she said. "I don't need your well-wishes from so far away."

"Momma." My voice reverted to a whining tone I hadn't heard in decades.

"What if your father divorces me? What will I do? I don't work. I can't work. My English is terrible. I'll end up in Old Town. And then you'll be sorry."

I grew heavy in my immobility. I could not help feeling that I could have done more, if I had truly wanted to. But she had chosen to stay with Saul all these years, knowing full well the man he was. Dare I say she was getting what she deserved?

Momma tugged lightly on my sleeve. "Don't go, Sully," she said. "Come home. Sleep in your old room. I am so alone." She held my hand. I allowed her, but did not close my hand around hers.

"Just for a few days, let's be a family again," she said.

So I agreed to stay with Momma after I was released from the hospital, just for a few days. Probably not my strongest moment, but if my sleeping in my old room would make her feel better, well, I rationalized, wasn't that why I came back to Bordirtoun in the first place?

I've always felt more pathos toward my mother than my father. One of my earliest memories: I was a toddler watching television in the living room, Momma was in the kitchen, and Saul was working at the dining table. Even back then, we were distant planets. We lived in a one-bedroom apartment; my parents were a young couple, moving up in the world. Momma inadvertently spilled milk over some of Saul's papers. Arguing ensued, and Saul punched Momma in the face so hard, she fell sprawled onto our living room rug, narrowly missing where I had been sitting. Legs wide, Saul stood, slouched and huffing, over my unconscious mother. I began wailing. The noise I was creating seemed to surprise my father; I recall him looking around the room as if there was someone watching us. Then he squatted and cornered me. He hugged me close and promised never to hit Momma again. Saul's first broken campaign promise.

Before I departed for college, back when I was far less cynical, I actually offered to help Momma leave Saul. I was packing some boxes in my room, and she was riffling through one of my crates marked for Goodwill. She retrieved a battery-operated dog whose white, nappy fur had turned sooty. She smoothed the fur and reminded me of the long-ago birthday when she had given it to me. I informed her I had no intentions of bringing toys to college. She sighed and laid the dog on its feet on the floor.

"Sully, so grown up now," Momma said. "You're more and more like your father. Always leaving."

I glanced at my empty desk, the barren closets, and thought of Saul and Momma arguing. The arguments ended as so many had ended—with Saul hitting Momma and Momma screaming for him to stop. A knot noosed in my throat. I returned to my packing, stacking a handful of CDs.

"Would you leave him?" I heard myself saying. "With me?"

The flicker behind her eyes, the rapid blinking. She was as surprised as I was by the question. When she didn't respond immediately, I realized she was considering my offer—imagining a life without Saul.

The more fully I envisioned Momma's escape plan, the more I believed it could work. She could rent an apartment, find a job. I could live on campus. Momma was only forty at the time, still young enough to start over. We could both start over. Of course, she never left. Yet another example of advice unheeded by a Pong. That summer, my final one at home, Momma chose instead to get a facelift.

Yes. If you're wondering, my father was once the type of man who taught his son how to ride a bicycle, shoot a basketball, and perform simple multiplication—all things I do now regularly in prison (yes, I teach basic math to a group of especially slow prisoners). Yes, I am reasonably sure that he was once a man I admired and looked to as a sage. Yes, there was some decency, even in Saul, if it makes you feel better. But alas, while I'm sure that other Saul existed, I can hardly remember him with any clarity—he was long gone by the time I was in middle school. The Saul I know is post-Atari, post-PONG, the Saul that decided that being middle-class in a lower-class border town was not good enough for him. At some point in my early years, Momma and I became obstacles in Saul's chase for the bigger, the better, and the more. Yet he never left us. Why? Why not just walk away?

I ask the same questions of the other Pong men. Millmore chose not to strike against the railroad company because he was afraid of losing his job. Yet, his fear ultimately cost him his life. Parris was afraid his "Beest Layddys" would desert, so he used his fists, hoping to strike, with preemption, fear in them just as they had struck fear in him. When Francisco was wrongfully interned at Rio River, he never even tried to protest. Why?

Because, I postulate, of the one trait all Pong men shared and nurtured, one of the reasons that I find myself behind bars: cowardice.

The morning after Momma visited, the nurse who had handled me in the ER entered my room. He had a patchy mustache, cumulus black brows, and a tattoo on his forearm of a forearm with a tattoo of a forearm. I guessed his age to be roughly thirty. He hoisted the trash bag out of the wastebasket without looking at me, without saying a word. I wondered if he was upset with me for snapping at him while I was on that gurney in the hallway. I cleared my throat and asked him if I could access a phone.

He replied that there was only one rotary phone for the entire hospital.

"Can I borrow it?" I said. "I'd like to call my wife."

He scratched his mustache and said he'd do what he could.

I thanked him and asked for his name.

"Jimbor," he said. "You the mayor's son?"

"Yes, that's me." I mentioned I had just returned to Bordirtoun from Europe after many years.

"My wife's been, but I never been," he said, tying up the trash.

"If you and the missus ever get a chance, you should go," I said, my old Bordirtoun mumble returning.

Jimbor frowned and nodded slowly, like he was chewing the concept and didn't like the taste.

"She talks about it a lot."

"I highly recommend it."

"I don't make enough money," he said matter-of-factly.

"Oh." I looked down. "Well, I'll follow up with my father about the wages of hospital workers." I cringed as the words spilled forth, never to be unspoken. Jimbor was too polite to laugh in my face.

"Thanks, Mr. Pong, if you need anything, you let me know," Jimbor said, throwing the belly-end of the trash bag over his shoulder.

"Please, call me Sulliver."

"Sull-ver."

"Thanks," I said. "Oh, and the phone, please."

He grunted and sidled out the door.

Eventually, Jimbor came through, rolling the rotary phone into my room on a nightstand with wheels. I dialed my Danish home and aimed to reassure Lene, telling her in my most upbeat tone that surgery had been successful, the staff had been immensely helpful, and I would be home as soon as they took the stitches out. Which, of course, meant up to three more weeks in Bordirtoun—not ideal, but sufferable.

Lene sighed. "The important thing is that you get better so you can come home."

"Luckily March is a quiet month in the PR world," I said. "Maybe when I get back, we can even go on a long weekend to

Bergen, Norway and have ourselves some whale steak."

"I don't sleep well when you're not in my bed," she said. "I've never noticed that before."

A warmth spread inside me. I was buoyed by the impression that Lene needed me in some way rather than vice versa. "We haven't been apart since we got married," I said.

"Do you have trouble sleeping without me?"

I had slept quite well the night previous. "Sometimes," I said.

She seemed satisfied with my response, and when she asked how my mother was, instead of telling her that my father had lied about the doctor, I answered that Momma was doing better than expected. I told Lene that my mother might not have been as seriously depressed as Saul made it seem, but that only time would tell how severe her condition was.

The day after my surgery was the sweetest I'd had since my father showed up in Copenhagen, life as it should have been: simple, uncluttered, time moving forward without the drag of mediocre personal dramas. I caught up on American television, hours of it: reality shows, sitcoms, crime dramas, Cartoon Network, TV Land.

But at night, when the clock struck the eleventh hour, sated on Percocet and meatloaf in a cup, I experienced unpleasant premonitions of the imminent arrival of Danish divorce papers.

It is infinitely easier now to articulate the truth of my marriage: I was not as happy as I wanted to believe. When I first met Lene, everything about her was imbued with seemingly infinite newness: the sunlit nights walking and dining on the Nyhavn harbor in alley restaurants I never would have found on my own, the marbly native tongue she taught me, even her habit of asserting truths about everything from politics to celebrity gossip as self-evident. With her in Denmark, Lene was my teacher, and I thought I might learn from her forever.

And I taught her a few things as well. Patience, poise and charm in the face of her adversities. Some might argue that these qualities that I tried to pass on to my more fiery Lene were the flip side of my relentless passivity. Nonetheless, when Lene's parents passed away, I was her tether. I kept our lives, our household, our world spinning. I don't want to make more of my contributions than I deserve. Deep down, I knew it was the absolute least I could do since I could never feel the same level of grief that she felt about her parents. After all, they were her family, not mine.

Gradually, like the rate of my absorption of the Danish language, as a marriage matures, the learning slows. And one day, you find yourself going to dinner with friends who speak English to you and hyperspeed Danish to her, and you wonder if they're speedtalking just to piss you off and you bike home beside your wife in silence and the only words you offer before bed are an insincere affirmative about what a good time you had, and soon the darkness falls early and the snow shuffles in from the sea and you feel like the only place you can be remotely comfortable is in your flat.

I was well on my way toward becoming utterly purposeless in Denmark. Even worse, I was losing the will to stoke the fires. Just the thought of groveling for new clients—seeing the door shut in my face nine times out of ten (*nej, tak*)—made me nauseous. Maybe Lene knew of my unhappiness; perhaps she wanted me to admit explicitly that I desired a return to America. But I never spoke of my feelings directly. How callous I would have sounded to say that I expected her to reciprocate, to repay me, even, for my eleven years as a foreigner in her native country.

On television, the Bordirtoun Nightly News came on. A rotund black woman, hair in curlers, shouted into a reporter's microphone that her home was being demolished by the city without her permission. The house was built in the '70s: flat roof, one story, monochromatic in its shit tint, black steel bars over the windows. It was an Old Town house, antiquated twenty years ago. A bulldozer's teeth bit into it; wood snapped and buckled.

"Oh my God!" the woman cried out, palms pressed together, arrowed toward the heavens. "Oh sweet Jesus Lawd God Jesus and Mary, they never told me! Mayor Pong, you mother—!" Her speech was interrupted by a lengthy stream of bleeps. She cantilevered at the waist, compressing a pillow of fat around her belly and beginning to sob. The Old Town woman drifted into the background. A young consoling black man embraced her. He looked like her son.

They cut to clips of the Pong Foundation press conference and my own red, slack-jawed face. The reporter said I was the man the administration had tapped to redevelop Old Town.

The woman's son looked into the camera and said that he personally planned to bleep my Chinese bleep up for what the city had done to her mother's home.

Jimbor walked in and looked at me, then he glanced at the television. "You look scared."

I swallowed a vomitous breath and turned the channel. "Scared?" I said. "Of what?" On the television, a music video. A portly lazy-eyed black man, wearing diamonds in his teeth and an oversized white coat, gyrated and rapped in front of a cream-colored Bentley and several voluptuous bikini-clad women, pumping their backsides up and down.

"I enjoy rap music," I said, nodding along as if I liked the song. I felt myself growing hard.

Jimbor began rapping along and claimed that the artist's latest album was great. I agreed.

He unholstered his bottle of blue cleaner and squirted one of my room windows. I chose not to ask why the nurses did double-duty as window cleaners.

"Say, do you know T.R. Grathe?" Jimbor asked, wiping figure eights of light froth.

"T.R.?" I repeated. T.R. Grathe was my best friend in high school. His father was Reverend Dohney Grathe, an Old Town district supervisor. His two children attended high school with me. T.R. was a fearless eccentric. He'd walk the quad with an acoustic guitar slung over his shoulder, and at lunch, he'd make up songs poking fun at the popular kids. Every fall, he'd run for student council president only to lose in a landslide to one of the jocks. I'd had a crush on his older sister Taryn, the chain-smoking editor of the high-school paper, *The Scaffold*. The three of us backpacked Europe after graduation on a trip that seemed less about sightseeing and cultural experiences and more about finding the next source of hashish and marijuana. It was that summer that I decided I would, one day, live in Europe.

"T.R.'s my brother-in-law," Jimbor said.

I was aghast. Taryn was married to Jimbor? While I was at a loss for words, Jimbor suddenly became quite talkative. He told me that T.R. had become an Old Town district representative on the Bordirtoun Board of Supervisors, and Taryn was working as a publicist at an environmental non-profit. He went on about how Taryn's pregnancy had taken him by surprise, and he wasn't sure if he was ready, and how his daddy had told him there was no such thing as ready. He said his daddy was in the penitentiary (I've since met the guy; he was in for a felony DUI and vehicular manslaughter—even he got paroled last year).

I maintained a firm smile. Taryn, married and pregnant. My, the horrors of reproduction. Yes, of course, quite mean-spirited of me to be so harsh on Jimbor as a progenitor, but the fact of the matter was, I simply expected more from someone as lovely as I remembered Taryn to be.

"She and T.R. asked about you," Jimbor said. "They want you to come over for dinner."

"Absolutely." I asked him how far along she was, and he replied three months. I congratulated him, and for some reason, I decided to share that I had no desire to have children due to my poor parental role models.

Jimbor's brow crinkled. "Well, I didn't like my dad all the time either. He had a drinking problem. Your wife have problems with her parents?"

"No."

"She don't want kids?"

"It's too late for her now."

"Oh."

An uncomfortable silence settled between us.

"Anyway, tell your wife and T.R. I said 'hello,'" I said. "And yes, I would love to come over."

Jimbor laughed. "Awesome," he said. "You know, T.R. and Taryn, they don't like your dad very much."

"That's okay." I chuckled. "Neither do I."

A few days later, I was released from the hospital, and I took the car service to the family house as I'd promised Momma. Inside the Lincoln Continental, an ad for The Pongel Horse, Bordirtoun's top-shelf gentleman's club, was screwed to the door. The promo featured two blondes, from my vantage pubescent, cheek-to-cheek ("Quality Quality, A Pong Promise!" —Saul Pong, Mayor, Owner). Directly below my father's quote, there was a transparent tray holding The Pongel Horse business cards. Twenty percent off all lap dances. Only three cards left. I recognized one of the girls in the ad from one of my weak moments on the internet. Lexus Lenoir, girl-on-girl specialist, reportedly eighteen. College Tryouts Volumes One through Four. Well, perhaps I was more familiar with Lexus's work than I'd like to admit.

"Have you been?" the driver asked.

I told him I was not like my father, meaning I was not the type of man to frequent that sort of establishment. I neglected to mention the ten to twelve bachelor parties I'd attended, the hundreds of lap dances I'd paid for over the years. Before I met Lene, I often sought out male friends and found ways to get invited to weekends in strip club capitals like Las Vegas, New York, and Atlanta. I used to make a point of getting at least three lap dances (each with a dancer of a different ethnicity) before leaving a strip club.

"Your father really outdid himself," he said. "Take a card. Call the service, ask for Delly, and we'll go sometime."

"No, thanks."

"What, I'm just a driver to you? A servant? God forbid we be buddies? I live on the North Side, you know? Come on, take a card!"

I emptied the tray and held the cards up for him to see. "I got three, okay? Maybe we'll go sometime and share a drink. Maybe we can get some lap dances together with the mayor. Hell, why don't I bring my mother too?"

The driver's face blanched. His eyes actually became red and filmy, and I thought he might cry. "Your Dad is the friendliest guy," he said. "I wouldn't guess you two were related."

"Look, I'm sorry," I said, slipping the cards into my pocket. "I've been in a terrible mood lately."

The driver didn't bother to reply and proceeded to take me on a white-knuckle, sound barrier-breaking drive to my family house. I stumbled out dizzy and was still trying to situate my crutches, when the car peeled out and left me coughing in a whirlwind of diesel fumes.

The sun was stark and raw, and the sky was the color of sandpaper. As I crutched up the steps, there was a faint sizzle in the distance, its source unidentifiable. Our residence was a two-story home with a four-car garage, clay-tiled roofing, just like all eight on the street. The lawn looked like it hadn't been mowed in weeks, and a toppled sprinkler lay in a pool of muddy stillwater. My mother's rose garden shriveled from neglect. There were tiny cracks in the paint. Not what I expected from my fastidious mother. I rang the doorbell. No one answered. I rang again.

Momma opened. She wore pajamas, and her face appeared gray without makeup. She smiled weakly, and it seemed to take her several seconds to recognize me.

"Are you okay?" I said.

"Why didn't you tell me you were coming today?"

I shrugged as I entered the house. I removed my shoes, left them in the foyer, and lowered myself onto the living room couch—like a guest. The ivory walls badly needed a fresh coat of paint, and there were a few odd ornaments I didn't recognize but most everything else was the same, but older: the same white porcelain mask on the mantle, the same fake birds of paradise, the same fake fruit centerpiece on the glass coffee table. Lene had impeccable interior design taste. Plastic fruits and plants would never find their way into our flat. I wished she was with me. Well, perhaps not right at that moment. Juggling Lene and Momma's attentions would have been a chore. But I did find myself suddenly missing her.

Something else was missing. The noise. I listened for sounds upstairs, in my father's home office. Silence.

"Dad's not here?" It was Sunday.

"Why don't you go to your room and rest?" Momma said. "I've unpacked for you."

"You didn't have to do that," I said. "I'm not staying long."

"All your clothes are upstairs."

Sighing, I slowly crutched up to my room, but I stopped on the way when I noticed that my father's home office, where he had spent most of my childhood nights, behind closed double doors, was abandoned. On the desk, a leaning tower of obsolete software manuals sprouted from a tangle of network cords. Millmore and Francisco Pong's black-and-white framed photos were gone, the nails still in the wall.

Momma walked in behind me.

"Did Dad move out?" I asked.

Momma's eyes began to mist. "He moved into the hotel," she said quietly. "He built it so he could sleep with young girls. Let's not talk about it. I'm just glad you're back. With you back, maybe your father will think twice about sleeping with girls half your age. With you back, I won't be alone."

"What happened?"

"He says he can't stand to touch me anymore," Momma said. "I'm old. I offer him all the sex he wants, and he refuses. But let's not talk about it anymore."

I put my hand on Momma's shoulder. "Okay."

"He says he likes them twenty-five and younger," she went on. "He told me he likes tighter pussy. Can you believe that?"

My mouth soured. "Let's not talk about it."

Momma placed a bony hand on my knee. "Don't be like Daddy," she said.

"I'm not like Daddy."

"I hope you don't like to fuck young girls like Daddy," she said, sighing. "But I don't want to talk about it anymore."

When I was in grade school, my father was driving me home one day when I excitedly shared with him the legend of George Washington and his cherry-tree-chopping confession ("I cannot tell a lie!"). When I repeated his father's alleged response (that the truth was worth more than a thousand trees even if they were blossomed with silver and had leaves of purest gold), Saul guffawed and guffawed.

"I can't wait to move you to a private school," he said, mussing my hair.

That summer, we took a family vacation to Hong Kong. While Momma visited her side of the family, Saul took me on a walk. I followed him, not knowing where we were going. He would point out an occasional landmark, like the Clock Tower at Tsim Sha Tsui or a Chinese junk in Victoria Harbor. Soon, the storefronts and boulevard traffic disappeared, and my father and I were walking narrow streets and alleys. I remember the sewer stink of the streets, the Chinese characters I couldn't read in red and green neon. There seemed to be three or four girls in hot pants in front of every door. Many years later, on a business trip with a client who enjoyed underaged Filipino girls, I would discover that my father and I had been in Wan Chai. After Saul shook his head at the girls in front of several of the clubs, he finally picked one to enter. He introduced two of the girls to me. I was ten years old at the time.

My father and I sat at the bar, and the four girls gathered around us. They loomed over me, one with an arm on my shoulder, another with a hand on my thigh. My father had a girl on each arm.

"Sully, would you like to buy these girls a drink?" he asked.

"I don't have any money."

"Well, of course, I'll pay," he said. "But only if you want to buy them drinks."

"I don't care."

"No, Sully, I want you to decide."

I shrugged. "Sure."

My father glared at me, grabbed me by the arm, pushed aside the girls, and dragged me toward the exit. Behind us, I could hear an older woman shouting in Cantonese for us to come back. My father turned around and cussed at her. Soon, we were heading back the way we came.

"They were trying to cheat you," Saul said. "If you buy them drinks, they come back with a glass of water and charge you a hundred dollars. Three or four drinks later, you're paying them four hundred dollars for nothing. Not even a lousy blow job. Always go to the expensive clubs for women. Anything worth having is worth paying for. In this world, people will try to cheat you. Only dumb people let themselves get cheated. Remember that."

"I didn't know," I said.

"I have to get you out of that white school," he said. "These white people are teaching you nonsense. Do you think the truth is really worth gold?"

"I don't think my teacher really meant gold."

Saul stopped in his tracks, and I stopped with him. A young apron-wearing man with a cigarette dangling from his lips bumped into my father and proceeded to cuss him out with a medley of colorful Cantonese insults (your mother's pussy stinks, fuck your sister). My father cussed him back with his own medley (I hope your whole family dies, fuck your mother). Then he turned to me and said:

"Sully, if we went to the bank and tried to deposit truth, they wouldn't take it."

Almost thirty years later, it is I who sit in a cell, scribbling my version of the truth, hoping someone will take my deposit.

My cellmate Manny, ironically, is here for bank robbery. During the stickup, on a 95 degree afternoon in Old Town, he kept complaining that his ski mask was making his face hot and sweaty. In full view of the cameras, he put his gun down at the teller window and started clawing at his face with both hands until the mask came off. How relieved Manny was to free that meaty face! And how chagrined he was to find the teller pointing his own gun back at him!

Manny and his fellow robbers looked at the woman. She was a tiny, old lady. Manny's gun was shaking in her frail hands. Manny and his friends exchanged glances. Then they unloaded their weapons on her.

To hear Manny tell his story, you might think that the woman was a steroid-taking ex-bodybuilder-turned-bank-teller who decided to hop the counter, wrestle the gun from his grasp, rip the ski mask off his face, and stick the pistol into Manny's mouth before his fellow thieves blew the woman's brains out and saved his life.

Yes, the security cameras don't lie. But even Manny, whose IQ is in the double-digits, is smarter than I am. He is from the Saul Pong School of Life. The truth ain't worth much.

Saul agreed to meet us for dinner at a Chinese restaurant named Barry Buck Roger Fong's. A giant red and gold papier maché phoenix dangled from the ceiling. It reminded me simultaneously of Oscar Wilde's tomb and a piñata. Momma went on and on about how she didn't know why my father always chose this restaurant, the food was awful, and she hated running into the wives of the other city officials. I waited in silence, nonresponsive; I let her blow off steam. When Saul finally arrived, he was wearing a long dark wool coat and leather gloves despite the fact it was ninety degrees outside (Momma and I were wearing shorts). Saul greeted a patron and shook hands with a server before finally joining us at our table.

"How are you feeling, Sully?" Saul undid his coat, took off his gloves, unbuttoned his suit jacket, and proceeded to inadvertently knock over my crutches, which had been leaning against the edge of the booth. He motioned for a waiter to pick them up. "So good to be together as a family again."

"Why are you dressed so warmly?" Momma asked. "Did you

just come from the hotel? I'm surprised you're not naked underneath the coat."

My father glowered at her. He smiled at me and said, "The air conditioning is very cold at City Hall. So many meetings. So many people want to see me." He picked up the teapot and tried to fill my cup, but Momma placed a hand over it.

"I'm his mother," she said. "I pour his tea."

My father shook his head and rested the pot. Momma poured my tea.

"Why isn't Elena coming?" Saul said. "What kind of wife doesn't visit her husband when he's in the hospital? Do you need me to pay for the flight?"

"Are you kidding?" Momma said. "That's too expensive. We have no money left because you're out wooing younger women."

"I can afford the flight," I said.

"Why are you in such a bad mood, Sully?" my father asked.

Why, I wonder, father? Why might I be in such a bad mood? Could it be that I had been coaxed on an 8,000-mile journey under false pretenses? Or could it be that I had unwittingly walked into a press conference where I'd been appointed to some city job I didn't fully understand? Shouldn't I have been in a gay mood? Shouldn't I have been skipping fields of poppies hand-in-hand with my father while we inspected the new showgirls at The Pongelliano?

I chopsticked a salty peanut and filled my mouth with tea. I looked my father in the eye, thinking I had truth on my side. The tea scalded, but I gave it a rinsy swish and swallowed hard.

"Momma says she never saw a doctor."

"I never saw a doctor," Momma repeated.

My father examined me, brows furrowed, and the sagging skin of his face contrasted with his bleached teeth and made his face look like a rubber mold. He was wearing makeup.

"What about Dr. Quango?" Saul asked Momma in Cantonese. He tossed his hair and turned an ear toward her.

"He knows nothing," she spat. "He's black."

"He's from France!" my father barked. Several patrons looked at us. I told my parents to quiet down. Saul said that Quango suspected Momma was a manic depressive, but couldn't be certain without further evaluation. Quango had scheduled monthly appointments Momma never kept.

"Is this true?" I asked Momma.

She ignored me. "You paid your black friend to poison me," she said to Saul.

He threw his hands up and shook his head to the heavens, his complexion purpling. "See what I have to deal with, Sully? All she does is sit around and watch TV. She doesn't take care of the house, or do any of the gardening or cooking. And she hates the blacks. She's the one that's lying. She knows nothing about what I do, what you and I are planning."

"We're not planning anything."

"You know I love the blacks, Sully," my father added.

"Why don't you tell Sully where you're sleeping?" she said.

"Bitch," my father muttered, his lower lip protruding and mouth hanging open.

"Dad—"

"Tell him where you bring all your whores."

"Cunt," my father whispered.

"Stop!" I said. More patrons' heads turned.

My parents glared silently at each other again.

"You've lied to me, both of you," I said. "Again and again and again. I'm not here to get involved in your lives. I am a very, very busy business owner in my own right. I don't have time to care about your business or your politics or, frankly, your marriage. I've always thought you two should get divorced."

Momma began to cry softly. I looked away and told her to stop crying.

Saul stared at his joined hands as if he were praying. "A divorce would hurt my numbers," he said quietly. He glanced askance at me. "The Pong Foundation will be good for both of us, Sully. I need your help."

Saul went on about how the redevelopment would benefit Old Town economically and how he had a lot of his own money invested in the project, which meant it was practically my money since it was family money. I shook my head, sipped my tea, and waited for him to finish. I refilled their cups and looked at Momma, who was red-faced with tears, then Saul, who was licking his teeth.

"If anything ever happened to either of you, I would be here," I said. "For instance, if Momma was sick— "

"Momma is sick," Saul said.

"I am not."

"Let me finish," I said, holding a finger up. "If either of you were sick, I would be here. I know we've had our tough times, but you are my parents. It is my obligation. It would be the right thing to do." How insincere I sounded! I might as well have been reading aloud from an unfamiliar book. I reached out to both of them, found a neutral fleshy part of their respective shoulders to pat.

"You sound so happy about it," Momma said.

"What the hell do you expect?" I said. "Have you ever supported me? No. You just send your little pictures of Cantonese girls."

"They spoke so well," Momma explained.

I turned to Saul. "And you! I walked into a press conference!"

Saul rolled his eyes. "You're still talking about that? I've already apologized."

"No, you haven't."

"I have!" he said. Then his eyes narrowed. "Haven't I?"

"No."

Saul pursed his lips. "Oh. I thought I did."

"Look, I don't live here," I said. "I don't work here. My wife lives in Denmark." I said the words extra slowly and loudly this time because clearly my message had not been getting through.

Saul sniffed and looked down into his teacup, swirled the liquid. "I don't know what's so great about Amsterdam. Everyone speaks English anyway."

"Copenhagen."

"I'm not lying to you," Momma said. "That doctor was not a real doctor." She stabbed a finger at my father. "He is looking for an excuse to fuck young twat."

Saul slammed both palms on the table, toppling our cups. He backhanded the soy sauce bottle, sending it bouncing and spilling on the floor. Patrons and staff alike gasped. He stood and retrieved his lengthy billfold from his jacket and flipped two hundred-dollar bills on the table. "How often does Sully come home? You are determined to spread your crazy lies and make me look like a fool."

"Because you are!" Momma screamed.

"I can't talk to a crazy woman." Saul tried to look me in the eye, but I would not meet his gaze; I was seething.

"I'm not the bad guy, Sully," he said. He huffed toward the exit, then slowed. He waved and shook hands with the maitre d'. Made some smiling small talk, shook hands again, and squeezed the man's elbow before walking out.

I stared at the tint of the spreading tea on the tablecloth, the dark leaves clumped at the center of a sagging amoeba shape. My mother's shoulders trembled; she was silent save the occasional sniffle. A baby began to cry in the far corner of the restaurant. I loosened my jaw and looked hard at my mother.

"Dr. Quango?"

"Your father ordered him to drug me and put me in the crazy house." Momma said, her eyes darting left and right. "Talk to him yourself."

She rummaged through her purse and handed me a business card of thin stock and bent corners that read:

Murray Jean-Baptiste Quango, M.D.
Quango Psychiatric Services
Clinical Care. Consultation. Collaboration. C You There.

Quango. Even his name was mysterious in origin, sounded like a tropical fruit. But alas, the word "quango" is British—an advisory board financed by the government but formed to act independently—a definition that turned out to be absolutely appropriate to Dr. Quango's small part in helping put me here in prison.

At the time, Quango was an unexpected sign that my father had been telling the truth all along. Maybe Saul hadn't been as calculating as I thought, and my mother was indeed depressed.

The morning after the disastrous dinner with Saul and Momma, I called Quango's office. A female answered. There were multiple voices in the background; it sounded like a crowded waiting room. I asked for an appointment with Quango and told the woman who I was.

I heard a man yelling repeatedly that he was Ezekiel. "So this is about the Mayor's wife?!" the woman shouted.

"My mother, yes!"

"Dr. Quango is very busy this week," she said. "This month, in fact."

"Is there any way he can fit me in?" I said. "Fifteen minutes. Thirty, tops."

Someone began singing what sounded like Queen's "Bohemian Rhapsody" ("I am a poor boy, nobody loves me").

"Sir!" she exclaimed. "Sir!"

"Yes?" I said.

"Please take the *Vogue* out of your mouth," she said. "There you go. That's right. Thanks so much. Dr. Quango will be with you momentarily." She groaned. "Sorry, Mr. Pong. You were saying?"

My desire to pow-wow in Quango's place of business suddenly flatlined. "Any way I can meet him outside the office?"

We settled on fifteen minutes at the nearby Starbucks. I took the car service there and was on my third venti and had been going to the bathroom every ten minutes when the good doctor finally walked in, thirty minutes late. He was a dark man with short blond (heavy, blindingly dyed) hair and a silver beard. He was dressed in a navy suit and pink tie and wore heavy gold chains on his wrists and several thick, shiny rings. Not like any doctor I'd met. His sunglasses were yellow. I could tell he was much older than his face appeared. His cheeks looked laminated, the texture of vacuum-sealed beef.

"So very nice to finally meet Saul's son," Quango said with a trace of what I assumed to be a French accent. He beamed (gold bicuspids?) and shook my hand. "Your father is a great man. You are lucky to come from such accomplished stock."

I asked him how he knew my father.

"We were at the University of Utah together," he said. "We were on the same table tennis team. Go Utes!" He laughed. "I remember when you were yay tall." He put his hand out level with the table. "Do you remember me?"

I shook my head.

"Really?" Quango said. "You don't remember the jazz club in Old Town?"

"How would I get into a jazz club if I were yay tall?"

Quango glanced skyward, pondering. "Maybe that wasn't you."

I swilled cold coffee.

Quango smiled at the attractive brunette barista (high schooler?) and requested his usual: a venti quadruple Americano. He crossed his legs, folded his hands over a knee, and eyed me intently. "What can I do for you, Sully? Can I call you Sully?"

"Depends on what you say about my mother."

The barista rounded the counter and hand-delivered Quango's Americano.

"Why, thank you dear!" Quango said. "Table service today?"

"Only for you, Jean-Baptiste," the barista said with a smile.

"I love it when you call me that! *Je vous trouve très belle!*" I didn't speak French but I could tell from the predatory gleam in Quango's eyes that he was telling the girl she was beautiful. He continued to ogle her as she wiggled back to the register, tittering. "They love me here," he said to me, before licking his lips.

"About my mother," I said.

Quango sipped his coffee and finally stopped beaming. "Right, yes, well, I just talked to your father this morning about her. I guess he has not made any progress in getting your mother to return for another session. As I understand, your father has been under a lot of stress. He has not been happy in the marriage recently."

"Recently meaning 'the last forty years.'"

Quango had nothing to say to that. He turned to his coffee, and as he swallowed, his dark gullet skin flapped.

"Can you tell me what you told her?"

"I'm afraid I can't really discuss the specifics due to patient confidentiality."

"Can't you tell me anything?" I said. "She's my mother."

"Your mother clearly has some sort of mood disorder."

"My father said 'manic depression.'"

Quango chuckled. "Your father did always want to be a doctor; he certainly wanted you to be." He observed me, seeking a reaction. I gritted my teeth and waited for him to continue.

"The fact is, I never had a chance to give her a thorough examination," Quango said. "She was raging at your father when she came into my office. She refused to participate in the interview process or the physical examination. I need more time with her to gauge the right type of treatment. To be candid, I pity your father. Maybe he loved your mother once, but a man can only do so much."

"My father is not the victim here."

"Your mother is obviously not well."

"My father is not the victim here," I repeated more firmly.

Quango paused. "Perhaps you'd like to schedule a consultation, and we can explore your feelings about this topic further."

I told him I had not come for a consultation.

He raised the coffee to his lips. "You really should consider it."

"I'm not staying in town long."

"You're not?"

"Let me guess. My father told you I was moving back."

He nodded. I shook my head.

"Aren't you leaving a lot of money on the table?" he said.

"You mean the Pong Foundation?" I laughed. "I didn't even know one existed until I landed."

Quango's expression darkened. He twisted the ring on his middle finger and checked his watch. He began downing his coffee, bubbles of sweat multiplying on his forehead. I sensed he was hiding something he previously thought I knew.

"So about this money I was supposed to make," I said.

"Your father made me think that you two...well, the three of us, were in the deal together."

"A deal?"

Quango cleared his throat. "My time is nearly up."

"Why, I am the president of the Pong Foundation!" I said sardonically. "I want to know what's going on within my organization."

Quango got up and straightened his suit jacket. "Very nice to finally meet you. Please tell your mother I said 'hello.'" He put on his yellow sunglasses and hurried out the door, leaving his venti half-finished.

At physical therapy, I was lying on a mat, with Jimbor on his knees beside me (due to budget cuts, he informed me that he played numerous roles at the hospital: nurse, part-time janitor, and unlicensed physical therapist). He raised my leg to a 45-degree angle, then lowered to 30. Raised again, then lowered. Reliving my visit with Quango, I shared with Jimbor that my mother didn't seem any more unhealthy or depressed than usual, and that Dr. Quango appeared to be one of my father's cronies.

"He and my dad are up to something," I said. "I just need to figure out what that something is. What's 'the Deal?'"

"More RICE," Jimbor said, his eyes following a passing female nurse. She was young, long-haired, long-legged. Reminded me of the intern who worked the personals at *Ekstra Bladet* in Copenhagen. "Rest. Ice. Compression. Elevation. You don't have much mobility. You're not healing right."

"Oh?" I said.

He inspected my pelvic region and puckered his mustachioed lips. "Scar tissue."

Jimbor raised my right leg and folded it over my left, stretching my lower back. I heard a spinal pop and groaned with pleasure. He cupped my right glute.

"You guys enjoying yourselves?" someone said.

Over Jimbor's shoulder, I saw the smiling face of a man I

recognized as a clean-shaven, short-haired version of an old friend.

"T?"

Jimbor got off me and helped me to my crutches. T.R. hugged me; he smelled of tobacco.

"I nearly lost all bladder control when I saw you on TV last week," he said.

I laughed uncomfortably, reminded that it had already been over a week since my father had rolled my piss-wet self around on the ground while I cursed all things otherworldly in agony.

"I called the old house but your mother didn't understand what I was saying." T.R. slapped Jimbor playfully on the chest. "And this guy didn't tell me you were in the hospital for days!"

Jimbor shrugged. "I didn't know you knew him." He eyed the doorway. "Hey hon."

Taryn. She walked in, wearing jeans and a summer maternity blouse, her hair much longer than I remembered, down over her shoulders like lax mattress coils; she was just starting to show. While her skin sagged around the chin and beneath the eyes, and she was bordering on heavy-set like myself, she was still pretty. I identified several buxom actresses in their early twenties she vaguely resembled. She embraced me. Her hair smelled of sweet milk, and she was soft in my arms.

"You look well, Sully," she said.

"You too." I looked into her eyes, the color of machine-washed money, and then at her rounded belly.

She chuckled and patted her mound. "Oh, yeah," she said. "The little one."

T.R. palmed the back of my bald head. "Good to have you back."

"Good to be back," I said. It was the first time I'd actually acknowledged that there was any good to this trip. I explained to the three of them that contrary to what they may have heard in the local news, I wasn't working for my father; I had unwittingly walked into the Pong Foundation press conference. Taryn and T.R. laughed.

"You did look a little stunned," she said.

"How could you not know he was up to something?" T.R. said. "He's Saul Pong."

My face warmed. "I've been gone so long that I've forgotten," I joked.

"I ran for mayor against him four years ago," T.R. said.

"Wow! Really?" I said. For some reason, I was surprised my friend was experienced enough to run. I felt suddenly old and unaccomplished.

"He slaughtered me," he said, making me feel less unaccomplished.

"T.R. did well for his first time," Taryn said. "If he ran again, he'd do better."

"Somebody's got to get him out of office," I said.

"I think I'm done," T.R. said. "I'm not polling well anyway."

"You should give it a chance, T," Taryn said.

"I'd work for your campaign," I said. "I'll dig up all the dirt on Saul for you."

T.R. shook his head and smiled. "Naw, I don't play your father's game."

That's probably why he lost, I thought.

Jimbor took the rest of the day off and drove the three of us across the bridge into Old Town, where the Grathes lived. The pea river glistened in the periphery, pushing its moldy odor through the AC. We passed Old Town's main drag, where all those jazz clubs I'd supposedly frequented with Saul and Quango were located. Protesters jammed the streets. The storefronts were dark and empty; the stoplights turned green to no avail. There were several groups of protesters: one sitting and snacking on PowerBars, another standing and holding signs reading pithy phrases like "GAME OVER,

MAYOR PONG," and still smaller groups playing acoustic guitar and singing.

"They're going to be evicted," T.R. said.

"Evicted?" I said. "All of them?"

T.R. nodded. "Your father did the same thing with the hotel. He razed the houses and moved the residents. That was just a few homes, though. This is going to be much larger."

I mentioned my meeting with Dr. Quango and my intuition that Saul was going to make a lot of money from the new Old Town development.

What I said was not a revelation to T.R. "He'll have one of his companies buy the land surrounding the development site for cheap," he said. "He'll tell investors, 'if you want to build over these poorer neighborhoods, I'll help you, but you have to take the land I own at my price.'"

I recalled thinking bitterly that of course, Dr. Quango and T.R. Grathe knew infinitely more about my father's dealings than I did. I was only Saul's son, not one of his precious cronies, after all. I took tiny consolation in knowing that my father would chafe at the idea of me socializing with his political rivals. When I was a senior in high school, Saul ran against T.R. and Taryn's father, Reverend Dohney Grathe, for a seat on the Bordirtoun Board of Supervisors. When my father realized the Grathes were my friends, he ordered me to stop seeing them, saying it was shameful for his own son to be so close to his rival's family. Naturally, his objection only made me want to hang out with the Grathes more often, and Saul refused to speak to me for the rest of the campaign. When he won, Momma and I were not invited to the celebration. As an adolescent, I remembered wishing I had been spawned by an upstanding, pure-intentioned person like Reverend Grathe. When my father routed him, the reverend even patted me on the shoulder and told me what a shrewd and able politician Saul was, even though my father had repeatedly falsely accused him of being a closet member of the Fundamentalist Church of Latter Day Saints.

We pulled up to the Grathe house, and I followed T.R. and Taryn up the adobe walkway to the porch where the three of us had loitered away many teenaged days and nights, drinking beers and smoking weed out in the open, stargazing while Reverend Grathe was away, attending City Council meetings. The house hadn't changed much, with its dark brown exterior, the green window shutters, the slate roof tiles. The reddish-green grass in the front garden had grown to the size of small hedges, longer stalks pointing south with the wind. Windblown dust and dirt swirled and skated across the landscaping and smelled vaguely of equine manure. I had always been the hopeless one, the one who ranted that Bordirtoun would never get better and that the only viable path for us was the path out. I never thought I'd be the only one to leave. T.R., I understood (he was too much of an idealist and optimist to leave), but Taryn?

That evening, she cooked a spartan dinner of spaghetti marinara, and by the time we got around to eating, I'd had too many glasses of red wine. The walls of the Grathe dining room appeared to be undulating. I found myself blabbering too much recent life information, including my opinion that my wife and my parents would never get along, the fact that I was nearly unemployable and on the dole in Denmark, and my opinion that the problematic roots of my chronic groin injuries were Lene's taste for yogic sex, and the unfortunate fact that we didn't have it particularly often.

There was an extended moment of silence. I realized I had created a bit of an awkward moment. Jimbor refilled my glass, and I drank more. He removed from his mouth what appeared to be a chicken wishbone in Taryn's chickenless entrée, and left it on the edge of his plate without comment.

I rested my fork, tine down, and raised my glass. "I want to give a toast," I said. "Unfortunate that it took such unfortunate circumstances to bring the three of us back together. And you too, Jimbor, of course. Cheers, everyone." I clinked glasses with Jimbor and Taryn. That's when I remembered that only T.R. and I were drinking wine, Taryn being pregnant and all.

"I'm so jealous that you're living in Denmark," Taryn said.

Grinning, I shrugged, careful not to make eye contact for fear of appearing too self-satisfied. "Of course, I miss you guys," I said. "But I have a good life there, and I shouldn't have anything to complain about."

"Ever think of coming back?" T.R. said.

"Sometimes," I found myself saying. "But I'm married now."

"What's your wife's name?" Taryn asked.

"Lay-na," I pronounced. "L-e-n-e."

"Is she nice?"

"Of course."

"Would I like her?"

"Perhaps."

"Do you speak Danish?"

"Horribly."

"All of a sudden, it's the Taryn Inquisition," T.R. said.

Taryn blushed. "I'm just happy to see Sully," she said. Jimbor's cell phone rang, and he excused himself and answered the call in the kitchen.

I caught myself staring at Taryn, my eyes drifting toward her chest. I experienced a boozy hallucination of entering her side-saddle and wrapping my arms around her belly mound. I felt myself growing hard. Tried to think about baseball. Parched and too warm, I pressed the cool glass against my cheek and took a drink. In my water, I noticed a lemon seed drowning beneath a diminishing ice cube.

Jimbor returned to the table, but didn't sit down. "I gotta go, hon."

"Again?" Taryn said.

"One of the girls called in sick." He kissed Taryn on the forehead, then he playslapped me on the arm. "I'll see you at PT, Sull-ver."

After Jimbor left, my phone buzzed, and I saw Momma's name on the caller ID. I took two gulps of wine and ignored the call.

"So where were we?" I said, looking at Taryn, then T.R. My cell buzzed again. "Goddamnit!" I shouted, silencing the phone, thinking the call was from Momma. But then, I noticed it was Lene.

"Excuse me." I worked my way up on my crutches, and I was so inebriated, I almost fell. I zigzagged out the front door and answered the call on the porch.

"*Hej, skat*," I said, panting.

"You sound like you're outside."

"I am." I leaned forward against the railing and shut my eyes, trying to still the quavering world. I inhaled the vaguely metallic night air and found myself tasting the grit in my teeth and coughing from the dirt in my throat. "I'm with friends," I eventually managed to say.

"You still have friends there?" Lene said. "You never told me you still had friends there."

"I did grow up here." I looked inside at the Grathes. Taryn mussed T.R.'s hair. Jesus, those locks, those eyes. I tried to remember what Lene's face looked like.

"You've been drinking."

"I only had a glass of wine at dinner."

Lene laughed. "Sure."

I shivered with exhaustion. Lene's indirectness was new to me. If we had been face-to-face, I knew she would have been unloading both barrels, accusing me of lying to her. Suddenly, all I wanted to do was get back to the Grathes. More accurately, to Taryn.

Lene said she had just returned from a conference in Stockholm.

"I wish we could buy a vacation home there."

I stared out at the dim lights of Bordirtoun's North Side neighborhood. The splashing of river water sounded like an animal quietly consuming its feed; the blinking buoys looked like dying candles. I was reminded of the Øresund Strait between Copenhagen and Malmö, Sweden. I rubbed my bleary eyes and told myself in Danish to get it together (*tag de sammen, Sully!*).

"We will," I said. "When business picks up again. I promise."

"Sully?"

The voice wasn't Lene's. I smelled sweet milk. "We're going out back," Taryn said.

"Your friend?" Lene said.

"Just a friend."

Taryn wandered a few steps away. I waited for her to go back inside. But she didn't.

"Maybe things aren't so bad there?" Lene said.

"Trust me. Things are bad. At the very least, complicated."

"Your lady friends are complicated?"

"That's not what I mean," I said, blushing. I watched Taryn scratch her left calf with her right foot, which required her to place a hand against the house and allowed me a view of the outline of her bosom. "Lene, I'll call you in five minutes."

"It's okay. Don't bother," she said. "I'm headed out."

"The conference?"

"To work!" she said. "It's seven in the morning."

I winced. "Yes, right."

"Your friends must be important," Lene said. "I can't remember the last time you called me Lene."

My stomach balled up. "Oh *skat*," I purred.

She flipped a chilly goodbye. I crutched to Taryn, who inspected my face. "I just wanted to make sure you're okay. You look like you've had too much to drink." She held my elbow, steadying me. "Was that your wife?"

"The wife it was," I said.

"Where have you been all night?" a hazy-eyed Momma said, after letting me into the house. "I called the car service, and I called you ten times."

"Dinner with friends," I mumbled.

"What kind of dinner is this? It's four in the morning!" She sniffed me audibly. "Have you been drinking? Are you chasing women like your father? Is she Chinese?"

"No!" I shouted. "I'm not like him, okay? I'm not! Stop saying I'm like him!"

"Shhh!" Momma said. "What's wrong with you? Quiet down and go to sleep." She headed back upstairs, shaking her head.

I managed to make my way into my room and onto my bed. My heart was racing. It dawned on me that, despite my exhaustion, I wouldn't be able to sleep. I dug through my desk drawers and found some old photos of Taryn, T.R. and me in a Barcelona bar. Three glasses of yellow absinthe on the table. In the picture, I was glancing askance at Taryn, and a stranger might have thought I was angry, but I was actually admiring that sinister skirt she was wearing.

I heard a lock snap, and the front door creaked open. The familiar throat clearing and clack of shoes against the marble foyer. Saul. What was he doing here? I hopped on my crutches and tried to shut the bedroom door. The footsteps approached. My room was large, the door far away. I had turned out the lights and was standing within arm's reach of the knob when Saul appeared in a pre-dawn shadow, his suit rumpled, hair frizzy and misshapen. He stopped when he saw me.

"Why are you still up?" he said, voice muted and phlegmy. Had he been drinking too?

"Can't sleep." I turned the lights on.

"Sull?"

"Yeah?"

"Learn only the good things from me, not my bad."

There was an atypical ruefulness in my father's voice, perhaps as a quiet hint of deference to my mother, whose faint rhythmic snoring could be heard behind closed double doors. I turned my crutches toward the bed and moved away from Saul. "Why are you here?"

"To pick up some things."

"Why didn't you tell me you left Momma?"

"Would it have changed your mind? Would you have come home right away to help me?"

I was surprised at his tone, surprised that it genuinely stung. "Help you do what? Maybe if you actually told me what you wanted me to do without lying, I might actually do it."

"Fine, can you take a call from a reporter about the Pong Foundation tomorrow?" he asked.

"No!" I said. "I just said I don't know anything about it!"

My father threw up his hands. "Do you think this is easy for me to ask?"

I reminded myself not to give him any ground. I leaned my crutches against the wall, hopped to the bed. He followed and sat next to me. He smelled of whiskey.

I sidled along the edge of the mattress, creating more space between Saul and me. "I saw your friend Dr. Quango today. He mentioned that he thought we were all in some sort of deal together."

My father slouched and sighed. "I know how this appears," he said. "Like I'm manipulating you."

"You should just admit that you lied to me. You're trying to involve me in one of your moneymaking schemes."

"Momma is having a difficult time—"

"Because of you!" I said. "You are her problem!"

My father stared at his feet; for once, he had nothing to say for himself. I enjoyed seeing him weak.

"Do you still hit her?" I asked.

Saul stood as if snapped up by his puppeteer. He mouthed several unfinished words.

"Get some sleep," he said, before leaving the room.

I fell into a deep sleep, feeling vindicated that I'd stood up to Saul. When I woke, it was nearly ten. I turned on the television and saw that the Republican candidate for President was appearing at a Bordirtoun fundraiser that afternoon. The local news interviewed my father, and he told reporters what a good friend and mentor the candidate had been, mentioning a gold mallet he had received for donating to the Republican's campaign. The phone rang, and I picked up.

"There he is," my father said. "Sully, this is Dora Tollworth from the *Bordirtoun Daily*. Dora, Sulliver Pong, my son."

"Hello, Mr. Pong," she said.

Before I could reply, Saul said, "Please excuse his limited availability for the past week, he has been recovering from a mountain biking accident. Sully is quite the adventurer, and we definitely worry about him quite a bit. My wife is always telling him to slow down, be safe, but that's just not Sully. He has always had a risk-taking, entrepreneurial spirit, and that's the leadership style he's brought to the Old Town project. He called me up a few months ago and said, 'Dad, you need to do something about Old Town. People are hurting, jobs are scarce.' I told him, 'I've tried. But I have North Side, Civic Center, East End, my airport, all the initiatives I've spearheaded during my administration, all very successful, all improving the lives of our citizens immeasurably.' Sully said, 'Dad, I'll do it. I can bring a new approach. I'll bring commerce, public transit, and new housing to Old Town. I'll come home.' And he's most certainly a man of his word. The next day, he started working with the planners at the Pong Foundation and now, he's here."

"How is your approach different from your father's, Mr. Pong?" the reporter asked. "Sulliver, that is." She laughed. Saul responded with a titter of his own.

I was squeezing the phone so hard my hand was shaking. My father started yammering about the Pong family's history of philanthropy. I also vaguely heard Saul's voice down the hall, in his abandoned office.

"Sully brings energy, vitality, youth, new ideas, all of which I possess in fair quantities, but I'm simply overextended—"

"I am returning to Europe," I said.

"Really?" the reporter said.

"His wife has already agreed in principle to move to Bordirtoun," Saul said. "She doesn't feel completely safe without Sully at her side, especially when it comes to traveling, and we all know the dark history of Europe with regards to immigration. It's much better that she moves here and becomes an American citizen."

"We haven't discussed that," I said.

Before the reporter could respond, Saul began talking about the groundbreaking, and as he spoke, I discovered that the Old Town project was well underway, and I had apparently signed off on environment impact reports and a variety of "purposeful initiatives for the purpose of health and safety purposes," including the relocation and shutdown of current businesses and homes located in the 500-acre redevelopment area. The reporter asked if the administration was concerned about the protesters gathering at the development zone.

"Concerned?" Saul said. "That's what protesters do. They protest and they gather because they are concerned. The administration is not concerned."

"I'm concerned," I said. "Where are these people going to live?"

"Shouldn't you know, Mr. Pong?" the reporter said. "Sulliver, that is."

"Because of the scope of the construction, Sully and I have decided that it is just not safe for residents to stay," Saul said. "We have examined all the data available from the health and safety experts, and they recommend that we relocate, at least temporarily, a select group of residents who are in the development zone. When the time is right, you can be certain that Sully will provide a more detailed plan."

"Sulliver will?" the reporter said.

"I will not!"

"Absolutely, he will," my father said.

"Then this question is for Sulliver," she said. "How does Quango Valley figure in your plans?"

I was silent, stunned. Quango Valley? As in Dr. Quango?

"We're not prepared to discuss specifics at this time," my father said.

"Quango?" I said. "The doctor?"

"Yes, Dr. Murray Quango," she said. "You sound surprised, Sulliver."

"Like I said, Sully has been in the hospital."

"How is Dr. Quango involved?" I asked.

"Are you asking me or your father?" she said.

"It's a rhetorical, even a philosophical question," Saul said.

"He is the lead investor in Quango Valley, the new housing development," she said. "I have the filing from the Housing Authority in front of me. You co-signed this document just yesterday, Mr. Pong. Sulliver, that is."

The previous night's wine backed up in my throat.

"Is that a question?" Saul said. "I don't think that's a question."

"I have nothing to do with anything involving the Pong Foundation or Old Town or Quango Valley," I said, the volume of my voice increasing. "Even the press conference was a surprise to me."

"Sully is so modest—"

"It seems my father has once again lied to me."

"He's lied to you?"

"Yes."

"Listen, Mr. and Mr. Pong, I think I have what I need," she said. "Thanks a lot for your time."

"You're welcome, Ms. Tollworth," Saul said. "And tell Kingsley that I love the changes he's made with the paper. Much more hard-hitting. Much more news-y."

"Kingston is on vacation," the reporter said dryly.

"Well, tell him to call me when he returns, will you?" Saul said. "I hope we've given you what you need to write a compelling article."

The reporter sniffed. "Maybe you and your son should talk to each other more often."

After she hung up, my father cussed loudly in Cantonese and I heard a bang, the sound of furniture, possibly a chair, puncturing a wall. My mother opened the master bedroom door and began shouting, asking my father what the hell the noise was all about.

The next moments happened so fast that it didn't occur to me what I'd set in motion until after it was over. To this day, when a prison guard slams a door, or if, on a rare overcast Bordirtoun day, a similar light filters through the Plexiglas in my cell, I see the following moments again, and the familiar fear rises within.

The office doors flung open, and my mother took one look at my father and fled into the master bedroom. He tore in after her and shouted, "Bitch, you turned my son against me! Cunt, you taught him to be this stupid!" Momma shouted back, and their warring voices rattled my insides. I got on my crutches and headed to them as fast as I could. Halfway between my room and theirs, I heard a thump; my mother yelled for help and started crying in earnest. Several louder thumps, my father grunting. My mother continued to wail, and I realized I had stopped.

Saul emerged from Momma's room, his head slightly bowed, face quite red, his crisscrossed bottom row of teeth visible. He galloped down the stairs, without looking at me. I stared at the ground as he passed, and only after he left the house did I allow myself to breathe.

I had just been standing there.

The bathroom door slammed, and I made my way through the bedroom and called out for my mother, who was muffling her sobs.

She told me to leave her alone, to leave the house, in fact. The faucets squealed and ran full blast in the bathtub.

"I'm calling a lawyer!" I shouted. "I'm calling the police!"

The door opened. Momma gripped the knob, wearing only a towel, her face wet and swollen, her right cheekbone already billowing, two new bruises on her upper arm. "You will not."

"You can't let him—"

She slapped me.

"Leave me," she said.

My face warmed, and my right eye blinked uncontrollably. I headed down the stairs and out of the house as fast as I could on my crutches, stumbling on one of the front steps and falling into the overgrown grass. I thought I might hear Momma's bray, calling out for me. Wouldn't she be just as concerned for my well-being as I was for hers? But Dartmouth Court was abandoned, and only the birds chirped. I propped myself up and called the car service.

THE MISADVENTURES
OF PARRIS PONG

THE YEAR WAS 1930, the Year of the Tiger. According to Parris Pong's Chinese astrologist, the Tiger Year forecasted to be a difficult one for a Pig like Parris, especially financially. But as he rocked in his chair on the porch of his palatial home (where The Pongelliano stands today), pen in hand and a sheet of paper nailed to a clipboard in his lap, Parris couldn't help but feel that he had been and would continue to be uncommonly lucky. Of course, it had been difficult to be Chinese in America for all of Parris's life (no open immigration for the past fifty years, no land ownership, and no marrying non-Chinese women—just rotten because of Parris's predilection for white ladies), but thanks to his highly successful chain of local brothels, Parris was now retired and quietly wealthy in the midst of a depression. Cash, gold and silver in whiskey barrels were buried deep in the ground beneath his locked basement.

Today's primary task involved Parris's will. Even though he was in superior health, Parris knew that death could strike like a closed fist, and decisions regarding his estate would give many people tremendous comfort and fortune in the hard, dusty times ahead. On his paper, Parris scribbled the following note:

"*1. the assholshacion.*"

Parris wrote in phonetics because he was nearly illiterate. Every morning, he conferred with his assistant Frank, who would translate the misspelled notes into documentation or actions. Without his literate, eighteen-year-old friend with the endearing bowlegged walk and unusually short neck that made his shoulders appear to directly jut from his ears, Parris would not have been able to run the Chinese Happiness, Fortune and Precious Metal Association, a formidable group whose charter was to protect the interests of Chinese merchants in Bordirtoun. Before Parris sold the brothel, every few years a new white businessman would question Parris's right to have a cathouse on Main Street. Parris chose never to fight. He'd just open up in a new location. And what happened? The customers followed. Why? One, his product was superior. Two, people liked Parris. And three, the association was incredibly adept at committing arson and other business-destroying incidents (mass grave of dead skunks in the chimney?). Suffice it to say, Parris's brothel never drifted too far from the main drag.

"*2. Phrank.*"

At Parris's urging, the association had adopted Frank from an orphanage when he was three. Frank helped keep Parris in touch with the Pong family in China. Despite being American-born, Frank had learned to read Chinese from members of the association, and he had read Parris the many letters he received from his cousin Wei Pong (Sulliver Pong's great-grandfather). Once a family of educated and privileged aristocrats, the Pongs in China had lost everything, thanks to Wei's father Yixin and grandfather Feng's ruinous level of opium addiction. Their imperial posts had been revoked; their land confiscated. Wei often blamed his family's woes on the corruptive influence of the West and the Chinese Christians. While somewhat moved by his relatives' struggles overseas, Parris found many of their letters, especially Wei's commentary, painfully dull. Best not to get involved in political matters, Parris thought. In response to one of his cousin's letters, Parris once asked Frank to write, "If everything is in such turmoil, why not just pay and smuggle your way to America? It's a dangerous and lengthy journey from what I hear. But I can tell you, it's worth it. I can also tell you that we have the best ladies in Bordirtoun." Parris considered offering to arrange for his cousin's passage. Because Parris was classified a merchant, his relatives in China would have been exempt from the exclusion laws. But in the end, he decided against offering help. If Wei were so fervently opposed to opium and Christianity, what would he think of Parris the hard-drinking, fun-loving cat ranch proprietor?

Parris's eyes skimmed the clear surface of the river and its winding path to Mexico as he pondered what to write next. Frank would be arriving soon for their morning meeting. He needed to clarify his thoughts. Finally, Parris wrote:

"*3. Famullie??*"

He had never been married, had no wife or family with whom to leave a portion of his fortune. Over the years, some of his well-to-do friends at the association chose to return to China in search of love and family, risking that they would never be able to return to America. Those who made it back brought wives and sons, even other people's sons who joined their new American clans as relatives on paper.

At the time, Parris was glad that he didn't go to China. Born in America, Bordirtoun was Parris's home. He loved living most of his life within a three-block square. Swing by The Castle Saloon on Main Street in the morning for a whiskey, head into work at the brothel down on the corner, back to the Saloon after hours for a little poker and more drink, stumble back home with a beautiful woman in tow, keep a gun beneath the pillow. Parris had never left Bordirtoun, and he never would.

After his mother died in 1900, Parris began to feel the weight of having no family of his own. His mother Martha had always been a burden, a harsh woman. She became very resentful of having to take care of Parris on her own after his father Millmore died. She had named him Parris because she had wanted to, one day, visit the correctly spelled city in France. Born in San Francisco to a restaurateur, she had run away from home for adventure only to find that without a husband, there were few life paths for a Chinese woman that didn't include prostitution. After Millmore died, Parris's mother became the sexual target of every Chinese man in town. After all, it was the 1870s, and there was one Chinese woman to every twenty men. Young Parris witnessed his mother entertain a different Chinaman every day, sometimes several times a day, for money, for pleasure. She was convinced that her life took this unlucky path because, in Millmore, she'd married the wrong man.

"Who in his right mind would choose to work in railroad and bridge construction?" Parris's mother said. "Your father was so emotionless in his face, like he knew the best path better than anyone else. Now I realize he was just slow."

Before she finally succumbed to syphilis, on her sick bed, Parris's mother confessed to her son some of the mistakes she had made in her life.

"I was a slut," she said in Cantonese. "I was easy. I was a floozy. A tramp. A harlot. Gave my pussy to any Chinese man who would smile at me. Gave my pussy to lots of Chinese men who didn't smile. I had so many abortions, I stopped counting. I was lonely when your father wasn't around. I don't even know if he was your real father."

"You're not being funny, Mother," Parris said, twenty-five at the time.

"I'm not trying to be funny, boy," she said. "I'm trying to be sorry."

"And I'm trying to say you don't need to be."

"I liked the sex," she said. "I'll admit it. I don't subscribe to any God. I liked the cock."

"Okay," Parris said. "You better get your rest."

"I never thought we'd stay in Bordirtoun, this sinkhole," she said. "Your father knew I wanted to travel. Why did he have to die?"

"I know, Mother," he said. "I miss Dad too."

"Really? How?"

"Well, not literally," he said. "I never knew him."

"Promise me you'll get out of this shitty town," his mother said. "Promise me. Go to Paris, Parris."

"I promise."

"I've heard they've got great cock!"

Growing up, Parris found himself consumed with a rage he didn't fully understand. In matters of business, mathematics, and finance, Parris would be calm, rational, focused. But regarding matters of the heart, Parris was often not so lucky. Spurned by those he wanted and too quick to submit to the desires of those he didn't, Parris would inevitably find himself in arguments with women. During those arguments, he would feel a shudder inside his head, lose focus, and his fists would fly, and he wouldn't feel release unless he connected and someone was hurt. Sometimes he would remember how the men who plowed his mother had treated her when they came over. The yelling, the screaming, the beatings.

After Sunblaze Wilde, Parris decided that he would spend the rest of his life alone, no matter the cost.

She was the love of his life. She wore her hair up with soft orange ringlets that caressed her lengthy neck. She had a pale, lightly freckled face with searing blue eyes, and when she smiled, you felt like she knew something good about you that you had yet to discover. She had an unusually large bosom that even the top-heavy, mutton-leg-sleeved dresses of the era failed to hide.

The year was 1902, and Sunblaze was the most frequently requested woman at the brothel. Raised in an orphanage, Sunblaze had started working for Parris when she was only sixteen, and her arrival coincided with the rise of Parris's Bordirtoun Brofful. Though the girl was his biggest draw, Parris took precautions to protect her against the town's worst slime. He had each of Sunblaze's customers take off his belt and leave his shooter at the door. Often, he interviewed the johns before taking their money to make sure they weren't psychopaths and brutes. He interrogated them at such length, many lost interest and left or were certain that Parris was going to rat them out to their wives. He even cut discreet holes in the walls so he could monitor any truly deviant and potentially dangerous behavior.

Every Sunday morning, though neither observed religion, Parris and Sunblaze would walk hand-in-hand along Bordirtoun River and palaver about the latest goings-on about town. Perhaps a market owner had been out sick due to blood poison or the house of a well-known resident had burned down. All week Parris looked forward to those clear, warm mornings, waiting outside the room Sunblaze rented at the local inn on Main Street. He'd have his bowler hat in hand and wear his finest sack coat with a matching vest and floppy bow tie. She'd appear, wearing her hair up and gathered beneath a hat, dressed in her high-necked Sunday best. She was a vision. Her skin so smooth and creamy. Her eyes made the white sky look dingy. Together, they walked along the river, the dappled surface of which stirred in the light, cool breeze. She made Parris feel small, unworthy, like a scoundrel.

"Are you happy, my dear?" Parris asked. He wanted to make sure Sunblaze would not leave Bordirtoun. She often talked about going to San Francisco or New York for a fresh start. Maybe applying to nursing school. She did not want to be a Bordirtoun whore forever, as Parris silently wanted.

"I am," Sunblaze said.

Parris sighed with relief. "Is there anything I can do to make you happier?"

"Well, I need to save up more money for school," Sunblaze said. "If you can spare a little bit on every john—"

"I don't want you to leave," Parris said.

"There are no schools nearby."

"Surely there must be," he said, stroking his hefty mustache and pointed beard. "You haven't searched enough."

Sunblaze paused, measuring the temperature in Parris's voice. "No, perhaps I haven't," she said.

"Maybe I can search for a school closer to Bordirtoun."

"I would much appreciate that, Parris."

Had Sunblaze been leading him on all along with their Sabbath morning walks? Did she view their dates as a duty because Parris paid her way? As he remembered Sunblaze now, clipboard in hand, Parris no longer viewed his life as so lucky. He went inside his house, and with a screwdriver, he undid a floorboard beneath his desk and retrieved a bottle of Old Overholt straight rye whiskey, and began drinking. On his list, he wrote the following note:

"*4. Sonblaze.*"

One time, after Parris had made love to Sunblaze at the brothel, he asked her if she loved him.

Sunblaze lit a cigarette. "Oh, of course, I love you Daddy," she replied. Still only nineteen, she called every john Daddy.

"Don't call me Daddy."

"Parris."

"Say, 'I love you, Parris.'"

Sunblaze hesitated. "I love you, Parris."

"Why did you hesitate?"

"Oh come on, Daddy, stop."

"Stop calling me Daddy!" Parris smacked Sunblaze across the face, knocking the cigarette out of her hand. She scurried naked to the corner of the room, folded herself small, and began to sob. Parris sagged with self-hatred as he watched his angel shivering in pale cold and fear. He pulled his trousers up. "Why do you make me do this?" he muttered, before leaving the room.

Instead of waiting for Frank to arrive, Parris left the house, strangling his whiskey bottle. He had tears in his eyes as he drank and drank. He had been a lucky man. He had been lucky that the sheriff had never found any evidence that he killed Sunblaze. Her body was never found. After the sheriff had first questioned him, Parris had considered fleeing to China and visiting his cousin. But he was scared. Afraid of China more than he was afraid of jail or a hanging. Killing Sunblaze was only the worst of the many bad things he'd done. He had slept with all his whores, making many of them pregnant. Who knows how many abortions he'd seen to? He didn't believe in God for this reason. If there was a God, why had he lived so long? Why had he lived such a lucky life? He'd never been sick. He gambled and won more than he lost. He drank at least a half bottle of whiskey a day (even in the recent Prohibition years), and yet he was completely healthy. No benevolent God would have resisted the urge to strike him down and shove him into the rectum of Hell.

Parris walked down the staircase that led from his house to the banks of the river. The water's edge was flat and rocky, and this was where he and Sunblaze had walked on that fateful Sunday morning, after Parris had been playing poker and drinking shots of moonshine all night, when Sunblaze finally told him that she had decided to quit the brothel.

"You can't leave," Parris said.

"I won't be here for the rest of my life," Sunblaze said. "I have a cousin in San Francisco."

"San Francisco is a terrible place," Parris said. "It's overrun with Chinese people and people who hate Chinese people. I know. I hear the stories from the association all the time."

"I'm sorry, Parris," Sunblaze said. "I know how you feel about me."

"Marry me," Parris said. Though the urgency of the words surprised him, Parris had planned this moment for some time. For a full year, he had kept a ring with him in the breast pocket of his vest. Reflexively, he reached for his gun. Then he realized his error and showed her the ring instead.

Once she saw the glint of the metal, Sunblaze turned her gaze to the river and to the west side of town, where Old Town sprawls today. "I can't, Parris."

"Yes, you can," he said. "There are ways. People have done it. We can enter into a contract. It's not legal in the eyes of the law, but it can be legal in our eyes, the eyes of people."

"I don't want to," Sunblaze said to the river. Then to Parris, she repeated. "I don't want to."

He let the pain settle in his gut. Of course, she didn't want to. How could he have not seen that she didn't love him? She was his prostitute, nothing more. He put the ring back into his pocket. Sunblaze said, "I'm sorry," and began to walk away. He grabbed her arm hard. She cried out. To keep her quiet, Parris hit her with a closed fist. She fell to a knee. "Please," she said, her white teeth coated in bright blood. Parris hit her again. This time, when his fist re-cocked, he stopped himself and reached for his holster.

"Parris!" Frank called out from the top of the steps.

Halfway through his whiskey bottle, Parris was crouched at the riverbank, crying where he had bludgeoned Sunblaze with his gun and dumped her body in the water over a quarter century ago. He had watched her billowing dress drift downstream toward Mexico.

Frank finished walking down from the house. Like Parris, he was a short, stocky fellow. He had a habit of repeatedly adjusting his bifocals and hiking his nose. "Did you forget our appointment?"

Parris teetered over to the young man. "No, I remembered."

"Shall we walk back to the house?"

"No, no need." Parris wiped his eyes with the heel of his palm. "I only have a couple of tasks for you today."

Frank balled his hands behind his back and nodded. "Tell me."

"My will," Parris said. "I want to leave eighty percent to you."

Frank's hands unclasped. "Sir?"

"I'm your father," Parris said. "Your mother worked for me. She died giving birth to you. She named you Francisco. After San Francisco, where she landed when she came over from China."

The boy backpedaled and swayed. His mouth fell open. His nose jittered double-time, making his spectacles appear to vibrate on his face. Even when he was telling the truth, Parris felt he was committing a cruelty. He drank deeply from his bottle.

"Ten percent to the association," he said. "Ten percent to my cousin Wei's family for their passage to America. I want all the Pongs here. You're a Pong now."

A confused Frank kowtowed to Parris. "I don't know what to say, Sir. I don't know whether to be angry or happy."

Parris's hand quavered on his son's shoulder, and for a moment, he thought the boy was going to faint. "Don't kowtow in America," he said. "You can be angry at me when I'm dead. I've done many bad things. Forget the bad. Learn only about the good. Be the best man you can be and live a lucky life. That's all I can tell you."

"You were never a father to me," Frank said, his voice cracking. "Why?"

Parris let his son go and pulled again from his bottle. "Because I had both the Devil and God on my side."

He wobbled up the steep steps with one hand on his whiskey bottle and the other on the railing. He left Frank on the banks of the river and reentered his house. He finished the rest of the bottle and was now in a fully drunken daze. He flopped into his chair, unlocked the top drawer of his desk, and pulled out the gun with which he killed Sunblaze. Parris loaded six bullets, touched the barrel to his heart, and rested his finger on the trigger.

He closed his eyes and whispered, "Sunblaze."

4.

JAYNUSS CALLED ME AGAIN TODAY. "Do you want *more* time in prison?" he said.

"What do you mean?"

"These pages make me want to kill myself," he said. "Are you sure you're not depressed? The art of denial? Cowardice? Domestic abuse. Luckily, I'm the only person within five hundred miles who doesn't own a gun, otherwise I'd have long since blown my brains out."

"You told me to tell my story," I said. "Leave no story stone unturned."

"Don't mock me," Jaynuss said. "Can't you be more positive? Show how you've reformed! No fucking wonder you haven't been paroled. I bet your other attorneys didn't even let you speak during the hearings. Your depressed ass would have hung yourself. Fuck!"

"Is this the only reason you called?" I said. "To cuss me out?"

"I called to tell you you're losing my fucking case!" Jaynuss shouted.

"Maybe if you did something with my fucking case, Anus, you wouldn't be fucking losing it!"

"Fuck you!" Jaynuss hung up.

Fine. Deep breath. Screw Jaynuss.

I can be more positive. I have reformed. For example, I've lost thirty pounds in the last eighteen months on the prison's "Body by Incarceration" weight-loss plan. The combination of prison gruel and seemingly infinite time to do pull-ups and push-ups has me looking svelte these days. Standing up, I can even see my gnarled toes again. Why did I begin exercising, you ask? To defend myself against inmate ambush. For the first year, if there were a Bordirtoun Correctional Bullied Inmate of the Month award, I would have been on that plaque twelve months in a row. My fellow prisoners were quite creative as well, utilizing a myriad of media and stages with which to batter and bruise the mayor's son. One time, my face was mashed against Plexiglas by one attacker and I watched the crowd in the prison yard cheering and laughing as the other attacker (who was a punter for the University of Texas at El Paso Miners for one year before being booted off the team for point shaving) kicked me repeatedly in the testicles from behind.

But now, the other inmates leave me alone. There are new transgressors for them to abuse. The pimply 19-year-old son of Dr. Quango, for instance—effete Ramesh, inside for repeated DUIs and angel dust possession.

When I first joined the Bordirtoun Correctional therapy group, the leader (his first name is Dr. Darrell; no one knows his last name) asked me to introduce myself and tell everyone why I thought I was unique in this universe. I was in an angry, frothier state at the time.

"I hail from Bordirtoun, U.S.A.," I said. "Approximately twenty miles from an internment camp, in a country that dropped two A-bombs and a billion firebombs on Japan."

"You're Chinese, right?" Miso, a man with one brow (the right one), inside for check forgery and bank fraud, said.

"Let me finish," I said. "I hail from a country that is currently engaged in an illegal war in the Middle East, and a city that elected my turpitudinous father mayor."

"Turpitudinous?" said Foley, carnal connoisseur of boys ten and under.

"I'm finishing!" I barked. I told them I was a spawn of mediocre Bordirtoun, a corrupt America, and a morally bereft Chinaman named Saul. I saw blinking all around. Even Dr. Darrell was looking out the window, quietly giggling at the cheering that had erupted around a fight that had moments before been a prison badminton tourney.

One inmate, however, was rapt. I would come to know him as Manny (he would move into my cell after my first mate broke his neck trying to do a headstand because he insisted that "all Chinese liked acrobats").

"Can't blame anyone but yourself for your actions, *cabron*," he said.

Sure, I told him to fuck himself, and yes, I paid for it dearly (ruptured spleen). But after my recovery and given the time to reflect, I have a better understanding of who I am penning this for. Not just for the parole board. Not just for wronged Chinese people, not for racist whites, not for my prison therapy group, not for Manny or Jaynuss, not for Momma, not for my once-again estranged father, not even for Lene (though I hope and, in weaker moments, pray she will read this one day), but for others, like myself. Those who lack foresight. Those often overwhelmed by the present. Those ignorant of and indifferent to the past. Those whose worst qualities come to the surface when tested. Those who are fertile ground for dubious moral judgment. Those who feel, in some mysterious but common sense, *unmoored*.

In the limo, I sat, Momma's slap sizzling on my cheek. The mere sight of the toilet bowl whiskey made me nauseous. Traffic slid to a halt on Francisco Pong Boulevard, and there were detour signs and a parabola of orange cones ahead. A crane hung high over a block of low buildings. A police car, siren lights flashing but silent, squeezed past the line of automobiles on the shoulder.

"Sorry about this," the driver said. "Some demonstration. Is there somewhere else you'd like to go?"

I told him to keep driving and turned on the small television embedded in the passenger seat headrest. I flipped through the daytime talk shows to a news station's live, local coverage. The footage showed protests blocking traffic on both sides of the bridge, police standing side-by-side, batons lowered, cordoning off a construction site. According to the Pong administration, a reporter noted, the protests would be allowed to continue peacefully. A woman with long hair, striped alternately black and white like a zebra, led the chants. Were it not for her enormous buttocks, she could have been Mrs. Marquis, my father's former executive assistant, a woman who insisted I take her extra Jolly Ranchers (though I hated candy) while I Xeroxed flyers for my father's campaign one high school summer. Upon closer examination, I realized it was Mrs. Marquis, her hair tousled, her head significantly meatier than my recollected version.

"You worked for Mayor Pong for a number of years, correct, ma'am?" the wide-eyed blond reporter asked.

"Yes." She smiled, staring into the camera. "Twenty-three, to be exact. I was forced to retire last year." She waved and mouthed a hello to a viewer she knew.

"Why are you here today?"

"I'm here to protest the Old Town redevelopment," Mrs. Marquis said. "They have no housing plan for the residents. Where will we go, Mayor Pong?"

"What do you have to say to the man leading the Old Town redevelopment?" the reporter said. "Sulliver Pong, the mayor's son."

"*Sulliver?*" Mrs. Marquis began to laugh so loudly the driver turned around. I hit the mute and perused the closed captioning as she opined that, during our summer working together, I had demonstrated such a singular lack of initiative and aptitude that she was surprised I graduated high school. She topped off her rant with an unfortunately lengthy anecdote about my inability to work an office copier.

"HE ISN""T CAPE^ABLE," I read. "HE SAULL'S POOPPIT."

I shut off the television and felt the blood rising to my head. I threw the remote against the front seat partition. The control bounced off the Plexiglas and hit me flush on the kneecap. I banged on the remote repeatedly with the gray rubber tip of one of my crutches.

"May I help you, Mr. Pong?" the driver said.

"Absolutely not!" I said, panting. "I'm perfectly capable."

"Of what, sir?"

"How is my father capable?" I went on. "Capable of what? Capable of beating my mother? Capable of hurting others? Capable of lying and cheating? And I'm not capable?!"

"Last Christmas, your father bought my wife some fine crystal," the driver said.

"He probably fucked her."

The heat vents went on full blast. "Your father apparently gave birth to an asshole."

"Fuck off." I noticed that my wallet had fallen out of my pocket, and the contents had spilled onto the floor of the car. My credit cards, my bank cards and sadly, The Pongel Horse business cards I'd taken from the previous car service. I reached down and gathered them, staring at the purple and pink neon lettering. My father's strip club. I must confess that while I had taken the cards to make a point, I had not discarded them on the off-chance I might use them before I left Bordirtoun. I put my crutches aside and slouched in the seat. Maybe I was Saul's puppet, I thought. Saul's puppeteering had kept me rooted to the ground while he was pummeling my mother. Saul's puppeteering brought me back to Bordirtoun. I rubbed my pate, depressed, deflated.

A sting pierced my inner thigh. There was a dollar-coin-sized spot of blood on my trousers; I had popped a stitch. Sighing, I knocked on the partition between me and the driver.

"Listen, I'm sorry I blew up like that," I said, sweating profusely from the heater. "I've been under a lot of stress lately. Can you drive me to the hospital?"

"You gonna walk around with a limp for the rest of your life, if you ain't careful," Jimbor said, after cleaning up my re-stitching.

I sighed, getting back on my crutches. "I'm going to need a place to stay for a little while."

Jimbor's mustache squirmed. "Yeah?"

"I hate to impose," I said. "My mother kicked me out of the house."

"Was it because you went home drunk last night?"

"Kinda," I said. "Long story."

Jimbor nodded hello to a female co-worker passing in the hall. She poked her head in the doorway and said, "Thanks for coming to Knit Group last night."

Knit Group? Wasn't he supposed to have been working? Jimbor smiled at the nurse and said, "It was fun."

"Come back next week," she said.

"I will," Jimbor said.

The nurse bade farewell, and Jimbor smirked sheepishly at me. "We're always looking for ways to kill time on the night shift."

"Oh, absolutely," I said, nodding vigorously. "We used to do similar things when I worked."

"Sounds like it's been a long time since you worked."

"At an agency, I mean," I said. "I work for myself now."

Jimbor cleared his throat. "You can stay with us as long as it's okay with Taryn."

I thanked him. After an uncomfortable pause, he said, "Say, did you and Taryn ever, you know?"

"No!" I blushed. "I mean, not that I didn't want to. I mean, not that I wanted to."

"You had a crush on her?"

"No, absurd!" I said. I desperately wanted to leave. "We were all good friends. The three of us. And you too, of course, Jimbor."

"I didn't know you back then."

"Any friend of T.R. and Taryn, or her husband, I guess, is a friend of mine," I said, the skin above my upper lip moist with sweat. I put a limp hand on Jimbor's bony shoulder. "What I'm trying to say is I really appreciate all your help since I arrived."

Jimbor nodded and smiled. "No prob'm, Sull-ver." He slapped me on the shoulder. "Taryn seems to like you."

I laughed. "Does that mean you don't?"

He didn't laugh.

"Jim?"

A corner of his mouth rose. "Any friend of Taryn is a friend of mine."

Jimbor called T.R., who came by and picked me up. I decided, at the time, not to tell T.R. about Jimbor's possible knit club fib. I took Jimbor at his word—a night shift knit group, it was. Just as I thought that it wasn't my place to tell Taryn that she married beneath her lot, I decided it wasn't my place to insert myself in the middle of their inexplicable marriage by making insinuations regarding Jimbor's devotion to his wife. Besides, I had no idea what even the most mullet-blind nurse would find attractive about the man.

I told T.R. what had happened at the Pong family house the previous night. Like a true friend, he mostly nodded and listened. It felt good to simply complain for a while, without being judged, without facing probing questions. I shudder to imagine how my fellow inmates in therapy group would react if I confided in them—they'd line up to make me pay for any demonstrated weakness.

We dropped by a shopping mall, and I purchased a few outfits. Then we returned to the Grathe house, where I took a shower. I felt like I hadn't showered in days. I leaned against the tiles, closed my eyes, and listened to the steady wine-borne throbbing in my head. I inspected my groin. My repaired stitches stung upon rinsing and seemed inflamed and encrusted with a mysterious yellow substance. Favoring my leg, I stepped from the shower and dressed. My cell phone beeped. Probably a call from Momma. Or was it Lene? I checked—Low Battery.

I felt a sudden deep bone-cold, not unlike the cell-block cold of desert nights during Bordirtoun Februaries, a trembling beneath my soft layers, a throbbing fear. For the first time, I imagined explaining to Lene that I had to stay awhile, to extract Momma from my father's grasp. Surely, she would be upset. With all she'd had to put up with lately, I wondered if my staying longer might be the last straw. A few small, dark parts of myself—the parts that were lazy (marriage is hard), vengeful (Saul must pay for what he's done to Momma!), sentimental (I actually have friends here)—would have been relieved if Lene decided to leave me then and there. Though, for the record, I must state that I never wished for such an unfortunate result.

I got on my crutches and made my way into an empty living room. The television was on (*Mad Max: Beyond Thunderdome*). I wobbled through the kitchen and out into the backyard, where the jungle gym, metal slide, and tanbark box were still there as I remembered, now warped and pocked with rust. Taryn was sitting in a lawn chair in the shade and staring out at the clear, white afternoon sky. She was wearing a distressed pair of Capri pants, and her legs were crossed, her pale front shin swaying. She held an unopened pack of Gauloises and rotated it like a deck of cards. When we traveled Europe, she smoked only Gauloises.

"You don't still smoke, do you?"

Taryn shook her head. "I ordered them online before I got pregnant, and they just came today. Guess they got lost en route. Six months. I completely forgot I'd ordered them. Jimbor couldn't even pronounce Gal-wah when he met me."

"They make cigarette brands easy in Denmark. Everyone can pronounce 'Prince.'"

Taryn smiled and scraped a finger over the seal of the pack. "I've been there. With you, remember?"

Her answer prompted a sudden silent stirring in my organ. "Of course, I remember."

"Remember when we slept outside that train station in Oslo?" Taryn said. "I remember thinking, 'being homeless is so cool.'"

"I remember thinking something similar," I said. "We were stoned out of our mind though."

"Yeah," she said, shaking her head. "I don't know what we were thinking."

"We were silly and young."

Taryn's gaze returned to the darkening sky. "What are you going to do about your mother?" she asked.

I felt heavy on my crutches, watching the wind clip the dead and unruly grass. When I was younger, T.R. and I used to play wiffleball on this very patch of now-decrepit lawn. The vague smell of burning rubber from the nearby plastics plant made me want to wake up in a familiar bed.

"I miss my wife," I said. "I want to go home."

I recall sounding very firm about this, surprisingly so. Yes, I remember thinking, that's what I truly wanted, deep down—to go home and sleep, to sleep next to my wife! Taryn's lips pursed, and she went a little soft in the eyes. I'd heard once that few characteristics make a man more attractive to women than a professed devotion to his wife. Had I heard this from my father? Taryn seemed to be thinking what a genuinely caring person I was. This is the Sully I know, her eyes read! Not the drunken, lecherous, lying one!

"But I'm not letting Saul get away with being Saul," I said. "I want to hit him back. Just not sure how."

Taryn stood with effort, releasing a puff of breath. "Come inside," she said with a quick tip of her head. She reminded me, just then, for some reason, of a missionary.

The Grathes and I spent the rest of the day plotting the first attack in the Saul v. Sull war. It was Taryn's idea that we would change the locks on the family house, install cameras, and hire a private security team to monitor the property for future Saul invasions. When she asked if I was willing to pay for it, I looked her firmly in the eye and answered yes without hesitation, without asking the cost.

"No price is too high to pay for my mother's safety," I declared.

If Saul persisted and tried to walk in and out of Momma's house as though he owned it (which, of course, he did), the Grathes would file a restraining order on Momma's behalf.

Naturally, I knew Momma would hate this plan—wriggle, yelp, and bite like the cornered animal she was—but, true to Pong family form, I didn't care what she thought. A restraining order would hurt my father politically, and that's what I cared about.

The next day, a quarter past three, the temperature was at least 110 when I rang the bell at the family house. Momma opened the door, wearing sweats, her hair unbrushed, undyed, and streaked with gray. Her swollen cheekbone was coated with a foundation that called to mind mannequin flesh.

"You," she said, her voice gravelly.

"Momma."

She blinked slowly. "Where have you been?"

"I want my things."

Momma turned and walked away from the door, leaving it open. I followed her in and left the door unlocked behind me. The vertical blinds were shut, and the air-conditioning blasted; even the coffee table's fake mixed bouquet centerpiece shivered. Momma returned to the family room and curled there, fetal at the other end of the sofa, eating dried fish strips out of a Ziploc bag and watching television. She looked so small. The blinking lights from the screen threatened to render her invisible against the fading white leather. A DVD case gaped open on the table. An old Andy Lau romantic comedy, the plot of which involved him dressing as an elderly woman to woo a young one.

I sent a text message to T.R., a signal that the locksmith and handyman could begin their work. Meanwhile, I sat next to Momma on the couch and watched the movie, pretending the beating had never happened and that I was spending time with her just because I wanted to. I glanced at my cell every few minutes, waiting for T.R.'s call that all was ready.

"Have you eaten?" Momma said.

I told her I had.

"Do you want some orange juice?" she said. "I'll squeeze you some juice."

"I'll be leaving soon," I said. "I'm staying with friends. In a few days, I'll be flying home."

Momma didn't look at me. I examined her for further reaction, but there was nothing.

My phone vibrated. I answered and told T.R. to come in.

She finally raised her head from the arm of the sofa. "What's that?"

I heard loud claps of dress shoes against the hardwood floor. T.R. walked in, holding a large envelope. He was dressed in his only suit, the gray tie much too short, his slacks billowed with mountainous pleats. He handed me two sets of new keys.

Momma shot up with a scowl. "Why didn't you tell me someone was visiting?" she said in Cantonese.

"This is Teaver," I said, using his unfortunate first name. "An old friend from high school."

T.R. stepped forward and shook her hand vigorously. "Hello, Mrs. Pong."

Momma pointed at his face. "He ran against your father," she said in Cantonese.

"I ran for mayor against your husband," T.R. said in English.

I handed her the new keys and proclaimed that Saul Pong would never set foot in the family house again. "Teaver will be helping me make sure you're safe when I'm gone."

Momma's face reddened. "You useless idiot," she said in a trembling but controlled Cantonese whisper.

T.R. opened the envelope and laid blank forms in front of my mother. His business card was clipped to the papers.

I informed Momma that if Saul Pong ever threatened her safety again, we would file a restraining order against him.

Momma began rocking back and forth with folded arms. She was nibbling her lip, her cheeks reflective with tears. I might as well have been telling her she was under arrest.

"You'll never stop him," she said to me in Cantonese. "What are you going to do, lock me in this house forever, you stupid, useless, fat idiot? Why did I have such a dumb son like you? You think this hippie is going to help me?"

"He's not a—" I began in English, then stopped.

"What's she saying?" T.R. asked.

"Never mind," I said.

I stared at Momma, who was staring at the papers. She darted for them but I got there first and snatched the forms. She pummeled me with her fists but I was not going to let go; I crinkled them if I had to, all the while smelling the rankness of her milky breath and feeling the stinging in my groin more than the blows of her tiny hands. I shoved her, sending her sprawling across the sofa as T.R. watched, mouth open.

"I'm not leaving him," she screamed. "You can't make me!"

"This is your last chance!"

Momma began cackling, rolling around on the cushions like I was being funny. All the while, the tears she had cried were still wet on her face.

"You're crazy," I said, shaking my head.

She stopped laughing and looked up at me. "Why can't you be smart like Daddy? Why do you have to be stupid like me?"

I told her that she had to choose between my father and me, and I didn't care who she chose. Her demise was her responsibility. I sat, huffing quietly, trying to ignore the trilling of Momma's whimpers.

"Mrs. Pong," T.R. said, with a solemnity I'd never heard from him. "I know this is a very difficult time. But no one deserves to be treated the way Mr. Pong has treated you."

"This white man's not even smart enough to shave," Momma said to me.

"He shaves," I muttered in broken Cantonese.

"Your Cantonese is terrible."

I got a pen from T.R. and signed the papers for her, just as my father had signed that housing authority filing for me. A fairly reasonable forgery, considering how long it had been since I'd done it. As a teen, I used to emulate Momma's signature, whenever and wherever my father asked. I never questioned what I was signing, or why I was signing it.

I handed the forms to T.R., and Momma didn't stop me. I'd like to think she was choosing my way in that moment (or at least the wisdom of it), a life in which she didn't have to be battered. I'd like to think she was choosing freedom, peace, and a future.

"This is for your own good," I said.

"I wish I never had you," Momma said.

Was I hurt, you ask? When your mother wishes you never existed (out loud), you feel a particular hard pinch of the testes. The relevant question was not whether I was hurt; it was how I would react to Momma's latest affront. Could I be Zen and choose not to retaliate? Could I remain stoic, like I often am now when a fellow prisoner spits in my face or deals me a racial epithet? Could I channel my inner Mahatma and make my life my statement? That was the relevant question, and the answer was no.

Taryn arranged a press conference for the next day, during which I would resign from my post at the Pong Foundation. When we brainstormed talking points that would hurt my father most, we discovered that we were surprisingly uninspired. There were the usual suspects, of course: Saul was a liar, a morally challenged politician; Bordirtoun deserved better. But there was nothing newsworthy there—everyone knew Saul was not an admirable person, and still, he was re-elected. We needed a hook, a smoking gun, a damaging revelation.

Since I'd allegedly signed some sort of housing filing with Dr. Quango, T.R. suggested we pull the forged documents from the Bordirtoun Housing Authority. Surely, we would be able to discover Saul's shady plans by following his various forgeries.

We got to the Housing Authority just before it closed. There was a single wood-paneled counter with several oscillating fans trained on the one working clerk. He was a bespectacled, gray-haired man who had the longest, thinnest fingers I'd ever seen. When I told him who I was, he let me know that every other city worker in the building had either gone home hours ago or never bothered to show. He didn't understand why my father would tolerate this level of slothfulness in the city administration.

"He's probably at the strip club," I said.

"That ain't a nice thing to say about your father," the clerk said.

"He could be at the blackjack tables," T.R. said.

The clerk frowned at T.R. "I expect you to take your cheap shots, Mr. Grow-Zone. Bordirtoun survived the heat and drought cuz of hard work 'n sacrifice. Not from selling your marijuana to Mexicans."

"I never sold...ugh, never mind," T.R. said. He explained to me that, during the last mayoral race, Saul had repeatedly accused him of being a marijuana dealer. The police chief even held a press conference showing expanded aerial shots of the Grathe house and referring to it as the Grow Zone. Hence, the nickname: Mr. Grow-Zone.

I asked the clerk for the Quango Valley documents. After a lengthy search, he told us that no Quango Valley papers had been filed with the Bordirtoun Housing Authority. He recommended we check with the county.

T.R. asked him to call the county for us and get us a copy of the filing. The clerk planted his elbows on the counter, took off his glasses, and looked at T.R. then me with bloodshot eyes.

"You forget something?" He patted his back pocket, made tumescent by his wallet.

"Is he asking for money?" I asked T.R.

"You can talk to me, Sonny," the clerk said.

"It's Sully."

"What happened to hard work and sacrifice?" T.R. said.

"Hard work and sacrifice makes a man awful hungry."

T.R. offered a twenty, and the clerk laughed. I didn't have any cash. I told the clerk I would come back and give him a hundred dollars after I visited a cash machine.

He opened his mouth and breathed on his lenses before wiping them on his shirttail. "I best be getting home, boys."

"I'm a man of my word," I said.

"Like your father?"

I stiffened. "No, not like my father."

"You better not be." The clerk put on his glasses, slapped a carbon-copy notepad onto the table, clicked his pen, and wrote "IOU. $100."

The clerk printed out a copy of the abstract of the Quango Valley housing development filing. The development zone was located just west of city limits, and the objective of the project was to "refurbish existing structures to create affordable housing for low to middle income residents." The construction start date was the January after the election.

I asked the clerk if I could keep the copy.

This time, he pulled out his wallet, opened its mouth, stared into it, and sighed loudly.

"Okay, okay," I said. "No need for the histrionics."

"I know more history than you'll ever forget, you goddamn fancy pants," he snarled.

Shaking my head, I promised him $200.

The clerk delivered a gap-toothed grin and handed me my filing. And a copy of my corrected IOU.

According to the location description, Quango Valley was ten miles west of city limits, but there was no address, only GPS coordinates, so we headed for an electronics store, where we bought a GPS navigator. Then we drove towards Quango Valley.

We went well past ten miles. I had never been this far west of the river. The only business we saw was a neon-lit liquor and porn store with a new promotion (Gin and Jenna Sundays: Any Gin and Any Video with a Pornstar named Jenna 30% Off). We passed what appeared to be an abandoned traffic accident scene. On one sidewalk, a smoking Buick pointed back toward Bordirtoun. Across the street, an Impala was missing a bumper, and the windshield was caved in. On the horizon, I saw only more road and telephone lines stretching into a bleached, heat-warped azure. To the left, down an embankment was the border wall, crowned with shards of glass reflecting sparks of sun. We passed two dead stoplights, a couple of houses, and the stony, graffitied barb-wired walls of the now-familiar Bordirtoun Correctional Facility. Soon we were on a long empty stretch of sandblown road, the black mountains in the distance.

"Is it much farther?" I asked.

Just then, the GPS responded, "Turn right in zero-point-five miles."

We turned and rocked and rattled onto a dirt road leading to a stone structure with a single window. It looked like a guard station. A wide area surrounded by a chain-link fence, topped with barbed wire. Behind the fence, row upon row of flat-roofed barracks and bare and leaning telephone poles.

The GPS said, "You have arrived."

We got out of the car and walked up to what was supposed to be

Quango Valley. Judging by the dirt-caked windows of the barracks, this place had been here for decades. We called out hello, and our voices echoed. Dust and dirt swirled and skated across the ground, got in my eyes, and made my mouth gritty. A blistered wood signpost leaned in front of the guard station. The sign itself was metal, rusted at the edges. The letters were so faded that they looked like a procession of tiny ghosts.

The Rio River War Relocation Center. Property of the War Relocation Authority.

Rio River, the internment camp where my grandfather's cousin Francisco died. As a kid, I never paid much attention to my father's cautionary tale about Francisco the pastor. "Never trust the white man," my father would say. Or the adjunct moral, "never count on God to save you." I had some idea Rio River was nearby, but since history was never my favorite subject in school (or ethnic studies for that matter), I had never even bothered to ask where it was. On the drive back to Bordirtoun, T.R. said the Board of Supervisors estimated that ten to twelve thousand residents would be affected by the Old Town redevelopment project. He worked himself into a lather, equating the relocation (which was planned for October—before the election) to the forcible internment of the poor. I had to acknowledge that, despite my indifference to whatever historical significance this Rio River situation might hold to someone with more depth than myself, sending any person to live in these un-refurbished, dilapidated "existing structures" for any amount of time seemed inhumane. Silently, I thought that this was exactly what we had been looking for: the hook, the smoking gun, the damaging revelation that would knock Saul to the canvas.

"You have to talk to Saul," T.R. said. "You know him as well as anyone, and you know he's never going to refurbish those camps. This is outrageous. Maybe you'll have some sway."

I felt a sudden desire to urinate. Knocking my father to the canvas was one thing. Getting embroiled in the controversial relocation of residents to an internment camp was another. I had hoped I wouldn't have to see Saul before I went back to Copenhagen. "Me?" I chuckled. "Trust me, I am without sway."

"We can't let this happen," T.R. said.

Had he forgotten that I wasn't here to stay? "We?" I said.

T.R. shot me an annoyed look. When the GPS navigator kept uttering that we were drifting farther and farther away from Rio River, T.R. ripped its plug out of the cigarette lighter and tossed the navigator over his shoulder.

"Well, *I* won't let this happen," T.R. said.

I felt guilt and thought of ways I could appear to do my best to prevent the relocation while avoiding deeper involvement. After all, I needed to get back to Lene, and my father wouldn't stop his plans just because I said so. But if it made T.R. feel better to see me try and fail, well, why not pretend to try and fail?

"Drop me off at the hotel," I said. "I'll talk to him." I sounded surprisingly determined.

"No, no, I can tell you don't want to get involved," T.R. said.

"No, I want to."

"No, you don't."

"I do!"

"Are you sure?" T.R. said.

I paused. "I want to hear what he has to say for himself."

At The Pongelliano, the lobby concierge directed me to my father's private elevator, which I rode up to his suite. I called for him several times as I crutched from room to room. No reply. Even though it was ninety degrees outside, the electric fireplace was on, and I had a sudden fear that I'd catch Saul copulating with one of his Pongel Horse employees. I found my way out to the expansive deck where there was an oval swimming pool, a Ping-Pong table, and a massage platform. That was where Saul lay under a red towel, face-down, his long flap of hair facing me. A masseuse, wearing a linen tunic that was open-chested to his waist, emerged from the suite, rubbing his oily palms together, wearing a bowler hat. He didn't so much as glance at me as he walked past and went to my father.

"Dad?"

"Mmm?"

"It's me, Sully."

My father got up, secured the towel over his nethers, and sprung into his slippers. He told the masseuse to take a break, and smiled at me, but not with his usual high beam smile; this one was notably half-hearted.

"How are you, Sully?" he asked, as if we hadn't talked in months.

"I just visited Quango Valley."

Saul stretched his neck, and there was an audible pop. "Good visit?" he asked.

"Illuminating."

My father went to the Ping-Pong table and slapped a button. One side rose and locked at a right angle. Saul took paddle and ball out of the table holster, tossed the ball in his palm a few times, and began hitting, the polyrhythmic clicking loud against the silent, hot breeze. He was still as quick as I remembered, in that light crouch, his hips rotating and whirling with sharp movements, the scrape of his slippers against the concrete. I was reminded of the times in my childhood when he would defeat me 21-nil and tell me he was doing it to make me better. Saul began whaling away at the ball—his swing not unlike a boxer repeatedly throwing his knockout right hook.

"Relocation happens all the time in Europe," he said as he played.

"The facilities don't look good now, but we have a refurbishment plan in place. We've hired hundreds of luxury buses with bathrooms on board. Besides, thanks to our president's bill to preserve those internment camps as historical landmarks, we will get federal funds to make Rio River like new."

"You'll never refurbish Rio River," I said, borrowing liberally from T.R. "You'll pocket the money. You're basically interning these people."

"Interning?" My father laughed. "Like at all the medical schools you never applied for?"

My pulse pounded beneath my tensed jaw. "We'll see how your jokes go over at my press conference."

Saul swung and the tiny ball glanced off the tip of his paddle and bounced toward me. I let it roll past.

My father twirled his paddle and rubbed ball marks off the table. "Press conference?"

"Press conference," I repeated.

Saul's nostrils flared, and he licked his shriveled lips. "The Grathes have turned you against me."

"Knowing you, you'll probably leave those Old Towners to rot."

"Maybe if you would commit to working with me and the Pong Foundation instead of wasting time with your friends, you would know exactly what we're planning."

"I'm going home."

"We need you here," Saul said, shuffling toward me. "Our family is going through a very difficult time." He spoke as if he was informing me of genomics or some other area of study about which I knew nothing. A waft of coconut massage oil made me queasy. He placed an arm around me; his limb felt like hollow plastic tubing.

"One day, you and Elena might go through what your mother and I are going through," he purred in my ear.

I threw his arm aside, one of my crutches dropped. "Don't you ever speak about Lene again," I shouted. "You've been trying to sabotage my marriage for years! You are not to even come close to the family house anymore. Do it, and I'm filing a restraining order from Momma. Try me, old man! You touch her, and I'm going to put you in jail! Do you hear me? What's wrong? No speakee English?" I stood there, clinging to the rail, hopping on one crutch, waiting for my breathing to return to normal. My words—the volume, the growl—sounded like Saul barking at Momma.

One of his cheeks palpitated, and his eyes were glossy with rage. He bent over, picked up my fallen crutch, and handed it to me. "When you go back to your old barren white wife and pay your high socialist taxes, I'll still be here, serving my citizens." Then my father marched into his suite and slammed the bedroom door.

I wake to the sound of a broom sweeping concrete. That's what Manny sounds like when he's stifling his laughter. He's not particularly proficient at being quiet. He's reading my pages again. No matter how many times I tell him not to, he pulls my manuscript from under my mattress and after lights out, beneath his blanket, out comes the keychain flashlight one of his boyfriends from the outside has smuggled into the prison for him. I inform him that I am trying to sleep.

Manny guffaws raspily. "Pong Duk Dong gonna put Daddy in jail! How did that work out, Pussy Pong?"

"Fuck you, Manuel."

I hear my unfinished manuscript slap the cold concrete, and before I can sit up, he's on top of me, his gigantic belly knocking me breathless. One of his forearms presses against my collarbone, and I'm staring at his raised fist. "I told you never to call me Manuel."

"I told you never to read my pages."

Manny's arm cocks back, and I shut my eyes, preparing to lose teeth. Instead, I feel a light slap on the cheek. My eyes open. Manny is laughing, his mouth a black hole of toothless gums. His breath makes me gag. He hops off me, and his feet thump on the concrete.

"Pong Duk Dong gonna put Daddy in jail!" Manny shouts. He begins bellowing this repeatedly and jumping up and down.

The other prisoners laugh. The laughter rises in volume and richness and soon, the inmates are repeating Manny's mantra ("Pong Duk Dong gonna put Daddy in jail!"). The guards yell at them to quiet down but it's too late. For hours it seems, the other inmates are hollering and rattling their cages like a colony of baboons at a zoo.

Yes, I confess that I lost composure and used poorly chosen words when I told my father that I was going to put him in jail. We all know things didn't quite work out that way. But I meant those words. As with Momma, every hurtful word I used against my father, I meant. While I may have resisted deeper involvement, make no mistake, I felt like a bigger, better man claiming moral superiority over Saul. It gave me pleasure to have a hand in any of Saul's failures, big or small, and it gives me no pleasure to admit that I am that type of person, that type of son. Regarding my actions, I am contrite. Sometimes.

I stood alone behind a podium in the Bordirtoun Hyatt conference room, preparing for my press conference. I was wearing a somewhat ill-fitting suit I'd just purchased and hadn't had time to get tailored (sleeves too long, a little tight in the waist). I was skimming the statement Taryn had prepared for me, trying to register the words. T.R. was glad-handing a small band of local reporters. Taryn approached me, and I noticed that I'd never seen her in a business suit. She was curvy, not like my sinewy, cylindrical Lene.

"Any questions?" she asked, looking over my shoulder.

I told her I was questionless. I tried to think of something witty to say. "Back in my consulting days, I was the person behind the person on the podium too," I said.

"It's a comfortable position to be in," Taryn said. "You're responsible for things going well in the spotlight, but you never actually have to perform."

"I used to tell nervous speakers to relax by counting to three before saying anything."

"Typical advice."

"But what if you're so nervous, you can't count?"

She laughed, touching the middle of my back. "Oh, enough, Sully. You'll be fine," she said. "You're better than Saul could ever hope to be."

I wrapped an arm around Taryn's waist and pulled her close. I looked her in the eye and joked that the jury was still out, before I let her go, before the moment became more than an innocent flirtation.

The reporters began to take their seats while I glanced at my talking points and realized I'd been rumpling the papers in my hands. I smoothed them against my chest and stepped to the podium, my fingers trembling as I adjusted the microphone. "Thank you for joining me today. It's a pity that only now, several weeks after the fact, do I get the opportunity to speak publicly regarding my appointment to the Pong Foundation. After performing further due diligence on the Old Town redevelopment plan, I've decided to resign from my post with the Pong Foundation, effective immediately."

Reporters began scribbling, and flashbulbs popped. "As a Bordirtoun native, I will always want to see the best of futures made possible for its residents." I'd delivered that line surprisingly well. My voice had become clearer. One might have even mistook it for genuine. "But I recently discovered that my father has plans to relocate residents affected by the Old Town redevelopment to the Rio River War Relocation Center."

Gasps and murmurs rolled through the room. "I went to visit the existing living structures cited in the Mayor's plan and discovered these structures are, in fact, unrefurbished internment camp barracks."

Soon, reporters were firing off questions, and I was answering them easily, having practiced my responses with T.R. and Taryn the night before. Yes, Mayor Pong had masterminded the Pong Foundation's relocation plan. Yes, Rio River would be renamed "Quango Valley." No, he had not consulted with me. No, I did not know if my father stood to gain financially, but he had mentioned on one occasion that the project was eligible for federal aid since the internment camp was a historical landmark. While I couldn't speak for my father, I could only guess that he appointed me because he didn't want to take responsibility for his controversial decision. Yes, of course I was hurt he'd put me, his own son, on the firing line without telling me, but knowing my father, I could not put anything beyond him.

I was on such a roll, I even ad-libbed a bit. "Bordirtoun deserves a mayor who is more interested in the welfare of its citizens," I said. "A mayor who's not on the take from every private developer who wants to put a hotel, casino or gentleman's club near the border. Even though the mayor is my father, I'm not afraid to be critical of his choices."

A reporter in the back raised her hand, and I called on her.

"Hi, I'm Dora Tollworth from the *Bordirtoun Daily*," she said. "You and I have spoken on the phone."

She had long waist-length hair and was, to be frank, bordering on morbidly obese. I said, "Nice to put a face to the name."

"You and your father seem to have very differing political views, and you sound quite passionate about the type of city Bordirtoun should be," she said. "Have you ever considered a career in politics, maybe even running against your father?"

I glanced at Taryn and T.R., who were standing by the wall. They appeared equally puzzled by the question. Not one we'd prepared for. Deciding on honesty, I replied, "I have no intentions of running for mayor at this time."

"Are you certain?" Dora said. "With your father practically guaranteed a third term against the weak field of opponents, wouldn't this be the ideal time and the ideal way to serve the citizens of Bordirtoun?"

I smoothed my tie and looked at my helpless talking points. I briefly visualized myself, living here. Sulliver Rockefeller (yes, that's my middle name) Pong, wearing a suit that fit, pointing to Old Town, directing change! Changing things like — well, whatever it is a mayor changes. At least I would have a purpose, something guiding my days other than Danish daytime television and the occasional foray into internet pornography. Run for mayor? Lene would be horrified!

I took some water and cleared my throat. "My wife and I are going to sit down and talk when I get back to Copenhagen, and we'll make a joint decision."

There is something about standing in front of a group of people who are waiting on your every word, with the microphone inches from your lips. I can't deny I felt charged in a way I hadn't before. I did not want to disappoint them; I aimed to please. It was the vainglorious side of me that wanted to leave open the possibility of a mayoral candidacy. Suffice it to say, the Grathes had quite a long laugh afterward at my expense. And though I certainly do not find my behavior so funny now, at the time, I laughed with them. Small slip-up, I thought. No one would hold me accountable if I never returned; I told myself I'd be old news by the time I boarded the plane.

A few days later, my stitches were removed, and I retired my crutches and scheduled my flight home. I decided not to let Lene know I was coming; I'd surprise her. At the airport, T.R. and Taryn walked me to the security line. I would be boarding a commuter plane from El Paso to DFW. From there, a separate plane to JFK, then another to Heathrow, and another to Copenhagen.

Taryn and I hugged. I left my hand on her flank an instant longer than I would have were she someone else. I stored the feeling of her softness in my mind.

T.R. handed me a black box, about the size of my open hand. "A going-away present," he said.

I opened it and pulled out a gold mallet like the one my father received for donating to the Republican Party.

"For when you come back and run for mayor," T.R. said, with a smirk. "When I ran, your father whipped out the gold mallet story every couple of days to prove how Republican he was."

I laughed, and we hugged. As I invited the Grathes to visit, I noticed how weak my embrace was compared to T.R.'s.

I went through security, already feeling freer. On the plane, the engines wheezed, and my seat began to vibrate. The flight was less than half-full, my row empty, and the plane smelled of baby puke and jet fuel. I rested my head and took what seemed to be the longest exhalation of my life. My visit, originally planned for one week, had lasted nearly three. I thought of Lene and her silence in recent days. Had she gotten used to life without me? Would she cheat on me? Had she ever? Had she ever cheated on anyone before me? Eleven years and this was the first time I'd wondered. Shouldn't a husband know this answer about his wife?

On the other side of the window, Bordirtoun transformed into a series of flat brown grids, like an unimaginative, poorly sewn quilt. I tried to feel good about my trip, proud of my primary accomplishment: pulling myself out of the quicksand that was my hometown. My answers at the press conference made for good headlines ("Mayor Pong's Son Denounces Father's Plan to Intern Old Towners, Leaves Open The Possibility of Mayoral Run"). I was proud to think that I might have hurt my father politically even more than I had initially intended. I chose not to think about the many negatives: the constant warring with my parents and the fact that I was naïve enough to think my father wouldn't retaliate. Accentuate the positive, I told myself. Be glad it wasn't worse.

The worst was yet to come.

THE MISADVENTURES OF FRANCISCO PONG

THE YEAR WAS 1940, the Year of the Dragon. For Francisco Pong's sign, the Monkey, the most fun-loving and weak-moraled of the Zodiac animals, a Dragon year forecasted to be replete with good fortune on all of life's many fronts. But Francisco didn't believe in Chinese astrology, and 1940 was not a time for the fun-loving, morally weak as Francisco opined in his letter, written in Chinese, to his cousin Ri (Sulliver's grandfather) on February 20:

Many call America the land of opportunity. It is also a nation of people who know right from wrong, and unlike China, America is a nation that is not at constant war with itself. Despite tough laws, it is easier than ever to come to America. One day, fifty years from now, I predict there will be no borders, and the Chinese will freely travel in and out of this great country. It was my father Parris's dying wish to see all the Pongs in China come to America for a better life. Cousin, in honor of my father's request, I am offering to arrange for passage for you and your family. I urge you to take this gift and join the other Pongs in America.

Francisco inhaled the fresh air from his church window, which overlooked Main Street and the statue of Leland Stanford. What a prescient man, that Leland Stanford! Mr. Stanford's nearby railroad company and the Grace of Jesus Christ had helped Bordirtouners survive and even thrive during the Depression. Now that America was increasing its support for the European war effort, even better days were ahead for Bordirtoun's new cattle ranches and copper mines. As he had tried to explain to his cousin, between America and China, there was no contest! Francisco had already successfully arranged the immigration of numerous Pongs. Thanks to his connections to associations in Seattle, Portland, San Francisco, Los Angeles, and San Diego, Francisco was able to offer Pongs the option of settling in a city of their choosing. Though Francisco was determined not to become a man who had both God and the Devil on his side like his father, he decided to fulfill Parris's last wish to the best of his ability and had traced the genealogy of hundreds of Pongs in China. The branch of the family tree with the most fruit, by far, was Pong Feng's. The man had forty-five children (forty-three girls) with twenty women in four provinces. Every month, Francisco wrote ten, twenty, sometimes thirty letters to extended family members, enumerating the values of life in America and extending his immigration offer. He also included a Chinese language pamphlet promoting the greatness of Our Saviour and Lord, Jesus Christ.

He expected Cousin Ri to be an easy win, since Ri's father Wei had written Parris begging for emigration help. Unfortunately, the letter arrived after Parris's suicide, and Francisco didn't find the correspondence until years later after he'd returned from seminary school. Wei, a Nationalist sympathizer, died in a Communist prison.

Francisco sealed the letter to Cousin Ri with a rubber stamp and turned his attentions to his completed sermon, the pages of which were fanned on his desk. He stood in the middle of his sparsely furnished room and began to read aloud:

A woman asked me the other day, why must man wrestle with the same problems from generation to generation? Why must we be at war with each other again and again? Perhaps you are burdened by similar questions today.

I'm glad to tell you that the answers lie in the world's bestseller, the book that all Americans, all Bordirtouners, should turn to when these human anxieties visit upon them: The Bible. The Word of the Living God. According to the teachings of God's Word, our burdens and sorrows are rooted in Sin. Sin separates us from God like Bordirtoun River separates Downtown from Mexicotown.

There are some nations and nationalities that are currently suffering more directly due to Sin. For example, the Japanese who have invaded China, the country where many of us have ancestral ties, the country that is now a good friend of the United States. With all due respect to our congregants from Japan, these Jap invaders are likely to suffer greatly in the eyes of God. So shall the Germans who go about invading peace-loving nations like Denmark.

Let us turn to that glorious verse in the Bible, John 3:16, "For God so loved the world that He gave His only begotten Son that whosoever believeth in Him should not perish but have everlasting life." Some have called this verse of scripture a tiny pocket Bible, the Gospel in a small radio, a glowing star you can hold in your hand, a chosen, blessed toy you never outgrow, a perfect statement. Indeed, it is the warm pulse of a loving God.

No one knows what burdens you carry today. No one knows who you are warring with and why. Perhaps you are even warring with a loved one or family member. But God knows, and His love can reach down into the ache inside your heart and turn on that small radio Gospel and get the glorious music of Life singing its pleasure inside you again. By the blood of His only begotten Son whom He gave as a ransom for us all, you tonight can have your sins and even the sins of the Japs washed away and eternally forgiven. I do earnestly commend Him as Saviour and Lord.

After the sermon, Francisco stood outside the church, shaking hands and talking to people who alternately praised and asked him for spiritual advice. The Holy Moly of Holiness Baptists congregation was the largest in Bordirtoun and drew from swathes of the population on both sides of the river. Most of his congregants consisted of Chinese and Japanese immigrants, though there were an increasing number of white and Mexican families. Francisco took great pride in the congregation's diversity and popularity, and he saw himself as an instrument of God designed to spread His and America's message of love and equality for all of God's children, no matter the creed or race.

As Francisco idly watched members of his congregation spill out into the street, a woman approached and complimented him on the sermon. She was in her fifties and nearly brown in complexion, which made Francisco surmise that she worked at one of the cattle ranches. She had high mongoloid cheekbones that reminded Francisco of some of his family members in China, the ones he'd seen in photos. Her teeth were crooked and mottled with mysterious black shapes. He had not met this woman before.

"Are you new to the congregation, ma'am?" Francisco asked.

She said she was, and her name was Chun Fah. "Are you not filled with anxiety?" she said in English.

"Well, of course, I occasionally feel anxious for events that have transpired and perhaps even for events that have yet to be resolved within my personal history," Francisco said, thinking about his father, a consummate sinner. "But that was the central thesis of my sermon. That one can overcome these anxieties by seeking comfort in God's Word."

"I understand," Chun Fah said. "Of course, I understand. Your sermon was not difficult to understand. I'm not stupid."

Francisco was taken aback by this woman's tone.

"What I'm trying to say is," she went on in Cantonese. "That maybe you are ignoring what's going on here in Bordirtoun. There are plenty of sinners. They're waiting for the right time to put us away. They're waiting for the right time to blame us."

Who's they, Francisco wondered? "Turn to God, Chun Chun," he said in English. He realized he had misspoken her name but didn't bother to correct himself. He squeezed her shoulder and winked into her roaming, pulsating eyes. "Turn to Him. Thanks for coming."

"You believe you are American," she said in Cantonese. "But you'll find out the truth."

Francisco was already looking at the next person in line, a brunette woman in a pink petticoat and divided skirt. She smelled like rosemary. Francisco wiped his cheek of sweat and the Chinese woman's spittle. "Jesus is the way, the truth and the life," he said in conclusion to the strange lady, who had begun walking away and appeared to be hissing to herself.

Cousin Ri's response arrived several weeks later. Francisco eagerly opened the envelope, having already received three letters that week from other Pongs ready to board the liner to San Francisco. This letter was short:

Cousin,

I think that calling your offer a gift might be an overstatement. I am very, very busy with my art here. We are not as affected by the war, famine, and depression as you think. You may be reading propaganda from your Western newspapers. My wife and I will not be able to take you up on your offer. Furthermore, we have just learned that she is pregnant. Furthermore to the furthermore, I've heard that America is very, very unfriendly to Chinese people. I hear that they blame us for all kinds of diseases, and we have not been able to emigrate easily for nearly sixty years now. Perhaps I am reading propaganda from my Chinese newspapers?

Despite the day's scorching heat, Francisco started his fireplace and threw his cousin's letter in the roiling flames and watched the paper wither and shrink. Why did his cousin have to bristle so at Francisco's attempts to help him? Francisco couldn't help but feel hurt. Every other Pong he'd successfully contacted had said yes with little hesitation. By their own accounts, China was a horrible, horrible place. A weak country. A dead empire. Destitute. Starving. On the verge of being colonized by the Japanese. If not the Japs, then the Brits or the French. Fifty years from now, China would certainly be carved into five or six smaller countries. Why was Cousin Ri hanging on?

With a parched throat and fogged spectacles, Francisco riffled urgently through the many papers on his beaten desk to find his Bible. He threw sheets on the ground until his precious Book filled his hand. Francisco scurried outside to the church garden to read His Word where he had always read His Word: by the row of tall cacti that offered him quiet shade and respite from the growing heat in his room and his overwrought mind.

Like any other Friday afternoon, Francisco took a walk down Main Street, looking for inspiration in the faces of the town's citizens for his Sunday sermon. He wasn't feeling particularly well. He had indigestion after dining in Mexicotown with a family from the congregation (beans and sour cream never agreed with Francisco). After evacuating his bowels, and after sitting in the cactus shade to read passages from The Bible only to go back inside and evacuate his bowels some more, Francisco had become possessed with rage and had written a scathing retort to Cousin Ri that included a number of embarrassing and misapplied passages from The Book including every priest's favorite, "As So You Sow, So Shall You Reap." He basically implied (okay, directly stated) that if his cousin's wife died of famine or got raped by Japanese soldiers, blood would be on his cousin's hands. Francisco didn't know what came over him. He pushed aside a vision of his father swilling whiskey straight from the bottle.

As he rounded the Leland Stanford statue and headed into town, a large brown DeSoto cruised slowly beside him. The passenger side window opened.

"Hey Chinaman!" the man barked.

Refusing to respond, Francisco hastened his bowlegged steps. The redheaded man inside the car began heaving tomatoes at him.

"Hey Chinaman!"

Frightened and busy dodging softly tossed produce, Francisco still refused to respond.

"Maybe he's not even a Chinaman!" the driver said. "Maybe he's a Jap."

"Hey Traitor Jap!" the man barked.

"God sees no color," Francisco said, ducking, then hopping. "Come to my congregation, and you'll see members of all races in God's great family."

"Traitor Jap thinks it's Halloween!" the redhead said, referring to Francisco's pastor robe. This time, the man pitched a baseball, and only the quickness of Francisco's reflexes allowed him to deflect the ball with a forearm.

"Jiminy!" Francisco exclaimed, rubbing his arm. His old habit of hiking his nose returned, jittering his spectacles and making him mildly dizzy.

The car drove off, taking a hard left to avoid Main Street and its pedestrian witnesses. A sheet of tire-thrown dirt blinded Francisco momentarily. After he doubled over, hacking repeatedly, Francisco removed his glasses and wiped his watering eyes. He had experienced racism before, but never quite in such an upfront manner, and certainly not during an upset stomach. Instead of walking down Main Street, Francisco headed right, down a side street, around the back of City Hall, and hurried to his church. He needed to lie down, he thought.

As he walked, he felt the wet heaviness in the rear of his trousers and realized that he had defecated in them.

On the Sunday morning of December 7, 1941, the day the Japanese bombed Pearl Harbor, before news of the attack became widely known, Francisco gave the following sermon:

Judges 5:28: "The mother of Sisera looked out at a window and cried through the lattice. Why is his chariot so long in coming? Why, tarry the wheels of his chariot." Sisera's mother waits, wearily watching in vain for one who will never come.

Thousands and thousands of Americans are waiting in the same way for their call to a war overseas. Perhaps you are sitting idly by while great spiritual unrest roils inside of you and tears you asunder as if you had swallowed shards of glass. Perhaps you are waiting passively while invaders attack you, lob weapons at you, and call you names. Perhaps you are waiting and in the interim, you are traveling the higher road, the quieter path of the supposedly noble.

A man walks in solitude on a bright cloudless day. He's a preacher of the Gospel. He is ridiculed for preaching on the streets. Perhaps he is even being ridiculed for being a Chinese man. He begins to sing and to praise God while he's attacked. While he praises God, a dust storm comes and sends his attackers scurrying away like cowardly mice. He is free!

One of the attackers slips and falls in the sudden swarms of dust. The preacher walks up to his attacker and offers a hand.

"Sir, what must I do to be saved?" the fallen man says.

The preacher gives him one concise answer. "Believe in the Lord Jesus Christ and thou shalt be saved. Believe in Him and you shalt wait no longer for the truth."

After the sermon, a white man wearing a blue Standard Oil uniform and cap came to Francisco and said, "The war's coming to us, whether we like it or not."

"That may be the case," Francisco said. "But the thesis of my sermon still holds."

"We're going to fight a war against your country," he said. "I feel it."

Francisco chose not to correct the man, who was broad-shouldered and carried an unsettling intensity in his stooped posture that frightened Francisco. "My country is America," Francisco said.

"Rather than feeling things that may be untrue, perhaps you should focus your efforts on feeling the heartbeat of the one true God."

"Our reckoning is coming," the man went on. "We've already drafted people. There's going to be war. Our boys are going to die. We're just waiting for it. Your sermon was right."

"That's not exactly what I was intending."

"Then what was your intent?" the man said. "Are you going to fight for us, or are you going to fight for your peoples? Are you my brother or are you the enemy?"

"I'm God's brother," Francisco said. "I'm your brother. We're all brothers. One another. All for one and one for all." Francisco cringed. Was that from the movie *The Three Musketeers*?

"Have you registered for Selective Service?"

Francisco was silent. He had meant to. He was of age. He had come close to doing so several times. Knew there was a lottery. He had been busy. He was a community leader. No one had insisted. Okay, he was deeply afraid.

"Have you?" the man repeated.

"I have," Francisco said. "Absolutely, I have. But as luck would have it, I have not been selected. It is a very selective service indeed!"

The man didn't laugh. Instead, his upper lip arched into a snarl, and he nodded as if he had discovered via telepathy Francisco's draft-dodging secret.

A letter arrived from Cousin Ri on December 20, 1941.

Dearest Cousin Francisco,

I understand you have generously offered to sponsor our passage to America. The hearts of me, my beautiful wife Suen, and our newborn son beat in unison with great anticipation that we will see you in person when we come to America. Life has gradually become unbearable here. We have no money. I have discovered that painting is absolutely useless and that it is time for me to grow up and develop some practical ways to make a living, which is very important now that we have a newborn child. I would like to meet you in person, in Bordirtoun, to show our gratitude and apologize for any misunderstanding I may have caused. I have appreciated your persistence and generosity regarding this matter, and we may very well owe you our lives should you ensure our safe passage. We are looking forward to meeting our cousin for the first time.

The letter brought a much-needed smile to Francisco's face. He put the letter in a wood frame and hung it over the mantle of his fireplace. Of all the letters of gratitude he had received, this one was the most hard-earned, the most satisfactory, and surprisingly well-written and articulate. Yes, he found it strange that Ri's letter would include no mention of his prior reservations, no well-wishes regarding the Pearl Harbor attack, and in general, the tone of this letter seemed so different from the previous correspondence that it felt written by another person entirely. Regardless, this was the letter Francisco felt God would be most proud of should he ever get the opportunity to humbly kneel before His glorious gates and tally his many good efforts in the expression of the Gospel.

The day was February 20, 1942. A Friday afternoon. Francisco Pong received the final paperwork for Cousin Ri's family, and they had boarded the ocean liner to San Francisco, where they would pick up railroad tickets to Los Angeles and Bordirtoun. They would arrive in roughly two weeks.

It had been a deeply unsettling time since Pearl Harbor. Francisco felt like parts of Bordirtoun were slowly separating from its moorings in a way that was imperceptible to most residents but obvious to a community leader like Francisco, whose finger was forever on the public pulse. The congregation now consisted of roughly one-third Japanese families, and many of them requested counsel regarding the rumors of relocation centers and evacuations and the questioning and unfriendly looks they were getting from the whites and even the Mexicans in town. The great America, God's country, had arrested Tony Ishikawa, the head of the Japanese business association, within hours of the Pearl Harbor attack. Hundreds of whites had marched down Main Street with signs that read, "MOVE ON JAPS," "TRAP A JAP TODAY," and "THIS IS A WHITE MAN'S TOWN." A Japanese storeowner had posted a large sign that read, "I AM AMERICAN." Another was found disemboweled and hanged from the bridge that ran over the river. There were rumors that the government had constructed a place named Rio River approximately ten miles outside of town. Francisco just kept advising his congregants to seek solace in God's Word and the blood of Christ. Believe in Him and the truth will reveal itself. A dust storm might come to save them. Whatever else he could think of. During cold desert nights, however, Francisco prayed for better answers. He spent many evenings unable to concentrate on the Scripture, unable to sleep. His sermons had never felt as empty.

He left the church and took a walk around the statue of Leland Stanford as usual, to search for inspiration for Sunday's sermon. He noticed a large black DeSoto parked near Main Street. A man and a woman were talking to the people inside the car. The woman was talking to the driver; she was brown-skinned, and as Francisco approached, he recognized that she was Chun Fah from the congregation. She wagged her finger at him. Francisco didn't think much of it at first. He was a very recognizable figure in town. Perhaps they were just discussing the moving nature of last week's sermon.

Talking to the passenger was a gas station worker. Dark hair. Standard Oil. A snarl in his expression. Again, from the church. Francisco waved a greeting to all of them. He couldn't very well ignore their presence.

The car hissed to a start and drove off, leaving his two congregants planted in the road. Francisco thought the car had left until it drove around the statue and pulled up in front of him. Two men got out. They were wearing topcoats, skinny ties and bowler hats in the blazing heat.

"Are…you…Fran…cis…co…Pong?" the large-bellied one said, taking breaths between syllables.

"I am," Francisco said. He wondered if this was about the Selective Service for which he'd failed to register.

The taller, willowy one opened the door to the backseat. "Can you come with us, please?"

The bigger man flashed his badge. "F…B…I."

"Is this about the Selective Service?" Francisco said. "I'm sorry. I've just been negligent. Very busy with the congregation. Holy Moly of Holiness. You ever heard of it? It's the most popular church in town. You should come by on Sunday. Draws from both sides of the river. It's been a very trying time for all Bordirtouners now that we're at war."

The two men exchanged glances as Francisco went on. The taller man grabbed Francisco's wrist. "Not the Selective Service, Pastor Pong."

5.

MY PAROLE HEARING is only a month away. I have been sending Jaynuss my weekly pages, and lately, he hasn't been returning my calls. Given the way we left things the last time we talked, I'm concerned. It's like he and I are in a relationship in decline, not unlike the way things were with Lene while I was in Bordirtoun.

Pity Jaynuss isn't calling me back, because I suspect he and the parole board would be happy with the progress I'm making here in the penitentiary. There are days in the prison yard when I feel fully rehabilitated, when I feel that I am finally the man that I thought I was when I married Lene. This feeling, equal parts joy and relief, usually arrives in the mornings, in the summer, before the sun blazes high and hard above us inmates in the perpetually cloudless sky.

I've learned to navigate my surroundings here over the past two years. I read a lot, work out more, and play wiffleball most (though due to my rice-paper groin muscle, I often require a pinch-runner). On Tuesdays, I teach tai chi as an homage to my great-great-granduncle

Millmore, who was, reportedly, an enthusiast. On Thursdays, the inmates who have earned sufficient points for non-violent cellblock behavior, are allowed to team up in the yard and play tennis, softball or basketball. Since anything tennis-related spurs nausea and hatred in me, I typically choose the sports with the larger spheres.

I am a quieter man. Gone are the outbursts for which I was known when I first entered Bordirtoun Correctional. But since I started writing these pages, I find that when I do speak, I am more articulate. Some of the newer inmates, like Ramesh, Dr. Quango's kid, even look up to me and listen as if my lips round only to spout wisdom. The other day, I told Ramesh that he should avoid making the same mistakes I made; he should not allow his father's loose ethics to ruin his life. His fingers threaded in front of his crotch, Ramesh fidgeted and blinked at his nervously shuffling feet like an admonished child. When he looked up again, he had tears in his eyes.

"You're right," Ramesh said. "You're so right. My father has been dictating my life."

Saying no more, I hardened my face with gravitas and cast a solid hand on his Shiva-thin arm as if to say, "You've absorbed my wisdom now. My job is finished."

It feels good to be seen as wise. This must be how my granduncle Francisco felt before he was interned. Listened to. Admired. Seen as an exemplar, a role model, an instrument of the community. I am sure that Jaynuss will bring numerous anecdotes like the one I just related about Ramesh (fabricating them, if necessary) to the parole board. Sully is an avuncular presence at Bordirtoun Correctional. Some inmates even see him as a very young father figure. Now, if you don't mind, ladies and gentleman of the board, since he means so much to his fellow criminals, please let him resume a free man's life!

Do I care whether Ramesh makes the same mistakes I did? Of course not. In my forty years on this Earth, I have done nothing of which I should be proud. I have made some money. I am well-educated. I have lived in several large cities. I have been married once. I have made love countless times to a grand total of three women. And now I am here, in a cell, only fifteen miles from where I was born. If this is a sum of a proud, wise man, then the sum is set quite low indeed. I try to help my fellow inmates, if nothing else, to expiate my own guilt.

Yes, you read correctly. Guilt, I wrote. Am I confessing that I committed the crime for which I was convicted, you ask?

Am I confessing that I conspired in the attempted murder of my father?

Am I CAPE^ABLE?

I will let you be the judge.

I consider the hours after I got off the plane in Copenhagen among my finest as a man.

It was mid-morning Saturday when the cab pulled into the alley in front of my salt-washed green complex. Per my instructions, the driver helped me onto the hood of the car and handed over the two sizable bouquets of sunflowers that I had purchased on the way home. I got down on my knees and closed my eyes.

"Lay-na!" I howled toward our third-story balcony, a tortured, star-crossed, bowel-quivering love-howl. "Lene!" I opened my eyes. "Lene?" The lights weren't on; the shades were pulled.

"Are you sure she's here?" the driver asked.

"Lene!" I tried a few more times until my voice grew hoarse. No one came.

"I can't wait all day," the driver said.

"I'll pay you, okay?" I said.

"You damn well better pay me," he said.

"Fuck off!" I said. I moved to the edge of the hood and the ground looked too far for a jump for my recently repaired groin. "Fuck," I muttered. I was forced to ask the driver to help me down.

With my flowers, I went up to the flat. The apartment looked more or less as I had left it, beds made, not a pillow or book out of place in the living room. I inhaled deeply the scent of pomegranate soap I'd come to identify with home. I limped around the office and noted that our pictures had been removed from the bookcases. My steps slid against the creaky hardwood as I approached the bedroom. I pushed aside random images of my father fornicating with Lene.

Our bed was empty and made. Sigh, relief—she wasn't here. I had more time, so I went back downstairs, and the cabbie drove me to a nearby florist, where I bought more flowers, candles, and baubles. I bought much of the inventory and paid the driver 5,000 kroner to help me cover the hallway with my purchases.

After we were done, the hall looked like white fabric, not unlike the aisle I walked down on my wedding day. I gave the cab driver my home number and instructed him to wait downstairs and call the house if a middle-aged blonde woman entered the building. The driver replied that, in Denmark, many women were middle-aged blondes. In Danish, I told him I was quite aware how many middle-aged blond women there were in Denmark—I had lived here for eleven years. He informed me my Danish resembled that of a retarded Muslim and asked that I pay another 1,000 kroner. I told him to go to hell, then assented to 900. On the street, the driver kept his engine running.

It had been quite a long flight, and I had worked up a heavy sweat hobbling to and fro. I decided to take a shower. The familiar pulsating massage spray loosened the clenched muscles in my neck, and for the first time since my father showed, I felt at ease. Lene might not welcome me, flowers or no flowers, but I chose to be optimistic. It had been several weeks since that last copulation with Lene, so I braced my palm against the soap holder, closed my eyes, and tried to squeeze in a quick, motion-confined wank, deferential to my new stitchless groin—Taryn's softness in my mind.

The bathroom door hinges squealed.

"Sull?" Lene said.

I unhanded myself.

"Lene?"

The shower curtains snapped open, and I faced my wife. Her face was slick with perspiration, and she was holding up a broom like a baseball bat. She was wearing jogging sweats, disturbingly reminiscent of one of my mother's outfits. I was naked, one hand on my hip, the other on the soap holder.

"I'm sorry, *skat.*"

Lene slammed the broom handle on the floor.

I stepped gingerly out of the shower and embraced my wife. Her arms remained at her side. "I won't leave you again," I said. "I promise."

She noticed my semi-hardness and cackled open-mouthed, not unlike Taryn. "I don't think so," she said.

I apologized over and over again. She said, "You don't even know what you're apologizing for."

"I know that I love you."

Providence. I was finally home, albeit thousands of kroner poorer as the taxi driver made off with my exorbitant fare. I resumed my routine, telling myself I was a better man for having gone to Bordirtoun. In the following days, to make up to Lene, I cooked dinner every night and called her several times a day to coo, "*Jeg elsker dig,*" which means "I love you" in Danish.

I talked to the Grathes the following week via speakerphone, while slowly riding my new exercise bike. All seemed to be going well. My father hadn't shown at the family house, and the number of protesters had doubled since my Rio River press conference. Saul had been forced to order the Bordirtoun police to guard the development zone.

The only negative was the one I chose not to discuss with T.R. or Taryn: the outrageous invoice for Momma's private security company. Why didn't they tell me that having a security guard surveil a home 24/7 was so expensive? More importantly, why hadn't I asked? The first month's fees came out of our joint savings account. Due to my period of extended unemployment, it would not be long before we ran low on funds. Lucky for me (unlucky for Lene), I managed our finances.

"What's wrong?" Taryn asked.

"What do you mean?"

"You seem tense," she said. "I can hear it on the phone."

My laugh took on a high, false pitch. I pedaled harder. "I'm just on my exercise bike."

"How are things with your wife?"

"Good again," I said. "How are things with Jimbor?"

"The same. He's working a lot of nights."

Knitting, no doubt, I thought.

"When are you two coming to visit?" Taryn asked.

"I'm sure we'll get out there at some point," I said, thinking there was little chance Lene would ever desire a Bordirtoun visit.

My groin grew sore, so I got off my bike, toweled off, and sat at my computer. I logged into my bank, examining the pending debit from the security company. I had already seen it several times that morning. I was just hoping the number of figures to the left of the decimal (five) would change.

"Can I talk to T.R. alone?" I said.

"Sure," Taryn said. T.R. got on the line.

"Hey T.R.," I said. "Is the security company invoice correct?"

He confirmed its correctness.

"Wow."

"We went through the numbers, remember?"

To this day, I have no recollection of running through any numbers. What I do recollect from that evening of planning was that I had had quite a few glasses of cheap red wine and that Taryn was wearing an especially low-cut V-neck top.

"Can we get a discounted rate?"

T.R. replied that we could replace the current security consultant with a lower priced one (i.e. one with special needs).

"Is there a problem?"

"Not at all," I said, logging out of my bank's website. "Just making sure the bill was correct, that's all."

"Well, let me know if you want to switch to the Secure Special Package instead of the Secure Premium," T.R. said.

I scoffed. "My mother's safety is first priority."

Jeg elsker dig, I said to Lene, before I closed my cell and exited Nørreport Station. I had a lot of time during the day, waiting for my dole check and thinking about all the jobs I wasn't applying for.

On this afternoon, I chose to wander downtown. Had a falafel for lunch, bought a shirt på Strøget, sat outside, and savored a bottle of Tuborg at Café Europa. I hadn't been down near the Royal Palace in quite some time. The sky was brightening, only weeks before summer began, but it was unseasonably cold. I watched a scarf-wrapped, mink-wearing blonde woman with shoulder-length hair and smart knee-high boots pumping her way up the walking street, and I was reminded of what Lene looked like many years ago.

Lene and I almost never got together. After several months of admiring her in my Danish language courses, I finally worked up the courage to ask Lene out to dinner as my consulting engagement at Bang and Olufsen neared an end. I had already made my travel arrangements to return to Manhattan, where I would resume my position at Ogilvy and Mather. I was not looking forward to returning to New York and walking home from the blue line to my empty apartment near DeWitt Clinton Park, where I'd listen to the nightly message from my mother flashing on my answering machine about eating more fiber, drinking more water, and sundry other ways to ease bowel movements. If it were up to my mother, all people would be having healthy firm (but not-too-firm) bowel movements as many times a day as possible; there would be no unhealthy limit. My father also seemed to feel that my apartment was his second home in those years. Whenever he had any business in the area, he asked to stay at my place. "Business" and "area" were words loosely defined. Areas might be New Jersey, Connecticut, even Massachusetts and Pennsylvania sometimes. He never told me specifically what his business entailed, but he did invite me to meetings, which I repeatedly declined. "Business" may very well have been a high-priced prostitute he particularly enjoyed or a weekend trip to Scores. During the Bang and Olufsen engagement in Copenhagen, my parents contacted me much less frequently, and I was a better, more confident and fulfilled person for it. I had purpose, long work hours, colleagues to laugh with, drunken getaway weekends with other ex-pats.

After one of my last classes with Lene, I waited until the rest of the students left and walked Lene to her bicycle. I told her I was planning to return to New York soon, and I wanted to take what might be my final opportunity to thank her for her instruction.

Lene's hair was long back then. She was wearing knee-high boots with her jeans tucked in them. "Can you ask me in Danish?" she said with a smile.

"*Må jeg tagen dig ud for mad?*" I said, knowing I was butchering the pronunciation and using all the wrong words.

Lene laughed and laughed until she turned red.

"What's so funny?" I said, smiling. "*Hvad så sjov?*"

She laughed even harder. "You should stay in Copenhagen just so you can take my class again."

"I wish I could."

After she composed herself, Lene nodded and said, "*Ja, selvølgelig, jeg ville elske hen til nyde middagsmad hos jer.*"

And so we began with lunch, then dinner, then drinks, and two weeks later, we began making love, and I was only days away from flying home. Should I stay, I wondered? Was Lene worth it? She was Danish. I was an American. She was older. I had not been in a relationship in years. Still, we couldn't get enough of each other in those early days. Yes, you read me correctly. For reasons that remain somewhat mysterious to me, *she* couldn't get enough of *me*.

I called in sick on my last Monday and took a bike ride around Faelled Park, my groin sore from screwing. With the wind in my face on a sunny day and the bebopping trees and verdant blankets of sod on either side of me, I decided that I simply couldn't leave; I needed to allow this new relationship with Lene to run its course. If I left, I would always wonder about her, I reasoned. And, of course, I was very enthusiastic about the other benefit of staying: continued, limited contact with Saul and Momma. The next day, I began to make arrangements for the six-month sabbatical Ogilvy and Mather owed me, the sabbatical from which I never returned.

I did love Lene, I thought as I watched the woman in knee-high boots disappear around a corner. I do love Lene. I wasn't lying, I told myself. But why did I only feel certain then: alone, aimless, spending my wife's money, and ogling someone else? The wind intensified, and I downed the rest of my beer with gloves on.

I meandered past the Studenterhuset, recognizing the harsh surface of a young American accent. A tall, red-bearded man wearing what looked like an elf's hat spoke English with a Danish but distinctly American lilt (he'd probably lived in the States, and his conversational tone sounded quite dramatic in contrast to the lower, mumbling tones of spoken Danish). He was telling the young brunette woman in red-and-white-striped wool gloves and a vomitous green kangol that in Danish culture, what an American might view as professorial sexual harassment (say, inviting her to dinner at his house and offering her a therapeutic, full-body Swedish massage), was simply native hospitality or *hyggelig*. I sat on the bench around the corner, under a bare-knuckled tree, and for awhile, I listened to them speak, gauging the possibility they'd eventually fuck each other blind. I had had a cigarette outside this very place as a young man, with Taryn and T.R., during a two-day backpacking stop. It was a different bar then. An Italian traveler with a ponytail and sizable mutton chops was smoking with us, trying to make bedways with Taryn. He had called her "bootiful" and put an arm around her, testing whether she'd retreat. She did not. In fact, she laughed at his incomprehensible jokes. I tried to look cool, smoking with increasing Chinaman-without-a-cause aloofness. T.R. and I shook our heads at each other. Look at this spectacle, we said without speaking. But after we staggered back to the hostel without Taryn that night, I tried unsuccessfully to masturbate to visions of the Italian administering cunnilingus to Taryn (I couldn't get help imagining his mutton-chops chafing her thighs).

Beneath the tree, I rubbed my gloved fists against the corduroy chassis of my legs. The North Sea chill had seeped into the air. The brunette American and the tall Dane walked past. Judging from the distance between them, I'd bet against them fucking. A biting gust hit me in the face, blowing dirt in my eye. I got up and started walking north toward Nørreport Station, my eyes watering. I retrieved my phone and called Lene yet again.

"*Hej?*"

"*Skat,*" I said. I realized I didn't have anything more to say. Everyone on the street seemed to be walking the opposite direction.

"Hello?" Lene said. "It's very loud."

"I feel lost," I shouted over the wind. I ducked inside the Round Tower.

"I can't hear you."

"Can you come home?"

"You can come and wait for me," she said. "I'll find a substitute for my four o'clock."

I looked at my wrist for my watch, but remembered I wasn't wearing one. In fact, since my return, I had rarely needed a clock. I asked her what time it was.

"It's almost two."

A lump grew in my throat. I told her I'd meet her after her class.

I reversed direction, headed south toward the Number 8 line. Maybe I'd buy a book and read it at the bookshop, I thought. I couldn't remember the last time I'd read a book.

I never made it to the university. My palms sweat at the thought of the bus ride home. Lene would ask me what was wrong. I'd tell her nothing, then we'd sit in silence the rest of the way.

I walked past the Museum Erotica, and in the window was a brown-haired woman made of wax. She was wearing black garters and glittery star-shaped pasties. I ducked in for a quick tour. Inside, I stood for quite some time in front of the sculpture of a woman wearing a pencil skirt, a leather corset, and a suit coat. She was leaning back in a chair, her legs dangling, her head thrown back. A man in a business suit was on all fours, administering cunnilingus, his hands preventing the chair from toppling. His suitcase was on the ground next to him. It looked rather acrobatic, physically unlikely. According to the plaque, it was a new installation, donated from America, called *bordersandboundary.com, a social commentary*. Social commentary, eh? I put on the headphones to listen to the sculptor explicate the inspirational origins of his supposed art.

"Hi, this is Saul Pong, founder of The Pongel Horse, a full-service, global chain of gentleman's clubs in North America, Asia, and soon, Copenhagen!" the audio said. "I took the opportunity to sponsor Nigel Koch Reimers's sculpture *bordersandboundary.com* because of the evident two-way metaphor of wealth as a form of rapture. Some may see it as social commentary, I, however—"

The room began to spin. I ripped off the headphones and rushed out the door, past the ticket counter, and into the brisk wind outside. I staggered to the nearest tree and dry-heaved. Even in Denmark, my father! I looked at the canals through tear-blurred eyes. Was I still in love with Lene at all? Was I ever? Was I capable of love? Was I just another Pong man most at home with the cocks and beavers?

I sat at the foot of that shadeless tree for some time. The sky was dark, and I was still there, ignoring the people walking past. My tears dried cold on my face as my cell buzzed, Lene trying to reach me. What was I supposed to say? That I was bumbling through Denmark jobless and doing nothing about it besides wasting her money? That just moments after I'd been waxing about our love, I walked into a sex museum?

I headed home, wondering if I'd ever know what happiness or love was. Before, our moderate happiness seemed acceptable, more than I deserved, but now, it wasn't, and I wasn't sure why.

I was slumped in my office armchair when Lene returned home. The house was silent, and I'd allowed myself a single bourbon. She came no closer than the doorway, her arms crossed. I peeked at her face—tense, but slackening. Had I not looked so stricken, she'd probably have been more upset.

"I called you," she said.

"I know."

"What's wrong, Sully?" she said. "Tell me. Please."

That last word struck me in the chest. Please. Why can't we please each other? The word reminded me of my mother beseeching me to call her back. Was I the one depressed, not her?

"I'm not sure," I said.

She approached, striding forward without so much as a wobble on her dark platform boots. Kneeling beside me, she touched my neck with surprisingly warm hands and smiled with teeth stained deeply yellow by years of smoking. "Laugh, Sully. When was the last time you laughed?"

In Bordirtoun, I thought.

"What happened back there?" she said. "In Bordirtoun. Tell me."

I was spending our savings to protect my mother from my father. My mother, who didn't want to be protected. I was infatuated with a pregnant, married friend. "You'll be angry."

"If you've done nothing wrong, what would I have to be angry about?" She kissed my hand, her lips moist. Then she stared me in the eye. "You haven't done anything wrong, have you?"

By wrong, she meant cheating. I laughed and told her I had absolutely not cheated. In fact, I told her I'd never even thought about cheating. "What about stupid things?" I said. "Will you be angry at me for stupid things?"

"For today," she said. "I won't."

So I proceeded to tell her some of everything. I said I had not been motivated to look for work since I got back. I didn't even skimp on how I still kept in touch with the Grathes via phone every week. As for my hot flashes in the presence of a certain preggers and the big checks I'd been writing. Well, those bits remained obscure.

"You don't have many friends here," Lene said.

I glanced out the window. The fog hovered above the gray and roiling sea. Eleven years and no friends. I'd had a few, but they were casual; I'd lost the will to maintain them. Since I got back, Lene'd been going to those dinner parties in Nørrebro or Amager on the slushy S-train by herself; I'd preferred the television.

"I don't have *any*."

Lene stroked my round face. "You're not happy here anymore. So what would you like to do?" She backed away, as if discovering a bug. "You want to move to America," she stated hesitantly.

I studied my wife's face, the faint crenellations around the mouth, flecks of brown against the eye whites, her lashes so short they were almost non-existent. I knew the idea of moving to America was unpleasant to her. She wanted to spend the rest of our lives in Copenhagen, but there it was, the unspeakable future consideration, the player to be named later, the payback for us settling down where Lene was comfortable, where Lene had lived all her life, where I had no roots. I never knew when I'd want to go back and for how long, but now that she uttered the words aloud, the desire to return to America flushed fresh and warm through me.

"New York, San Francisco, Washington D.C.," she said. "Those places, I'd be willing." Lene sat in my lap. I grimaced, my groin tightening, but I held her close. I pressed my face against her bosom. Her breasts seemed saggier.

"What about Bordirtoun?" I mumbled.

Lene loosened her hold. "No way! That sounds like a horrible place."

I reassured her I was jesting, and we would never, ever move there.

"Good," she said, getting off me. "If you want an adventure for a couple of years, I would want an adventure too. I just want you to be happy, Sully."

I tried to smile. "I'll be okay," I said. If only it were that simple, I thought. I had become unhappy enough to consider a move to Bordirtoun! Horrifying! I decided to drop the subject. "I'm just getting stir crazy."

"What crazy?"

"Stir crazy. Restless. I just need to find work."

The next day, I arranged what both of us needed least: a vacation. A premium Paris weekend package, the five-star Hotel Pont Royal on the Left Bank, and a first-class flight. No more backpacking for Sull and his lovely wife!

How could we afford such an extravagant trip on one meager income and my new Bordirtoun expenses, you ask? When Lene asked a similar question, I replied that I was blowing through my personal savings to motivate me to dive back into the job market.

Shameful, the way I actually funded the vacation: dipping into Lene's inheritance funds, our retirement money.

We flew to Paris on a gray Saturday morning. After we checked into the hotel, Lene and I strolled from the Notre Dame to the Concorde. On the Seine, we hopped on the covered tour boat, snapped a few pictures, and I put my head on Lene's shoulder and napped. On Sunday morning, we rose in a crowded Eiffel Tower elevator that smelled of wet asphalt and sweat. An older woman was chiding her weeping husband in German while the woman next to them sang some French song aloud with headphones on. The man in front of me was reading a *USA Today*. *Taliban Attacks Spur Troop Calls*.

"What's 'End of Days' Security?" Lene asked.

That was the name of the security company I had hired to protect

Momma. "End of Days?"

"Yeah?" Lene said. "I saw a letter addressed to you. Looked like a bill."

I cursed the security company silently. I had registered for online billing and even called their customer service line to make sure I wouldn't receive paper invoices. I shrugged while I considered quick lies. *Junk mail. Credit card promotion.* But we were in Paris at the Eiffel Tower—a romantic destination. Did I really want to start a getaway weekend with yet another shameless lie? Though it might be difficult to explain, I decided, for once, to tell the unedited truth. "It's the company I hired to monitor my mother's security."

Lene's eyes narrowed. "Your mother's security."

"They notify me if my father comes to the house."

"Okay."

"When I was there, there was an argument and a fight," I said. "Very ugly. I told my father not to come to the house anymore."

Lene searched my eyes. "You didn't tell me about this."

"I forgot."

"You forgot."

"Why do you keep repeating what I say?"

"I don't understand why you keep forgetting to tell me things."

"The alternative was to stick around longer and guard the house myself."

"How much does all of this cost?" Lene said.

I told her.

"Sully! That's a lot of money!"

My heart banged in my ears. A sharp odor of flatulence rose in the elevator, and the iron and light made me dizzy. The door opened, and the crowd squeezed us deliberately out into the cold.

"You would do the same for your mother," I said, cringing with guilt as the manipulative words left my mouth.

Lene sighed through her nose. She cussed at me quietly under her breath.

"I've got it taken care of, okay?" I said.

That night, Lene forced me to cancel our reservation at the Grand Vefour, a Michelin three-star restaurant, and we dined on street-bought paninis.

While we packed for our morning flight back to Copenhagen, Lene and I made love for the final time. I hardly remember the details. We'd been steadily drinking red wine since dinner, and as she bent over our zipped luggage, I embraced her from behind, fondled her right breast, and she slapped my hand away. I understood her resistance given the way I'd behaved, but eventually, after a few whispered apologies and additional kisses on the back of her neck, she acquiesced. I climbed onto the bed and stood straight on my knees. She remained standing, bent over a chair, her behind thrust before me. This was one of the rare times we had sex in my preferred position. I see now that this may have been the way Lene was trying to reach me—by sacrificing her pleasure for mine.

The rest was a dizzying, rather listless blur, and soon, we fell asleep, bottoms off, bodies apart, atop a blanket-less bed, the heat turned up to 35 Celsius (Lene was anemic, always cold) and a TV3 drama on. We arrived home, our minds in separate places, silent and smileless in our false marital acceptability. I handed her our rolling case to unpack and watched her wide hips as she sashayed down the hall into our bedroom, running a hand through her hair, the small of her back exposed when her blouse hiked with her raised arms. Why couldn't I be a better husband to this good woman? I was spending our modest life savings, ruining our marriage. For what? For who? For my pathetic mother? For my married and pregnant crush?

In my office, I had eight new messages.

"Sully, this is T.R.," the machine blared. I lowered the volume and shut the office door. "Call me back. It's urgent."

I didn't sleep that night, but I pretended to, so as not to alert Lene. I waited until she left for work in the morning and returned T.R.'s call. It was nearly midnight in Bordirtoun.

"Where have you been?" T.R. said.

"With my wife," I said.

"Don't get pissy," T.R. said. "I'm just asking because it's been a few days."

I realized I'd sounded like I was talking to my father. I apologized and asked him what had happened.

"Your mother went to the hotel and saw your dad with one of the showgirls. Hit her with a chair."

I shot up, my Adam's apple pulsating. Our so-called security plan had failed to secure Momma from her biggest threat: herself. T.R. went on to say that Momma had broken the showgirl's nose and had to be tasered into submission. She was arrested, and my father refused to put up bond.

"Can you guys get her out?" I said.

"We don't have fifty thousand dollars."

"Fifty thousand dollars?!"

My fists were balled and shaking, and I was having trouble breathing. I turned down the thermostat and opened a window. On the street below, a procession of Danish soldiers jogged past. I looked for my Prince cigarettes, the ones I only smoked with Lene, on the balcony, during relaxing, happy times. These were not those times.

"Sully, you there?"

I imagined my mother getting tasered, her screaming and falling. I thought of having to withdraw fifty thousand dollars from Lene's inheritance money. "He should be the one in jail," I said, starting quietly. "There has to be something we can do. I want to destroy him, T.R. I want him to fucking suffer sometimes, I swear to God!"

T.R. was silent for awhile. By the time I was done talking, I was nearly shouting. I could hear T.R.'s breaths over the phone. "Sully? Your mother."

"I'll wire the money."

"I'm sorry, Sully."

After I hung up, I walked out to the balcony, phone in hand, and lit a cigarette. A weekend vacation, I could reasonably repay. Fifty thousand dollars, however, would be more difficult to explain. I put out my cigarette, went inside to the bathroom, and vomited.

Every once in a while, back when I was a free man, I wondered what it would be like to have an entourage of kin and kinship. The good times, the camaraderie, always having people to choose from when you were required to list emergency contacts. That said, I did not miss people problems. Like close friends asking you for money or a mother expecting you to bail her out of jail. I know now that this is why I have always had so few close friends or family. They were too inconvenient.

Spent from getting sick, I decided to take an afternoon nap. I was disturbed by a violent nightmare in which I was running from shadowy, slouching figures firing scissors at my genitalia. It was nearly one in the morning in Bordirtoun, and Saul would be asleep. Call him when the sun rises, I rationalized.

When I woke several hours later, I made the required phone calls, gave the necessary ID numbers, birthdates, and passwords to liquidate seventy-five grand from Lene's inheritance (fifty for bail, another twenty-five for future expenses).

How oddly casual it all was, systematically dismantling my marriage, filled with yeses, thank-yous, and have-a-nice-days to polite female voices. One might have thought I was changing my cable service. This was the man Lene had married: a casual, polite degenerate.

That evening, light snowflakes melted against my face as Lene and I walked glove in glove by the Nyhavn harbor and watched the listing surface of the sea, rainbow black in the twilight as if coated with oil. The pastel buildings looked warm in the streetlamps, and the din of the restaurants made me reconsider my recent weariness of Denmark. All evening, I held secret the distant turmoil. I reported to Lene that I had spent the afternoon sending out a number of resumes and followed up with a number of already submitted ones.

"Something will happen soon," Lene said. "Shall we stop here for dinner?"

I wrapped my arm around her waist and stopped walking. I stepped onto the flat deck wood at the edge of the pier. I looked into Lene's face, and on tiptoe, I was nearly nose to nose. She and I both had wide, meaty noses, a fortunate attribute in Chinese culture. I considered telling her what had happened, that Momma was in jail, and I needed to go home again. But I thought of the money—Lene's inheritance. My breath spewed white in the cold. What had I done?

"I'm not hungry anymore," I said.

"What's wrong?"

"I'm afraid I've caught a chill."

"Is it your stir craziness?" Lene said with an empathetic smile, putting a hand on my forehead to feel how hot I was. Was it a fever or was I just hot from the hell I was about to bring upon our marriage? I couldn't look her in the eye. "I've always expected to die miserable and alone," I said suddenly.

She backed away as if I was a baby who'd just defecated on her. "Sully, why do you say that?"

"I just know."

The next morning, T.R. called and told me that the police had moved in to break up the protests in Bordirtoun. Hundreds were arrested. Rubber bullets were fired into the crowd, injuring many. Instead of sending the arrested to Bordirtoun's already crowded prisons, the police had put them on Saul's one-way luxury buses to Rio River. The *Bordirtoun Daily* had published an editorial condemning Saul Pong's leadership and calling for a credible alternative to emerge. I asked about my mother.

"Challenges on that front, Sully," T.R. said. "I put up the money, but she won't leave. She wants your father to come get her."

After I hung up with T.R., I spent most of the day on my headset cajoling penitentiary officials into letting me have a five-minute conversation with my voluntarily incarcerated mother. It was five in the morning in Bordirtoun when I finally got to her.

"Are you okay?" I asked Momma.

"I've been in jail for a week," she said, sounding congested. "What do you think?"

"Then leave!"

"No!" she said. "Your father had me arrested. He has to fix this."

"You're the one who went to the hotel!"

"How can I stay home and do nothing?" Momma said. "Soon, you'll have eight stepmothers. Is that what you want? Eight stepmothers? Your father is not even a man. He's going to leave me in jail, you watch. Did he call you? You should have heard how loud he yelled at me."

"I told you to leave him, but you didn't listen."

"That purple-eyed whore!" she went on as if I'd been silent. "If they didn't stop me, I would have clawed her eyes out. I would have killed that bitch. I would have ripped her cunt open with my bare hands."

My lips parted, and my eyes shut. "Don't say that to the judge."

"What, Sully?" she said. "I don't understand what you're saying."

"Never mind."

I did not know what to do next. I knew I wanted Saul to pay, to hurt, to suffer. But how?

I started the day by taking the S-train to the gym where I played a pickup racquetball game with a daytrading Danish man (I was in no mood to ask about his occupation but he seemed eager to tell me). I earned his ire because I had no intention to have a good rally. I smacked ball after ball against the man, in the head, the belly, groin, the shins, grunting and cussing as I pretended I was whaling away at my father instead of my ball. He left after one game and called me a Chinese asshole on the way out.

While I was at the gym, I decided to take a kickboxing class where I was the only man in a class of twenty-five, and I punched and kicked a bag for ninety minutes until my groin and knuckles were swollen and sore.

Still, I found no relief.

Sometime that afternoon, I purchased two plane tickets to Bordirtoun and reserved a penthouse suite at The Pongelliano. I don't remember what I was thinking. Perhaps I was in a fugue state. At first, I'd only bought one ticket, then I decided it would look better to Lene if I just went ahead and purchased both. Surely, she'd have no desire to join me. Her work, her conferences would be far more important than my mangled family, the family she'd never even met. I confirmed thrice that her ticket would be refundable.

I spent the afternoon shaping "our" supposed reasons. Our weekend in Paris had whet my appetite for a longer vacation. My father gave us a deal at his resort. If we don't like it there, we can take the car service on a road trip. I needed a little America, a little home, for my peace of mind, for our peace.

It's difficult to believe this story ever seemed plausible to me. I certainly considered telling the whole truth and nothing but—but what was that truth? How would I have explained that I wanted to go back to destroy my father, and I had no clear plan on how to accomplish that? Just the thought of her second-guessing made me nauseous.

By the time Lene returned home, I had cooked a spice-rubbed tri-tip with roasted potatoes and prepared a side of pickled herring. The platters were laid on the Turkish rug in front of our fireplace. I had set several logs ablaze and unplugged the television. *Meget hyggelig, meget romantik.* Lene was punching the remote through the air, trying to turn on the television when she noticed the platters and Chenille pillows on the floor.

Lene beamed. "I do not like surprises much."

I told her to look beneath the platter. She discovered the envelope with the stuffed billfold holding our vacation package. The hearth crackled. Sweat bubbled on my pate.

Her smile flattened. "*Another* vacation?"

"*Der Americanishes Sudvest,*" I said.

"Sully, we can't afford this." Lene's eyes bulged upon closer inspection of the package details. "Bordirtoun?" She began pacing.

I took several gulps of red wine. "We'll be back in a few weeks."

When she unearthed The Pongelliano brochure at the back of the billfold, Lene chucked her surprise, hitting me in the chest. Her face alternated between red and redder with the flickering fire.

"Did your father arrange this?"

"Don't be ridiculous." I grabbed a poker and prodded the flaming log.

Lene walked behind the couch, her eyes distant, as if trying to recall something. "You're involved in one of your father's schemes."

I stopped poking and made sure I made eye contact. "Absolutely not."

Lene squeezed a cushion, but said nothing. I could tell she was analyzing the situation, trying to read me. This is what we had come to: she knew that if she asked, I would not tell her the whole truth.

"I thought you wanted to go to America," I said.

"Not Bordirtoun! Not now, right after we just spent so much money on Paris!"

"I'm going with or without you," I declared.

Lene's chin jutted. "I see."

I went through my list of secrets and measured which one, positioned correctly, might help me explain this second trip. "Look, the truth is: things are not good with my mother," I said. "Very bad, in fact. She had an episode with her depression. A breakdown. I need to go home to make sure she's okay."

"Of course, you wouldn't want to just tell me that in the first place."

"Because I was sure you'd yell at me for getting involved in their mess."

"What kind of person do you think I am?" she said. "You make me sound so cold."

"I don't want to argue," I said. "I just wanted you to have the option of being there for me this time."

"The option?" she said. "First it's 'I know you wanted to go to America' and now I 'have the option?'"

"You're parsing my words, Lene," I said. "This is not just about you."

She rested her hands on her hips, faced the floor, and began to chuckle in disbelief. She was angry—that was clear—understandably confused about my intentions. I assumed she would tell me next that I should just go since I thought of her as such a monster, such an impossible person to be truthful to. I picked up the billfold and eyed the toll-free customer service number and envisioned dialing the Indian call center to cancel the ticket and procure my refund.

"Look, I understand if you don't want to go."

Lene was still for a moment. Then her eyes cleared, and she smirked as if she had finally gotten a joke. "No, you're right, Sully," she said.

"I'll be back before you know it," I said.

"No," she said sternly. "I'm going."

I glanced askance at her, my brows raised. "I'm not forcing you."

"Of course not!" Lene exclaimed. "We must support your mother in her time of need. She is my family also."

"Are you sure?"

"Tomorrow, I'll call the school."

Incomprehensible. Unfathomable. Baffling. Forcing a smile, I walked over to Lene and issued a cold peck on the cheek. "Oh *skat*, you are so understanding," I said. "*Jes elsker dig.*"

THE MISADVENTURES
OF ROBINSON PONG

THE YEAR WAS 1955, the Year of the Goat. Goats are creative thinkers, wanderers, sometimes high-strung and insecure. Robinson Ri Pong, born a Rat, considered himself a Goat at heart. His Goat-like characteristics were why he was alone tonight in his car, looking for a half-decent place to get some dinner after another argument with his wife, Susan Suen.

Robinson pulled his Lincoln Capri into the parking lot of Bordirtoun Steaks, which, thirty years ago, was Parris's Bordirtoun Brofful. Robinson didn't feel like steak, but he sure as hell felt like several glasses of sherry without having to deal a bunch of drunken saloon regulars. If that meant he'd have to stuff a side of filthy cattle into his craw to get some peace, well, that's what he'd have to do in wonderful, blessed America. Hey, he and Susan had just bought a new car they couldn't afford so why the hell not buy a whole bottle of liquor and a cow as well?

As he trudged into the steakhouse, his belly moaning and

defeated, Robinson asked himself, "Why so angry?"

Dinner, please, one, yes, I would like booth.

Tonight's fight had been triggered by a dispute over Saul's bedtime. The earlier Saul slept, the more quiet time Robinson had to spend on his art, but Susan never seemed to get enough Saul Time, and now they had begun to play chess with each other until well after midnight every evening. Naturally, his fight with Susan was neither about bedtime, nor chess. Nearly every one of their arguments over the past thirteen years devolved into a rehashing of the underhanded way his wife had manipulated their emigration from China. Writing as Robinson, Susan had forged a letter to Cousin Francisco asking for help, then told her husband that, while he was out during the day, the Communists had stopped by their home with the intent to arrest him, like they had arrested his father. That triggered their emergency plan to go into hiding and put the paperwork in motion to sail to San Francisco. Of course by the time they got to Bordirtoun, Francisco had been caged with the Japanese. How many times had Robinson warned his wife that Americans didn't care whether Chinese people lived or died? He and Susan would only find out weeks after the fact that Francisco had died in the camps. Robinson never got a chance to apologize to his cousin for the insults in his letters.

Three glasses sherry, yes, three, and New York steak, no, Bordirtoun Steak too big, New York, please, thanks.

Susan had ruined his life, Robinson was convinced. She had even ruined his name. At the immigration station, he had stood there dumbly as the sea-otter-looking fellow asked for his first name. Turned out Susan had decided on them already because that's what she did: decide things! She had this childish fascination with obscure Western culture. Susan because she liked Susan Hayward, Saul because she liked the way Saul Goodkind's name looked on screen during the credits of *Buck Rogers*, Robinson for her favorite book *Robinson Crusoe*. Of course, Susan didn't think that the name Robinson might be difficult for him to pronounce (Robinson often introduced himself as "Lobson"). Robinson never painted anymore, was stuck day and night at the general store now that his wife stayed home with the boy. Saul. The demon child. At age five, the kid was bilking neighborhood girls out of their money by selling piss and water as lemonade. At age eight, he was playing shell games with the kids at school and coming home with pants pockets sagging and swollen with coins. Now age thirteen, he was more focused on selling baseball cards than doing schoolwork. Robinson had already been summoned to school twice because other students had complained that Saul overcharged them for cards that were in less than mint condition. There was something wrong with that boy.

While he waited for his order, Robinson set his hat on the table and lit a cigarette. He had called his sixth sister, who ran a dry cleaner in Los Angeles, and complained that they had left China too soon. Had he stayed, his work would be showing at the top national galleries by now. He was forty-three, too old to dream a young man's dream.

"You've always been such a whiner," his sister said. "Better to light a candle than curse the darkness."

Robinson's glasses of sherry came, and he killed his cigarette in the ashtray. He slid the cocktail napkins to one side of the table, pulled out a charcoal pencil from his jacket pocket, and began sketching on one of the napkins. A horse, mid-gallop.

The waitress asked Robinson if he wanted anything else. He shook his head.

"That's a nice drawing," she said.

Robinson smiled, perhaps for the first time that day. "Thank you." He hadn't noticed the waitress until now. She was pretty in a plain way. She didn't wear makeup. She had a round face, bordering on plump. Her skin was the color of a fresh penny. A Mexican. Young. Not yet thirty.

"Do you draw a lot?" she asked.

"I paint," he said. "Before."

"Before what?" the waitress said. One of her bicuspids tugged at her lower lip, creating a small light-colored nub. "You don't paint anymore?"

Conscious of his accent, Robinson shook his head.

"Why not?"

"No place," he said. "No time."

"Have you ever been to Bordirtoun Art Studio?"

Robinson noticed the wisps of brown hair on the waitress's bare, mole-speckled arms, a contrast to his wife's supremely blemish-free, hairless and pale skin. He informed her he had not heard of the studio.

"I paint too," the waitress said. "I can show you where it is. It's free."

Free, like America, Robinson thought sardonically. "Yes," he said dumbly.

"My name is Edna." She held out a warm hand. Edna told him where the studio was. Not far from the Holy Moly of Holiness Lutheran Church, where Francisco once worked.

Robinson tipped an imaginary hat. "Thank you. Edna."

"You're welcome," she said, canting her head. One of her brown curls tumbled out of her bun and rested on her shoulder.

Robinson watched her as she walked away. He drew her curvy figure framed in the doorway to the restaurant's kitchen. Then he sipped the first glass of sherry.

"Studio?" Susan Pong said in Cantonese. "What for, studio?"

"To paint," Robinson said. "I was...I am a painter. Remember?"

A clang came from Saul's bedroom. He was always searching for something because his room was a mess. Because he tended to lose objects he didn't value, Saul was usually looking for something school-related, like textbooks and homework dittos. He never lost his precious baseball cards or cash.

Robinson informed his wife that he would begin closing the store an hour early so he could work at the studio before dinner.

"How are we going to make up the money?" his wife said.

"We get no business at the end of the day anyway," he said. "Maybe we should sell some of Saul's junk. It's all over the apartment."

"What kind of father sells his son's things?"

"A horrible one, I suppose."

"Don't sulk," she said. "Do you want to be called a communist? It's bad enough that we're Chinese. This is America. Americans don't care about art. They care about money and God. All you need to do is to find a better way to make money and make right with God. If you tried to deposit a painting in a bank, they wouldn't take it. Isn't that right, Saul?"

"That's right, A-Ma." Saul emerged from his room, wearing a short-sleeved button-down shirt tucked into khaki shorts. He was tall and gangly for his age and had a habit of slouching so he could look in the eyes of the shorter kids. Robinson found his son's excessive eye contact, lack of shyness, and confidence off-putting. What had he done to earn such confidence? Saul was done searching for whatever he was looking for. And he didn't find it. He was going to school with nothing but a box of baseball cards.

"Where's your backpack?" Robinson said.

Saul shrugged. "I can't find it."

"How do you go to school without a backpack, without writing anything down?"

"His teachers have notebooks," his wife said. "You'd know this if you ever took him to school."

"Someone has to work at the store."

"And paint apparently."

Saul laughed. "You paint?"

"Yes, son," Robinson said. "I paint. I was a very good painter in China."

"Are you a *gay*?" Saul said the word in English.

"Are you learning these words at school?"

"Is Dad a gay?"

"I am most certainly not!" Robinson said.

"Don't raise your voice at Saul," his wife said.

Robinson exhaled, his back curving with his breath. He wished he owned a gun. When his son and wife left today, he could place the barrel to his chin and squeeze the trigger. Perhaps in lieu of a firearm, he could hang himself in the shower. Then he remembered what his sister had said. Stop whining.

"Go to school," Robinson said to Saul. "You'll be late."

Saul trotted to his mother's side, taking the crook of her arm as she opened the front door. The two of them vanished into the blinding light of the morning.

"What do you think?" Robinson said to Edna.

She walked over from her canvas. Dressed in denim painter's pants, Edna blew a lock of hair out of her eyes and observed Robinson's painting with crossed arms. Robinson's work portrayed the banks of Bordirtoun River populated by horses and fishermen of all races.

"It's how Bordirtoun should be," Edna said.

Robinson understood that, in her terse way, Edna was criticizing his work. "That's not how Bordirtoun is, is it?" he said.

"I'm not saying that the painting is bad," she said. "There's a long history of art that depicts places as they should be."

"Dee-pics?" Robinson had never heard the word before.

"Showing," Edna said, her mouth rounded and her brows raised, like she was trying to feed an unfamiliar food to a baby. Robinson was surprised when the expression made his desire twinge.

"Let me see your work," he said.

Edna's canvas contained giant naked men of all races using tools to mangle black mountains.

"Like when Chinese people make railroad," Robinson said.

"Really?"

"My grandfather tell me his brother work railroad," Robinson said. "He die in accident. My grandfather tell me don't come to America because Americans don't care if Chinese people live or die."

"I'm sorry," Edna said. She put a hand on the back of Robinson's neck. "Do you regret coming to America?"

Robinson allowed Edna's smooth, warm hand to send pleasant sparks down his spine.

"Robinson?"

He had not answered the question. He wanted to say that he absolutely regretted coming to America. He wanted to say that his wife had manipulated him into giving up his painting. He wanted to admit that fatherhood hadn't brought the joy he had expected. But right now, at this moment, he couldn't say he regretted America, because he was trying to make the best out of a bad situation. Because if he weren't in the U.S., he wouldn't be here, painting in this otherwise empty studio. With Edna.

"No," he said. "No regret."

Robinson and Susan spent the Sunday afternoon after church in the park by The Castle Tavern. Susan brought her picnic basket of cold noodles and slices of chicken roasted in soy sauce, garlic and ginger. Robinson carried two baseball gloves, a ball and a bat. He knew that Saul had grown to love America's game, and though Robinson didn't understand the appeal and had never understood the appeal of sports in general, he had decided to get closer to his son by pretending to like the sport. Saul's favorite player was Duke Snider of the Dodgers, and Saul even threw and batted left-handed like the Duke.

Susan began laying out lunch at one of the picnic tables. Saul loped off, and while Robinson watched his son's deliberate, kangaroo-esque gait, he thought about Edna. He knew that she was at the studio. It was a matter of great controversy to her extended family, especially to her husband Jaime, that she preferred to paint rather than attend church on Sundays. While his mind was on Edna, Robinson failed to see Saul whirl and throw the baseball toward him, and it smacked Robinson flush in the kneecap.

"*Dieu!*" Robinson cussed in Cantonese.

"What's happening?" Susan said.

Robinson limped toward the rolling ball. He noticed that his son didn't apologize. He couldn't remember the last time Saul apologized. Cannot be a good quality for a man, he thought.

"It's nothing," Robinson said.

"If it's nothing, why do you use such language?" his wife said.

"I'm sorry," he said. "I'm very sorry."

"Now you're just being angry."

Robinson threw the ball, and Saul ran after it, but when Robinson's throw fell short, Saul stopped in his tracks and flopped his hands to the heavens as if to say, "Why couldn't God have given me a Dad who knew how to throw a baseball?"

A boy approached Saul, and they started throwing the ball to each other, leaving Robinson out. Robinson just stood there, glove in hand for several minutes, watching the two boys throw the ball to each other before realizing he'd been excluded. He meandered back to the picnic table.

"It's good that he has friends," Robinson said to his wife.

"Of course he has friends," she said. "He's very popular at school. You would know if you ever joined the PTA."

"I'm at the store all the time."

"You mean at that studio."

"I need to paint," Robinson said. "You know that. You knew that when you met me. I was a painter, remember?"

Susan sighed. "Yes, I remember," she said, as if she wished she didn't.

"Wife, I cannot be happy without painting in my life," Robinson said. Susan continued to remove the plastic wrap from the paper plates of food. Robinson lightly grabbed her wrist and looked his wife in the eye and repeated himself. "Do you understand?"

She softened. "Of course, I understand, Ri."

"Thank you." Robinson relished this moment of victory between him and his wife, and in the silence, he saw the woman he'd fallen in love with years ago. Suen's parents had owned a small hotel that catered to foreigners in Guangzhou. She had a harsh mouth on her, and Ri liked that. On their first date, they had shared dan-dan noodles from a food cart.

His reverie was interrupted when he noticed Saul faking a throw. When the other boy raised his mitt, Saul stepped back and fired the ball as hard as he could, over the boy's head, out of the park, and across the street. Saul doubled over in laughter while the boy chased the ball.

"Saul," Robinson said quietly, shaking his head.

"I understand your desire to paint, and I know I haven't always been honest with you," Susan said. "But we're here now, and nothing is going to change that. Saul wants things. He's not like us when we were young. It's our duty to make him happy."

Robinson watched his son running back toward their picnic table and felt a weight on his chest. He did not know if he was capable of giving Saul all the things that he wanted.

"Saul, come get your lunch," Susan said.

"I want a ping-pong table," Saul said in Cantonese.

"A ping-pong table?" Robinson asked. "Why?"

"So when I serve the ball, I don't have to chase it."

"You know that wasn't nice to throw the ball so far that your friend has to run."

"He's not my friend," Saul said. "He's Mexican and gay."

Robinson shot a commiserative glance to Susan but she was already serving food to Saul and stroking his hair, which stuck up tent-like on the top of his head.

The boy ran up to them, baseball in hand. "Saul, do you still want to play?"

"No," Saul said in English. "I don't play with the gays."

The boy threw the ball down on the ground. "I'm not gay."

"Gay!"

"Okay, Saul, no more," Robinson said in English. He turned to the boy and said, "I'm sorry. He's—" The boy pivoted and ran off.

"That's not nice, Saul," Robinson said in Cantonese.

"The world's not nice," Saul said. "Even the pastor said so in the sermon today."

Robinson creased his brow. He did not remember any such statement, but then again, he wasn't listening particularly closely. He was thinking about painting with Edna. "That's not what the pastor said."

"He said that all we do is fail in God's image because of sin," Saul said. "We're all going to fail, and it's just a matter of who fails less and wins more."

Robinson felt the onset of a headache. He looked at his wife. "Who's teaching him this?"

Susan was staring off at the boy, who was bringing his father into this dispute over his gayness. "The boy does act like one of the gays," she said contemplatively.

"Hey, Mr. Fong!" the boy's father said. "What's wrong with your kid?"

Robinson sighed and stood up. "My name is Pong."

"I don't care what your name is." The boy's father was at least a head taller than Robinson with thick arms that stretched his white t-shirt. "Why's your kid saying that my kid is gay?"

"I don't know," Robinson said.

"What do you mean you don't know? Are you saying that my kid is giving you reason to call him gay?"

Susan and Saul laughed. Robinson wasn't sure what was so funny. The man was speaking English too quickly for Robinson to fully understand, but he comprehended the situation enough to say, "No."

"Timmy, show Mr. Bong," the boy's father said. The boy picked up the fallen baseball and fired it point-blank at Robinson's genitals. He felt like someone had removed his groin with an ice cream scoop. He crumpled to the ground, groaning. Susan and Saul stopped laughing.

"You're lucky the boy's mother ain't here," the boy's father said, looking at Susan and Saul. "She'd have taken you two with one arm tied behind her back."

Robinson and Edna laughed about this incident several months later, late at night, while sitting outside the back entrance of the art studio. Facing an empty parking lot, they were smoking and sipping sherry out of paper cups. Turned out that the father and boy were Edna's husband and son.

"I'm flattered that Jaime thought I could take your wife," Edna said.

"He underestimate my wife," Robinson said.

"From what you've told me, I agree with you," Edna said, laughing.

Robinson was painting nearly every day now. And though Susan didn't like it, she no longer protested verbally. Maybe she was giving up on him, Robinson thought both with sadness and hope. Over the past several months, he had completed three paintings. One of the empty Rio River internment camps. One of the border traffic at the checkpoint just south of town. And one from a photograph that Edna had taken at a school playground of a lone black kid being ostracized by the other children. Saul was among the ostracizers. Wonderful, Blessed America, Robinson had named this series.

"Are you happy?" Robinson said to Edna.

She blew smoke out the side of her mouth and hugged her knees to her chest.

"You forgot answer," Robinson said.

"I know," she said, refilling their cups. "I'm thinking about your painting of Rio River."

"What do you think?"

"Did you know that FDR once said, and I paraphrase: I know many educated and delightful Japanese, and they have all told me that they feel the same repugnance that I do about having thousands of Americans intermarry with the Japanese?"

Robinson drank the sherry down and held a sweet burn in his chest. "And you are surprise?"

"You aren't?"

"No," Robinson said. "Look what they did to fourteen year-old Negro in Mississippi just for whistle at white woman."

Edna sipped her cup. "America isn't what it says it is, is it?"

"Countries always all same."

Edna put a hand on Robinson's leg. He rolled awkwardly away and stood. "I go now."

"I'm married too," Edna said.

"Are you drunk?" Robinson said. "Yes, I know. We just talk about your husband."

"What if I told you that I felt that I was born to wander and create, no matter the cost?" Edna said.

Like a Goat, Robinson thought. "What is 'What if?'" he asked rhetorically, finishing his cigarette.

"'What if' meaning I would leave Bordirtoun with you if that was what you wanted too," Edna said.

"I know what you mean."

"Then why did you ask?"

"Never mind," Robinson said. Edna looked small and plump in her painting clothes, her hair an unkempt nest of tangled ringlets. He sat by her side again. "Leaving your family is not right."

"I've been a bad mother and wife."

Robinson nodded knowingly, as if to say "Me, too." Edna did not misunderstand him.

"I never wanted to come to America," he said.

Edna touched Robinson's leg again. This time, he did not move away. Wonderful, blessed America, he thought as she laid her head on his shoulder.

BEHOLD AN EXCERPT from the court transcripts of the public defender's closing statement during my trial: "My client has exercised horrible judgment and borderline mental incompetence in my humble opinion. During the course of my lengthy, four-year legal career, I have never seen a worse series of decisions. But good people, my client is a good person. He's just like you and me. His heart is relatively pure. His mind is somewhat strong. His intent is even, on occasion, benevolent. He just doesn't test well."

Eventually, he got around to mentioning that I would plead "not guilty."

Despite being terrible at his job, I will admit he had a point: my decision making up through this chapter of the story had been poor to say the least. And of course, I had to concede to my current lawyer, Jaynuss, that this process of reliving my journey from contented, average husband to convicted felon has, even if it doesn't help me get out of jail early, been quite edifying. This process of defining my moral borders and boundary, as my father might say. Had I been provided more information, might I have acted more virtuously, more like the man ruled by decency I wanted to be? Or would I have continued to act nefariously, when pressed, when tested?

Today, I am writing, belly-down on the top bunk, alone. Manny is no longer my cellmate. In fact, he's no longer alive.

One of my fellow Chinese inmates, Meng, a squat, tattooed member of the violent Chinese supremacist group named the Chinois Brotherhood, asked me in the lunch line last week whether Manny had indeed called him a "chink." Though I had never witnessed my cellmate cum literary critic display anything but the utmost respect for Meng, I had become a bit tired of his snoring, his masturbating, his reading of my manuscript without asking. As a prison basketball league referee, he never gave me any foul calls either. Manny and I just never got along. We were never *hyggelig*.

So I lied and confirmed that Manny did indeed frequently use the epithet "chink" for many a Chinese brother, including myself. Several mops and buckets were needed to clean his blood from the showers—I didn't wash for a week. My role in Manny's murder, like my decision to liquidate Lene's inheritance, was another one of my insouciantly cold decisions, made by a man with a corrupt soul.

Of course, I know now that Lene agreed to come back with me to Bordirtoun to find out for herself why I had been behaving so strangely since my first visit. On our transatlantic flight, there she was, sleeping beside me in the window seat I would have occupied had she not come along. Her mouth was slightly open, leaking a worm-shaped sliver of drool. Her head was tilted far from me, jacket and airline blanket draped over her chest. I stared at her for some time, my idle hand on her cold thigh. Lene stirred awake, and I turned my attention to the movie on the screen: a smiling Asian man helping an anxious but handsome white man find a pensive, pretty white woman. Soon, the whites face each other, smiling. Pan out to the ice skating rink at Rockefeller Center, credits roll.

"How was the movie?" Lene said, issuing a foul-breathed yawn.

"Awful," I replied.

"You're so negative."

"You asked."

"You're in a sour mood."

I blurted that I was not in a sour mood just as she said, "Don't deny it." Lene looked out the window. "This trip was your idea."

I didn't respond, trying to avoid further unpleasantness. Then Lene turned, and her eyes were upon me. "What actually happened?" she asked. "With your mother?"

"I thought I told you."

"No, you didn't."

"The breakdown?" I said. "I told you."

"You told me she had a breakdown," Lene said. "But what kind? Where? What happened? Did it involve your father?"

After a pause, I said, "Yes, my father was involved."

"Why are you being so secretive?"

"I don't know many details myself," I said. "All I know is that she and my father got in an argument. She had some sort of nervous breakdown and now, she's recovering at home."

"I thought your father wasn't supposed to see your mother."

"What do you mean?"

"The security company we're paying for?"

"Oh, right," I said. "It happened over the phone. The breakdown. I mean, the argument."

"Then how did you find out?"

"The security company alerted me."

"They tapped her phone?"

"Look, are you done with the interrogation?"

Lene muzzled a retort, then snapped the in-flight magazine out of the pouch. I could tell she didn't believe my answers (all lies), but her questions stopped, for the moment at least. She flipped through the magazine, muttering softly in Danish to herself.

My stomach churned with nerves as our connecting flight landed at Saul Pong Airport. I was sweating profusely, and the cabin started to cook through as we taxied to the gate. In a phone conversation with T.R. before the flight, I'd requested that the Grathes not discuss recent events until I'd gradually educated Lene on the big picture of what was happening in Bordirtoun. Inexplicably, when T.R. and Taryn welcomed us at arrivals, T.R. looked like he had just come from a protest. The bedhead, the acoustic guitar slung over his shoulder, the harmonica sitting on a neck holder, the leather vest he was wearing, the fact that he hadn't shaved—I wondered if it was Halloween, and he'd intentionally come dressed as Bob Dylan. Taryn was evidently preggers now, and she donned a rather pretty baby blue summer dress, unusually feminine for her. She wore makeup, which I'd never seen on her before, and when I saw Lene looking at her looking at me, I wished Taryn hadn't made the extra effort. I gave T.R. an awkward wave since his musical instruments were in the way, and Taryn hugged me tighter and longer in front of my wife than I would have liked.

"*Hej, hej,*" Lene said, offering firm handshakes all around. "It is very nice to meet you. I am so glad to be here."

Taryn launched into chit-chat about how Lene looked like many of the Scandinavian immigrants who lived in the nearby town of Alberg, while T.R. looked at me and said:

"Your dad had your mom picked up from jail yesterday."

"Jail?" Lene said. My stomach plummeted.

"Oh." T.R. blushed. He had forgotten my request.

As I placed a hand on the small of Lene's back, I felt her move away; my ever astute wife, omissions never unnoticed. She eyed Taryn, who, unfortunately, at that moment was smiling at me and trying to change the subject again:

"I'm so glad you're back, and you too Lene," she said. "And Jimbor, my husband, is really glad too."

In our suite at The Pongelliano, housekeeping had left the AC off, and the room so sweltered that my armpits quickly became slick. As I slid open the door to the balcony, I could hear Lene's stifled breaths. She gunned a flapping magazine through the door I'd just opened. The glossy landed face-up. *Things to Do in Bordirtoun.* My father's smiling mug was on the cover, one foot on a park bench, his elbow resting on a knee, City Hall in the background. Lene accused me, once again, of lying to her.

"My mother hit a showgirl in the face with a chair."

Lene stormed into the bedroom. "I always get half the story! Even now, you won't tell me everything. Admit that you lied to me. I've been thinking about this a long time, Sully. Why do you keep lying to me? What are you hiding? Are you having an affair? Why have you become such a different person since you returned to this place?"

Gritting my teeth, I sat at the dining table, staring at the matching salt and peppershakers—piglets. The warm draft pushed at my back. Lene continued to berate me from the bedroom. She rattled off a number of choice attributes, as if she'd been studying flashcards on the topic during the flight. Coward. Weak. Spineless. Passive-aggressive. Pathological. With each pejorative, the draft seemed to grow warmer, my breath shortened, and my fists closed while my heart galloped toward a quaking horizon.

Lene appeared in the doorway, red-faced, draping a blouse on a hanger. "You are such a child!"

I whipped the salt and pepper piglets off the table, sending them bouncing across the kitchen tile. "Then leave!" I shouted. "Leave if I'm such a monster. If this resort is such a hovel for you, leave!" By the time I finished speaking, I was toe-to-toe with her, looking up at her chin. I had grabbed her hard by the arm and my fist was raised.

Her eyes became teary. "Look what you've become."

I let her go and lowered my fist. My arms felt heavy and useless at my sides, and I felt the elevated beating of my heart and the blood of my father, and perhaps of past Pongs, coursing through me. I croaked an apology, trying to throw my arms around her. She forearmed me in the chest. "How dare you make this about accommodations? What are you planning, Sully? Tell me. Why can't you tell me? Is it the pregnant woman?"

"Don't be ridiculous."

"Then what is it?"

I stood there, silent. What to say? Certainly not that I wished to be in the presence of a certain old crush. Certainly not the truth about tasers and bail money. Can I fault Lene's questioning? Why couldn't I tell her the truth? Almost any situation in Bordirtoun seemed moist soil for lies, half-lies, and more lies!

Lene continued to unpack. I saw this, momentarily, as a good sign. Then she scooped a pile of clothes and shoved them at me. She was expressionless, her face already dry of tears.

"Just go. Go play detective or whatever you and your friends are planning."

"*Skat.*"

She tossed my clothes into the living room, grabbed my shoulder, and started pushing me out. I tried to resist, but she leveraged those thick Danish legs and with a final plow, muscled me backward and slammed the door.

"I'm not going anywhere!" I shouted. "I'm paying for this trip."

"Oh, shut up about the money already! I'm the one that makes all the money!"

I piled the clothes on the couch and turned on the television. I decided to wait her out. Sooner or later, she'd have to emerge. While Lene slammed drawers shut, I discovered a channel that disturbed to no end: PongTV.

"Today, Mayor Saul Pong completed his five-country European tour by cooking a Bordirtoun Omelette for a group of British investors—" I watched a chef hand a steaming skillet to my father as cameras flashed. A Bordirtoun Omelette was an angioplasty-waiting-to-happen consisting of beef tripe, pork's blood, chicken's feet, sliced Oscar Meyer wieners, and guacamole. Saul jiggled the pan back and forth lightly and beamed, careful not to move the food. I turned off the television and threw the remote against the wall.

"Be quiet!" Lene shouted.

"I'm not going anywhere!"

The phone rang.

"Sully?" Taryn said. "Hey, T.R.'s sorry. He forgot she didn't know."

I relished her conspiratorial tone. "I'll work it out."

"Why didn't you tell her about your mother?"

"It's complicated."

Taryn informed me that she, T.R., and Dora Tollworth of the *Bordirtoun Daily* were waiting for me in the lobby.

"Now is not the best time," I said, looking at Lene's shut bedroom door.

"Dora's on deadline."

I wished Taryn had instead expressed her personal desire to see me. "Yes, of course." I glanced again at Lene's closed door. Inside, classical music played. I gnawed at the end of a Pongelliano pen. I told myself I'd make things up to her later.

"I'll be down momentarily," I told Taryn.

I descended the spiraling marble staircase into the lobby and saw Taryn, T.R. and Dora sitting in armchairs, shielding their eyes from a leaning column of sunlight coming through giant gridded windows. Dora was wearing an unfortunately short pencil skirt that made her pale thighs look like sacks of flour. I looked around The Pongelliano for spectators and security cameras to which I knew my father would have access.

"So Mr. Pong, you have returned," Dora said.

"With my wife."

The concierge walked by and said, "Good afternoon, Mr. Sulliver." I nodded a hello.

"Your father's men are watching you," Dora said.

I took a second look at the concierge. Sure enough, he was glancing sidelong at us, leaning against the front desk instead of sitting behind the concierge's post.

We followed Dora to the parking lot, got into her SUV, and she drove us over the river. At the construction site, the protesters were gone, the shops and roads dug up and fenced off beyond the lone standing stoplight. We passed one of the razed residential blocks, now a stretch of rubble and exposed foundation. All that was left was an immense oak tree and several dumpsters brimming over with wood and dirt. The dumpsters had Pong Foundation signs branded with Saul's face. Someone had sprayed red graffiti X's over his eyes and blacked out his teeth. Only now did I see how massive the redevelopment zone was. Clods of dirt spiraled sideways across miles and miles of flatness.

Soon, a deep orange dusk fell, and we headed down a winding road toward the flickering lights of the camps of Rio River. Because

Dora took a different route, we were able to get an elevated view. The barracks were not empty anymore. Residents milled around cylinders of burning trash. People walked in and out of many of the housing units; they looked like ants. There were many more than a few hundred residents. There must have been thousands. Over the camps, dark birds flew low ovals. Above them, the light poles were lit, and armed guards stood at elevated stations. The relocation had begun.

Soon, we pulled up to a guard booth, approximately fifty feet from the front gate. Dora rolled down her window. A long-necked guard craned his head out of the booth and ordered us to turn the car around.

"I'm with the *Bordirtoun Daily*," Dora said.

"Sorry, ma'am," the guard said. "No one gets beyond the point."

Two machine-gun toting guards walked in front of Dora's car. They were wearing navy blue uniforms with the embroidered EOD logo of End of Days Security, the company I had hired to monitor my mother's house. In the distance, I heard a pop and a woman's scream. The guards didn't move.

"You best turn your car around, ma'am," the guard in the window said as the others fingered the safeties on their weapons.

Dora did as told and headed back toward the river.

"For such a long drive, we didn't see very much, did we?" I said.

"That's exactly what we wanted you to see," she said. I expected Dora to go on, but when she didn't, I realized she hadn't brought me here for a story about Rio River. I was Dora's story.

"You want me to announce," I said.

"When your father returns, he'll begin his campaign, and he will win, and those people will never leave Rio River," Dora said.

"I'm not qualified."

"You must be angered by your mother's situation," Dora said. "He left her in jail. You paid the bail. And now, his people take her home. He's treating the citizens of Bordirtoun like he treats your mother. Like he treats you."

"We've been looking at your polling data," T.R. said. He showed me a binder-clipped sheaf of graphs and charts. "You're rising, Sully. You can win. My numbers were never this good before I decided to run. People think you're going to save the city."

"Wouldn't you like to make your father pay?" Dora said.

"Wouldn't this be the best way?" T.R. said.

My heart was pounding hard. How nice of T.R. and Dora to put together a plan to make my father pay when I hadn't been diligent enough to do so myself! But was this the best way? Was this the only way?

From the back seat, Taryn said, "Make your own decision, Sully, and don't let them pressure you."

"Hold him accountable," T.R. said. "For what he's done to your mother. For what's he's done to Bordirtoun. For what he's done for you."

I squirmed in my seat, my eyes shut.

"We can start prepping the announcement right away," T.R. said.

The candidacy was becoming real. Me against my father, beneath the bright lights, inside the ring, for my hometown. I opened my eyes and nodded once.

"Is that a yes?" T.R. said.

My chin tipped downward a second time. "Okay."

Dora's face remained unchanged, as if she hadn't heard me. Perhaps she was as surprised as I was that I finally made a decision. T.R. was the first to crack a smile. "Lene's going to hate us," he said, laughing.

Ah, yes, the small matter of the wife. After the visit to Rio River, I told Dora, T.R., and Taryn that I needed time to tell Lene before we announced. Taryn suggested that delaying could work to our advantage. Because I had been gone for two months, many voters had forgotten me. She recommended we reintroduce my image to the public with a few well-placed human interest profiles before I announced my intent to run.

So I gave Dora something to use for the morning edition. I told her how I'd witnessed my father beating my mother for years. I described the bruises on her arms and neck, her screams, and how, as a child, I'd prayed for Saul to stop. I told her that I'd just witnessed the latest beating several weeks ago, that at nearly seventy, the Mayor of Bordirtoun was still a wifebeater. I told her that Saul's abusive ways and Momma's refusal to leave were why I'd left home at first opportunity to Boston, then New York, and finally Copenhagen. "For most of my life, I could never get far enough away," I was quoted as saying. "But I've come home because recently, I've realized that I can't just stand by and let my father do whatever he wants anymore."

Back at The Pongelliano, I stood outside my penthouse door, in front of which lay a bulky white trash bag filled with my clothes. My plaid boxers were visible through the plastic. When I put my keycard in the door, the lock flashed red. I knocked a few times, then called out for Lene. No response. I grabbed the bag and went down to the lobby, where the young woman at the front desk informed me that Lene had requested new keys, claiming she had lost the previous set. She had been last seen leaving The Pongelliano Spa with an all-day staff masseuse named Archipelago. I imagined this Archipelago to be tall, dark, angular, and wet.

"Can I get the new key?" I asked the woman.

The woman's eyes bulged as if I'd asked her if she was a prostitute. "Your wife said you were stalking her."

"I was not."

"Don't make me call security."

"Don't make me tell the manager how rude you are," I said.

She looked over her shoulder at an older woman who was staring at me with her arms crossed. "I'm her manager," she said. "Please step back. What would your father think of this?"

"He'd probably think you were too old for him."

"What was that?" her manager said.

I walked away, saying nothing. Aimlessly, I roamed the lobby. I ordered a whiskey at the bar. As I reached for my wallet, the bartender, thumbless as it turned out, wrapped four fingers around my arm.

"Saul Pong's son is not paying," he said. "Not at my bar."

"I can pay, you know."

"Doesn't matter."

"It does to me." I handed him my last ten.

"It's $10.50, Mr. Pong."

"Damn!" I handed over my credit card.

Moments later, the card was returned, declined, and I told the bartender that what I had wanted all along was a glass of tap water.

Someone sat next to me. I smelled sweet milk. "I'll have a water too, please," Taryn said.

"What are you doing here?"

"Waiting for T.R.," she said. The bartender pushed two glasses toward us. "He and Dora are still talking. Actually, it's more like he's still talking."

We laughed. I drank the water in numerous gulps without taking a breath. Taryn was doing the same. The air was so dry and dusty that I could chew the debris. What a strange sight Taryn and I must have been! Two people in some sort of water drinking contest.

"Man, am I thirsty!" she said, handing her empty glass to the bartender. Taryn looked at the trash bag of clothes at my feet. "Your wife must really be upset. What happened?"

"She's on an Archipelago."

"What?"

"Nothing." I chuckled. How ridiculous, useless my marriage had become. "She doesn't want to see me. We're having some communication issues. I haven't been straight with her lately."

I replayed what I had just said in my head. Had I ever been straight with anyone, Taryn included?

"I'm surprised you were able to get her to come," she said.

"Me too."

"If it's any consolation, every marriage has its issues. Jim's always wanted lots of kids. I've never felt particularly maternal."

I glanced at her belly. "You seem to have resolved that issue."

"But lately, I've wondered whether I wanted to have a child all along, and I just didn't want to have one with him."

I raised a brow. "Ouch."

"I don't mean that with malice," she said. "It's just this feeling I have. It came on very suddenly a few weeks after I learned I was pregnant. I started becoming uncomfortable with the idea of him being a father." She shrugged and sighed. "It's probably nothing."

I must confess, with guilt, that her small confession made me feel good. Cracks between Taryn and Jimbor? An opening for me, perhaps? An opening for the adultery I would supposedly never commit? Like the many adulteries my father committed. Like the adultery Jimbor might have been committing.

"Marriage will play tricks on you," I said. "Like marijuana."

Taryn laughed. "And we've had quite a bit of that together, haven't we?"

I placed a hand on her leg, just long enough to squeeze once. "Yes, we have."

Taryn blushed, then looked around the lobby for T.R. Silence bloomed between us. I worried I'd gone too far. I noticed our bartender was just sitting on a stool by the register, his thumbless hands folded in his lap, watching us like Taryn and I were a television show.

"Hey," I asked Taryn. "You want to go for a stroll?"

I handed the bartender my bag of clothes and asked him to watch it. Taryn and I walked outside, and the sky was a faded orange, the hills a dark ellipse against a starless sky—dusk. Two elephantine mosquitoes hovered around the large and garish sconces above the drive-and-drop. I took a deep breath. Exhaustion. I had been on the go for over forty hours, and I felt suddenly that, with Taryn beside me, I could go forty more.

"You want to go there?" Taryn said, pointing to the hills. "I know a way up."

"I'll follow you."

As we walked, a pair of bright headlights sped past, leaving a bitter trail of exhaust. We crossed the road and hiked up a newly built concrete path I'd never seen, lined with gas lamps and benches. The trail wound around the hill on a slight incline.

"Your dad had this walkway built," she said.

We approached a vista point. Fireflies flitted in a triangular formation around a streetlamp. I heard the thrum of machinery nearby. How the city had changed in twenty years! The side of the river on which I grew up was speckled with the nightlights. The head of my father's statue was spotlit.

I walked over to a small statue nearby. It was my grandmother, my father's mother, wearing an argyle sweater and pleated skirt. I had no recollections of her. She had died shortly after I was born. The statue had my father's slight hunch. She was smiling. Not unlike my father's fake politician's beam. Her name was Susan Suen Pong, and I placed a hand on her bronze shoulder. Was she a good, decent woman? Would she have been disgusted by what we Pongs had become? Had I known more about the dubious intentions and the miserable legacy of the Pong family, would I have been more successful at avoiding the same mistakes?

"Were you and your grandmother close?" Taryn asked.

I shook my head. "I didn't even know her name until now. I didn't know my grandfather either. I guess he left when my dad was young."

Taryn and I sat on a bench next to my grandmother's statue. I reclined, my arms across the bench's back. To an outsider, it might have looked like I had my arm around Taryn. A haze moved across the night sky. The pungency of cattle excretion weighted the air. Taryn drew closer. We had never been this close. I looked into her eyes for a long time—how green, how clear.

"I'm not sure I'm in love with my wife anymore," I said.

Perhaps I was stating the obvious. Perhaps I should never have uttered the words. After all, once you say them aloud, you can't take them back, you can't deny them; the confession sits forever between you and your confidant. To this day, I can't decide whether I regret the confession or not. Perhaps I was hoping Taryn would reciprocate and say she wasn't in love with Jimbor anymore, followed by something to the effect of "I've always loved you."

Taryn said nothing. Instead, she hugged me close, and I placed my head on her shoulder, shut my eyes, and inhaled her scent. We sat there, embracing for some time. It took all my moral fortitude not to kiss her neck and bring a hand to her breast. She let me go, and we stood. I turned away from my bronze grandmother and watched the opaque layer of dust rise over the cityscape.

"Thank you for listening," I said.

"Of course, Sully," she said. "Let's walk down."

I stayed at the Grathe house that night and tossed and turned on their couch, soaked with jetlag and guilt. My mind overflowed with imaginings of Lene's anger and memories of Taryn's embrace, and my ears brimmed with the sound of Jimbor's streetsweeping snores.

I called the car service and headed back to The Pongelliano before dawn to investigate ways to penetrate my wife's new Bordirtoun fortress. When I asked the front desk to call her, the Pakistani man on the graveyard shift responded by unfurling a yo-yo with a flashing orange light.

A scowl twisted my face. "This is a misunderstanding. My wife is angry with me, and she has locked me out of the room. Can you call her? I must speak to her."

He did not move.

"You know who I am, don't you?"

He nodded.

"I'm practically your boss," I said.

"We'll call Mrs. Pong in the morning, Mr. Pong," he said. He wrote nothing down.

I trudged away and checked my bank balances at the lobby ATM. The numbers were alarmingly low. I quartered my transaction record and flipped the pieces in the nearest wastebasket, giving it a quick kick for good measure.

I found myself next at the bar, pondering a conspiratorial giggle between the bartender and a patron. They were watching the large screen television. The local morning show. Above the anchorman's shoulder, my digital mug. The caption read, "Son Denounces Mayor Pong."

"The mayor's office issued no comment," the anchor said. "Mayor Pong is due to return from his European tour later this morning."

As I approached, the patron left. The bartender looked at me. "That's you, isn't it?"

I nodded.

"Rumor has it your marriage ain't going so hot either," he said.

"That's none of your business."

"I apologize." The bartender offered me a stool. "Sit and let me buy you a drink."

I rubbed my bleary eyes and was briefly hypnotized by the tinkle of the distant slot machines in the casino. A drink didn't sound bad (especially if it was free); sleep would be better, but I took his offer and ordered a Glenfiddich on the rocks.

The bartender poured three scotches. Another man sat next to me. The newcomer picked up his drink with two hands; he was the thumbless bartender from the night before. The duo looked quite similar. They were dressed in Pongelliano work attire: white shirt, dark slacks, and red suspenders. One parted his thin silvering hair to the right. The bethumbed bartender parted his to the left. Both were slim, roughly the same build. I rubbed my eyes again.

"He's Drew," the bethumbed bartender said. "I'm Werder."

"Can we turn on a light in here?"

"Light won't help," Werder said. "We're twins."

"Oh, that's great," I said, as if there were some inherent and obvious value in twin-dom.

"So, Mr. Pong," Drew said. "Taking after your old man? Running around on your old lady?"

"Absolutely not." I took a closed-eye swill of scotch that seared my empty stomach.

"Taryn Grathe, the publicist," Werder said, raising his chin as if he had confidently answered a game-show question.

"We are both married," I said. "To other people."

"Unhappily—" Drew began.

I informed them that she and I had been friends since high school. Platonic friends.

"Must have been love, but it's over now?" Werder said.

I drank my scotch until there was only ice and slammed the glass on the table. "Thanks for the drink."

"Hold on, Mr. Pong," Werder said.

"Your father liked to tell his mistresses that he only hired me because he felt sympathy for my—." Drew held up his eight fingers.

"That's terrible," I said.

"He's never even asked me how I lost my thumbs."

"So how did you—"

"Not your business!" Drew said.

"We can help you," Werder said.

And that was how I ended up, two hours later, sitting in a golf cart with Drew and Werder, atop a course foothill, in a circle of yellowing fairway grass, the tepid breeze blowing water into my face from a nearby sprinkler. Drew handed me a telescope, and I aimed it at my wife's balcony. I saw my disrobed Lene, lying belly-down on a massage table, covered with a towel, getting a morning shiatsu from a ponytailed man wearing a bowler hat, likely Archipelago. I moved the telescope and saw a heat-lamp, a tray with a bucket of champagne, and a silver dome of hidden food. Only one glass, one dome. A rather early morning in-room spa appointment, I thought. I muttered that my wife was a cheating bitch.

"She left the room only once yesterday," Werder said.

"Why are you spying on my wife?"

Werder nodded toward Drew. "He brought it to my attention."

I asked Drew the same question.

He shrugged. "Since you're running for mayor, I would think your wife cheating on you helps you in the polls, doesn't it?"

"One, I have not announced a run for mayor."

They laughed.

"Stop laughing," I said. "And two, under no circumstances would my wife cheating on me be a good thing."

"She wasn't wearing a wedding ring," Drew said. "She told me she wasn't married."

"Why are you talking to my wife?"

"She had a drink at the bar last night," Drew said. "Not long after you left with your mistress."

"I do not have a mistress," I said. "I didn't cheat. I don't cheat. I have never cheated."

"We believe you," Werder said.

Sarcasm detected. "Do you know anyone who can get me near her?"

"I can alert you when she leaves the room again," Drew said.

I gave him my cell number. Drew wrote it on his arm.

"What's in it for us?" Werder said.

"I'll pay you."

"With what?"

I patted myself down for something of value. I removed my wedding band.

Drew laughed. "That's it?"

"Christ! That's all I have."

Werder pocketed the ring. "Your father gave me his wedding ring once. It was a lot nicer than yours."

I kicked the glove compartment. "Stop comparing me to my father!"

"Shhh!" Werder said. He grabbed the telescope and pointed it at Lene's balcony. "Shit." He chopped the telescope down on my thigh, and I cried out in pain. The golf cart jerked forward. I grabbed the hood. The next thing I knew, we were getting drenched. The cart was slaloming through sprinklers. My cell buzzed. Unknown ID. My stomach dropped. Was it Lene? I answered.

"Sully?" T.R. said.

The cart rolled into the shadows of tall trees, jostling as we came to a stop.

"The hell you do that for!" Werder slapped my arm.

"Stop hitting me!" I said.

"Where are you?" T.R. asked.

"I'm indisposed," I said.

An audible exasperated sigh. "Just meet me in the lobby," T.R. said.

I was soaked head-to-toe when I returned to the hotel. T.R. was nowhere to be found, and there was a crowd standing in front of a flatscreen at the bar. When I saw my father on television, microphones jammed in his face, I realized I was the Pong family member having the best morning.

"Well, I deny it...I deny the allegations," my father said, his eyes bloodshot. His voice was so soft I could hardly hear him. "I have never laid a hand in a violent way upon my wife."

"Why do you think your son would accuse you of such things?" a reporter asked.

"I can't even begin to speculate."

The caption at the bottom of the screen read, "Son Alleges Mayor Pong of Spousal Abuse."

"Please respect our family's privacy during this difficult time," Saul said. "I have no further comment until I speak with them."

My phone buzzed in my pocket. The caller ID read "Momma." When the new message notification flashed, curiosity got the better of me, and I traipsed the lobby, trying to find a quiet place to listen to the voicemail. Finally, I chose the bathroom.

"You useless retard!" Momma shouted. "I knew I shouldn't have had that cigarette when I was pregnant. Dump our family secrets to the world like a communist! You are responsible for everything bad that happens to our family! Remember that when I'm dead and poor. Why didn't you just stay away? Huh? Why? Why didn't you just leave us alone?"

Leave *them* alone?! I hung up and proceeded to scream "Fucking bitch!" several times at the top of my lungs.

After I splashed some water on my face, I toweled off and felt better. That was when I noticed, in the mirror, the stunned and frightened female attendant cowering in the corner. I had inadvertently entered the women's restroom.

I apologized and walked out and into T.R.

"What were you doing in there?" he asked.

"Never mind."

T.R. said the phone had been ringing since dawn with people wanting me to run for mayor. "Now is the time," he said.

"I still haven't talked to Lene."

"Tell her now."

"We're not on speaking terms."

"Maybe if I tell her, she'll understand," T.R. said.

"I'm not sure *I* understand," I said. I walked out of the lobby and into the cloudless polyester blue. How the brightest of colors could seem flat in my eyes! In the garden, I sat in a teak chair and slumped, feeling suddenly like a long, warm nap. The sun warmed my wet clothes, and the mistmaker drizzled over my face. I inhaled deeply the smells of chlorine and wet grass. I could have sat there for the rest of my aimless and disappointing days.

"I'm concerned I don't hold up to scrutiny," I said.

He stood in front of me with his arms crossed and told me to get up.

I didn't move. "I'm tired, man. Jimbor was snoring—"

"Look at me."

"Don't be gay."

T.R. grabbed my hand and pulled me off the chair. He looked me in the eye. "If you didn't want to run, you wouldn't have come back," he said.

I knew T.R. was right. Hell, I was *born* for the job—my fat face and last name were enough! Though I wasn't qualified, had no particular passion for politics, and really didn't care much about people or the problems of people, I thought I could learn these attributes as I went along as if I could simply purchase *Small Town Mayors for Dummies* from a chain bookstore.

T.R. left to start working on the announcement, which meant I could no longer procrastinate on telling Lene. I returned to the bar and to my thumbed and thumbless bartenders and asked them for the latest on Lene's resort whereabouts.

"Hot tub, private appointment, one p.m.," Werder said.

I nodded, noted it was almost noon.

Werder filled a scotch glass with no ice and slid the drink across the bar. An hour later, I had had several more cocktails and ignored repeated voicemails from both parents. As I took free drink after free drink, I started feeling homesick for my favorite Arab-run burger place in Copenhagen on Østerbrogade, then for Bordirtoun Steaks (there were no good steakhouses in Denmark), then back to my favorite Arab-Danish hamburger. I began to feel nostalgic for the other places I'd lived (Cambridge, how I missed the red brick, the icy Charles in the winter). I felt briefly horny while I ogled a showgirl or two. But finally, and least trivially, I started feeling this was my last chance to serve up a coherent explanation of my actions to Lene.

Werder shook my shoulders. "She's coming down," he said.

I tried to stand but wobbled.

"You want some water?" he asked.

I braced myself against Werder's arm. He nodded to Drew and held me by the waist. "There she is, by the stairs. Your wife."

Lene was wearing a swimsuit and holding a towel. Her hair was wet, and her face glowed pink and shiny. Drew handed me a glass of water.

"Get yourself together," he said.

I closed my eyes and downed the water. Werder nudged me away from the bar. Lene headed outside toward the pool, and I followed. Pushing through the glass doors, I smacked into a blur of white. I had knocked over a towel boy, spilling his inventory on the ground. I heard gasps and crouched down behind the hedge where he'd landed.

"Jesus Christ, motherfucker," the boy said. Then he saw who I was. "Oh, I'm so sorry, Mister—"

"My fault," I said, holding a finger to my lips. "Is the tall blonde woman watching us?"

The boy peeked and said she was not.

Attention averted. I got up and continued to tail my wife, down a declining brick path, toward the private pool and hot tubs that overlooked the golf course and river. A young woman waved and smiled at me. I gave her a thumbs-up. In fact, I gave several more as people continued to stare and smile as I walked by. I remember being happy that none of these people actually stopped to talk to me. My eyes locked on Lene's wide back, hoping she wouldn't turn around. I wasn't ready to plead my case just then. We had to be alone. I had to be ready. During my hour of drinking and ruminating, I hadn't really given much thought to what I would actually say.

Lene pulled open a latched gate and entered the pool area. I followed, the chlorine mist stinging my nostrils. A teenaged boy cannonballed into the water and splashed my just dried pants, but I kept quiet. Lene laid her towel over a deckchair and stepped tentatively toward the pool, dipping a toe in the water. The line in her upheld calf flexed, the hollow of her gluteus cheek puckered, and I felt a twinge in my member. My wife was so much more than I deserved. In our primes, we could not resist. Where did our primes go, and how did it go so fast?

She entered the water slowly, and for a moment, she propped her elbows on the concrete and held her upper body above water.

Then she dropped, all the way, rising above the surface to clear water from her eyes. I stood a few feet away, in the shadows, watching. She smiled and greeted a lean, muscular man wearing just board shorts labeled "STAFF" over his groin. He was Archipelago, the ponytailed masseuse I had seen through Werder's binoculars. Twice in one day?! Archipelago rubbed his palms together and spoke to Lene for some time. His posture was lax. Lene stayed still, listening and nodding. Their interaction appeared instructional. Nevertheless, I could feel my nostrils flaring. Such a reaction was ridiculous, but why was Archipelago now sliding into the pool himself?

"Lene," I said sharply, walking to the pool's edge.

She looked up, one eye closed, her face moist. Archipelago backed away from her.

"What do you want?" she said.

"Whatever it is you're having."

She rolled her eyes.

The man thrust his hand up at me. "You're Saul Pong's son, right? I'm Archipelago Villalobos, licensed hydroyoga and massage therapist."

I left his hand hanging.

Lene puffed her lower lip at Archipelago. "I'm sorry, we'll have to reschedule."

"No problem! You know I'm flexible for you." He idly massaged his firm pectorals. Then they hugged for a long time. Eventually, Archipelago noticed I was standing there.

"Good to meet you, Mr. Pong," he said as he climbed out of the pool. "Say hi to your father for me."

I glared at him as he left, and when I turned back to Lene, she was glaring at me. She folded her arms and backed against the edge of the pool. I sat beside her, on the concrete.

"*Skat*," I said.

"No," she said. "Don't call me that."

"We need to talk."

She guffawed. It occurred to me I should have had more to offer. Flowers. Jewelry. Something.

A young Latino family of three walked by. The staggering toddler strayed from his staring parents and promptly started hitting me on the back of my neck.

"No, Stefano, no!" the boy's mother said, picking him up. "Bad boy, that's the mayor's son. I'm so sorry, Mr. Pong." The father was pinching his nose to restrain laughter.

I said it was nothing in Spanish, and the mother gave me a withering look.

"Funny how you want to talk now," Lene said finally.

"One more chance," I said. "I'll get it right this time. I know there won't be any more chances." Funny, no matter how many times one relives such conversations, it always sounds like Air Supply.

My wife got out of the pool and picked up her towel.

"Lene, please," I said.

She wrapped the towel around her chest and refused to look at me.

"If you had told me that you wanted to move home to help your mother, I would have supported you," she said. "Even if you told me you wanted to run for mayor against your father, I would have supported you. But you didn't tell me that. You tell me this story and that story. After eight years, what else do I have to do to convince you that I will support you?"

I told her that I was convinced. But words had never felt meeker.

"Even if you had told me you wanted to spend much of our inheritance on a run for mayor, I would have supported you," she said.

The morning's scotch backed up in my throat. She had known all along.

"I am not like your mother," Lene said. "I will not let this pass."

She began to walk back to the hotel.

I got up and felt my groin grab. Lene didn't stop, and I didn't ask her to. She was already halfway back to the lobby. I limped after her. Had I felt forgiven, I might have asked her to wait. But I knew this was a reunification borne of pure matrimonial exhaustion, a reunification that just as easily could have been separation. Lene seemed past caring whether I followed or not.

Never had I imagined myself as a divorcing type. "I'll be your family," I had said to Lene; it was one of the few fundamentally sincere statements of my life. Was I always in love with my wife, every minute of every day? Of course not, who is? But before my father reappeared in my life two years ago, calling, showing up on my doorstep, I never, ever envisioned that I would one day know what divorce was like. And yet, there I was, sleeping on the couch of our penthouse suite, a melted icepack puddling my crotch, with my estranged wife locked away in the master bedroom. Let me be clear. I am not blaming my father for my decline. Those choices were mine. But before my father re-entered my life, adultery, divorce, forgery, spending my wife's life savings without telling her, conspiracy, press leaks, none of these were satellites in my universe. I was not supposed to become Saul Pong. I was the Bordirtoun hick done good. An obese, bald, expat dullard on the dole. The better man.

I hobbled into the bathroom, popped a couple of Advil and blow-dried my genitals before finding my way back onto the couch. Lene walked out, mussing her hair and yawning. She sat in the armchair with her hands folded, and her bare legs crossed.

"What are you going to do today, Sully?" she asked.

This wasn't a generic question. Her caustic tone made that obvious. I sat up straight and knew I had to deliver a satisfactory answer.

I cleared my throat. "I'm going to run."

"So you're staying."

"What do you think I should do, Lene?"

She laughed. "Now you ask?"

"I feel this is the right thing to do."

"You should just admit you're staying for that woman."

"We're just friends."

Lene marched onto the balcony without shoes. "Everyone in this hotel sees you with her. How do you think that makes me feel?"

"Lene," I said. "I'm sorry."

My wife continued to look out over the balcony. "How did we get to this horrible place?"

It took me a moment to realize Lene wasn't referring to Bordirtoun. She was referring to our marriage.

"I'm here to win," I said.

"Isn't that exactly what your father wants?" she said. "He's always said this is your city."

That afternoon, Lene packed and prepared to check out. She was flying home, and we were separating. At the front desk, I tried to settle our hotel bill. The woman handed me a stapled ten-page list of charges for our three-night stay. My eyes bulged.

"Mayor Pong would like to take this opportunity to speak with you regarding your—" She plucked a Post-It note off the monitor and read, "*debt* to him."

The woman led me past the lounge and through a pair of double doors into the Bistro de Pong. In the purple velvet corner booth sat Saul and Momma. Goiterous bodyguards stood on either side of them. The restaurant was otherwise empty of patrons. Saul's shoulder-length perm had a fresh wave, and my mother's jewelry glinted on her arms, ears, and neck. One of the bodyguards placed a barstool at the head of the table.

"Sully!" my father said, beaming. "My only son, home where he belongs." He noticed my limp. "Your leg again?"

I didn't reply. My mother looked at me like I was disappointing theater.

"Some tea, son?" my father said, pouring a cup.

"No, thanks."

"How's Elena?" he asked.

"He's never even brought her to the house," Momma said. "I've never even met her."

My blood began to boil. "I have nothing to say to either of you."

My father put his arm over the back of the booth, around Momma.

"Sully is very busy destroying the family," Momma replied.

My father laughed. "She's so funny sometimes." He swallowed. "Sully, I'm happy to announce that Momma and I have decided to seek maritime counseling."

"*Marital* counseling," I corrected.

"With my long-time friend, Dr. Quango," Saul said.

"Is this what you want?" I asked my mother.

"Tell those people outside my house to leave," she said.

My jaw flexed. And there it was, at long last, my mother's official choice. My return trip to Bordirtoun to no avail, my efforts for naught, my concern wasted. Given the choice, she would always choose to be with my father, no matter what he did, no matter what I did.

"During my trip to Europe, I realized how much I missed the feeling of family," my father said. "One cannot live forever alone, don't you agree?"

"No, your son doesn't agree," Momma said. "He likes to put his face on TV and tell everyone our problems so he can be famous."

My father shook his head, smiling. "That's not the way I feel, son," he said. "But your mother has her opinions. I understand that you care deeply about the Bordirtoun people just like me, and now you want to do a better job than me, isn't that right?"

I told him that that was not the case, that a sedated monkey could have done a better job than he'd done.

"Very funny, Sully," Saul said, not smiling, his words sharp. "Why would you want to embarrass me like this?"

I looked down at the table, trying to find words for my answer, for my rage. "Because you need to be punished."

Momma eyed the heavens. "What have I done to deserve such a stupid son?"

My father finished his tea, and as my mother poured him another, he stared hard at me while he tapped two fingers slowly on the table near the cup.

"Is what I hear correct?" he said. "That you want to run for mayor."

"There are people who wish I would."

"If you do, I will not run against you."

"You won't?"

"This is your city, too," Momma said. She was suddenly smiling. I hadn't seen her smile in quite some time. Even as she did, grimace lines cracked on her face.

"I'll endorse your candidacy," Saul said.

"I won't take it."

"I'll advise you on the areas I'd like to see addressed by your administration."

"No."

"Namely this Old Town development, which has really gotten out of hand," Saul said. "I have many ideas about how to turn that project around. It would have been much farther along had you taken the reins as you had promised. But I think it's great that you're coming back. I'm getting old, and Momma and I would like to retire soon and maybe do some traveling."

I looked at Momma. "I can't believe you're letting him do this to you."

Momma said nothing and sipped her tea.

"I'll feel so much better knowing you will be my successor." My father nodded and winked at me. "I'll show you my tricks. No one will run against you, I promise."

"I said no!" I shouted. "You and I will never be close. We will never work together on anything. Do you understand me? Never."

My father blinked hard as if I'd slapped him. "You have your opinions or beliefs or distortions, and I understand." He cleared his throat and shrugged. "I haven't been the best father, and you resent me for that. I understand."

"I don't give a shit what you understand," I said. "I will ruin your legacy. The Bordirtoun people will learn every last truth about you." I limped off, like some peg-legged working class hero walking away from a pyrrhic horizon.

I almost got out of the restaurant without comment from my father until he uttered, "Son?"

I stopped.

"Don't forget to settle your bill," Saul said.

THE MISADVENTURES OF SAUL PONG

THE YEAR WAS 1969, the Year of the Rooster. Roosters are practical, honest, neat and conservative, and if you had told Saul Pong you were a Rooster, he would have called you weak. He was riding south from Salt Lake City on Route 15 on his Harley, wearing his long hair tied in a ponytail and sunglasses so big that they covered his cheekbones. He had all of his earthly possessions with him in a knapsack, two changes of clothes and a week's worth of tighty whiteys. With the wind pounding his checks, Saul felt free. He felt that nothing bad could ever happen to him on this open road, the desert and its endless shrubs and cacti on either side, the warmth blanketing his bare forearms. He felt big against the world, like Gary Gulliver compared to the Lilliputians in the cartoon *The Adventures of Gulliver*. "I am Gulliver the King of Lilliput," he said to himself, referring to one of his video game concepts, which he had described in detail (Gulliver would be attacked by swarms of Lilliputians!) to his roommate Nolan. Nolan had pooh-poohed the idea.

"Gulliver wasn't the king of the Lilliputians," Nolan had said. "They were friends and teamed up against the evil Captain Leech."

"It's a video game!" Saul replied. "Players don't care about friends. Players need lots of enemies."

Nolan said they'd discuss the Gulliver idea later. The whole fraternity was distracted; they were about to break into the university's mainframe center to play Space War. Saul decided to stay in and work on his game. One day, the world would realize that Saul Pong was the video game king! Like Nolan, Saul had had his share of engineering job offers in California. Unlike Nolan, Saul turned them all down. He didn't need a day job to distract him from his goal: to get rich from games. In one year, he and Nolan planned to reconvene in Santa Clara, where Nolan and his wife Paula had moved. Saul would pitch two or three good ideas, and if they agreed on one they could commercialize, they'd start a company together. That's what they'd promised each other. They'd shaken on it.

Saul was on his way to his mother's apartment in Bordirtoun. Even though she was frail and blind now, she still possessed a thousand wisdoms that Saul used to live his life. She had often reminded him that life was a game. Every game had winners and losers. Every game could be cracked; every game had a winning approach. She called America a game. You won by having the most money and God on your side.

When Bordirtoun appeared in the valley below, Saul revved the throttle. "I've always been good at games," he said to himself. The new Dow Chemical plant streamed smoke skyward. On the horizon, a gray cloud hovered over the Mexican border. Saul felt comforted. He was at the edge of darkness, the edge of a shitty country like Mexico, but still on the side of winners, on the side of America.

Saul's mother had a Mexican caretaker named Juanita. When Saul arrived at the apartment, toting his knapsack and in desperate need of water, he asked Juanita how her family was doing but before she could get out a comprehensible answer, he requested agua.

Juanita laughed and waddled to the kitchen, returning with a full glass. "Good to see you again, Sow-ool."

"Thank you, Juanita," Saul said, gulping the tinny water. To Saul, Bordirtoun water tasted sweeter than water in Salt Lake City. "Might I add that you are looking lovely today?"

Juanita tittered. "Your mother is still sleeping."

"No, she no sleeping," Saul's mother said in a mock Spanish accent. She slowly shuffled forth with the aid of a cane. She wore a thick diamond-patterned argyle sweater despite the summer heat. "My baby is here."

"A-Ma." Saul hugged his mother.

"Don't believe a word that bitch says," Saul's mother hissed in Cantonese. "All the Mexicans are the same. Just like the one who took your father away."

Saul nodded another thank you to Juanita and asked her to be on her way.

"We miss you, Mister Sow-ool," she said, closing the door behind her. "See you tomorrow, Mrs. Pong."

Saul's mother waited silently for Juanita to leave. "Do you like her? Is she pretty?" she asked when she was gone.

"She's very fat," Saul said.

"Mexicans tend to be very fat. It's their diet. Never marry a Mexican. Only marry Chinese."

"Yes, Ma."

"Do you like fat girls?"

"No, Ma."

"Do you have a girlfriend in college?"

Saul found himself laughing uncomfortably at his mother's light pressure. He had never had a girlfriend. But he'd had far too many beer-blinded regretful encounters with girls with aesthetic deficits.

"I haven't found the right one yet," he replied. Saul led his mother by the elbow to the kitchen table. "All the women are married in Utah. Many are married to the same man."

Saul's mother groaned. "Why did you have to go to that school? They believe in that crazy pervert."

"As long as we believe in the right God, who cares if their God is wrong?" Saul said, sitting with his mother, his hand on hers. It pained him to see his mother's cataracts clouding her eyes; the darks of them were marbly gray.

"My grandmother was a concubine," she said. "Terrible, terrible life. Bound feet. Addicted to opium. That's why I came to America. Because I didn't want to take care of her."

Saul had never known this about his great-grandmother. He worried that his mother was telling him these facts now because she felt she did not have long to live. "We are very lucky," he said. "We are very lucky that you are still so healthy. So strong. So vibrant. So beautiful." He kissed her hand, the skin of which was translucent, revealing a vast network of purply veins. "You are my family."

The whites of his mother's eyes pinkened. "You are my good boy," she said. "No thanks to your father. Now go get a girlfriend! Get married and have some grandchildren. I want grandchildren before I die."

To say that there was a paucity of useful computer electronics equipment in Bordirtoun would be an understatement. Saul had to cobble together working parts from various junkyards and pawn shops. He made lengthy day trips to Tuscon on his motorcycle and would strap monitors and motherboards to the rear seat. Eventually, Saul gathered enough equipment to piece together a lab in his old bedroom.

One day, on his way back into town, Saul drove through a McDonald's on the Old Town side of the river. In the drive-through window worked a young Chinese woman who, beneath her orange baseball cap, wore her hair quite long. Thick tendrils fell to her mid-back. Saul thought she had a pretty face. High cheekbones. Perfect skin.

"Good afternoon," Saul said, as he quieted his bike.

The woman giggled and exchanged looks with the homely coworker on the fryer, but neither woman appeared to understand what he had just said.

"Hi, my name is Saul," he said in Cantonese.

The woman nodded and asked what he had ordered.

"Hamburger, small fries and Coke," Saul said.

The woman left the window, and Saul caught a glimpse of her backside in those ugly, polyester uniform pants. Nice and round behind, he noted. She was slim, too. She returned with his order, and he paid her. Behind Saul, a Camaro pulled up, its engine spluttering like a frat boy's post-bender diarrhea.

"What's your name?" Saul said in Cantonese.

The woman spoke but too quietly for Saul to hear. The Camaro honked. Saul ignored it.

"What's your name?" he asked again louder.

"Mary!" she shouted in English, punctuating her name with an embarrassed laugh.

"Hey Kato!" the driver of the Camaro said. "The Green Hornet's hungry too."

Saul ignored him. "What time do you get off work?" he asked Mary.

"Five o'clock."

"Would you like to go for a ride with me?"

"No," Mary said, laughing.

"Please?"

"Your hair is too long."

"My hair is not even as long as yours."

"I'm a lady."

"If you don't like my hair, I'll cut it."

"But what if I don't like your hair short either?"

"I'll let you cut it so you'll have no one to blame but yourself."

Mary's eyes narrowed, but she was smiling. Saul had stumped her for the moment. The Camaro honked again, several times, with rhythmic vehemence.

Something snapped behind Saul's eyes, and he got off his bike, set his bag of food down, picked up a sizable rock and smashed the Camaro's headlight with it. Then he pressed a finger to his nostril and blew a stream of snot on the hood. The drivers began cussing and honking some more, but they didn't step out of the car to challenge Saul. He continued to stare down the drivers as he picked up his food, bounced on his bike with a flourish, and made it roar.

"See you at five," he said to Mary.

Saul brought barber's shears. If he could find computer parts in Bordirtoun, he could sure as hell find shears no problem. He had walked into a barbershop, feigned interest in a haircut, and while the barber turned his head, Saul stole the shears and slipped out the back door.

While Saul waited in the McDonald's parking lot, he tried several different relaxed poses against his bike. Hip against engine, hand on seat. Hip against seat, hands in the pockets of his bell bottoms. Straddling seat, hands on throttle. When Mary strode out of the McDonald's in a short orange day dress (nice legs, not too bony, he thought), Saul had chosen to stand beside his bike, hands in pockets. He held up the shears and smiled.

"I was just kidding about your hair," Mary said.

"So you like my hair long?"

"I don't care about your hair."

Saul straightened and pretended his feelings weren't hurt. "Fine," he said. He tossed the shears into the desert shrubs. He cleared his throat. "Have you ever been on a motorcycle?"

"Yes. Lots of times."

"Really?"

"There are lots of boys with motorcycles in Bordirtoun."

Lots of boys, eh? "Then why aren't they picking you up today?"

"Because they're losers."

"I can tell you right now I'm not a loser," Saul said. "I've always been good at games. I win."

Mary crossed her arms. "You talk a lot. Are we going to go for a ride or what?"

Saul whipped his leg over the bike and told Mary to get on. She just stood there, unwilling to mount the seat because of her short skirt.

"I won't look," Saul lied.

Mary hiked a thin, dark brow. "I don't believe you."

Saul looked Mary up and down. She was small. Not much bigger than his mother. He got off the bike and held out his hands. He told her he would lift her on.

"You just want to touch my girl parts."

"I won't touch your girl parts," Saul said. "Raise your arms."

Mary slowly did as told. Saul hoisted her onto the motorcycle by her damp armpits. She was indeed light and delicate like his mother.

Saul threaded his leg over the saddle. "Put your arms around my waist."

"No," she said.

"My belt, then," Saul said. He was surprised by how quickly he responded. He was already getting used to her objections. He felt her hands press lightly against his lower back. Every game could be cracked; every game had a winning approach, Saul thought as his motorcycle came to life.

Saul's motorcycle was parked at the top of the black mountain overlooking downtown. He laid a picnic blanket on the dry dirt and let Mary sit first. When he sat, she curled into his arms and threw her legs over his. He stared out at the Leland Stanford statue, a random protrusion in an otherwise flat landscape on the east side of the river. They called the sparsely populated sprawl on the west side "Old Town" now that more than just Mexicans lived there. It was a beautiful, clear dusk to be outside. Even the smell of sulfur in the air was sweet. For nearly a year, Saul and Mary had been dating. Saul was mostly happy. Mary was pretty, sweet, decent in bed, didn't try to get in the way of his work. He was only weeks away from trading his motorcycle for a Camaro and driving to California to stay with Nolan and Paula for a few weeks. He was bringing a very rough prototype of a simple game about table tennis. He expected Nolan to like the concept and that would mean that he would have to leave his mother and work in California. It would be hard to leave her again. The doctors were recommending a wheelchair, though she was resisting it. And what to do about Mary?

"What do you think about California?" Saul said.

"It's far away."

"I know," Saul said. "But that's where the work is."

"Who's going to take care of your mother?"

Saul remained silent.

"Maybe I can stay here and take care of her until you come back."

Saul looked at Mary. "You would do that?"

"Of course," Mary said. "Family is the most important."

Saul stiffened. He agreed that family was important, but he would not for one second consider taking care of Mary's parents were they sick or invalid or even troubled with a cold. Mary's family lived in Bordirtoun and ran a terrible take-out place. They were planning to return to Hong Kong in a few years when they retired. Saul hoped that would happen.

"You are truly a good person," Saul said, shifting with discomfort as his legs grew numb under the weight of Mary's lower body. Why did she have to straddle him like this? For someone who had so much attitude when they first met, Mary had certainly become clingy. "If you can just make sure she's okay for a few weeks until I figure out what Nolan wants—"

"If we get married soon, then it will be important for both families to be together and close by," she said.

Mary went on about family but Saul's attention wandered. There it was, the word marriage. Was he ready? This was the first time he had slept with only one person for so long. Lately, the sex had become a little routine. He was starting to want others. Not in a serious way, of course. He didn't feel like leaving Mary right this moment. They were still having fun. But even his mother had warned him that if you eat chow mein every day—

"Saul?" Mary said. "What are you thinking?"

"Nothing."

"Are you thinking about family?" she said. "Are you thinking about your father?"

Saul chuckled with rue. "No, why would I be thinking about him?" When he was ready to start a family, Saul would never abandon them like his father did. Even if things were bad, you had to stick them out. That's what family was all about.

"Don't you wonder about him sometimes?"

"Not really," Saul said. After a pause, he added, "I don't want to be like him, though. When I get married, I'm sticking with it. I'm not going to escape with the first Mexican that comes along." He liked how confident he sounded, and also thought it was a good point to touch upon to firm up Mary's commitment to watch his mother while he was in California.

Mary smiled. "I know you're not the type of person to do that. You're a good person."

Saul nodded and squeezed Mary closer. "I try," he said.

"Saul?"

"Hmm?"

Mary All this is not to imply touched her belly. Saul figured she had a stomachache. Just as he was about to ask her if she felt okay, Mary said, "I think I'm pregnant."

7.

JAYNUSS FINALLY RETURNED MY CALL today. He sounded surprisingly upbeat, but when I asked him whether he had been reading my pages, he answered no. I reminded him that my parole hearing was only a week away.

"Don't worry, Pongy," he said. "I've got a new angle for you."

"I'm listening."

"One of the parole board members is sssssmmmmooookin'."

"And?"

"I fucked her," Jaynuss said. "Last night. Twice."

"What's this got to do with me?"

"I still got game!"

"I'm going to be in here the rest of my sentence, aren't I?"

"My game is good for you, Pongy," he said. "I had her in every position. Hoooo! I left a message for my ex-wife and told her about it. Bull-fucking-shit I can't keep it up!"

"Please call me Sulliver," I said. "My name is Sulliver."

"Yes, Sulliver, yes it is," Jaynuss said. "I told her about you."

"Your ex-wife?"

"No, aren't you listening?" he said. "Ashlene, the parole board member! She'll be your champion at the hearing."

"But she's only one person."

"It only takes one."

"Actually, it takes three out of five," I said. "There's a vote."

Jaynuss fell silent. He released a lengthy belch. "Really?"

Anyone who is seeking evidence of natural selection need look no further than the collective IQ of Bordirtoun's legal community. Jaynuss mentioned once that he got his law degree from an American university in Cancun. "Haven't you ever been to a parole hearing?"

"Let me call you back," Jaynuss said. "I gotta pee. My cock's sore from fucking."

Back to Pong v. Pong. Five months before the election. Early July. I announced my candidacy shortly after Lene left. She was a superior estranged wife in every way: she settled my bill with The Pongelliano (with the remainder of her inheritance) and generously offered to fly back to Bordirtoun to appear as my wife once (and only once) before the election.

The irony does not escape me. Sometimes, late at night, I think about what I had said to my father ("The Bordirtoun people will learn every last truth about you") and cackle like a psychopath, waking my fellow inmates. Quite absurd I would say such a thing after my own equestrian course of lies. Marriage on the rocks, a candidate for mayor of a town whose citizens I have never respected. Well on my way, I was, towards becoming Saul. After a long campaign day, I would look myself in the mirror and see Saul's trademark slouch and bulbous eyes, and my breathing passages would narrow, my chest ache. I'd feel empty in the belly even after inhaling one of the many large late-night room service meals I was fond of ordering whenever I was lonely. Worse than becoming Saul, I feared I was becoming a lesser version of him. His dubious actions never appeared to cause him heartburn or chest pain, and yet, my various compromises torment me to this day.

The campaign was now all I had, and I threw myself into the work of becoming mayor. T.R. was my campaign manager, Taryn my publicist, and we called ourselves the SPB (the Sulliver Pong Braintrust). We turned a Courtyard by Marriott downtown into our headquarters. Living on public funds and contributions, my daily schedules looked something like this:

6am—7 am
Location: Fitness Center
Activity: Groin stretches
Participants: Sulliver Pong

7am—8am
Location: Conference Center
Activity: Daily Briefing
Participants: The Sulliver Pong Braintrust (SPB)

8am—11am
Location: North End
Activity: Sycophantic breakfast session
Topic: Donate and I'll stuff your pockets later
Participants: The SPB, North End business group of the day

11am—1pm
Location: East Side

Activity: Sycophantic lunch session
Topic: See prior appointment
Participants: The SPB, East Side business group of the day

1pm—5pm
Location: Old Town
Activity: Sycophantic praise session (note to self: keep eyes shut when praying)
Topic: Muffling my atheism
Participants: The SPB, Various ethnically segregated church groups

5pm—8pm
Location: Bordirtoun Two TV
Activity: Televised interview
Topic: Look at how hard I'm working while my dad is out free-fucking
Participants: The SPB, Bordirtoun Two reporter

8pm—11pm
Location: Miscellaneous
Activity: Town hall
Topic: Why I was a man of the people, and why the people should donate liberally
Participants: Me and "the people"

Please don't misunderstand my attempts at humor. All this is not to imply that I didn't *have faith* in small town politics. In my more robin-breasted moments, I wondered if I wasn't *naturally gifted* in the ways of the local politician. Firm handshake, look a person in the eyes, speak loudly, clearly, and contemplatively, use only platitudes so your words can't be used against you. I started falling asleep with the television on just to absorb the spoken rhythms of news anchors. Before I'd go to bed, in the car between campaign stops, or on the toilet, I skimmed urban planning reports, treatises on homelessness, environmental regulations, border patrols, and other dry documents T.R. said my father would never read. An Old Town church let us borrow one of its cars during the campaign; a Ford Explorer, a few years old, not as elitist as Saul Pong's car service, not ragtag enough to hurt us with the moneymen. Sure, the pandering and long hours weren't ideal. But if I wasn't naturally gifted as a politician, I was at least a born vacillator!

Let me speak briefly, if I may, about the plight of the noble, suffering Bordirtouners. My father had stepped up the Rio River relocations. Thousands had been told to get on luxury buses (destination: barracks) or migrate west on their own. My father issued an order to limit eastbound traffic on the bridge to "administration-approved" vehicles until the Old Town redevelopment was completed. Every day, it took us an extra two hours to circumvent the bridge to get back over the river.

A week after I announced my candidacy, we held a rally outside Rio River. That day was the coldest in Bordirtoun in two decades. Vapors billowed from my mouth as I waited, in my blazer and tie, a few strides away from our makeshift podium. The Bordirtoun Two news van was parked down the dirt road, and the camera operator tripoded his camera, cigarette in mouth. T.R. and Taryn were talking to him, giving directions, I presumed. I did a double take on my friends in their dark wool coats and scarves, both looking so grownup and determined, and I firmed my jaw and straightened my posture, trying to will myself to care about the people behind the chain-link fence.

I stared out into a diffuse murmuring audience of twenty or so, standing roughly thirty yards from the Rio River entrance. My father's people had erected a billboard above the gates that read, "Welcumm to Quango Valley, affordibble tounhousing for Bordirtoun." Uniformed guards loitered at their stations, cradling rifles. The relocated Old Towners crowded the fence.

Taryn handed me the speech. "Are you ready?"

"What's the name of this place again?" I said, smiling as I slid my gaze to the light fuzz on the meat of her cheeks.

"Ha-ha," Taryn said dryly.

"River Rio," I said. "River River."

"Close enough."

"But there's no river anywhere near here."

"Wait 'til the thumbs-up," she said.

"Aren't you going to wish me luck?"

"If you don't even know the name of this place, luck won't do you any good." Taryn guided me forward and issued a thumbs-up to the camera operator before walking away. I strode to the podium and unfolded the speech, written by the Grathes, and vaguely approved by myself.

"Ladies, gentlemen, fellow Bordirtouners," I began. "As we stand here today outside the blight that is the Rio River internment camps, I want you to imagine a new, better Bordirtoun. A Bordirtoun where hardworking taxpayers aren't trapped here because someone wants to build a giant shopping mall. A Bordirtoun with a leader who remembers what it was like to have principles. I am a Bordirtouner as my father before me. But unlike him, I will work for you day and night to make your vision of a better Bordirtoun come true."

I paused, annoyed at the "Bordirtouner as my father before me" phrase that sounded very Jedi Knight. I kicked myself for not reading the draft more closely. At least half the audience looked to be younger than voting age. I decided to dump the speech and improvise.

"When I was younger," I went on. "I watched my father, our mayor, abuse my mother. Physically. Emotionally. And I just stood by and let it happen. Right now, he is doing the same to you. While Old Town residents are being bussed here to Rio River, Saul Pong is spending your tax dollars traveling the globe and running a chain of strip clubs. As citizens, it is time for you to ask if he is the man you want to lead this town into the future. As citizens, it's time for you to say 'no more!'"

"Stop," a pubescent girl whined as her boyfriend tried to grope her breasts.

"That's right," I said. "Stop!" I pointed at the boy. He looked at me sheepishly, his oblong head upturned, hands at his sides.

"It's time for each and every one of you to stand up and say, 'Stop!'" I slammed my fist on the podium. "If my father won't tear down Rio River, when I am mayor, I will!"

I finished my speech to tepid applause and thunderous audio feedback. Taryn scurried into the news van. The red light of the camera went dim, and the operator started to dismantle the tripod. The audience began to disperse, and I was planted at the podium, not knowing where to go next. Most of the stump speeches to date had been similarly anticlimactic.

T.R. walked up to me. "Nice job!" he said. "That's going to make a nice sound bite tonight."

I waved at the people watching us through the fence. They were remarkably placid and well-behaved, like they'd been caged for years.

"Can we talk to them?" I asked.

"The guards won't let us get any closer," T.R. said.

The uniformed men informed us that we had to stay at least ten yards from the entrance. I held a thumbs-up to the people behind the fence. A few applauded and whistled. Someone shouted, "Way to go, Saul!"

"Please call me Sulliver!" I corrected. "My name is Sulliver!" Then I shouted, "I will get you out of here! Each and every one of you!"

When I walked back toward T.R., a bespectacled round Chinese man with slicked-back silver hair and a medium-sized paunch was standing next to him, waiting for me. He said he was Saul's cousin, my first cousin once removed. I looked more closely and recognized him as Cousin Sarly. I recalled visiting his apartment with my father when I was younger and discovering a gargantuan library of *Playboy*s in his closet.

"Sully," he said, shaking my hand limply. "I am so proud of you."

I thanked him. Cousin Sarly promptly informed me that my father owed him $100,000 on a real estate deal thirty years ago.

"That's without interest," he said. "My mother warned me not to do business with him."

"I'm sorry to hear that," I said. "But that sounds like Saul."

"How is your grandfather?"

"My grandfather?"

"Saul's father."

I told him that I didn't know my grandfather. All I knew about him was that he had left the family when my father was young.

"Ah," Cousin Sarly said. "He's a painter. Lives in Portugal. When my mother was terminally ill with cancer a few years ago, Robinson flew out to see her in Los Angeles even though he was in his nineties. He's my mother's brother. So my mother would be your grandaunt."

"Oh, nice," I said. "I mean, not nice that your mother passed away. That's terrible. I'm sorry about that." I wasn't sure what else to say. I couldn't be expected to know every living Pong.

Cousin Sarly put a finger to his nose and blew a stream of mucus at my feet. I looked away. "Nice to see you, Sully," he said, holding out his snot-trigger hand. "I just wanted to see if you knew if your grandfather was still alive."

Masking my disgust, I shook his hand and said, "I have no clue."

I seemed to meet someone like Cousin Sarly after every

speech: someone screwed by my father. There was an architect who had a lawsuit pending against Saul for stealing her design of The Pongelliano. The very attractive and articulate staff member who was suing for sexual harassment (Saul told her that her behind was so delicious that he wanted to bite it like an apple). The tea shop owner who was asked to pay Saul $40,000 in cash to expedite permits to set up shop at the airport. And then there was Drew and Werder, both of whom joined my team after they were fired when it was brought to my father's attention that they had given me free drinks. T.R. put them in charge of our rapidly growing PFO (Personal Foible Office); they were responsible for important campaign projects like digging up my father's former mistresses or finding out whether he had snorted cocaine.

The feeling of others counting on you, believing in you, being proud of you; well, for someone who hadn't worked at all in months, maybe years, you could see how I could enjoy this new sense of purpose.

Did I mention I was winning? Eleven points ahead in late July. Saul hadn't publicly commented on my candidacy. His spokesperson claimed the mayor was running unopposed, that my entrance into the race was a private issue between father and son, a misunderstanding soon to be resolved. I don't know why his campaign didn't move against me in those opening days. Whenever I am in a forgiving mood, I give my father the benefit of the doubt—I assume that he was genuinely conflicted about my continued antipathy toward him. I imagine he was frustrated by his inability to circumvent my stubborn opposition, to persuade me that my anger was misplaced. When I am in a less forgiving mood, I simply imagine that he was too busy cooking Bordirtoun Omelettes in bed for his showgirls in his penthouse suite to attend to his campaign.

Speaking of extramarital intercourse or the hope of such intercourse, in the early days of the campaign, Taryn and I were nearly inseparable. Between the daily press releases, interviews, and planning sessions, she worked long hours with the rest of us, despite her advancing pregnancy. I got the feeling that she also enjoyed a new sense of purpose, something she'd been missing since T.R. ran against my father four years before.

At first, I tried to keep my distance, without discouraging our closeness. Taryn had never been afraid of getting physically close to someone. We were often nearly nose-to-nose in public. Soon, I found myself encouraging her, noticing her first in a room full of staffers and volunteers, then sidling casually to her side at the first opportunity. I'd find her hand on my shoulder and my hand on her far flank and tell myself to stop there (don't pull her near!). I'd look into her eyes and smile and unload affected cringe-inducers like, "How's my favorite soon-to-be mother?" or "Ms. Grathe, you look lovely this evening," or "My, you certainly glow tonight," and Taryn would laugh open-mouthed, humoring me.

In the beginning, I stopped at benign flirting, a smidge of the victimless encouragement. Soon, however, the nightly fundraisers involved me partaking in a couple of glasses of wine or champagne, and there were enough people in a room to make talking to each other difficult, and I'd have to hold Taryn close as we alternately spoke loudly into each other's ears. I'd whiff the sweet scent of her hair and begin to wonder whether others noticed how close we were because it certainly seemed to me that Ms. Grathe was, indeed, in my arms instead of her husband's nearly every night of the week.

I had an idea we were becoming a topic of gossip when my staff would ask where Taryn was whenever I entered the room alone—day or night—and when I replied that I didn't know, the room fell quiet, and no one looked me in the eye.

One night, Taryn and I found each other at the hotel bar, the last to leave a town hall meeting, and she confided in me that she'd become concerned that Jimbor no longer found her attractive. In recent months, he had stopped touching her with affection.

"I'm sure it's because you two have been busy," I said. "You're pregnant. Maybe he's afraid to hurt the baby. It's perfectly natural."

Taryn nodded. "Maybe."

"Have you talked to him about how you feel?"

She said she had not.

"Maybe you should."

"I know I should."

"Of course. I never tell you anything you don't know already."

"Oh!" Taryn grabbed my hand. "I accidentally checked his email the other day. He's in a knitting group. How come I didn't know he was in a knitting group?"

How come I knew, I asked myself. Her hand was soft and warm. "There's nothing untoward about knitting." I stroked her supple knuckle with my free hand.

"Then why don't I know about it?"

"Maybe he hasn't had a chance to tell you."

"So you think I'm being paranoid."

No, I thought. "Perhaps," I said. "You guys just need to spend more time together."

We unhanded each other. "You're right," she said. "After all, he doesn't know I'm here tonight. I forgot to tell him I'd be out late."

"Tit for tat."

Taryn laughed. "Did you say 'tits for tats?'"

I snuck a glance at her breasts, ample, fuller than Lene's. "I'm running for mayor. I can't talk about tits." I put my hands to my flabby pectorals. "If anyone asks, I was talking about my tits."

On the first day of August, outside the hotel window, white flakes spiraled deliberately through the air. Snow? The ground was frosted, and a car below scraped and fishtailed as it left the parking lot. I turned on the television, and the news said it was the first snowstorm in Bordirtoun in over a hundred years. Looking out at the sludgy river and flat landscape of Old Town and the black mountains beyond, I thought: this was what I had traded my marriage for. A starving man's Reno.

I phoned Lene, as I had daily since she'd left, trying to restart a friendship and keep my marriage alive. Unfortunately, on this day, she didn't answer, and unfortunately, during our previous calls, I would learn that Lene's friends and family had never understood what she saw in me and were genuinely surprised our marriage had lasted as long as it did. Lene had returned to her life of dinners with colleagues, weekends alone (as far as I knew), and trips to the countryside to visit nieces and nephews. Occasionally, there were even longer getaways to Malmö and Oslo with unnamed *venner* or "friends."

The unexpected snow shut down the bridges, and we had to cancel the rest of our appearances that week. We met over a few brews on the patio of The Castle of Pong Tavern. Inside, Atari memorabilia covered the walls. Missile Command dart boards. Old Atari VCS ads. Posters for Yar's Revenge and Star Raiders. There was a vending machine with game cartridges from the 1970s. No video poker or shuffleboard here. Each table featured an operational, vintage PONG console. At our picnic table, Werder and Drew played PONG with nail-bit intensity. T.R. and I watched the midday news on the beer garden telly. The latest poll showed that my lead had increased to fifteen points.

T.R. led the patrons in a cheer.

"We haven't won anything yet," I said. But I soaked it in, beatific, and falsely modest. In the polls, I could find solace. I stared out across the street at a small park, blanketed in white. Even the cactus was frosty. Two arrays of bundled-up children pitched snowballs at each other. In an attempt to dodge an offensive, a child in a crimson scarf inadvertently ran into the cactus, collapsing in the white.

T.R. sprung from the table and trotted across the street. I regretted, in that moment, not doing the same. He lifted the child to his feet and dusted snow off him. The boy wobbled, but straightened. T.R. applauded, and the children followed. I found myself thinking that, in a better world, a better Bordirtoun, someone like T.R. would be mayor instead.

Someone placed a hand on my shoulder. It was Taryn. I half-stood, prepared to put my arm around her and give her a peck on the cheek (a greeting I had become especially fond of reserving for her since we began spending so much time together), but out of the corner of my eye, Jimbor appeared, holding a pint and sporting a lengthy, newly braided goatee. Quite the craftsy fellow, that Jimbor.

I aborted my greeting and reached to shake his hand instead. "Jimbor, how are ya?" I said loudly in my campaign function voice.

"Sull-ver," he said.

Taryn lowered herself onto the bench and grimaced a greeting to Werder and Drew, both of whom lifted their gaze from PONG only long enough to nod.

I asked Taryn how she was feeling.

She rolled her eyes and said she felt like a whale as Jimbor answered, "Can't wait."

"No, he can't," Taryn said.

"You're in a bad mood," Jimbor said to her.

"This weather is ridiculous," she said.

Jimbor reached for his pint. In three gulps, he finished half his beer.

Taryn exhaled suddenly. "I wish I didn't have to miss part of the campaign," she said.

"The campaign is the last thing you should be worrying about," I told her.

"Sull-ver's right," Jimbor said, suppressing a burp. "Worry about the baby," he added just as I said, "Worry about your well-being."

I tried to exchange eye contact with Taryn, but she tucked a lock of her auburn hair behind an ear and stared blankly at the PONG screen. I told Jimbor yet again how happy I was for them.

"I hear you've been busy, Jim."

"Lots of night shifts," Jimbor said.

"Knitting," Taryn said. She laughed to herself.

Jimbor and I exchanged a look that I'm ashamed to confess contained equal parts fear and conspiracy. The secrets we men held from our women.

"How's the groin?" he asked.

"Little sore and tight today, thanks for asking," I replied. Taryn smiled, and I felt warm.

"Must be the cold," Jimbor said, without noting my irony. "Keep it stretched." He stared into the tavern. I turned to see what he was looking at and saw five figures approaching. They wore long dark wool coats with fur collars. The man in the middle was my father. His cologne and hairspray smelled fruity and strong. I remembered that Saul had once brought me to this very tavern (which at the time did not have PONG consoles) to meet his political opponent, the good Reverend Grathe. Saul had tried to talk him into dropping out of the race for supervisor. It was then, when Reverend Grathe recognized and addressed me by name before I was introduced, that Saul discovered that I had befriended the reverend's children. My first betrayal of my father.

Saul nodded, flat-lipped at the others. He stared at Drew and Werder.

"I'd like a word with my son," my father said.

"You ain't the boss here, Saul," Drew replied.

The others looked to me. I nodded, and my team stood and left. Saul sat across the table where Jimbor had vacated. His men remained standing. They were all lean, tall Asian men with stiff orderly coiffures parted right of center, like clones of the son my father wished he had. They marched across the wooden deck, their boots thumping, before stopping and blocking my view of the park. Saul cleared his throat, his sagging, crinkled Adam's apple not unlike a testicle.

"Why does your team get to stay?" I asked.

"Why do you say such mean things about me in your speeches?"

"Because I'm honest."

My father harrumphed. A vapor spouted from his lips and disappeared as quickly as it came.

"What can I do for you?" I said.

"I want a truce."

I laughed.

"Do you really think you have what it takes to be mayor?" Saul said.

"We'll let the people decide."

He snickered. "And you criticize me of hoo-brisk."

"Hubris," I corrected.

"I don't understand why we can't work together instead of fighting."

"We're not fighting."

"We are fighting."

"No, you fight Momma," I said, putting up my fists and mocking a left jab.

My father's expression soured. "You are so unpleasant."

"I've learned from you."

"I didn't pay for your education so you could lecture me," Saul said.

"Are you going to hold that over me for the rest of my life?" I said. "Christ, I'm sorry I ever went to school. Maybe I should be illiterate like you. Everything would have been different if I had just gotten that student loan." I immediately regretted raising my voice when I noticed Saul suppressing a smile.

"I propose we have a press conference," he said. "I'll retire and endorse you as a continuation of the Pong administration, and I'll train you, ensuring a smooth transition. Like a proper father and son."

"Why would I do that?" I said. "I'm winning. Haven't you noticed?"

"You don't understand what you're doing," Saul said. "The Old Town redevelopment cannot be disrupted. It cannot even be *threatened* with disruption."

"What about the people at Rio River?"

My father laughed. "You don't care about those people."

"I care more than you."

"You have the luxury to play the maybe mayor. 'If I were mayor, I would have done this. If I were mayor, I would have done that.' If you knew all the facts, you would understand that I have no choice. The Quango Valley housing development is my only option."

"You mean the Rio River internment camps."

"Quango Valley."

"Rio River."

"You seem to relish hating me and whatever it is I've done to you," Saul said. "I've always been there for you. I never loved your mother. So many times, I wanted to leave, but I stayed for you. I never even laid a hand on you."

I applauded mockingly. "Wow. Congratulations. Do you think that just because you didn't leave or hit me that you've been a good father?"

Saul pounded a fist on the table. "Stop talking about how I hit people!"

"Does it shame you?"

"*You* shame me."

"Finally, something we agree on."

Both of us fell quiet, resting, our breaths visible in quick clouds. The PONG console reverted to its demo mode, the white square slugging back and forth. I heard Taryn laughing and T.R. playing loudly with the children in the park. Saul's men stood between me and my friends, rigid, a black wall that kept me in my filth, my genetic filth.

"Not every development has been as successful as my hotel," Saul said finally. "The Old Town redevelopment is payback to my investors for the failures. They will get almost all the revenues from the project for the first five years. I know very well that normally a redevelopment of this scale would come up for a vote as a proposition. And we would have a better plan for housing for the displaced. But we simply didn't have time. My investors want their returns now."

"Sounds like your problem, not mine."

"It's your problem too. These investors will be very invested in my winning if we don't work together. You'll find this out soon if we don't team up."

"So you're here for my benefit, right?"

My father rolled his eyes. "Do the press conference, Sulliver," he said. "We put forth a united front. Then I will tell you everything."

I could not remember the last time he used my full first name. "The only reason people support me is because I'm against you," I said. "If there's no difference between me and you, I might as well drop out. Tear down Rio River and find housing for the people you've displaced. Then we'll talk."

"Are you crazy?"

"What do I get for helping you, then?"

"You're not understanding me." He glanced at his men and lowered his voice. "These people, my investors, do not react well to losing. Do you understand?"

I was not sure I did.

"Do you hate me so much?" he said. "Would you even care if I was in danger?"

If my father was in danger and asked for my help, I would have liked to think of myself as a person who would have said yes without hesitation. Just as I said yes (with numerous hesitations) when Saul asked me to visit Momma because she was allegedly (not at all) depressed. At that moment, with my father sitting across the table from me, his nostrils flaring, I remembered I had felt similarly guilty, similarly conflicted in my flat in Copenhagen during my father's first visit. I would not be fooled again, I decided.

"I don't believe you," I said.

"Goddamn you," he spat, his large hair flopping forward.

"Do you want me to list your lies since you called me in Copenhagen?"

Saul shook his head and sighed. "Amateur," he muttered.

"You're losing," I said. "Lose like a man, old man."

My father's men leaned forward, one of them edging toward Saul. The mayor held up a hand, his fingers quavering. Snowflakes flitted randomly and sideways between us, melting against my father's cheeks. I puffed my chest. For once, I had silenced him; I had rightly responded to his barb. This was the changing of the guard, I told myself, the moment in a man's life when he officially becomes more capable than his father. I was Mr. Fifteen-Point Lead.

He stood and motioned for his men to follow him out. I kept my gaze on the steady, falling snow, hoping he would leave saying nothing more. But before he walked back into the tavern, Saul said in a low, shivering voice:

"I'm sorry, Sully. I really am. For what's about to happen."

As mistakes go, where would I mount this mistake in the pantheon of Pong mistakes? Because that's what my decision to assume that my father was lying about the criminal ties of his investors was: a mistake. Does it beat Millmore Pong's decision not to strike with his fellow railroad workers? Does it surpass Parris Pong's misspelling of Bordirtoun or his ill-fated Sunday morning walk to Sunblaze Wilde's house on the day of her disappearance after he'd spent all night gambling, taking shots of moonshine, and hollering and firing his gun at the full moon for no discernable reason? Does it outrank the morning that Francisco Pong decided to take a walk down Main Street even though the entire town was abuzz with Yellow Peril, and most Asian-Americans, Japanese or Chinese, were staying indoors at night because of lynchings and "Keep Bordirtoun White" campaigns? Well, sadly, I think my decision not to help my father was a mistake that would make a Hall of Fame of Pong mistakes. There were still many to come, of course! Had I decided to team up with him then and help complete his Old Town project, I would not be in jail today. I would be the mayor of Bordirtoun, and all of my father's stakeholders would have gotten their returns and promises of future business in Bordirtoun. We, the Pongs, would have had our happy ending.

My father would not give up his mayorship without a fight. He had only been waiting to see if he could work out a deal with me. But once I rejected him, Saul knew he would have to campaign as if his life depended on it.

The cold weather persisted but the snow had stopped falling,

long enough to create a dark ground slush. After my early morning
groin stretches in the fitness center and four plates at the breakfast
buffet, T.R. and I headed out the revolving door to the car to begin
our day. The morning was brisk and bright, and I looked down
the lengthy sag of Main Street, the alternating red brick and adobe
buildings on either side. My father's statue rotated squeakily in the
horizon. To my right, cars on the bowed highway overpass were
hardly moving. A patrol car drove on the shoulder, sirens flashing,
lisping past the traffic. An accident, I thought. My foot hit the
sidewalk and fishtailed. I told myself to be careful. Then my other
foot hit and gave, and very quickly, the scene blurred. I landed on my
tailbone with a crack and immediately knew something was broken.

"Sull!" T.R. promptly grabbed me with both hands and tried to
hoist me up. But the pain blazed in my lower back, and my legs went
numb. I screamed for him to let me down.

I would find myself in the same hospital room I'd stayed in
during my first visit to Bordirtoun. When the doctor walked in, she
was chewing a half-eaten stick of beef jerky as she stared at my chart.
Her leaning tower of peacocked bangs threatened to collapse over her
face but held. She asked me to lie on my side and inserted a gloved
finger (sans jerky and not so gently) into my rectum. I had fractured
my coccyx, she told me. I'd have to spend the next few days in bed.

"Why does this always happen to me?" I asked.

She swallowed her jerky. "You are carrying some extra weight."

Later that day, T.R. and Taryn arrived with flowers and cards,
and I was thinking about what my father had said. I told them that I
was convinced that Saul would launch an offensive, and I'd be unable
to respond since I was lying in a hospital bed struggling to poop
without pain.

Taryn sat in a chair, bracing her abdomen. "Worry about getting
better," she said.

"You're in good hands," T.R. said. "When you're better, you'll be ready for the stretch run."

"Can you get me a phone to call Lene?" I asked. "Please. Thanks."

"Sure," T.R. said, leaving Taryn and me.

I looked Taryn up and down and noticed how her flushed and bloated expression didn't stop me from looking her up and down. My tailbone throbbed, and the painkillers were wearing off.

"When are you deserting me?" I said, referring to her upcoming maternity leave.

"Probably at the end of the week."

"I'm going to miss seeing you every day."

Taryn stood and put her hands on her buttocks. "Ugh, I'm so big!"

"So am I. The doctor said that my extra weight made the fracture worse. Bitch."

"Thank God I didn't slip and fall."

"You're not that huge," I said with a smirk. She slapped my arm. Then we both laughed for a bit until the laughter trailed off into silence and awkward separation.

"How are things going with your wife?" Taryn said finally.

I exhaled. "It's been tough."

Another silence. Outside, the hiss of a car going too fast in the snow. "I'm sorry," I said as she said the same.

"What are you sorry for?" I asked.

"About your marriage," she said, eyes averted.

Was that all, I wondered?

"What are you sorry about?" she asked me.

"For bringing you into my marital problems."

"Don't be ridiculous," she said. "You've listened to me complain about Jimbor."

"Things better?"

Taryn shrugged. "Tough to tell," she said. "We never seem to be in the same place at the same time anymore. Look, here I am at the hospital, and it just so happens that he's not working today."

"Next time, I'll break something when he's around."

She laughed.

"I never, ever thought I'd be separated," I said. "I was never, ever going to be like Saul. It's hard to get up in the morning. If it wasn't for the campaign, I'd be in bed all day."

Taryn palmed my pate and said nothing. "You're not like him."

"Thanks for saying that." I put my hand on her forearm, and her hand moved down to my cheek.

"I'm not just saying it," she said.

I took her hand off my face and held two fingers. I started growing hard. "I don't know if I'd be able to get through this without you."

Her face darkened. Then she winced and pulled her hand away.

"Big kick," she said.

In the hall, the roll of the phone stand grew louder and closer. T.R. entered the room and plugged the phone into the jack beside my bed. I cleared my throat.

"The baby's kicking," I told T.R. Loudly.

Was I actually in love with Taryn, pining for her in the way Wordsworth might? I'm not certain. Were there commonalities between Taryn and me that Lene and I didn't share? Absolutely. But did that mean I had found a new love, a better love than Lene? Unclear. Was I curious what it'd be like to be with Taryn, after all these years? Of course. I was searching, I realize now. I was tempting and teasing adultery because I was searching. For something pure, perhaps? Some idealized version of love? Or was it cultural sameness?

Romance? A joining of the loins? I don't pretend to be sure. But I was hoping a transgression might happen, though I was not courageous enough to let her know that I wished to have her ass up, her breasts in my hands, and maybe, if we had time, I also desired a go at her sizable pregnant tits, as someone like Saul might do.

"I think you should push this storyline further," Jaynuss said to me today.

"My desire for Taryn?"

"No, the titty-fucking."

"Janning!" I said.

Jaynuss cackled, describing in detail how the parole board member, Ashlene, had sizable tits, and he had just had a go at them the previous night. Twice.

I didn't respond, and Jaynuss sighed. "You're not someone who is capable of planning a murder," he said solemnly. "Contemplating adultery is one thing; murdering someone, like your relative Parris did, is another. First, you are an innocent man. Second, you are an innocent man who has served most of a guilty man's sentence without complaint, like that guy Millmore who worked the railroads and got syphilis from his slutty wife. Third, you've embraced your avuncular role in the penitentiary and mentored other inmates, like that fucker Francisco the pastor who loved to give shitty advice to his congregation."

"My granduncle Millmore got syphilis?" I asked.

"You didn't know this?" Jaynuss said. "James John Jang, the curator of the Museum of PONG, recently self-published a book named *The Misadventures of the Bordirtoun Pongs*."

I told him I hadn't read it and that I'd heard most of my family stories in oral snippets from either Saul or Momma.

"It's a good read," he said. "You come from generations and generations of idiots and jerks."

"I'm afraid I don't need to read a book to glean this knowledge."

"Finally and most importantly," Jaynuss continued. "Ashlene is in love with me, and she's currently trying to use her feminine charms on two of the board members. So, Sulliver, I'm optimistic."

I wanted to believe him. "Thanks, Janning."

"Look, Sully," Jaynuss said. "When I was married and things got tough, I fell in love with another woman, an old married friend. Real love. Emotional. I had this affair with her in my mind. Sure, there would be the sexual fantasies, but the fantasies that stay with me even today are the ones I had doing silly things to make her smile, all the things I'd stopped doing for my wife. I never acted on my impulses, even though I sensed that my friend was interested too."

"Do you regret it?"

"Sometimes," Jaynuss said. "In the end, we both got divorced anyway. She remarried and moved away. The moment had passed us by."

I started thinking about all the potentially life-changing moments I had let pass me by. The many loves that I hadn't acted upon. Even the many times I chose not to mend my relationship with my parents. The sheer number of moments, the nature of them, overwhelmed me into a long silence.

Jaynuss cleared his throat. "I think you should volunteer to teach English to the inmates," he said, his voice cracking. "It would be good PR."

In my hospital bed, nursing my broken tailbone, I idly channel-surfed and saw my parents on television, sitting beside each other on a bright orange couch, holding hands on "The Remus Sans-Lubé Hour," a highly-rated local talk show. Latino and middle-aged, Sans-Lube was one of those hosts who made it a point to look as smitten with his guests as possible—he salivated over my parents like they were pigs at a luau.

The camera drew close on Saul as he talked. He doted upon Momma, holding both her hands and occasionally allowing his eyes to grow misty while biting his lip. "We've worked out our differences," he said. "Divorce was never an option. It's a lesson for anyone in Bordirtoun who's had marital problems. Work it out. Blame is tempting, but it's never the fault of one person only."

"What do you think is motivating your son?" Sans-Lubé asked.

"I don't know," Saul said. "I do know that with the proper guidance of someone with political experience, like myself, Sulliver could be a fine mayor."

"His friends, bad people," Momma said in English, issuing a pained smile as the camera turned to her.

"That's my wife's opinion," Saul said. "She looks at his campaign team and sees T.R. Grathe, who has always been an outsider, a marginal city politician with no notable accomplishments. I can see where my wife is coming from, but I'll reserve judgment until Sulliver allows me to speak to him further, maybe during a family vacation or a long dinner or perhaps a minor league baseball game. Go Bordirtoun Bombers! I'd like to know what he's thinking."

"So he won't speak to you?"

Saul shook his head and sighed. He moved my mother's hand to his knee and squeezed. "He's very angry at me for reasons I don't fully understand. I think he and I would make a great team, if he'd only let me in."

"Fucker!" I pounded my fists on the bed. Then my surroundings turned red, and I was soon grasping for my bottle of painkillers.

The phone brayed beside me. I picked up, and without thinking, unleashed a stream of racial epithets about Chinese people. Had I been overheard, my brief political career would have been over.

"Sully?" It was T.R.

"Fucking family!"

"Relax."

"Relax?" I barked. "This is just the beginning!"

"Calm down," T.R. said. "Take a deep breath. Seriously. You're scaring Taryn's unborn child."

I did as T.R. suggested and felt momentary relief. "You, of all people, should know this is about to get ugly," I said.

"Don't get ugly with him," T.R. said. "You're the better candidate."

My campaign issued a statement regarding my accident and for twenty-four hours, I fielded interviews from news crews, during which I smiled broadly, gave thumbs-up, took pictures with hospital workers, and assured my supporters that before they knew it, I'd be back on the streets, fighting for the less fortunate Bordirtouner. My room filled with flower vases (which I asked to have removed due to allergies), cards and chocolates (never liked sweets), and several jockstraps from young voters who thought they were being funny.

Meanwhile, my father was on the evening news each night I was in the hospital, touting his record of redeveloping Old Town, refurbishing the airport, increasing awareness of Bordirtoun at home and abroad, and growing the local economy. He accused me of using Rio River as a political football and blasted me for having no other solutions. The day before I was released from the hospital, a front-page story in the *Bordirtoun Daily* reported that an independent audit commission was investigating several Pong Foundation executives for allegedly giving themselves large raises and bonuses. At first, I thought that was good news. Then I read that the audit commissioner was a "local business owner" named Dr. Murray Jean-Baptiste Quango, and I was on the list of the investigated.

I heard a knock on my door. It was T.R., carrying my breakfast.

I flung the newspaper across the room.

"Morning to you too," T.R. said flatly, as he rested the food tray with the hospital's version of a Bordirtoun Omelette, which smelled vaguely of anus and Lemon Pledge.

"Did you know about this?" I said.

T.R. picked up the splayed paper. "Whoa," he muttered after reading.

The lumpy, rheumy eggs on my plate reminded me suddenly of my teenaged complexion. "T, this is unacceptable."

"You haven't done anything wrong, have you?"

"Of course not."

"Then you have nothing to worry about."

"That's not the point," I said. "The point is, it's your job to know about this. It's our job to retaliate."

"We're trying to get people out of Rio River, remember?" T.R. said he had been working on a city council resolution to issue emergency funding for temporary housing in Old Town. A resolution, he reminded me, that I had supported in a recent speech. Naturally, I had no recollection of the resolution in question. "There are enough real problems in this city for you not to have to resort to twisting the truth like your father would."

"I don't care what I should or shouldn't be resorting to," I said. "Find something we can use against him! It shouldn't be hard. He's Saul Motherfucking Pong!"

T.R. scrutinized me as if I was speaking a mysterious dialect.

"Eat your eggs," he said.

By the time I was released from the hospital, Saul had cut my lead in half. He continued to conduct interviews on every local news program indirectly referencing my connection to the Pong Foundation and directly referencing Momma repeatedly. T.R. counted eighteen references to "Mary and I" or "my wife and I" or "my wife tells me" in a single three-minute spot. Meanwhile, I found myself defending my connection (or lack thereof) to the corrupt Pong Foundation, the Pong Foundation for which I'd never even worked.

Then, of course, there was the small matter of the unsubstantiated rumors of an extramarital affair I was (not) having with the pregnant sister of my campaign manager. It made good columnist fodder, and the photos of Taryn and me, hugging and laughing at fundraisers, our faces close, were very easily construed as something more than it was (whatever it was). If Lene saw them, sufficient explanations would be difficult. Both Taryn and I laughed off the rumors and issued the standard denials, and when Taryn finally took her maternity leave, she said she was thankful not to be hurting the campaign anymore. As for me, all the rumors just made my adulterous yearnings more intense. Not a night went by that I didn't try to find relief in visions of Taryn. One night, I even spent a few moments (perhaps hours) on a site that offered high-priced prostitutes. I shudder now to think that, had I found a redhead who resembled Taryn, I might have hit "submit" on that inquiry form.

A second heavier summer snowstorm moved in, and my new ambulatory self was confined to indoor appearances. Not a good thing in prefab, wood-paneled, pressboard-and-paisley Bordirtoun. An even worse thing for the people of Rio River, who were living in freezing barracks and had been nearly forgotten by local journalists who seemed to think this crazy snowstorm and the father-son mudslinging contest were more worthy stories. The snow made it difficult for either campaign to plan any appearances at Rio River. Despite that, my father had hundreds of generators trucked into "Quango Valley" and made sure the story was well-covered ("*Mayor Pong Brings Warmth To Quango Valley*," a headline read).

I further hurt my chances when I appeared at a Migrant Workers Union event and, during one of my ad-libs, repeatedly sprinkled gratuitous, misused Spanish in my speech ("*Los sientos* for Saul Pong's indifference to your cause! *Los sientos* for Saul Pong's devotion to special interests!"). After I was finished, Jonathan Menendez, the union leader, stepped to the podium and said, in perfect English, to his members, "I know full well that Sulliver's policies will be more effective than his Español."

At night, I'd watch my news sound bites and see myself hobbling around, making verbal gaffes, looking like I'd gained ten pounds, and I'd think that I had no chance of winning. Saul the Shiny Sino-Scoundrel vs. Sull the Sullen Sino-Schlub. I often sat alone in my hotel room, scribbling mediocre and hackneyed Better Bordirtoun ideas on hotel stationery, looking out the window at the white-capped flat roofs of the buildings beyond. On bad days, I would desire Copenhagen summers with Lene, holding hands and walking på Strøget. On other days, however, I'd call the lovely, blooming Taryn ostensibly to see how her pregnancy was progressing, and she and I would sometimes talk for hours, bantering over mundane matters like American reality shows and conservative media outlets, and what we'd do after the election. She was pushing Jimbor to go to business school; I kept talking about patching things up with Lene. We shared a certain wanderlust, a certain disappointment-to-date with how our lives had turned out. We also shared a somewhat delusional optimism that things were always okay and getting better. I missed this very American characteristic in friendships. The Danes tended to be bruisingly fatalistic; they expected very little and if life was going poorly, they would not expect it to get better. In fact, they'd be delighted if it didn't get worse. Casually ask a Danish couple trying to reproduce how they're doing, and they're liable to tell you cheerfully that their *in vitro* treatments would never work or that their sex lives had become quotidian. Lene and I aspired to very little. All we lived for was, well, living. Not so with Taryn. She cared about what most

Americans cared about: aspiring to the ever more.

As much as I enjoyed T.R. and even, on occasion, Drew and Werder (or Thumb and Thumber, as I called them behind their backs), I missed Taryn's presence on the campaign trail. Without her by my side, I was not nearly as enthusiastic about meeting with voters. My flagging energy showed, and by the end of August, my father was slightly ahead in the polls.

Two weeks into Taryn's maternity leave, I arranged for her to be driven to Bordirtoun Steaks, the best steakhouse in town, where I had reserved the VIP room, which had a private parking lot and entrance, and no windows.

There was a single table for two in the center of a room large enough for fifty. A real fireplace blazed. Mounted antlered heads of various sizes and species graced the walls. When the building was Parris's Bordirtoun Brofful, patrons were required to pay for every step they took in the room. The more they paid, the higher level of services they could demand. While I waited for Taryn to arrive, I had several glasses of wine. Courage juice, I thought. Courage to do what, you ask? Well, I didn't even want to admit it to myself.

A doorbell rang, accompanied by a bovine "moo." My tuxedo-wearing server, who wore white gloves, strode to open the door. Taryn entered, wearing a dark dress with a high waistline, and from my view, I could hardly tell she was pregnant. I stood and hugged her, kissing her lightly on both cheeks, before pulling out her chair so that she could be seated.

"Wow, Sully!" she said. "This is rather posh, isn't it? What's the occasion?"

"None, whatsoever," I said, pushing her seat in. "Just two old acquaintances catching up."

"Acquaintances?"

"Colleagues."

"Friends."

"Discussing business."

"The Bordirtoun Beltway."

We laughed.

The server asked Taryn what she wanted to drink. She requested a virgin daiquiri.

"A daiquiri?!" I exclaimed. When we were traveling together, there were nights when we would put away two bottles of absinthe at dinner. "The Taryn I knew would never have ordered a daiquiri."

"Well, the Taryn you know now is old and pregnant and in the mood for something sweet."

"Likewise," I said, draining my latest glass of wine. I motioned to the server for my own strawberry daiquiri.

"Is Saul's progress worrying you?" she asked.

"I'm counting on T.R. to tell me if I should be worried."

"We have to make this election a referendum on Rio River and Old Town," she said. "Not this back and forth about affairs and the state of marriages."

"I'm not winning if I run on the state of my marriage."

"Neither would I," Taryn said. We shared a chuckle, not without its rue.

We ordered our food, and Taryn revealed that she and Jimbor had begun sleeping in separate beds. She blamed it on the pregnancy and Jimbor's work schedule, but then she stopped, and her shoulders sagged. "I'm tired, Sully."

"Tired?"

"He comes home late, and I'm watching television, and he gives me his routine peck on the forehead, and he touches my belly and when he goes in the next room, I tell myself, I should want to make more of an effort. We are married. I should want to know more about him. More about his dreams and motivations." Tears blurred her eyes. "I just don't. *We* don't. I'm afraid we just don't want to."

I reached across the table, and she held my hand. "Try to remember the good times," I said. "That's what I do."

"All he ever wanted was to have kids and live here," Taryn said.

"Lene never wants to leave Copenhagen."

"Have you ever asked her to move?"

I shook my head. "Not really. I tell her I want to be back in America at some point. But I know she doesn't want to move."

"What are you going to do?"

"I don't know." Taryn and I were still holding hands. "Do you?"

She stroked my ring finger. "Where's your wedding ring?"

I peered down at my hand and remembered that I had given it to Drew and Werder as collateral.

Taryn pulled her hand away.

"I need to get it back from Drew or Werder," I said. "Can't tell them apart sometimes. I have to look at their hands. Isn't that horrible?"

Taryn didn't laugh. "What are we doing?"

"What do you mean?" I said. But I could tell from the hardness in her voice exactly what she meant.

"This," she said, wagging her finger in the space between us.

"We're just two friends having dinner with each other."

"Everyone wants this to happen, you know."

The server arrived with our daiquiris. "Nothing is happening," I said.

"But you want it to," Taryn said.

"No," I said, sipping the drink, which was nauseatingly sweet. "I just miss seeing you. That's all."

"What would Lene think?"

This was the first time Taryn had used Lene's name. "And Jimbor?" I added.

Taryn was silent.

"I'd venture to say that neither would mind much," I said, warming beneath my collared shirt. "Sometimes, my wife doesn't call me back for days. And Jimbor might well be knitting or nursing, nursing or knitting at this very moment. I find it hard to believe that either would object to us eating and talking as old friends."

Taryn leaned forward, her pale skin and light freckles lumined in the candlelight. "Is that all we are?"

"The issue isn't what we are," I said, placing my elbows on the table. "It's what we might want to be."

"And what do you want to be?"

"I must admit, I'd rather not say."

"Neither would I."

Our server arrived with our steaks. "Perfect," I said. "I am, as I hope you are, quite hungry."

And just like that the subject changed, and we ate and talked, as old friends, as colleagues, and we left each other that night, once again, our relationship undefined, with a long embrace and platonic peck on her fragrant cheek. Lovers? No, not yet. Sadly, I had to be happy with that, both with the "no," and the "not yet." Be clear that I am not proud of the way I behaved, but I might as well be truthful now that we're so near the bleak and bitter end of my story. I must also confess that later that night, when I called Taryn to make sure she made it home okay, I heard Lene beeping on the other line, returning my call for the first time in several days, and I let her call go unanswered.

Mid-September, roughly 45 days before the election. I sat at the head of the conference table at the daily Sulliver Pong Braintrust meeting and today, only T.R., Drew and Werder were in attendance. Just two months ago, when I had a fifteen-point lead, this meeting was standing room only, and volunteers flowed out the door.

"Where the hell is everyone?" I said.

No answers.

Werder turned on the television and played a digital video recording of a PongTV segment. After fast-forwarding through several commercials for various brands of cereal for the elderly, I saw my father and his fur-coated henchmen wearing hardhats and pointing at a single building skeleton at the Old Town construction site. There were actually men working on the beams, even in the cold. One of my father's henchmen was Dr. Quango. Saul pointed something out to him, and a squinting Quango nodded and stroked his chin.

"On another record cold day, Mayor Saul Pong visited the Old Town redevelopment zone this morning. He announced the appointment of local entrepreneur, Dr. Murray Quango, to head the Pong Foundation and replaced all the managers currently being investigated for compensation improprieties," the newscaster's voice said.

"Are you happy with the progress here?" the reporter asked my father.

"Absolutely." He nodded, arms crossed. "It's my top priority to get this project back on track. The people of Old Town need this."

The reporter turned to Dr. Quango. "Doctor, what did your commission discover about Mayor Pong's son, Sulliver?"

Dr. Quango smiled and winked at the female reporter. "First of all, I'd like to comment on how radiant you are, even on a cold day like this."

The reporter almost succeeded in suppressing an irritated expression. "Thank you, Dr. Quango."

"But yes, about my predecessor, Sulliver," Dr. Quango said. "The detailed findings of the commission will be published in an upcoming book coming out later this fall from my publishing company,

Quangohead Press. We discovered a number of improprieties approved by Mr. Pong, Sulliver, including his use of funds to hire private investigators to follow the Mayor, a case where he bribed a county clerk, and even an incident involving the possible solicitation of a high-priced prostitute."

I stared incredulously at T.R., who wouldn't look at me.

"Are you disappointed in your son's conduct?"

My father spewed a sizable stream of white-hot obfuscation into the cold air. "Look, my son is a good man. I think he is very conflicted. He just needs strong mentorship from someone like me who has accomplished so much and is a man of ideas and yet, I am still so young."

"Do you believe he's getting bad advice?"

"Please don't attack my son," Saul said, pretending to be vexed. "To be honest with you, I think he's been distracted lately by his marital problems. He and his wife have recently separated, and he's going through a bit of a rough patch. I've left many long messages with him and his people, and I've recommended the counseling Mary and I have participated in with Dr. Quango." He glanced at the doctor, who crossed his arms and stared grimly into the camera.

"Turn it off," I said. "We are the fucking Keystone Kops!" I pointed at Drew. "Where are Saul's fucking mistresses?" I turned to Werder. "And you! I don't even know what you're here for!"

T.R. said he was planning a large rally to reinvigorate the campaign, re-announce our presence: we were still here, we still wanted the people out of Rio River, and we still wanted a better Bordirtoun, remember? T.R. even suggested that we fly Lene out to attend.

I rolled my eyes.

"What?" he asked.

"Lene's not going to stop me from losing."

"I'm sure you're familiar with losing," Werder said to T.R.

"If you're not happy with the job I'm doing, just say it," he said to me.

"I'm saying it, T," I said. "You're my friend, but consider it said."

Drew cleared his throat and put a thumbless hand on the table. "We've had something for awhile," he said. "A game changer. T.R. didn't want to use it."

I looked at T.R. He was slouched in his chair, his hands folded over his stomach like he was suppressing diarrhea.

"You knew about this?" I asked him.

Begrudgingly, T.R. nodded.

"Is it the women?" I asked.

There was no response.

"Then what is it?" I said.

"Not just the women, Sully," Werder said.

My half-siblings. Six of them, in fact. Five under ten years old. Two stepmothers, one Japanese and one German.

Drew and Werder had contracted a network of private investigators to travel to Europe and Asia to track down Saul's precious Old Town investors. They discovered that Saul had moneymen in Tokyo (yakuza ties) and Berlin (neo-Nazi crime organization). Drew and Werder noticed that one of them (named Herzmann Suzuki) was in both groups. In Tokyo, Herzmann had asked the investigator (who claimed to be a friend of my father's) how Mr. Pong's "other son" was doing. Drew's investigator made note of the comment and one note led to another, which led to another, and soon, Drew and Werder had discovered my first half-brother. His name was Haruki. He was thirty-six years old, married with two boys, living in Osaka. He was also a gambling addict, an alcoholic, and perhaps most galling to my father who thought all creative activities were time-flushers, an aspiring artist. Unbeknownst to me, my father had flown Haruki to Bordirtoun when I was in junior high, and Saul, Dr. Quango, and Haruki had spent several nights drinking in Old Town, even frequenting several of its jazz clubs.

The discovery of one son led to another and another led to a daughter, and gradually, my father's global family tree surfaced. Saul Pong, a seminal participant in globalization.

Even when Saul had said I was his *only* son, he'd lied. I was given surveillance photos of my four half-brothers and two half-sisters. There was my father, cradling Helmut Pong, age six, the oldest of three Chinese-German children. There was a picture of my German stepmother, Frau Karolyn Pong and Saul together, sitting in a black Mercedes SUV. There was another photo of my father walking hand-in-hand with my half-Japanese half-sister, Junko, both bundled in wool coats. She would be a heartbreaker one day.

Was Helmut the son Saul always wanted? Would he grow to inherit my father's slithery business sense? Would he take care of Saul in old age? Or was he embittered that his father was never there for him? Was he embittered like me?

T.R. advised that the right thing to do would be to tell my mother first, before leaking the photos to the press. I briefly considered doing the right thing. But the rage settled like disturbed ocean dregs inside me, and I once again became consumed with the feeling that I was a superior man to my father in every possible way, and if my mother had chosen to side with him over me, then she deserved to pay the price for her poor judgment. That is how I rationalized giving my team the green light to leak the photos, ensuring that my mother would learn about my father's other families on television.

In the late morning, I walked up the slushy, murk-stained steps of City Hall. I had made an 11 a.m. appointment with my father, revealing none of my intent: to deal the final knockout blow to his re-election campaign. I wore a blazer, no tie—casual, relaxed, befitting a future mayor. The canvas of my father's portrait, which was hung over fluted Ionic pillars, was streaked gray with mud across Saul's illustrated cheek. I carried a manila business envelope with a single black-and-white photo inside. I'd chosen the one with Saul tickling his young son Helmut on a park bench. How happy Saul looked! My father's beam appeared genuine and was at maximum cosmetic wattage for his giggling, shut-eyed son.

The elevator bell rang, and I strutted down the heated marble hallways, my dress shoes clacking. On one wall, the painted portraits of past mayors. My father was the first non-white one and also, incidentally, the first without a sizable mustache. On the other wall, framed maps of Bordirtoun in different epochs, each succeeding frame growing more developed with real estate, the only constant the dark brown fissure of the river.

I remember thinking that, in a few months, this would be my place of work. This would be the place where I could erase all traces of my father's ignominious legacy. I thought of changing my last name, perhaps to Lene's (Sulliver Rockefeller Svanemüllerströp). Maybe I could borrow T.R. and Taryn's last name (SRG might make a good monogram). Or Smith, American as Apple Pie. Anything but Pong and its connotations of the morally wayward immigrant.

At the end of the hall, Saul's blonde hollow-cheeked secretary sat behind a gilded desk bending a flexistraw back and forth (no cup in sight) with wide-eyed amazement like the straw was some sort of invention. I asked for my father. She looked at me with purple contacts, pursing her protuberant, glossy lips. I wondered if she was alternately employed by Saul Pong's more lucrative nighttime enterprises.

"Mr. Pong is waiting, Mr. Pong." She delivered these words and the subsequent snigger as if rehearsed.

"Haven't I seen you at The Pongel Horse?" I inspected her face and watched it darken, her nostrils flaring.

In my father's office, he lay with his feet up on the brown leather couch by the window. A large white rug that seemed to be the pelt of some ursine beast stretched from his desk to a marble fireplace. Wall mirrors gave the relatively small office a look of one thrice its actual size. Notably absent? Any evidence of accomplishment. There were no degrees, newspaper clippings, nothing an elected official might display. My father was wearing his dark-rimmed reading glasses. In his hand, a pink hard-covered journal with a gold-ribbon page marker dangling limp. He closed the book, hiked his glasses, and sat erect at attention.

"Sully?" he said.

"Father."

"Good to see you standing after your fall."

"Good to see you reading."

He guffawed, a throaty scrape with each laugh. He held up the journal. "Dr. Quango recommended that I write down my reflections about my marriage, then read the previous month's entries, and meditate on my reflections." His residual smile broke. "Lately, my thoughts have been positively negative, even depressive. Sully, I do not like the person I've become."

I was surprised; I had come to talk business or anger or the anger of business or the business of anger but I didn't come to talk about my father's reflections.

"Before you say anything," he said. "I want to tell you something I've been waiting to tell you for a long time. I'm in my early sixties, Sully. Yes, I know. Shocking! I am actually sixty-two. The truth!"

I calculated his age based on what I understood to be my father's birthdate. I was thirty-eight at the time, born when he was twenty-nine. You do the math.

"I have only myself to blame for pushing you away, and I want you to know that I have always been proud of you," he said. "Perhaps I have not said it enough, but I am. If you feel strongly you must defeat me to be happy, than go ahead. Your happiness is all I want. Don't waste your time hating me. I am begging your forgiveness. I don't want to die not knowing you."

My father's voice cracked, and he took off his glasses and began to weep, his shoulders shaking.

I began to blink hard, pinching the corner of the business envelope in my hands. I had not seen my father cry since I was very young, at my grandmother's funeral. I felt a dull round emptiness in my sternum. Would I cry when Saul died, I wondered? The longer he wept, the lower my gaze dropped. I could not look my father in the face. This was not playing out the way I'd hoped. What did the Pongs do to deserve such misery per capita? Did we really need more public humiliation? I considered pulling the photos back; it was not too late to call the television station. I rested the envelope on his desk and sat in his mayoral chair with a sigh, a habit from my high school summer days, back when I worked for him, back when his executive assistants looked more like matronly schoolteachers than pole dancers. A quiet corner of me wondered if Saul's sudden confessional might be, in some small way, authentic.

Then my father whimpered, "You're my only son."

My hands went cold. I was his only son, he had said. Another lie. I opened the envelope and unsheathed the photo of Saul and my half-brother Helmut. Would my life be different now if I had found some hidden reserve of compassion, had I not, deep down, been so vindictive and angry, through and through, an eye for an eye, a tooth for the proverbial tooth?

"Sully, I love you," he said.

I got up, walked around his desk, my feet light on the pelt rug, and handed him the photo.

He put his glasses on again, and when his eyes came into focus, his face turned the color of ash and a single tear landed on the photo. He ripped it into scraps and threw them like he was pitching a baseball, but the pieces just spiraled in the air like confetti. He got up off the couch and swept a carriage of pens off his desk with such force that they rattled against the wall mirror like pellets. He swore in Cantonese, ironically asking the air to fuck its mother. I just stood there, my heart pounding, my jaw clenched.

"Sometimes you remember what you did and it's like someone else did it," Saul said, his back turned to me, looking out the window at his statue. "You know it's wrong, and you know no one else did it but yourself. I know you don't think so but it is suffering. Why do you insist on making things worse for me? My father deserted me. He basically told me he never wanted me. You're lucky to have a male model around at all."

"You mean, male role model."

"In my heart, you are my only son," he said.

"You'll always have Haruki."

"Fuck you!" My father barked, startling me. "You good for nothing fat fucking dumb son-of-that-goddamn-fucking-cunt!" He sat hard in the chair across his desk and exhaled through flapping lips, which made the sound of flatulence. I noticed, for the first time, the framed photo I had seen as a teenager in my father's home office, the photo of my father as a younger, ponytailed man, wearing bell bottoms, an oversized plaid shirt and caramel-colored sunglasses, looking into the eyes of Paula Bushnell outside an Atari office building. Forty years ago, was this where Saul thought he would be, steeped in regret and defeat?

I informed him that the photos had been leaked to the press and the story would run on the evening news.

My father looked at me, eyes brimming with tears again. "Sully. Please."

I walked out of his office, past his secretary, who looked frightened by Saul's outburst, and I continued down the hall. I never turned around. I entered and exited the elevator and walked out of City Hall and down those slushy steps. I never once gave any attention to my father's creaky statue.

The next morning, the staff meeting was standing room only again. New polls had us out front by seven points, and a stack of the morning's newspapers was fanned out on the conference table. The front page headline of the *Bordirtoun Daily* read "*Mayor Pong the Polygamist.*" I said a few words at the start of the meeting, telling the team that we were almost at the finish line and that we needed to stay focused on addressing the pressing issues of the Bordirtoun people.

Afterward, T.R. pulled me aside, sat with me in the cavernous, abandoned room, and told me he was resigning.

"Why now?" I said. "We're so close to winning."

"I hate to say it, Sully, but I think we've forgotten why we're running."

There it was, the truth. "We" meaning "me." T.R. had wanted me to run because he was outraged by the Rio River internments. But there we were, weeks before the election, and Rio River was the farthest thing from my mind.

"I think this is for the best," he said. "For me and Taryn."

"For Taryn?"

"You should be aware of how you two look together."

"But it's nothing," I said. "Just rumors."

"The phone calls?"

A bead of sweat traced the back of my neck. "We're friends. Friends call each other."

"You have a town car pick Taryn up and drop her off at the VIP room of Bordirtoun Steaks, where half the city officials eat, and you expect people not to notice?" he said. "You think Jimbor doesn't know?"

I kept my eyes on the parallel grains of the table. "Well, you can tell Jimbor that nothing is going on. And I'll have you know that Jimbor's not exactly an angel either. When I was in the hospital, I saw him making eyes with his fellow nurses. Let's just say he's a favorite of all the ladies."

"Jimbor's not running for mayor, and we're not talking about him," T.R. said. "Working for this campaign has felt like working on the staff of some gossip rag. You've made this race about you and your father instead of about the people of Bordirtoun. And you know what? I expected that. Anyone who talks to you for five minutes knows you've got issues with Saul like nobody else. But I'm not going to stand by and say nothing when you're asking my married sister out on dates. She's my family."

Family. That word again. Lene was my family, and she was mine. I had never been part of the Grathe family. Jimbor, no matter how dubious, would always be more family to T.R. than I was. I was just the friend, the acquaintance, the son of Pong, who reappeared after twenty years.

"I'm married," I said.

"Separated."

The word stung. I felt myself slouch like my father, the bags beneath my eyes swelling like his.

T.R. inhaled through his nose, and the noise sounded like a vacuum seal. "I didn't come here to scold you," he said. "I came to wish you good luck." His voice was deeper now. Like it belonged to a stranger.

"I'm sorry I've disappointed you."

T.R. stood and looked down upon me, pity in his eyes. "When this is over, we'll have a drink and forget all about this," he said. "When you win, don't forget to tear down Rio River, and when you do, call me. We have to find affordable housing for those people."

He shook my hand and nodded toward the television. "I left something for you to watch." Then he turned his back on me and left. As he disappeared, I noticed how straight his posture was, unlike mine, unlike my father's.

I turned on the television and hit play. Footage taken from a handheld camera. The snow-covered buildings of Rio River. Two families, eight people sharing a single barrack, huddled in horse blankets in the darkness, the light coming from the camera and a few candles set upon saucers. A father asked a whimpering girl to join him beneath a blanket. I could hear a male voice behind the camera, asking for permission to film the rest of their living space. The families agreed. The voice was unmistakably T.R.'s.

The lens turned to the bathroom: a single sink, a toilet, and a shower. T.R. gasped at its size and condition. One of the fathers said, "The boy Pong is going to get us out of here, right?"

"Yes, yes he will," T.R. said.

The next scene was day. Footage of dirt swirling down the wide street. A truck drove into Rio River with supplies, and the residents spilled out of their barracks to crowd the vehicle. The lens focused on a man unloading the truck bed. The man handed a box to one of the families and looked directly into the camera. T.R. must have sensed that he would be discovered, because that was where the footage ended. He had been filming from an open window.

I turned off the television and slumped in my chair. While I was arranging date nights with his sister, T.R. had found a way to sneak in and out of Rio River. While I was busy making political hay out of my father's second and third families, T.R. was documenting the living conditions inside the internment camps my father had revived. While I was telling our staff with squint-eyed gravitas to stay focused on the needs of the Bordirtoun people, T.R. was actually out there with the people who were suffering most under my father's administration. Never had I felt less worthy to lead. The Pongs didn't deserve Bordirtoun. We never did. We never will.

Over the next two weeks, the event that T.R. had proposed had been transformed from a mere fundraiser into a coronation. My lead increased to double-digits again after the bombardment of Mayor Pong polygamy scandal coverage. However, I was far from delighted. With T.R. gone from the campaign, there was no one with which to celebrate my success, except for Drew, Werder, and a bunch of volunteers I hardly knew. After T.R.'s upbraiding, I even stopped calling Taryn. I felt lonelier than ever.

I ended up taking T.R.'s advice and inviting Lene back to Bordirtoun. I was driven to the airport to pick her up on the eve of the campaign event. I ran my hands over the empty seat beside me, my sweaty fingers smudging the black leather. My phone began vibrating.

Momma calling. She had been calling every hour for the last few days, and I was tempted to finally pick up. The vibrating began to sound like her sobs. Had Momma faced my father's rage as a result of my handiwork? Was I a better person for what I did? Your father has two other families, she'd say. She'd wail that I *had* to help her, as if I had never before tried. The "New Voicemail" message appeared, and I did not check. Even if Saul Pong was on his way to the family house to pound Momma into a pulp, I could no longer be involved. I could no longer be asked to care.

The wipers started back and forth. Rain began to fall lightly. I received a text message from T.R. that simply read "Congrats"

"You are running against your father for mayor?"

I nodded and tried to ignore the female-female-male threesome (with toys) on the screen. "Come to our campaign rally at the Pong Paramount Theatre. It's just up the street tomorrow night."

"Thanks, but I have business," he said. He tried to hand twenties to Lene and me, but we refused.

Back in the hall, Lene and I walked back to our rooms, and the boy walked away without thanking us. I became aware that Lene was surveying me.

"I know," I said. "That was disturbing."

"No, not the pervert," Lene said. "We have been together over ten years, and I never would have imagined that you would do what you've done. This place has so much pain for you, and still, you come back. Why? Why, I wonder, would you choose to stay here, instead of come home with me? But then, I see you here, and you are a changed man. In Copenhagen, you are afraid. I feel like I need to protect you. I feel like I almost have to be your mother. Here, you are assertive. You are your own person. You walk with purpose. I see now that you don't have this purpose in Copenhagen. You only have this purpose here."

I felt my ears growing hot. And what purpose was that? All the good I had claimed I wanted to accomplish was still undone; all the harm I hadn't intended had been unloaded with a truck-full of campaign mud.

"I always thought that if the time came, if my parents really needed me, I'd do the right thing, without question." I said. "I wanted to be that person. No matter what happened in the past. Maybe I'm just not that person."

"Who says you have to be?" Lene said.

I wanted to close my eyes and start over, wake up in Copenhagen purposeless again. "What should I do," I said.

"Will you do what I say this time?"

"What if I did?"

Lene half-smiled. "What do you mean, 'what if?'"

I was informed by my staff that the Millmore Pong Paramount Theatre would be full, over two thousand tickets sold at twenty bucks a pop. Saul had not resigned but had not surfaced all day either. I sat backstage in the dressing room, taking deep breaths in front of the mirror, trying to ignore the audible cheers and occasional laughter from the crowd (Remus Sans-Lubé and a combination of mediocre comedians and activists were lukewarming them up). Lene stood behind me and picked some lint off my jacket collar. She was wearing a navy knee-length skirt and an off-white blouse. I told her she looked fantastic.

"Are you ready?" She smoothed my lapel, and I could feel the envelope in my left breast pocket. The speech Lene and I had written last night. I was dropping out of the race, and I would endorse T.R. for mayor. Lene had convinced me that it wasn't too late to pull out of my private quagmire, soak my losses, and go back to Copenhagen. From there, I'd try to find renewed purpose, and Lene and I would try to find each other again, first as friends who cared deeply for one another, then as spouses, if we got that far. No promises. But no Bordirtoun Pongs either.

A campaign coordinator whose name I couldn't remember darted into the room with a headset on. I asked him if he'd seen T.R.

"He said he wasn't coming, sir," the coordinator said.

"Oh," I said, disappointed.

"Did you receive a message from Ms. Grathe, though?" the coordinator asked.

I told him that I'd missed her call last night.

"She sounded frantic," he said. "I got cut off. There's no reception in here. I hope she's not delivering tonight."

"Well, if she is, she should be calling her husband," I said. I checked Lene's expression, and she didn't seem bothered by the fact that Taryn was frantically calling.

"How do we look?" Lene asked the coordinator.

His face relaxed for the first time. "Not bad," he said. "Congratulations, Mayor Pong. Congratulations, Mrs. Pong."

I smiled and recalled my first trip to Bordirtoun, how I'd torn my groin in a dressing room not unlike this one. Several months later, I was about to deliver a speech to two thousand people. Didn't my life at least resemble *an* American dream, even if the dream wasn't mine? Yes, it was only Bordirtoun, but could a man of my limited stature expect more?

"When you get out there, hold hands," the coordinator said. "Walk to the edge of the stage, smile, and give thumbs-up. Look gracious, together, point at a few people like you know them. It'll look good on TV." He demonstrated for us. The coordinator looked at his watch. "Ten 'til go time."

Lene and I headed out of the dressing room, walked down the corridor, and waited behind a large curtain in a dim blue light. I squeezed her hand.

"Thank you for being here."

"You don't need to," she said.

We kissed, soft and warm against cold, nervous lips. Our first kiss in months.

I felt a tap on my shoulder. I turned and recognized the round, bald black man from the hotel room the night before. Over his shoulder, in the shadows, I saw the golden glint of a necklace. The man wearing it had brightly dyed blond hair. It was Dr. Quango. Once he saw that I'd seen him, he pivoted and walked away.

"We must talk," the round, bald man who'd tapped my shoulder said.

"Five minutes," the coordinator said in the shadows.

I looked at Mr. Threesome-With-Toys, who looked like a darker, more muscular version of me and appeared to be sucking epicurean debris from his teeth. I told Lene I'd be back and guided him into the shadows.

"Do you know Dr. Quango?"

"Who I know is none of your business," he said. "Your father will lose, no?"

"Yes."

"I know people who will be very unhappy."

"Who are they?"

"The investors."

"And who are you?"

"My name is Herzmann Suzuki."

My father's investor. The one with neo-Nazi yakuza ties. My heart beat fast in my throat. "Nice to meet you," I said, though I'd met him last night.

"As mayor, will you support the Old Town redevelopment?"

I heard laughter from the crowd. I considered telling Herzmann I was quitting the race, but decided against it because I couldn't tell whether my quitting would be a good or bad thing to him. "I don't support Rio River," I said.

"Rio River?"

"The camps."

He stared blankly at me.

"Quango Valley?" I said.

"What valley?" he asked.

Remus Sans-Lubé began his introduction of me and my wife. He spoke of how I was going to make a better Bordirtoun. He shared anecdotes that my staff had conjured to demonstrate my populist appeal: I had visited sick children in a hospital, driven around in a Ford Explorer instead of a town car, and served room service in the hotel where I was staying. Bordirtouners were voting for a true plebiscite, Sans-Lube opined. The crowd was silent. Poor word choice, I thought. Unlikely they knew the meaning of the word "plebiscite."

Several enthusiasts began chanting "Sull Not Saul." As I edged toward Lene, Herzmann gripped my elbow hard enough to make me wince.

"What would you do if he took your money after he promised on his mother's grave that you'd see it return ten times over?" he asked into my ear. He was near enough for me to smell his rank vodka breath and stark body odor. Taken aback, I looked into his bizarrely jaundiced and bloodshot eyes.

"Say that you don't stand to benefit, Pong," he said, the spittle on his chin curlies trembling. "Say that you don't have other investors lined up to pay you off for the land."

"I don't know what you're talking about," I said. The crowd cheered again. Sans-Lubé called for me and Lene to take the stage. The coordinator started yapping, "Go-go-go."

I tried to shake my arm loose but Herzmann held fast. "What would you do, then, if you were me?"

"Make him pay," I said, and finally, he let go.

Lene and I walked on stage, holding hands, grinning, waving, issuing the thumbs-up. I took a deep breath, tried not to look like I had defecated in my pants. Near the podium, I saw a row of leather chairs, like ones typically found at a roast. Seated were the various comedians, local television personalities, all in support of the new Sulliver Pong administration. A banner ran over the stage reading "A Better Bordirtoun for Bordirtouners: A True Family Man." The crowd was standing and applauding. There were a fair number of college students; certain sections looked like the Future Pongel Horse Dancers of America. Where did we find all these people? Were they here because they believed in me or because they felt sorry for me? Let's vote for poor Sully with his polygamous, philandering, and abusive father! Me and my platform of pity! Lene and I continued waving and smiling and pointing to imaginary friends, as instructed. We walked toward the edge of the stage, and I clasped my hands over my chest and mouthed, "Thank you."

Lene took the empty seat in the row of chairs next to the podium. I cleared my throat and thanked the crowd again. I smiled at Lene and spotted the teleprompter and the blue words rolling up on the screen. I leaned into the mic and asked that the prompter be shut off. I retrieved the envelope from my breast pocket, took out my speech, and smoothed it on the podium.

"I'd like to begin by introducing my lovely wife, Lene, my guiding light," I said. "She is, in fact, my only wife. I'm one of the first Pongs to have just one."

The crowd made a noise that could be characterized as a combination of boos, cheers, and laughter.

"Sorry, bad joke," I said. "But seriously, I am not going to tell you what you need or what you want. I hate it when politicians get up behind a podium, and tell you that you need a candidate that is committed to building a better town, and a candidate that is not committed to himself or special interests. Of course, you want that type of candidate. Who doesn't? They are insulting your intelligence with clichés."

Tepid applause.

I mopped sweat from my brow. "What I'm trying to say is that you will show what you want at the polls, and it's not my job to tell you what you need. You know best. I guess what I'm saying is that I'm not what you need. You should know that outside of my father,

I may be the most selfish, corrupt person I know."

The crowd rustled lightly, and there were even a few gasps and nays.

"My friend, T.R. Grathe, should be the next mayor of Bordirtoun."

More gasps and nays. I urged the crowd to applaud T.R., even though he wasn't in attendance, and after a few broad priming waves, they finally did.

"I've learned so much about myself during this race," I said. "Over the past few months, I've sat through one meeting after another, with businesses, unions, and community organizations alike, and I must confess, I've been absolutely indifferent to each and every one of their causes."

Laughter, as if I was joking.

"But there are people who genuinely care," I went on. "People with principles like T.R. Grathe. T.R. Grathe is the type of person who would risk his own skin to help others. T.R. Grathe is the best person for the job."

The crowd was silent now. Sulliver the Party Pooper.

"I'm sorry to have to abandon all my wonderful supporters so close to the election," I said. "But I feel strongly that this is the best decision for you and for me and my wife. Bordirtoun deserves a fresh start, an administration without Pongs. On November 1st, please write-in my friend, T.R. Grathe, for mayor. As for my lovely wife, Lene, well, she and I are going home." I motioned for Sans-Lubé to take the podium to no avail. He was yawning. I motioned again and finally, he walked up and leaned into the microphone.

"Wow, this is a quite a surprise, isn't it?" he said. "Let's wish Saul and Elena a safe journey home."

Lene and I again held hands on the stage, waving goodbye to the politely clapping people we never knew. I had made one of my few correct decisions during this time in my life leading up to my incarceration. Bordirtoun's public stage would not (and still does not) miss me. I embraced Lene and kissed her on that stage, for what would be the last time. Under the hot lights, I could almost remember what it was like to be truly passionate. I could almost taste freedom, summers in Copenhagen again, the soft and sweet lacquer on Lene's lips. The catcalling of the crowd sounded like backup singers harmonizing. And when I looked into Lene's flushed face, I could see she was embarrassed, but we continued to wave, give thumbs-up, and hold hands as we walked off the stage.

I would and may never again feel so close to being the man I wished to be.

8.

AS AFOREMENTIONED, eight is a lucky number in Chinese culture because spoken aloud, the word rhymes with the Chinese word for "rich." Many well-to-do Chinese-Americans personalize their license plates using some combination of a surname and the number eight. The license plate on my father's BMW 755i reads PONG168. Spoken in Cantonese, the phrase sounds like "Pong will continue to get rich."

Eight is not a lucky number for the Pong family, however. Millmore Pong died on August 8. According to documents, Sunblaze Wilde was Parris's eighth hire. Francisco was born in August as well. These connections may seem coincidental, but all that counts is what one sees in them, no?

Chapter Eight is where the circumstances leading to my incarceration at long last reveal themselves. When I reflect on how close I was to finally escaping the trap I had gotten myself into and returning to Copenhagen, I feel an aching deep in my gut, as if I'd been impaled and had the misfortune of surviving, and the wound never healed. All I had to do was keep hold of Lene's hand, walk off the stage, and out of the auditorium.

Instead, I let go, and Chapter Eight is where my story ends.

Lene and I walked triumphantly back into the dressing room only to find Taryn, sitting in my chair in front of the dresser, her pregnant stomach hanging awkwardly from her like a giant stone. Her face was purple and wet with tears.

"Where the hell have you been?" Taryn whimpered. "I've been calling you!" She began to sob, her hair matted to her freckled forehead. I stared at her and felt a brief falling sensation, a vertiginous swirling before I drifted away from my wife to Taryn. I expressly told myself not to hold her hand. But she held mine.

"What happened?" I asked.

"Jimbor left me."

"How?" I asked, as if such matters required manual assembly.

She blubbered incomprehensibly for awhile before saying, "He was cheating. I saw him. With an intern."

I glanced at Lene in the dresser mirror. She was standing where I'd left her, arms crossed, watching me.

"What kind of man would leave his wife when she's practically in labor?" I said.

Taryn pulled me close, and I hugged her. She cried harder, releasing into my chest. I tossed a chagrined look to Lene, who stared icily at me—make no mistake, she was fuming. All the euphoria of the stage seemed years past. I told myself I was embracing Taryn out of sibling instinct, not that other sinister one. As she shuddered in my arms, I felt myself grow hard. I knew quite well what kind of man Jimbor was. Jimbor was Saul. Jimbor was me. And that was when

Taryn looked over my shoulder and whimpered words I didn't expect.

"Your mother," she said.

"What?"

Taryn and I separated. "Your mother," she repeated. "She's here."

I turned and confirmed that a shaggy-haired and weeping Momma was indeed standing in the doorway, next to Lene, who towered over her. My mother's face was puffy, and the skin around her eyes was chafed; she looked as if she'd been crying for days. Forces in the cosmos had conspired to bring Momma, Lene, and Taryn, the most formidable women in my life, into one room, at one time, of all times!

Momma stepped forward and clutched me by the lapels. "Why didn't you tell me about the wives?" she shrieked, shaking me. "You told the whole city and not me! I can't even look at my house cleaner. Even the Mexicans are laughing at me! Stupid son! Stupid!"

I grabbed her tiny wrists. "He has two other wives and you blame me?" I shouted. "I tried to help you! You're getting what you deserve! Lene and I are going home!"

Momma wriggled and looked around the room. First at Lene, then at Taryn. For a moment, there was silence save Taryn's sniffling and the faint echoes of one of the comedians plugging his set at The Laugh Ranch and Slaughterhouse, the local comedy club. Lene's mouth was open slightly; she looked stricken.

Momma's gaze settled on Taryn and her pregnant belly. "Is this your wife?" she wailed in English. "No, you can't go! My grandson! Elena, I've never even met. I am Mary Pong, Sully's Momma. I wait so long for grandson! Don't take him away!" By the time I realized Momma was talking about Taryn's baby, she was tugging on both of Taryn's arms as if she was a grandson dispenser.

"Momma." I had to repeat it several times, each time louder until finally, I pulled her away from Taryn.

"What?" Momma said.

I pointed at Lene. "That's my wife. Lene." My voice softened. Lene's shimmering, swelling face mottled with red, and her lips formed an odd smirk. I knew I was in the shit.

Momma eyed Lene like she was a zoo animal. "But she's too old," she said in English.

"*Havde du sammen med hende?*" Lene said.

"*Nej,*" I said. "*Min mor er sindsyg.*"

Lene unstrapped her heels, took them off, and smoothed her skirt. Then she ran out of the room. I chased her but with her long strides and with me slowed by my various lingering injuries, she was already well down the hall.

"Lene!" I shouted.

"Which white woman is your wife?" Momma shouted in Cantonese as I ran.

I don't know whether I took a wrong turn or if Lene was simply too fast for me, but I ended up standing outside, in the parking lot, squinting into several links of slowly moving headlights. Then I saw a shorthaired blonde trying to hail a cab in the distance. I ran after her.

"Lene!" I shouted, my pupils dilating from the glare of the brake lights on either side of me. "Lene!"

The woman looked at me, and I suddenly remembered that Lene no longer had short hair. How could I have forgotten? She'd been by my side almost every minute for the past 24 hours! I watched my imaginary Lene get into the cab. I began to run back from where I came, searching for my longhaired wife when headlights gaped and tires screeched, and a group of hooting male voices bellowed, "Look out for the Jap!"

Blood on the blazer is not mayorly. Nor are compound fractures of the tibia.

I had been hit by a speeding pickup overstuffed with drunken high schoolers. The driver had been getting a blowjob from the only female in the group, and the other guys were egging her on (the driver would wear nasty bite scars for life). I spent the next two days having multiple surgeries on my legs. I was eventually moved into a room with a single flickering halogen lamp and eight other groaning patients. There was one bathroom between us, and the urine stench burned my sinuses.

As I became more lucid, I noticed I hadn't received any visitors. In fact, no one received visitors. Even nurse visits were sparse. While the nurse was changing my bedpan one day, I asked for a phone to contact my wife. She looked at me like I was speaking in tongues.

"Please?" I asked.

"Who do you think you are?"

"I'm Sulliver Pong," I said. "Mayor Saul Pong's son. The candidate. I think I've been very patient with the subpar service I've received in this hospital. You guys moved me, and I didn't complain. My family practically built this town, for Christ's sake, and you've got me in here with eight other patients and no television."

The nurse looked at my chart. "Is the patient taking his dementia meds?" she asked herself, tapping a pen on the clipboard.

"What are you talking about?" I said. "I've just been in a car accident!"

"You're not diagnosed with dementia?" she asked, chewing on the butt of her pen.

"I'm not demented!" Had I missed something? "Am I? Where am I?"

The nurse sighed. "You're in the maximum security penitent ward." She recited this as if she had been asked the same question a thousand times that day.

"Penitent?"

She shot me a disgusted look. "If you wanted your own room, maybe you shouldn't have ordered that hit on your father."

Yes, you read correctly. A hit on my father. Had I walked off that stage and fallen through a trap door into Hades? I learned the details from T.R., in a letter I received three weeks after it was sent.

The morning after I quit the race, my father was scheduled to appear at a press conference announcing his resignation. When he was a no-show, his assistant reported him missing. Two days later, my father was checked into the same hospital emergency room, with a litany of broken bones, barely breathing. He had lost an eye from being bludgeoned repeatedly, apparently with a lead pipe. He had been tossed into Bordirtoun River and left for dead. Saul's survival instinct kicked in, and he decided to float instead of trying to swim. His belt buckle snared a branch and held him moments before his body crossed the border into Mexico. Ten hours later, dockworkers spotted him at low tide, two miles downstream.

I had been moved to the hospital penitentiary so my father could lay comatose on life support in my old room. Thanks to a tip from Dr. Quango, the police headed off Herzmann Suzuki at the airport. Herzmann promptly confessed that he was ordered to perform the hit, not by some neo-Nazi yakuza organization or Dr. Quango, but by yours truly. According to Herzmann, I had instructed him to "make my father pay." I had wanted to make my father suffer, and now, improbably, my wish had come quite true.

I learned from Ramesh recently that it was Quango who had led Herzmann to my father in the first place. Tired of being shut out of the larger payouts of Saul's business dealings, Quango stood on the docks, sipped an early morning venti quadruple Americano, and watched from a distance as Herzmann and his men dragged my father to the river banks and pummeled him within an inch of his life.

Momma was my first visitor. I crutched up to the tiny booth, wearing an open-assed hospital curtain. Visitors were not allowed in-room—probably a good thing considering the overwhelming stench of bleach and feces. A guard eased me down in the chair, making room for my various casts. I stared at Momma through the smudged Plexiglas. She looked down at her hands, picking at her cuticles, her chin quivering, lips moist with tears. Someone had scratched "Fuck Me, Mommy" on the partition. She picked up the phone.

"Daddy woke up."

I released a long breath. "Good."

"Why did you do it?"

"I didn't!" I exclaimed, stunned she would actually believe that I would do such a thing. "Tell him I didn't!"

"I don't understand you," she said, dabbing an eye with crumpled Kleenex. "I don't understand why you tried to kill Daddy."

"I just told you I didn't!" I said. "You can't possibly believe I did!"

Momma slapped the glass with an open palm. "I know you're lying!" she barked in Cantonese. "You tried to kill Daddy." She hit the glass again, even harder and louder. "Daddy blames me, you blame me, everyone blames me! After you told the world Daddy had three wives, he came through a window to beat on me. I had to lock myself in the bathroom." She kicked the wall between us. "This is your fault! You only want to hurt us! Are you satisfied now? Daddy almost died. I can't even play mahjong without women who drive Toyotas feeling sorry for me. Are you satisfied? You tried to kill Daddy!"

Stabbing pain blazed from my pelvis to the screws in my legs. "I didn't do it!"

"Then who did?" she shouted. "Daddy? Is that who? Daddy beat himself? Daddy scraped his own eyeball out of his head?"

The guard threw the door open behind me, hand on his belted club. "What's going on here?"

"My son is a murderer!" she said in Cantonese. Then mindful of her audience, she translated herself. "My son kill my husband!"

A guard grabbed her under the armpits and hoisted her up, knocking over the chair. She was still calling me murderer, swinging her elbows, and kicking her tiny feet as the guard dragged her from the room.

For all their talk of a reunited Pong family, when the time came to have faith in our better nature, there was no faith to be found. But now that I look back, was it that far-fetched that my mother would believe that I hated Saul enough to want him dead? I had come close to saying as much on numerous occasions. I can understand now that I had not been an ideal son, just as they had not been ideal parents, and I can't blame them for seeing this situation through warped lenses. Ironically, it was the warped lenses Saul, Momma and I ultimately shared. Our capacity to see the absolute worst in each other. Our blood ties did not save us then, and I would go as far as to say they would not save us today if we replayed the circumstances.

Shortly after my father parlayed his sympathetic brush with death into a narrow re-election with record low voter turnout, I would find myself on trial for the attempted murder of Saul Pong.

In a wheelchair, my father was rolled to the stand, and as he was sworn in over the Bible, he raised his left hand because he had lost use of his right. He wore an eyepatch, and there was a large surgical scar on the top of his shaved head. His good eye was still a puffy lavender.

The prosecutor asked, "Do you think your son wanted you

killed?"

He told my father to take his time—he knew this was a difficult question. I wanted to chuckle at the absurdity of all this but I'd been coached by the DA's team to sit quietly and appear attentive. This should not have been a difficult question. A year ago, I was his black sheep, incapable of making my own life decisions, and now he couldn't answer whether I had orchestrated his attempted murder!

"He's so angry," he answered quietly. "I don't know why. I don't know what I did to deserve this anger. I have always loved my son." His face puckered, and his eye shut, and he began weeping.

"He wanted you to ruin you, didn't he?" the prosecutor said. "In fact, didn't he want to, and I quote, 'ruin your legacy,' unquote?"

My father nodded between the whistling and slurping of his sobs. The prosecutor held up a bound stack of papers. "Please let the jury note Exhibit D, signed deposition transcripts from five members of Mayor Pong's staff who witnessed the mayor's conversation with his son at The Castle of Pong Tavern on August 8. Sulliver Pong said, and I quote, 'I want to ruin your legacy,' unquote, referring to the mayor."

The DA scribbled on his notepad and pushed it toward me. "Stop looking gillty," he had written.

"He wanted *you to pay*, didn't he?" the prosecutor said. "For your marital troubles, for your expectations of him, for all the times your professional success forced you to sacrifice father-son time."

My father stopped crying suddenly, as if he'd realized he'd forgotten his house keys in the midst of this emotional moment. He wiped the tears from his face with his good hand and glanced in my direction. Was that a smirk that surfaced on his broken face?

"Yes," my father said softly, with finality. "My son wanted me to pay."

Great tabloid material. "Emotionally Charged," one headline read.

I was the "Hamlit of Bordirtoun" (sic). The jury's deliberation was brief. I, Sulliver Pong, was sentenced to thirty-six months in prison. Somehow, during the appeals process, the DA succeeded in getting an extra year added to my sentence.

My father resigned one month after the verdict and left Momma for the last time, citing "spiritual exhaustion." The mayor's office went to Saul's second-in-command, Hunter Chang, a young Chinese-American Republican from central casting (a JDMBA with pomade-slick hair and a porcelain-skinned Taiwanese wife perfectly three-quarters his size). I'd met him at The Castle of Pong Tavern that snowy August day when I had the fifteen-point lead. He was one of my father's henchmen.

Naturally, Saul made quite a dramatic exit, doing an exclusive televised interview on the "Remus Sans-Lubé Hour" about how his near-death experience had changed his perspective, and he was moving to Japan to pursue Buddhist monkhood. T.R. mailed me the *Bordirtoun Daily* with the front-page photo of Saul waving goodbye with his good arm at the airport gate. He was wearing an orange sarong.

"I'm only a spectator in the grand teacup of life," my father was quoted as saying. "Now I pour my tea in another cup."

Do I think my father calculated his winning move on the stand? On certain days, yes, I do believe my father realized that by playing along with his attorneys, he could put me in jail and win the election, thereby controlling our little PONG console again. On certain days, I even believe that he wept on command. On certain days, I imagine that once my father's beaten body had been fished from the river, he'd called his attorneys and asked them to visit him in the ICU, where he promptly led a lengthy planning meeting with flipcharts, whiteboards, and dry-erase markers with the primary objective of jailing his own son.

But sometimes, I believe that his emotions were genuine.

Sometimes, I believe that he never intended for the trial to play out the way it did. Sometimes, I believe that he didn't intend, at the time, to leave Momma. This is the conclusion I'd like to come to. But I'm afraid I never will.

The day before my parole hearing, Jaynuss visited me in person for the first time. Not only was I surprised to discover a well-kept, sturdy individual with fine taste in designer suits, I was also surprised to discover that Jaynuss was Chinese.

"Adopted by German immigrants," he said on the other side of the Plexiglas. "I have to say, I'm surprised at the way you look as well."

"How so?"

"I expected a tragically slovenly lost cause." Jaynuss went on to say that he assumed that I would be unfamiliar with all tools related to grooming or hygiene. "You look trim. I definitely expected a fat fuck. Prison may have been the best thing for you."

"I hope that's not your argument tomorrow."

"I have news about that," Jaynuss said. Turned out Jaynuss's lover Ashlene decided to work two of the parole board members a little harder than Jaynuss had originally intended. She had left Jaynuss to date both of them. "But I'm over that used-up slut. Really. What kind of person has a serious consensual relationship with two men at once! Fuck her restraining order! Talk about unnecessary! Show up to her place drunk and crying one time and you call the cops?"

I clamped my temples and squeezed my eyes shut.

"That cock-holster is not why I'm here," he said.

"Educate me."

Jaynuss's lips parted, and his Adam's apple bobbed. "That's what Ashlene used to say to me in bed," he said, his voice cracking.

"Jesus Christ, Jaynuss!"

"Okay, sorry, I'm good, really," he said, scrunching his gel-spiked hair. He reached into his jacket pocket and pulled out a postcard. On the front, a print of a painting. A closed-down Rio River.

"Do you know a Robinson Pong?" he said.

My grandfather. He was ninety-eight years old, didn't look a day over seventy-five. Holding a cane that appeared to be only cosmetic, he walked into the parole hearing with the confidence of a man who'd completed his bucket list. He was tall, with a slight stoop, a slouch not much more pronounced than my father's. Like me, he had lost a ring of hair on the top of his head. He had deep pouches beneath his eyes, and liver spots speckled his forehead, but when he sat beside me, he didn't require help, and he smelled of fresh chrysanthemum tea.

"I am sorry I only get to meet you now," my grandfather said with a slight Cantonese accent.

"I am sorry as well."

"It's *lo siento, por favor*," my grandfather said, chuckling. "I read about your gaffes during the race. I've lived with a Mexican most of my life."

Robinson Pong and his lifelong partner, Edna Jimenez, had become successful painters after moving to Paris in the late 1950s. Their work had been exhibited in galleries throughout Europe, and a book commemorating their paintings had recently been published in France. Robinson and Edna were extremely private people, and only a few in the European art scene knew where they lived. After watching my campaign disintegrate, Cousin Sarly spent a full year searching for my grandfather because he wanted to tell him about the fates of his son and grandson. Cousin Sarly eventually found Robinson and Edna, living in a cottage in a remote Croatian village, and Robinson became so moved by Saul's near-tragic end and the jail time I'd endured, he contacted Jaynuss to find out how to help. Jaynuss had been feeding Robinson my pages for months with the hopes of getting him to travel to Bordirtoun to testify on my behalf.

The five members of the board filed in and sat at a long table on a raised platform at the front of the room. The infamous Ashlene appeared last, and with her big blonde hair, dark-rimmed glasses, and cheap business suit with a pencil skirt two inches too short, I couldn't help but be reminded of pornography in the age of the VHS tape. The other members were men, ethnically diverse. An older black gentleman, a lanky Mexican with a mustache so thick that even his bottom lip was covered, an effete white fellow who was dressed in stylish clothes a size too small, and a Chinese man who did everything he could to look like a round-faced, bewhiskered and bucktoothed cartoon on a Yellow Peril poster.

As my grandfather stood, the sun came in through the wrought iron windows and checkered all of us with tiny shadows. He walked up to the podium between the board and me and adjusted the microphone.

"Lady and gentlemen," he said without notes. "Over fifty years ago, I left my family. It was the most difficult decision of my life. And while I have personally benefited from the decision, it is still my greatest regret. Perhaps I am being egotistical, but I believe that had I stayed, maybe my son and grandson would have become better men. As you can plainly see, I do not have many years left on this Earth. I ask you to please release my grandson, so I can spend more time with him, as a free man, before I die."

"Your story is very moving, Mr. Pong, Robinson," Ashlene said. "And I'm aware that you've traveled a great distance in delicate health to be here. But I've read the documents—this story—that Mr. Jaynuss has provided on Mr. Pong, Sulliver's behalf, and I do not see evidence of the defendant taking responsibility for what happened to the former mayor, your son." She sighed and spread the collar of her blouse wider as if to aerate her cleavage. "And the documents are frankly a longwinded, pretentious, pseudo-intellectual stir-fry." She looked at me and added, "No offense."

"None taken," I said.

"Furthermore," she went on. "While he has not assaulted anyone in prison, the defendant basically admits that he conspired with the Chinois Brotherhood to have his cellmate killed. Perhaps you can educate me on why this board should parole Mr. Pong, Sulliver, besides your old age and your professed regrets."

Jaynuss slammed a palm on his legal pad. "You are a fucking bitch!"

"Easy, Mr. Jaynuss," the Mexican board member said.

"And you, Sanchez!" Jaynuss said. "You're her Dirty motherfucking S—"

"If you don't get ahold of yourself, I'll have you arrested!" Ashlene shouted.

I buried my face in my hands as Jaynuss began to whimper repeatedly that Ashlene had told him that she loved him and him only and that if she had just been honest about wanting to date two men, Jaynuss would have accepted being the third. I began to brainstorm new hobbies with which to occupy the rest of my jail term. Too bad they didn't allow crochet because of the needles, I thought, as the bailiff cuffed my inconsolable attorney and escorted him out of the hearing room.

"Mr. Pong, Robinson," Ashlene said. "I'm sorry you had to witness that. Mr. Jaynuss is clearly mentally disturbed. I'm also sorry that you came all this way without being better prepared by Mr. Jaynuss to explain why your grandson should be paroled."

My grandfather gripped the podium. "I am prepared if you will allow me to speak, Ma'am."

Ashlene apologized. "Proceed."

"I have read my grandson's story as well," he said. "I believe that he has changed and would do things differently given another chance. That is not important, however."

Ashlene put her elbows on the table and peered out at my grandfather over her glasses. "Your grandson's likelihood to re-offend is not important?"

"My sixth sister once told me, 'Better to light a candle than curse the darkness,'" my grandfather said. "You may or may not know that I've had a very successful career as a painter overseas, and if my grandson is released, I am prepared to leave a sizable endowment to this wonderful, blessed city."

Bordirtoun, population 99,000. My birthplace, a tiny depot on a long road destined for the new beginnings of the Pong family.

Rio River still stands today, renamed Quango Valley. Twelve thousand former Bordirtoun residents live there. A portion of the Robinson Pong endowment will be devoted to creating affordable housing so the city can shut Rio River down forever. One of the members of the endowment's board of trustees is T.R. Grathe. Ever the activist, T.R. recently organized the dismantling of my father's rusty old statue. He hooked one end of a carabineer to Saul's bronze thumb and the other end to a Honda Civic Hybrid and drove off with all but the statue's legs. On television, my father's monument looked like it had been made of licorice.

Taryn named her boy Dohney, after her father. He has her auburn hair and green eyes. She is dating an older man, a bookseller named Marco. She visited today, the morning before my release. I was allowed to walk outside with her, around a patch of well-supervised sod approximately ten by ten feet. I admitted to Taryn that at the steakhouse that night two years ago, I had wanted to confess that I was willing to leave my wife for her. I asked whether she had ever felt willing to leave Jimbor for me.

I saw discomfort in her eyes, and she turned her back to me and stepped away.

"We're moving," Taryn said. "Dohney and me. With Marco. To Madrid. He has family there."

I congratulated her, them, their new family of choice. Before she left, we did not hug. Alone, I benched myself and faced the penitentiary exit. I looked beyond the barbed wire fence to the new abscess in the formerly flat skyline of Old Town (the Ye Olde Towne Consumer and Office historical district had just opened). Tomorrow, the fence will swing open, and the car service will be waiting. My grandfather will be in the backseat. The car will drive us to Momma's studio apartment (she lost the house; my father used it as collateral on one of his shady deals gone bad), and she will meet her father-in-law for the first time. Momma still believes I ordered the hit on Saul. My grandfather and I will try to convince her that, as her only remaining family, we're here to help, but as I've learned repeatedly over the years, I can't force her to take my hand.

Beyond visiting Momma, I have no plans. During my time in prison, I've briefly considered a myriad of possibilities, including a return to public relations, maybe even another run at civil service. But after reading James John Jang's fictionalization of my ancestors, I've noticed that planning is counter to the way of the American Pong. Did Millmore plan to become a construction worker in America when he was doing backflips in the courtyard of his family home in China? Did Parris plan to punish himself for his sins when he woke to work on his will that morning in 1930? Did Francisco plan to become a pastor after assisting an alcoholic cat ranch proprietor? Did my grandfather plan to fall in love with a Mexican painter, his muse for over half a century? And did Saul plan to become a two-plus term mayor of uncommon corruption while he was riding his hog down Route 15 dreaming of video games? I don't know where this new railroad of misadventures will lead me, but I can only hope to dig my heels into the edge of the boxcar, watch the turdy river shrink in the distance, and think: I have finally grown up, and I am no longer here.

ACKNOWLEDGEMENTS

I'm forever grateful to the many individuals and organizations that have helped me complete this book. Thanks to The MacDowell Colony, Brush Creek Foundation of the Arts, i-Park Foundation, and the New York Mills Regional Cultural Center for time, space, and freedom to create. For the mentorship and insight that made this book better: Kris Saknussemm, Paul Cohen, Laurie Foos, and Michael Lowenthal. To the myriad of talented fellow writers who have made me better over the years: Benjamin Bac Sierra, Alex Behr, Charles Bush, Jane Cullinan, Paul Matthew Davis, Kristen Engelhardt, Melissa Hurley, Chaney Kwak, Brian Liddy, Nami Mun, Nick Petrulakis, Gus Rose, and Shawna Yang Ryan. Special thanks to Jason Pettus for believing in the manuscript. Finally, and most importantly, I'd like to thank my wife Jessi, without whom this book and I would not exist.

LELAND CHEUK has been awarded fellowships and artist residencies at the MacDowell Colony, I-Park Foundation, and Brush Creek Foundation for the Arts. Cheuk's work has appeared or is forthcoming in publications such as *The Rumpus, Kenyon Review, Valparaiso Fiction Review*, and *Tahoma Literary Review. The Misadventures of Sulliver Pong* was named a finalist for the James Jones First Novel Fellowship as well as a semi-finalist for the Big Moose Prize from Black Lawrence Press. His short fiction has been a finalist for the Salamander Fiction Prize (judged by Edith Pearlman) and the national Washington Square Review fiction contest (judged by Darin Strauss). He has an MFA in Creative Writing from Lesley University. He lives in Brooklyn and is always at work on a novel and a collection of stories.

Made in the USA
Lexington, KY
04 December 2015